Heart Legacy

Robin D. Owens

B

BERKLEY SENSATION, NEW YORK

BERKLEY SENSATION

An imprint of Penguin Random House LLC
375 Hudson Street, New York, New York 10014

This book is an original publication of Penguin Random House LLC.

Copyright © 2015 by Robin D. Owens.
BERKLEY SENSATION® and the "B" design are registered trademarks of
Penguin Random House LLC.
For more information, visit penguin.com.

Library of Congress Cataloging-in-Publication Data

Owens, Robin D.
Heart legacy / Robin D. Owens. — Berkley Sensation trade paperback edition.
p. cm. — (Celta ; 13)
ISBN 978-0-425-26397-6 (softcover)
1. Life on other planets—Fiction.   2. Man-woman relationships—Fiction.
3. Paranormal romance stories.   I. Title.
PS3615.W478H46 2015
813'.6—dc23
2015025739

PUBLISHING HISTORY
Berkley Sensation trade paperback edition / November 2015

PRINTED IN THE UNITED STATES OF AMERICA

10 9 8 7 6 5 4 3 2 1

Cover art by Tony Mauro.
Cover design by George Long.
Interior text design by Kristin del Rosario.
Penguin
Random
House

To the Writers of the Hand (Hotel):
I couldn't have done this without you. Thanks and
blessings and Merry meet and merry
part and merry meet again.

Characters

Draeg Betony-Blackthorn's Family:

Note: Draeg is undercover as Draeg Hedgenettle.

Corax: Draeg's new raven Familiar Companion

Straif T'Blackthorn: adoptive father, FirstFamily GrandLord, tracker (hero of *Heart Choice*)

Tinne Holly: cousin to Straif T'Blackthorn, Draeg's adoptive father. Concerned about the old Yew threats against his Family (hero of *Heart Fate*)

Ilex Winterberry: cousin by marriage to Draeg through Mitchella Clover D'Blackthorn, Chief of all the Druida City Guards (police) and formally in charge of the investigation (hero of *Heart Quest*)

Mitchella Clover D'Blackthorn: adoptive mother, interior designer, FirstFamily GrandLady (heroine of *Heart Choice*)

Antenn Blackthorn-Moss: adoptive brother, architect and inhabitant of the Turquoise House (hero of *Heart Fire*)

Nico: Draeg's full brother

Vesus: Draeg's full brother

Loridana Itha Valerian D'Yew's Family:

Baccat: Lori's cat Familiar Companion

The Yew Residence: the sentient manor house

Cuspid Yew: a distant cousin, a generation older than Lori, maître de maison; he and Folia Yew and the Residence run the staff of the Residence and preside over the Family

Folia Yew: thirty-something unmarried housekeeper

Vi Yew: daughter of Cuspid Yew, twin of Zus, about a year and a half older than Lori

Zus Yew: son of Cuspid Yew, twin of Vi, about a year and a half older than Lori

Everyone who lives on the Yew estate and works in the Residence are Family members.

Lori's Stridebeasts (two of six named):

Semper

Cana

The Horses:

Smyrna

Ragan

Others:

Cal Marigold: boy who is the reincarnation of Draeg's mentor, Tab Holly

Cratag Maytree T'Marigold: Cal's father, an ex-merchant guard (hero of *Heart Change*)

Garrett Primross: private investigator, informally in charge of the investigation (hero of *Heart Secret*)

Nuin Ash: Heir of the Ashes, son of GreatLord Rand T'Ash and Danith Mallow, friend of Draeg, a Fire Mage

Lahsin Holly: Lori's grandfather's (MotherSire's) ex-wife, Lahsin Yew; now Tinne Holly's wife

Marin Holly: younger child of Tinne Holly and Lahsin Holly

Anthema Mayweed: Lori's chance-met new acquaintance

GreatLord Rand T'Ash: jeweler, blacksmith, Flair tester (hero of *HeartMate*); his Fam is Zanth

GrandLady D'Grove: Captain of the FirstFamily Council

Avellana Hazel: youngest child of the Hazels, HeartMate to Muin (Vinni), T'Vine, holographic artist

GreatLord Muin (Vinni) T'Vine: the prophet of Celta

One

CELTA,
424 years after colonization by Earth,
Druida City, late winter

I want you to go undercover as a spy at the Yew estate." Tinne Holly, one of the best fighters on Celta, prowled his sparring salon, his bare feet making no sound on the wooden floor.

Wiping the sweat from his torso with a towel, Draeg Betony-Blackthorn watched the older man. He'd had to use all his strength, guile, and skill to keep their match even. "I take that statement to mean that the guards of Druida City didn't consider the button you found beneath the failed balcony as evidence."

Scowling, Tinne made a cutting gesture. "The button is inscribed with Yew leaves. The only enemies my wife and daughter—who could have died when that balcony gave way—have are the Yews. But the guards say the button isn't evidence. Who else would have Yew buttons?"

Draeg raised his brows. "No one received a psychic impression that it came from the Yews. No one could date that button, either. And how many shops might have old Holly buttons?"

"Don't know." Tinne waved that away.

Draeg shook his head. "Go undercover on the Yew estate? As far as I know, the Yews are completely self-sufficient. Not one of them has taken their place in FirstFamily Druida society." And the

FirstFamilies, the descendants of the Earthan colonists that had funded the journey to Celta, comprised *the* highest status on the planet. Another disbelieving shake. "You really think the Yews have allied with the fanatic fringe of the Traditionalist Stance?"

"Yes, the Yews are the most conservative Family, and the Traditionalist Stance prizes old ways."

"That's a leap of logic," Draeg said.

Tinne's face set. "Accidents are happening, mostly targeted at children. It's the Traditionalist Stance behind them." His shoulders straightened. "That political party wishes to preserve the status quo and is against Commoners testing to become Nobles, or moving up the social ladder in any other way. Commoners who have access to the strongest Flaired people in the world, the First-Families. People who shape society and the world. That can cause a lot of resentment in those from older Families who haven't been able to climb so high, that Commoners are better connected than Nobles who've had titles for three or even four centuries. And Commoner women like Danith Mallow and Mitchella Clover have married into the highest strata."

"They're *HeartMates* of FirstFamily Lords, *fated* mates," Draeg protested.

"They're Commoner women who have married FirstFamily Lords, borne children of mixed blood, Noble and Commoner."

Draeg's mouth dropped open at the wrongness of that statement. "Nobody cares—"

"Borne children with odd Flair, perhaps. Borne children who might be mutants."

"We're all fliggering mutants here on Celta. Probably were on old Earth, too. Nobody cares about blood." Draeg's words exploded, his body primed again to fight.

"Most people care about the strength of Flair, true, but I think those of the Traditionalist Stance care about mixing Noble and Commoner blood. And I think that movement has fanatics, and I think the Yews are mixed up with them, wanting to get back into political power, maybe."

"That's crazy!" Draeg objected.

"That's fanaticism."

Draeg scrubbed dried sweat from his face, then looked at Tinne. "You really believe this."

"I really do." Tinne's jaw flexed.

Draeg allowed himself a couple of paces, too. "Why me?"

"You're wasted here as an instructor. You should be doing more."

"Like spying on the Yews?" Draeg asked drily.

"Like working with your adoptive father with the T'Blackthorn guards." Tinne's white-blond brows came down. "And staying off the streets of Druida at night, looking for and finding trouble."

Draeg snorted, threw the towel aside. "Don't lecture me. And get someone else to handle this Yew business."

Tinne's pewter gaze drilled into Draeg. "And you are good for this job because you hired out as a mercenary guard and traveled protecting merchants. You know stridebeasts and horses."

"I know stridebeasts."

Tinne shrugged. "You can learn horses."

"What's horses have to do with anything?"

"The Sallow Family say that they've been contacted by the Yews, who are considering buying horses. The Yews want a stableman and horse trainer." Tinne's lips curved in a thin smile. "And a man who knows stridebeasts."

"Stableman," Draeg said, but he liked animals.

"The Sallows will work with you until you know horses well."

"Huh."

"And I'll remind you that your oldest adoptive brother is a Commoner and has thwarted the Traditionalist Stance before. He'd be on the list of people to remove, too."

Draeg's skin chilled. "No."

"Think not?" Tinne settled into his balance and stared at Draeg, and waited.

"I'll do it."

"Good."

Four weeks later, D'Yew estate within
the walls of Druida City, early spring

You should not be visualizing My FamWoman naked.

Draeg Betony-Blackthorn jolted at the disapproving mental
voice in his head and slid his gaze around the stable courtyard to
see who might have spoken to him telepathically. He'd had a *fleeting* nude vision of FirstFamily GrandLady D'Yew, imagined from
when he'd seen her and the cat slip out of the estate at night.

The cat!

*Loridana is MINE. Not yours. You do not get to have her in
any way, shape, or form. You keep your lascivious thoughts to
yourself.* The male cat's mental order rang in Draeg's head. He
zeroed in on the large gray tabby Familiar Companion. The tom sat
in a patch of morning spring sunlight on the wooden bench outside
the stable.

I haven't met you before, Draeg sent back. He didn't think anyone was checking up on him from the Residence, watching in the
trees, like they had been the first week he'd been here on the Yew
estate. Still, it was better to be safe and answer the cat with his mind
than talk to it aloud.

As far as he knew, the Yews believed him to be a man with low
Flair, psi power, whom they'd hired to take care of the stables.

He studied the cat with narrowed eyes. Draeg hadn't met
many Fams strong enough to pick up images from his mind. He'd
have to watch that.

And what else might the cat know? Both with regard to what
he'd pluck from Draeg's lax mental shields . . . and, yeah, Draeg
might be able to pump the feline about the people in the Residence, and Loridana D'Yew, the FirstFamily GrandLady.

With a bespelled broom, Draeg continued to damp-sweep the
red flagstoned courtyard in between the U of three brick stable
blocks, only one in good shape. *I just have your word that you are
the Fam of FirstFamily GrandLady D'Yew.* He added a mocking

note to his mental voice. *That is what you're saying, right? That you're her Fam? If so, why aren't you with her?*

The cat glared at him with unblinking yellow eyes and hissed, his nose lifting. *The Residence is unpleasant and disagreeable and mean. The Family is similarly so. I do not like them.* A short pause. *WE do not like them, My FamWoman Loridana and I.*

Draeg figured that meant that the Residence, an intelligent manor house, could sense the cat within its walls and didn't want the tom inside.

He got a blurred image from the Fam's mind of the cat getting kicked, and Draeg stilled. He didn't think he was supposed to have received that. Interesting. He might be able to receive more from the Fam's mind now and then. Useful for his mission. Which was to find out who in the Yew household had hooked up with the Traditionalist Stance fanatics and was engineering "accidents" for some of the younger members of the FirstFamilies, most particularly the Yews' enemies, the Hollys.

The cat leapt from the bench and strolled around Draeg, nose raised and sniffing.

Draeg leaned on his broom; the courtyard looked good. *So you're not allowed into the Residence, huh? Where have you been hiding?*

Jumping once more onto the bench, the cat circled and sent, *I reside in My very own shed in the garden that only Loridana and I use. It is My particular territory.*

Pretty fancy words for a FamCat.

My previous companion, a scholarly professor, raised Me from a kitten. I am an EXCEPTIONAL Fam.

Draeg snorted. Cats always believed that. *Yet you do not live in the Residence.*

The Fam just sniffed.

Draeg continued, *From what I understand, the Yew Family doesn't allow the young GrandLady much independence.* It was a deduction, and a leading statement to lure the Fam into talking about the woman. But it was based on the fact that Draeg had watched her leave the estate at night and followed her into Druida City proper four times in the two weeks he'd been here.

Like all FirstFamily estates, the Yew land was situated within the Druida City walls, but in a portion called "Noble Country," with the more populated areas to the east.

Unlike other members of the Family, Draeg hadn't seen her leave the Residence at any time other than late at night. He didn't think the rest of the Family knew of her nocturnal rambles.

As I stated previously, both Family and Residence are mean. They don't treat her as they should, so we are going to— The Fam stopped abruptly, glared at Draeg, then reiterated, *She is My person. You do not get to look at her or touch her or talk to her. Mine. I have observed you trailing Us when We go into the main city to scout.*

To scout? Draeg prodded.

The cat lifted his leg and began grooming, now ignoring Draeg. But a weird pattern transferred from the Fam's mind to Draeg's—like a bright blue rope snaking through dim alleys to the south city wall.

Putting the broom aside, he let the six stridebeasts out into the corral to enjoy the warm spring morning. The winter had been colder and harder and lasted longer than usual.

Beautiful animals, not nearly as hairy as most stridebeasts he'd ridden when he'd been a guard for merchant caravans. These were the greater species and appeared equal to those that he'd cared for at the Sallows', who had the best, when Draeg had practiced being a stableman before he'd hired on here.

Stridebeasts were a native Celtan animal somewhat like Earthan llamas but larger. Yeah, the more he studied them, the more he thought the Yews had been doing some selective breeding. These animals' hair wasn't as long as those stridebeasts the Sallows had, merely a few centimeters, and each appeared a solid color instead of patchy like most. The necks were long, the ears oval, the legs sturdy and widening to padded feet that appeared tougher than those he'd used before. *That* would be a boon to every rider on Celta.

Pretty beasts. Though not as pretty as horses.

The animals had been well cared for even before he'd come, and he thought—and those who'd sent him had heard—that the eighteen-year-old D'Yew had tended them herself.

Draeg had yet to meet her. He'd sure like to interact with her on a one-on-one, in-person basis instead of watching her from afar and not just because he liked the looks of her slim figure from the back and the way she moved.

Loridana is MINE! the cat yelled in his mind, and Draeg flinched. Seemed like his thoughts leaked to the tom as much as the cat's did to him despite mindshields. Dammit. He needed info. And he needed more patience. It had been a while since he'd had to practice patience, and he didn't much like it.

Look, cat, he began.

You may address Me as Baccat, the tom said, staring past Draeg.

And you can call me Draeg.

The Fam's tail flicked. *I know who you are.*

Draeg's gut tightened; he stared at Baccat. Did the cat really know that Draeg had come to spy on the Yews? That his name wasn't Draeg Hedgenettle but Draeg Betony-Blackthorn?

Baccat's whole head dipped and rose as he sniffed long. *Your clothes indicate that you usually live with three cats, two foxes, and a young dog.*

Sinking slightly into his balance, Draeg met the cat's gaze. The tom had listed all the Fams in the T'Blackthorn household, those of his cuzes-siblings. Draeg's mind clicked through all the information the Fam might be able to tell about him from that one sniff. Straif T'Blackthorn, who'd formally adopted all of the Betonys years ago, had one of the premier FamCats in Druida City, Drina. If Baccat even knew *of* Drina . . . well, Draeg would be paying blackmail to D'Yew's Fam to keep his secret and stay here at his undercover job.

He dropped his arms, laded his mental voice with admiration. *You speak well.*

Baccat sat straighter with pride. *I speak better than you do. I matured in a Noble Household.*

Huh. Is that so? Draeg's Dad had been a Noble GraceLord; his adoptive father-cuz was of the FirstFamilies, *the* most important Families of Celta. The ones descended from the colonists who'd bought the starships and paid for the journey from Earth to Celta.

With an inclination of his head, Baccat said, *It is quite so.* Then his face scrunched a little and Draeg felt a cloudy chill. Glancing at the sky, he saw it blue and cloudless, realized he'd experienced emotions from the cat. Again.

You lost your Family, Draeg murmured. He let his body relax.

My first FamMan was an old scholar and he died, the last of his Family.

Draeg swallowed hard. Celta could be a hard planet for Earthan stock. As a young man, T'Blackthorn had seen his whole Family die around him. His wife was sterile from a disease she'd contracted as a child. *Made* Families, like his own, were wonderful, but Draeg knew all too well that you couldn't count on being here tomorrow, or on anyone else you loved being here tomorrow. An inward shudder rippled his nerves.

But you've got a new FamWoman, he pointed out.

Cat eyes got lost in a grin. *Yes. She is very generous, kind, and beautiful.* The eyes opened to threatening slits. *And she is MINE!*

"So we've returned full circle to that topic, Baccat." Draeg shrugged. "I've got a job to do." He turned his back and went to the corral to look at the six beautiful stridebeasts. Still, even as he worked with them, continued to make friends with the non-sentient animals, he kept an eye on the cat. Draeg hooked a little mental thread onto that beast's aura to keep track of him, part of Draeg's Flair. Wherever the cat went, Draeg would be able to follow and find him.

Better wise than surprised.

*W*e have decided to accede to your request for a horse, *FirstFamily* GrandLady Loridana Itha Valerian D'Yew," the Residence, Yew Residence, said in its usual arrogant male voice. As if its words were a portentous announcement. The thick, rich fabrics of the furniture and rugs in the library, even the expensive wallpaper, softened its tone.

Lori kept her spine straight in the chair but answered with more force than usual. "Oh, thank you!" Since the Residence monitored her physical reactions, it would have noted her pulse leap and faster heart rate.

You are disturbed, FamWoman? questioned her Familiar companion, Baccat, in a thought to her. Naturally, he'd felt the spurt of her excitement and dismay. He was the only one she didn't keep a barrier of control between her mindshields against, didn't control her every thought and feeling with.

No, Baccat. Surprised. Apparently we are finally getting a horse, she sent to him mentally. *Can you check out the stables to see if the Residence is . . . fibbing to me again?*

I spent a septhour in the stables this morning and am enjoying the sun in Our garden, Baccat grumbled, but she sensed he rose to his paws from a flattened bed of catmint and stretched, rump up. *I will do this for You, MY FamWoman.*

Keeping a smile curving her lips, she breathed to regulate her emotions and hopefully her pulse, too.

This has delayed our plans to leave the estate. She kept her mind touch as light as her tone, though deep inside irritation rolled through her in a tight, hot ball.

A huge telepathic sigh from Baccat as he trotted to the stables. *I postulate that we must now take the horse when we depart, too?*

Yes. She glanced out the tall window at the rolling grassyard of the estate toward the stables, but couldn't see them. She'd fought a bitter battle three years ago to have the thick drapes on one window in the library opened when she attended the Residence for instruction. One window of six. Even so, the furniture had to be rearranged so sunlight wouldn't fade the fabric on the plush antiques or exquisite carpets.

Yanking her attention back to the Residence, she reiterated her gratitude. "Thank you so much."

She sensed the Residence preening.

"The stableman we hired two eightdays ago has proven competent with our stridebeasts and stated he could also handle horses.
We checked his bona fides once more and his references agreed, so
we purchased the animals from the Sallows."

"Animals? More than one?" Lori swallowed. Last year, even a
couple of months ago, she'd have been pleased. Before she'd made
the decision to leave her whole Family, let them trundle on in their
rigid traditional ruts that they'd insisted she live within. Not allow
her to *be* D'Yew.

Now she had to fake pleasure. "How wonderful!" she said
aloud, then sent to Baccat, *Two horses.*

She heard her Fam sniff. *I heard the Residence in your mind.*

With a nod to him and to the Residence, who watched her from
a crystal embedded in the walls, she stood. Sweeping a glance
around the room, she saw that the chamber and *sensed* that the rest
of the large manor house held not the tiniest dirt or grime—her
duties today were done. She'd used a lot of Flair, psi power, but the
real surge of delight at the thought of her own horses mitigated her
weariness.

"May I have permission to visit our new arrivals?" she asked
the Residence.

"You may, D'Yew," the Residence said in plummy tones.

Being addressed as "D'Yew," a FirstFamily GrandLady's title,
meant less than nothing. Or rather it meant, "You are the daughter
of a FirstFamily, the highest of the high; you must believe as we wish
you to believe, comport yourself as we have trained you, and live
your life in the manner we approve."

"My thanks again," she said. She hadn't encountered the new
stableman yet. This last week had been the one designated for spring
cleaning, and the Family and house tapped on her Flair to power the
spells. Not that the Residence itself, or all the other members of the
Family couldn't handle the cleaning. But as soon as she'd finished
her First Passage—a dreamquest to free her psi power—at seven
and had enough Flair, they'd begun siphoning it for all the major

spells. She'd been told she was giving back to the Family who housed and fed and cared for her needs.

Her physical needs. And no one had ever mentioned love. She wasn't quite sure how that might feel, at least from people; she'd learned to love and receive love easily enough from the stride-beasts.

As for love between two people, which was shown in the limited vizes and books she was allowed, she thought it was just an aspect of sex and seemed to make people act stupid.

Baccat snorted in her mind distantly.

What? she asked.

These HORSES. Laughter traveled down their link.

She suppressed a sigh. Her high hopes at having something special crashed again.

The Residence went on. "The horses arrived early this afternoon. You may go see them." Its tone was indulgent. "Be sure to return in time to bathe before dressing for dinner."

"Of course. I'll take my calendar sphere." She never left the house without it. When she was a child they'd attached it to her clothes. Now she used it to schedule her free and daydreaming time and to arrive precisely at the correct moment to whatever event the Family wanted and be the person the Family expected.

She donned the proper manner and inclined her head, then proceeded across the room with back and shoulders straight, chin high. "Thank you, Residence, and please disseminate my gratitude to all the Family members who approved my request."

"Done, GrandLady D'Yew."

She hesitated; maybe she should try one *last* time to claim her proper place in the household.

Clearing her throat, she winced at showing weakness, then pushed on. "At Samhain in the autumn, New Year's, we spoke of having a ritual celebration of my adulthood, since I am eighteen and finished my Second Passage, which signified that I'm an adult. Spring Equinox is coming in three weeks and—"

"We will discuss this later, D'Yew, with the whole Family and when our duties are not pressing," the Residence said. It always felt able to interrupt her. Again, hurt and irritation surged, and again she pushed them down.

The Residence opened the door and she left.

The maître de maison, Cuspid Yew, a cuz of her mother's, stood outside in the hallway, posture stiff enough that Lori straightened her back even more. He and the housekeeper, Folia, were the real people in charge of the house, and the powers in the Family since Lori's mother died when she was five. Lori hadn't interacted with her mother much and didn't remember her . . . except she'd always scowled and looked scary.

Lori nodded to him. "As you may have heard, I intend to bring up the topic of a celebration for reaching my majority again this evening. I believe at drinks before dinner would be appropriate."

His face remained in deep frown lines. "Your cuzes Zus and Vi will not be at dinner tonight, but at friends', and because they are the members of the Family closest in range to you, we would like the twins to act as Priest and Priestess in such a ritual. Their input is vital."

She'd heard that before and couldn't think of anyone less spiritual than her twin cuzes, the maître de maison's children. "Ah, well, perhaps it's time I met their friends."

The man's jaw clenched. He started a cutting gesture, then dropped his hands. "We are not ready to present you to Druida City society, yet," Cuspid intoned.

So it always went, had gone since she'd wanted to attend grovestudy with other children in Druida City when she was ten. As for now, Cuspid ruled the household and he didn't want to give up that power to her.

"I hear you," she said, ascending the massive marble staircase in smooth steps to her rooms—not the MasterSuite or MistrysSuite. She must dress in clothes good for the stables. The acquisition of the horses she'd been campaigning for throughout the last two years must be a sop to keep her happy. So the Family and Residence had noticed her restlessness—and hopefully hadn't realized how determined she was to leave.

Silence fell, and only her steady footsteps and the ticking of the antique clock broke the quiet. She kept her footsteps light as she finished ascending the stairs.

Nothing changed, and nothing she could do would change anything. She was done.

Two

*F*amWoman? *Baccat questioned.* <u>You are dejected?</u> *She sensed he* hissed. *THEY have scraped your feelings again!*

Since no one was in the corridor, Lori picked up her pace and managed a shrug at her Fam's words. *I'll get over it.*

We will decamp SOON.

Yes.

Sometimes fighting is not the answer and, as we have experienced here with your Family, can make matters worse. Sometimes walking away from a situation is the best option.

Yes.

A few minutes later she drew in deep breaths of still-cold fresh spring air. Outside at last! No warm and heavy odor laden with the faint scent of incense that her Family preferred.

I am on my way, she told Baccat telepathically.

I support My FamWoman, physically, mentally, and emotionally.

Her walk continued as a stately tread until she knew she couldn't be seen from any window or tower of the Residence or any scrystone in the walls that the Residence monitored . . . then she ran, free of restrictions and constrictions. And, yes, she ran through the edge of the grove, a zigzagging path that she'd learned through trial and error was private.

As she drew close to the stables, indecision tore at her. With the animals, the stridebeasts she'd been raising and training according to ancient methods, she was completely herself, Lori Valerian Yew. No pretense, no masks, all love.

This new stableman . . . who and what kind of person; might she want to be with him? The Family approved of him . . . but as far as she knew, he wasn't allowed in the Residence. So the real question was whether he'd take tales to the Family and Residence if she acted like the woman she was, the one she wanted to become, instead of the arrogant GrandLady persona the Family preferred her to be . . . like her mother had been, and her mother's father, Mother-Sire, and probably all the previous generations back to the original Earthan colonists who'd funded the starships and journey. That was what "FirstFamily" meant. Her ancestors had had enough psi, psychic power, and enough gilt, old-time money, to buy their way onto a starship and berths in the cryonics tubes.

What do you think of the new stableman? she asked Baccat, though she wasn't entirely sure of his judgement. The cat had shown up at the stables at the beginning of winter, and though they were in concert about their ideas of her various Family members, Baccat had told outrageous stories of other Fams and people he'd known.

A hesitation before a rush of emotion came her way from the cat slyness, laughter, the hint of a secret. But she'd become accustomed to beings having secrets, and, after all, she had her own.

He is capable and efficient and speaks well. Another snort. *The horses like him.*

She slowed, pondering. Perhaps the stableman shouldn't be treated like her Family, with cool distance. She knew little about horses, and this new man did. If she wanted to learn from him, or would be working with him, she should be herself . . . the person she liked being, not the D'Yew the Family had molded.

Soon she came within sight of one side of the stables, and she smiled. Of all the estate, this place reflected her the most.

Like everything else on the estate, the stables were built on a grand scale, and Lori had used that reason to prod the Family into renovating one block of them, and keep the others from falling down. Lady and Lord knew, the Family had plenty of gilt.

The U-shaped stables loomed between the trees. Unlike the flat gray stone of the D'Yew Residence manor house, warm red brick composed the buildings. Her heart leapt a little seeing the corral with her six stridebeasts.

There she'd find love. There she'd give love to the stridebeasts. Though they weren't sentient animals like some other hybrid or Earthan animals, through her breeding program they'd become more intelligent. She'd have liked to compare her statistics and lines with others but was allowed no contact with the outer world—with "lesser" people, or other FirstFamily Nobles "who don't have our standards."

Lori believed only her Family followed some sort of hard-edged rules that were far too strict for human beings. *She* found them stifling.

She did want to be loved, and the stridebeasts gave her that. She hoped the horses would, too.

Rounding the last copse and seeing the full stable block revealed, she skidded to a halt. In the gravel courtyard, a man looked to be practicing some sort of fighting pattern. She just stared.

He didn't look like her relatives. At all.

She thought he stood as tall as she, so medium height for a man, but his muscles were certainly bigger. She didn't think she'd seen a man with developed muscle that went from his shoulders to his neck. He had a strong back, then.

Yes, she could see it very well since he wore no shirt. A very triangular sort of upper body with ridges of muscles. She swallowed.

She slid her eyes lower than his back and chest. His legs looked like all muscle, too. His backside tighter than anyone's she'd seen. She patted her own. Solid, but nothing like his, and she thought she was the most physical person in the household. Surely she'd been exercising more so she'd be tougher when she left with six stridebeasts.

He looked like a guard. The Residence and the Family had debated having guards for a long time as she grew up. But none of her cousins had wanted to take the training . . . and the Yews' archenemies were the Holly warriors, whom everyone in the household despised.

Catching a movement from the corner of his eye, Draeg Betony-Blackthorn whirled. Saw the young woman lingering in the deep black cold-winter shadows under a stand of conifers. The trees blocked the view of D'Yew Residence from the stables. He continued his spin, worked in a kick that had him grunting with effort. Just the notion of having female eyes watching him pushed him into flashier moves.

So this was FirstFamily GrandLady D'Yew, the threat to the fighting Hollys.

Like hell. He went with his previous impressions, with his gut. No threat to the Hollys from this one. Had to be wrong.

But this slim young woman, six years younger than he, decades younger than he in experience, would be the outward spearhead of whoever threatened the Hollys. Any results of her relatives' actions would be blamed on her. He was damn sure that her folks remained ultraconservative and were associated with the ugly Traditionalist Stance political party sprouting in the last few years. Maybe the fanatical, violent edge of that party. At least the Hollys thought they were behind some "accidents."

He glanced at her clothes. Worn and shabby and not a button to be seen. All fastenings seemed to be hidden tabs.

All his instincts told him this woman was innocent. Not this Yew, but who?

While he thought, he'd kept on going with his training. He flowed into another fighting exercise, angled more to the side of her as he studied her in glimpses. She continued to move like a self-conscious woman with a hitch of hesitancy. Like she wasn't sure of herself, or who she might be.

Since he figured he'd changed mightily several times during his life, he understood that. He continued through the level until she stepped into the sunshine and walked with soft and quiet steps toward him.

As the stridebeasts in the corral caught her scent, they got noisy and pressed against the fence to greet her.

The cat, who'd trotted in earlier to sniff at him and the horses, left the patch of sunlit ground to saunter toward the paddock.

She met Draeg's eyes, then looked away, her gaze sliding once more over his bare chest, and that clued him in that she was as naive and isolated as he'd believed. Stuck here on the estate with no contact with anyone but her Family—except when she snuck into the city of Druida at night.

Lori nodded to the stableman, ignoring the heat she felt in her cheeks, then went up to the fence and greeted the small stridebeast herd. They looked good, cared for over the last two weeks as well as she would have done. She'd grabbed a precious few minutes in the dawn and after dark to check on them but hadn't spent as much time as usual with her beasts.

Yes, he'd tended them well, so she approved of the man. He stood near the opposite end of the stables and had donned a tunic, which was a pity. She could have studied his chest more.

I am here also. Pet Me! I did well and deserve your attention! Baccat's haunches tensed, and then he leapt for her shoulder. Lori stood straight and still, muttering a couplet for the invisible shelf that set on her shoulder to take her Fam's bulk. He thunked down. *Thank you for coming and telling me about the horses.* She scratched the side of his head. She hadn't seen her Fam since she'd slipped from the Residence before dawn to feed him proper Fam-Cat food.

One of the stridebeasts hummed at her and she turned her attention to them, feeling Baccat smirk at each of her other beloved animals from his position on her shoulder.

She took the time to pet each one's nose and say words of admiration, though the smell of a different scent drifted to her nostrils. The horses were here. Somewhere.

They are situated around the end of the stables in a temporary pen. Draeg is getting them and Our stridebeasts accustomed to each other's smell, Baccat said.

"All right, then," she murmured.

When she was done with the stridebeasts in the paddock, she waved a hand and transferred a couple of bales of the feed they particularly liked as a treat from the storage barn.

The outside stall doors stood open and she glanced in them. They appeared well tended, too.

I merit a treat, too, Baccat said, once again rubbing against her cheek; she thought he sneered at the stableman. With a snap of her fingers, she translocated a thin sheet of papyrus folded into a tiny envelope with catnip inside.

MINE! You gave Me the most excellent and efficacious and ecstasy-producing nip! I LOVE YOU! Her Fam snatched the packet with his mouth, then sailed from her shoulder using his Flair and a trickle of her own to land in a dry patch of dirt that looked like his personal wallow.

She didn't often give her companion catnip, perhaps twice a month, and while she smiled as he tore into the papyrus that would quickly decay, and he rolled around in the leaves, she kept hidden the fact that she wanted time with the horses without cat comments. Baccat should be happy with the nip for a good septhour.

Whuffles, horse noises, came to Lori's ears and she hurried to round the stables, looking eagerly for the animals. Beyond the far edge of the large door, the stableman had erected a smaller pen and outdistanced her to stand straight and proud near the gate.

He was prime. The horses weren't. They looked old and tired, and Lori stared. She'd heard that the Sallows prized their animals.

With a nod to the man, she projected calm, part of her Flair that she'd inherited from her father, a Valerian. Her mind focused on the horses she'd wanted for so long. She strolled to them; one mare was gray with a black mane and tail. She watched Lori with wide eyes but didn't seem to be afraid. That was good, at least.

"That's Smyrna," Draeg said.

"Greetyou, Smyrna," Lori said in quiet tones, reaching out a slow hand to brush her neck. Smyrna arched into Lori's hand, no doubt still feeling the calm she sent to the beasts.

For an instant, she thought she saw a faintly visible iridescent arc of a bubble curve over the mare's head. Lori tried to hold still, but the image vanished within a blink. She thought that the bubble might be a manifestation of her adult Flair since it had begun to occur after her Second Passage, but wasn't sure what it meant.

"Here." The man handed her an apple and Smyrna's soft lips took the fruit from her with greed.

The other mare was reddish brown, the color called roan, but didn't look like the gorgeous beast in her horse book.

"And this is Ragan," he said.

Lori nodded, and though she focused on the horses, she wondered that he didn't offer his own name. She should have known it—the head of a Noble household should always know her staff— and he was the only one who wasn't a Yew, but she didn't recall anyone telling her his name.

Ragan snickered.

Yes, the horses remained beautiful animals, but not the kind of beasts she'd imagined. She slid her hand down the roan's strong neck, and the mare turned her head to sniff and lip her hair and Lori felt the gentleness of her spirit, the greatness of her heart.

Irritated, she turned back to the gorgeous man and said what she'd thought. "Why do we have these ladies?" she demanded. Her notion of riding across the land at speeds a stridebeast couldn't match faded. "The Sallows are supposed to be excellent judges of horseflesh."

His brows raised in a look questioning her that she herself would never be allowed to get away with inside the Residence with any member of her Family. He scratched Smyrna's forehead.

"The Sallows are wonderful horsemen, and careful of their

charges," he said. "But these are the beasts that could be purchased from the Sallows with the amount of gilt you were willing to pay. Even then I had to guarantee I'd take care of them on my solemn vow of honor."

Lori suppressed a sigh; she should have expected something like this. She continued to stroke the mare, then felt the intensity of the man's eyes on her. "And you are?"

His brow rose again, and then he swept her a flourishing bow. The kind of bow she'd been told was her due as a FirstFamily Grand-Lady. If she'd been in a ballroom. "Draeg Hedgenettle," he said.

That should have been followed up with something like "at your service," or "your humble employee," but wasn't.

Nothing humble about the man.

Three

As her gaze scanned the area again, the horse pen, the stables, the corral, she saw that he'd already done her excellent service. That it might be because of the horses rather than just because of his job made her think better of him.

She sighed. "So the Family paid the smallest amount they could to purchase the horses."

"You sound as if you didn't make the decision," he stated.

She shrugged. He blocked the gate, so she teleported into the far side of the pen, then walked toward the horses who'd turned. She learned from Ragan's mind what kind of seed the horse liked, translocated some to her hand, and held it out. The horse stepped quickly to her and slurped them up.

When she met Draeg's deep-blue eyes, he emphasized, "I do not give my solemn word of honor lightly." His lips set in a grim line. "No one does after hearing the tale of the Hollys."

That distracted Lori. Her mother and her MotherSire had been enemies of the Hollys, and the whole Family and Residence continued to rant about them. Most often she could automatically turn her mind to other topics for a good five minutes. She thought back but didn't recall any stories of the Hollys and Broken Vows of Honor, which she should have if it showed that Family in a bad light.

Hot eagerness spurted through her, then innate wariness cooled that. What if he *was* in the pay of the Family to test her loyalties? Had they seen through her pretense and figured out that she planned on leaving them and *their* plans?

She couldn't take the chance that Draeg Hedgenettle reported to the maître de maison or the housekeeper or the Residence itself—those who ran the Family.

A tiny, niggling thought in the back of her mind calculated that his showing up at this particular time, within a couple of eightdays before she left this restrictive place forever, was not a coincidence. If he could tell her of the outside world, that could be too good to be true. So was the virile man himself.

As she'd considered him, she'd fallen into his intense gaze, couldn't tell what *he* was thinking. Wrenching her glance away, she said, "I understand about vows and how they can adversely affect whole Families if broken." She switched her scrutiny to her horse's ears and frowned. "It looks as if the horses have ear infections." Lori scowled at him.

He opened the gate and strode through. Neither of the horses shied at his presence. Lori got the feeling that they had been found wandering and were relieved to have been discovered and would be cared for. They saw the stridebeasts and how nice they looked and how Lori had given them food and pats.

Draeg tilted his head as if he sensed the horse's emotions, too. He left the gate wide open. Neither Smyrna nor Ragan headed toward the gap.

The stableman came over to study Ragan's ears. She butted him, then turned her head pointedly back to Lori, who laughed. One of the reasons she loved animals. All of them saw *her*, just her, and they loved her back, and loved her *first*. Not the Family name, the Family traditions. They schemed for nothing more than her time and her love and more food and more play.

"I'll medicate the horses. The Sallows had just picked them up from the late GraceLady Alexanders's land." His expression darkened further and she sensed that he expected her to comment. He added, "No one knew the Alexanderses kept horses until the NobleCouncil reps went to that estate and found them. As expected, the reps declared the Family dead, the line extinguished."

Again his eyes bore into her as if she should comment. She went with one of the things her father had recorded on one of his spheres she'd found and hidden. "Celta is a harsh planet. We descendants of the Earth colonists still only have a toehold here."

Draeg jerked a nod. "Too true."

Yet he didn't seem satisfied with her response. Too bad.

"You don't find it disturbing that a Family has died out?"

Lori shrugged and saw from his expression that the movement seemed too callous or casual to him, so she didn't say that she wouldn't care if her Family died out.

"It's sad." She drew in a breath and met his watchful eyes. "But it's Celta." She waved vaguely. "Things happen." Another tiny pause. "I don't have any immediate Family—that is, parents or siblings or even Sires or Dams of my parents. Some G'Uncles and G'Aunts and cuzes who are their children and grandchildren."

Eyes still matched with hers, Draeg said, "I'm sorry." He didn't sound it—odd. Was he working for her Family or not?

Then he continued, in a dark, rich tone that sank into her skin and tingled her nerves. "Family is the most important thing on Celta."

She didn't know why tears backed up behind her eyes, maybe because he sounded absolutely sincere spouting what he believed to be a truth, and it wasn't, not to her. She leaned in and rubbed her face on the mare's neck, breathed in the horse scent, so different from stridebeasts, so innately pleasing to her—because horses had been brought to Celta along with the colonists? Stridebeasts had been here, or their ancestors that the colonists had bred, part of the flora and fauna close to Earthan due to the planet seeding of some ancient race.

"Don't you agree, GrandLady Loridana D'Yew?" the man asked softly.

Another breath of horse smell and she stepped away, began circling the beast who'd welcomed her touch, seeing the rough coat, the occasional sore. Terrible. She cleared her throat and looked at him over Ragan's back. "I think love is the most important thing. On Celta or off. Period."

He just stared at her and gave a crack of laughter, then shook his head. "You're such a girl."

Anger fired in her. Though perhaps it was hurt that he was just like everyone else she knew, dismissive of her. She might be stuck on this estate with no outside influence allowed in, but she was remedying that and would be gone soon, and those who thought Family should rule their lives could let it do so. And she wasn't a girl!

Impulsively, she pulled herself onto the back of the horse, narrower and more comfortable than a stridebeast's without a saddle. She leaned forward to whisper in the ear flicking back toward her. "Let's run!" She sent a vision of them—an amended one she'd had all her life but this one featuring Ragan—of running. Long strides but not as fast as she'd imagined. Grabbing fistfuls of Ragan's mane, Lori gave a gentle press of her legs and they took off. More in symbols than in words, she sent telepathically, *Let's show him what we can do, together!*

Learning to speak in animal pictographs hadn't been easy, but she'd persisted, *made* her standard Flair follow her wishes.

The horse neighed in agreement and off they went . . . first at a walk straight through the gate. Lori pointed her to a well-traveled path and Ragan picked up her pace to a jouncing trot, then long strides as they reached the edge of the groomed portion of the stables and the estate and headed into hedgerows.

She sensed Ragan had missed this, too.

Lori didn't push the horse, let her canter at her own speed. Smoother than even Lori's best stridebeast's gait! A feeling of freedom, of exultation flowed through her, and she shared her emotion with the horse.

They continued down the hard, wide path until they were within sight of the edge of the band of thick forest that separated this part of Noble Country from the rest of Druida City. Smaller, lesser Nobles' estates sat beyond the Yews'.

Time to turn Ragan around, let her walk back, though Lori's eyes felt wild and her grin huge. The first time she'd ridden on horseback had been everything she'd imagined, had craved. The wind had swept her hair back from her face and whisked away the tears of pure joy.

She and Ragan were only halfway back when Lori's calendar sphere chimed. She had twenty minutes before she must descend the grand stairway dressed formally for dinner. Teleporting to her waterfall room, putting her clothes in the cleanser, and showering wouldn't take too long. Dressing and skin care and facial enhancements longer. If she did a Whirlwind Spell to take care of everything, it would be noticed by the Family and she'd be disapproved of for having to use a spell to be presentable instead of managing her time wisely.

Unclenching her jaw, she checked on the horse's energy and asked Ragan if she could canter back, reassuring the mare that the path was wide and clear.

Baccat? she sent to her Fam.

Lorrrrri, he purred in her mind, drunk on nip.

It's dinnertime for me. If we go into Druida later, it will be when Eire twinmoon rises.

Yesss. This afternoon sun is very nice and warm. Spring weather should be here soon!

Until later, my Fam, I love you.

Until later, FamWoman. I love you, he replied.

She and Ragan made the stables. Lori slid from Ragan with a wince, then inclined her torso in a slight bow to Draeg Hedgenettle, who had put Smyrna in a free stall. "My apologies. My enthusiasm overcame my sense and I have no time to care completely for Ragan." Though Lori set a hand on the horse's withers and sent a brisk cleansing energy down Ragan's hide.

That one brow of Draeg's rose in commentary and she just refrained from biting her lip, a habit her Family had broken her of, though she wasn't accustomed to controlling all her emotions here at the stables.

"I'll handle that," Draeg said.

Lori nodded and settled into her balance. She closed her eyes, found the well of her inner peace, and sent it out to blanket the stable area. She always said good-bye to her stridebeasts this way. When her lashes opened she saw a near comical expression of surprise on Draeg's face. His mouth actually hung open.

Bringing her hands in front of her and pressing the palms together to continue the cycling of her energy, she teleported to the waterfall in her rooms. It continued to irritate her that, again, the Family had failed to recognize her as D'Yew in all but name and give her the MistrysSuite. They'd used her title since she'd been a toddler to beat her into compliance.

Annoyance smudged the joy of her first time horseback. *That* she could blame herself for—not continuing with the pleasure of the ride and the peace of sending love to her beasts—and she even owed grudging gratitude to her Family for purchasing Ragan and Smyrna.

Hot water pounded down on her and chased away the aches of riding a horse bareback instead of a stridebeast.

As she dressed, she wondered if she could, if she should, slip out of Noble Country and into the more populated portion of Druida City tonight. When she'd started, it was to scout out a good path from the estate through the city and away. Since six stridebeasts would be with her when she finally made her escape, she had to choose her route carefully. No matter what hour, she would be remembered if they were seen. And six stridebeasts left a trail.

Now escaping into the city, even if she only observed other people, was an adventure. Yet the more often she did it, the more chance she'd be caught. She'd noted that she wasn't the only one of the Family leaving for city amusement. Her twin cuzes, Vi and Zus, had used the gleaming polished and refurbished Family glider to sweep into the city on several occasions. At least at first, now she thought they teleported to some place they knew to meet their friends.

I wish to prowl the streets of Druida City together tonight!
Baccat sent her.

She grinned. *Yes! Always a thrill in Druida City! We should
go over the route once more.*

*It is good that you continue to prepare diligently. I will meet
you just within the east garden gate at Eire moonrise. Later, My
FamWoman.*

Later.

As Lori stopped to breathe and steady her hand applying the
enhancements, she smiled, then sent to the Residence, who would
have noted the spike in her heartbeat, a mental lie. *I've been
remembering my first horseback ride, D'Yew Residence. Thank
you again for procuring the horses for me.*

You are welcome. A child should be rewarded for good behavior.

Lori swallowed annoyance. The antique clock on the mantel
of her sitting room chimed fifteen minutes before dinner. She had
to leave now for all the little rites the Family insisted upon, and
where most of them who taught her would scrutinize her. For
proper behavior.

*W*hat had just happened? Draeg stared at the spot D'Yew had
teleported from until Ragan stepped daintily up to him and nick-
ered. He ran his hand down her back, noticed that some of her
sores looked better, her coat a little healthier. Had D'Yew shared
energy with her mount when they'd raced away?

Maybe.

Smyrna made a disgruntled sound, like she envied her stablemate.
But Draeg had no doubt that whatever emotional balm D'Yew had
sent through them all, Smyrna had felt, too. He stretched, his muscles
feeling warmer and looser than he'd experienced in a long while. That
was the physical effect he was perfectly able to admit to himself.

He didn't really know what the emotional—no, the *mental*
effect was. He'd felt at peace . . . but also with a slight zing that
seemed to travel like a ruffling breeze over his nerves.

Interesting.

He finished rubbing Ragan down—not that she needed much—and put both the horses in the last two empty stalls of the stable block, then moved the stridebeasts in from the paddock. All the animals had studied each other, and it seemed to Draeg that the stridebeasts wouldn't mind having the horses in the corral with them tomorrow, and those animals were familiar to the horses. Time would tell.

The one issue that nagged at Draeg during the rest of his chores was the simple fact that he'd seen D'Yew use a good amount of Flair, and she gave absolutely no indication that it had wearied her a bit. From observation, he had to think she had a great Flair, more than he—and the people who'd sent him here to check out the Yew Family—had anticipated. Too bad the Yews hadn't allowed T'Ash, the best tester of the strength of Flair, near the young woman.

And some tightening at the back of his neck told Draeg that Loridana D'Yew would be slipping out of the Residence and the estate tonight, as she'd done several times in the last two weeks.

He'd be ready to track her and find out exactly what she did in the city.

Four

Baccat leapt down from the ivy-free spot atop the wall that Lori had cleared previously for him and into her arms, a tiny tradition of theirs, reaffirming their connection. The warmth and weight of him, and his purr against her heart, made her smile. He stretched and licked her chin, then said mentally, *We do not need to traverse the roads through Noble Country tonight on paw and foot. Let us teleport through it.*

Lori raised her brows; she'd planned on walking the full escape route to set it in her mind, but that could wait for another time. *All right.*

I have plans for Us, he said smugly. *Let Us get beyond your substandard estate spellshields.*

They were substandard because the person with the best spellshield Flair disliked the Yews.

The gate didn't creak, didn't even whisper against frost-stiff grass and old fragments of leaves dead since autumn. She and Baccat had slipped away from the estate over the last month when weather permitted, but being outside the Yew walls remained an adventure.

They could teleport in small jumps if she used his visualization. Baccat often left D'Yew's grounds, teleporting out and in, and he knew the city well.

At first it had been difficult adjusting to his view of the world, though she'd had experience working with stridebeasts. But she and her Fam both desired to roam the city, so they practiced. They'd become adept at reaching Apollopa Temple in a midlevel Noble section of town with three hops.

Baccat had chosen the refurbished temple, and told her unbelievable stories of the site and the nearby Turquoise House and murder and mayhem. She found the Temple soothing and thought that within a short time she'd be familiar enough with it to teleport to it directly from D'Yew estate.

Soon they arrived in the Temple and Baccat's loud rough purr echoed, adding to the atmosphere of solace. They'd used the main teleportation pad, a small area outside the circular ritual chamber, and she heard voices beyond the open double doors. She tensed until she understood the questions and responses and the singing lilt of a wedding.

Baccat lay heavy in her arms, but his weight wasn't as much as she wanted to hold. Her chest tightened. Suddenly her animals didn't seem enough and she swallowed with a sudden *need* for a human love, a man in her life.

Her whole body rippled with a wave of emotion. *Stupid* yearning. She had her own *plans*, her own life to live, her freedom to grasp; why would she want a guy messing that up? And she didn't know one man outside of her Family, and the men she knew in her Family, the distant cuzes who worked in the Residence and on the estate, she didn't respect.

Wrong. The image of Draeg Hedgenettle rose to her mind, how he looked bare-chested, how he moved with masculine vigor and efficiency, his black hair shining in the sunlight, his blue eyes looking at her with appreciation as he smiled. Her next swallow was more of a gulp as heat flushed through her and settled moistly between her legs.

She had to draw in a couple of deep breaths before her mind stopped buzzing.

A third swallow as her throat tightened when triumphant musical notes surged, then segued into a ritual dance tune. People celebrating together, perhaps joyfully. She led and participated in the formal rituals of the seasons and the phases of the twinmoons, a *celebration* of her faith and religion, but not joyfully.

FamWoman? Baccat sniffed and his eyes widened. *There is food here! A full repast of wonderful dishes, meats and sweets—*

No, Baccat, Lori said, though she felt a rumble of her stomach. Keeping her hold on him, she stepped from the pad and reset the switch, indicating it was available. Baccat seemed happy to rest in her arms as she walked to the rear door and out into the straight path into the herb garden, trim and tended with deadfall cut away. Some beds held turned earth, others rows of tidy crocuses sprouting above the ground. She liked her own wild garden better.

Sweet and savory spice smells of previous plantings in the tumbled dirt wafted around them and she relaxed more. She heard nothing from the temple and left unruly emotions behind, fixed her thoughts on her goals.

"Now that we have horses that we'll be taking with us, we should double-check the route to make sure it's fine for them—look at the width of the alleys and streets." A boon, for sure, having horses! Thank the Lady and Lord, but it did change her plans, and thank the Couple that she *could* alter her plans at this time and that the horses hadn't appeared the day she'd decided to leave.

But wait! Baccat leapt from her arms, set himself directly in the one-person garden path, and puffed up, raising his hair in emphasis. *I would like to show you ALL of Druida City before We leave.*

"No," she said aloud.

You should SEE Druida City, KNOW it and its various cultural and historical places before We leave. To educate yourself. You should not believe just what the Yews and Yew Residence teach you.

"I don't," she said curtly. "I haven't since I was young and my nurse told me to think for myself, and not to believe people who were mean to me." Since her Valerian nurse had been dismissed within a week of that warning, it had truly stuck with Lori.

Along with the kindness of the old stableman who'd died when she was a child and finding her father's memory spheres and recording spheres, she'd been able to block most of the toxic negativity of her Family and their teachings. Lately she'd considered that her heart and spirit had been saved from tainting by her nurse and the stableman, and her father's spheres.

But Baccat's words that she lacked a wide education flicked her on a raw spot. It hadn't been easy, analyzing the Residence's and her teachers' words and figuring out what might be true or not.

She looked down at the cat. "I'm not interested in staying in Druida City. I'm determined to *leave* it. Living in the country at the Valerian estate my father left me will suit me fine. Once I'm gone, they won't be bothered to come after me. They'll have the power they want." She snorted. "Every one of the Yews is distrustful and isolationist. I don't know of anyone but the twins even coming into the city. No one will follow us." Her lip curled. "And they won't hire anyone to bring us back because they don't trust anyone outside of the Family."

So we can spend a little more time in the city, not just tracing the route! Baccat gave her big kitty eyes.

"The more time we spend near Druida, the more chance we will have of getting caught. And I don't want to even think of the consequences of my plans being discovered."

Her memory shied away from the hardest punishments in her life—whipping when she was young and, after she'd developed her psi powers, having DepressFlair bracelets manacling her wrists. Both had been awful, first the physical and emotional hurt as she wondered why her mother would whip her when Lori hadn't thought she'd been bad.

Then, later, the psi-blocking cuffs used by Cuspid and Folia that shut off all sense of her magic, being unable to use an integral part of herself.

How scary that there'd even been DepressFlair bands small enough to go around her nine-year-old arms.

No, she didn't want to discover what her Family would do to her if they caught her. "They might kill *you*, you know," she murmured to Baccat. He hissed and hunched in energetic anger.

Staring at him, she continued, "I'll try my best to protect you. To translocate you away if we're caught, but Cuspid and Folia, and especially the twins, can be sneaky."

I agree. They can be sneaky and mean. Your Family is mostly unpleasant and all are sneaky and mean.

She sighed. "Yes, they are." And she appeared to have gotten the sneaky gene. Maybe if she were away from her Family, she'd do better. A slight *whoosh* came and she glanced back at the Temple to see that the dome had opened to the starlit sky. "We need to move on."

I can show you the hidden sanctuary of FirstGrove, the Public-Library, The Green Knight Fencing and Fighting Salon, the Turquoise House—

"No!" That came out louder than she'd thought, and she glanced around the Temple grounds, back at the door. Nothing stirred. "You've already told me about the Turquoise House. And we have a plan to implement if we're leaving within two eightdays at the soonest, perhaps three if the weather doesn't warm sufficiently. There's no time to tourist around the city."

You have not even seen CityCenter, the great buildings of the new GuildHall, or GreatCircle Temple or the starship Nuada's Sword.

She set her teeth, shut down temptation. "Stick with the plan." *She'd* be joyful if her scheme worked.

I like CityCenter at night. Very attractive lights, and there are food trucks. He slid his eyes toward her in a sly glance. *When was the last time you ate any food not prepared by your kitchen staff or from the Residence no-time storage units?*

No-times kept everything, particularly food, at the same temperature it went in, but, always, she'd only ever eaten Yew food.

Her mouth watered and she ran her tongue around her teeth. "Never." This time the word squeaked out as a whisper. The scent of food came from the open temple dome. And she'd also been thinking of food and the no-times since she and the Residence and Folia would be doing the quarterly inventory tomorrow.

Imagine it. Baccat's voice in her mind came as a whisper, too, a lilting, seductive one. *You have never had fresh baked furrabeast meat pies.*

She swallowed again.

With thick gravy and mushrooms and scallions grown on other estates than the Yews. Exquisite, DIFFERENT flavors.

Lori had a weakness for mushrooms, their rich, earthy taste. Her stomach growled. The lure of Druida's core tested her resolve to continue checking out the path she'd take with her animals. Her prospective route would take her nowhere near CityCenter.

"All right," she said aloud.

Baccat trotted through the gardens and around to the front of the Temple and the street beyond and she followed—just in time to see the PublicCarrier to CityCenter pass by.

We will teleport. He paused and licked his muzzle. *I will show you the area of food carts.*

"Will we be seen?"

Your padded winter clothes are long out of fashion, old and shabby; we will not be noted.

"I don't have any gilt with me." She should have been full from dinner, but that had been septhours ago.

Her Fam put a little swagger in his walk, a wave in his tail. *I have credit with some vendors. From rat catching.*

"Zow."

Would you like to view the Turquoise House? It's just up the street from here.

"No, why would I? You've told me of the Turquoise House often enough," Lori said. "Let's go explore!"

That shut the cat up.

*   *   *

They were gone. Both woman and cat. Good thing Draeg had a hook in the cat's aura.

He'd finished a round of the stables, mentally keeping track of the cat until the Fam had vanished. Then Draeg swore and used the scouring Whirlwind Spell to cleanse and dress himself in his mercenary leathers.

He teleported outside the Turquoise House, where one of his brothers lived, just in time to feel Baccat and D'Yew move to the southern edge of CityCenter. She must be depending upon Baccat for images to teleport, and that wasn't an idea Draeg was comfortable with: trusting a cat, not even a Fam bonded to you.

A few minutes later he found them and stood back in the shadows of a deep storefront doorway. He watched Baccat outrageously making up to a street vendor who sold meat pies, and D'Yew staying out of sight as she ate one. To Draeg's surprise, the cart advertised food from Darjeeling's Teahouse so the fare would be hearty and of good quality. His mouth watered, but the woman running the food cart handed over two pies to D'Yew as if they were the last of her inventory, paying more attention to Baccat as she closed up her mobile stall.

Then Baccat and D'Yew stepped into darkness unlit by streetlamps or moonslight and disappeared.

The carts and the shops in this area had shut for the night, and Draeg expected cat and woman to teleport back to the D'Yew estate after a small fling at CityCenter. But their next hop took them to a wide business street that was rarely used after the stores closed. A north-south directional street; they'd gone south.

When he caught up with them, he saw D'Yew breaking off pieces of the pies and tossing them to Baccat, who tidily fielded them. She spoke quietly, and Draeg supposed she conversed with the cat, answering her Fam's mental comments aloud.

Baccat turned into a narrow way between two buildings and so did D'Yew, and caution prickled through Draeg. He didn't like that the cat showed the naive woman the not-so-safe back alleys of Druida.

Keeping his steps light, he prowled through the skinny crack, came into the alley, and turned after them. Ahead of the pair, lurking against a wall, he noticed a moving shadow—no, more than one!—freeze and wait.

"I don't know about this shortcut to that boulevard, Baccat," she said.

The cat yowled.

"We can use it now, but not later."

She should get out of the place altogether. Draeg had just opened his mouth to yell at them, when two guys rushed him, one from the side, one from the back, and the fight was on. He dropped low, and neither of his assailants found him where they'd expected him to be. They tangled together and Draeg yelled a fighting cry and put them out with a few blows.

As he fought, he heard a cut-off squeak from D'Yew, sensed her and the Fam teleporting away.

Five

T*oo busy with the men he knocked out, and rushing the others of the* same group farther down the alley, Draeg paid little attention to where the woman and cat 'ported, just glad they'd left so he could concentrate on fighting.

These continual fights became tiresome.

Nope. He lied to himself even as he grinned, showing his teeth, to the three men facing him. He welcomed the fighting, dirtier and meaner than he could get away with at The Green Knight Fencing and Fighting Salon run by Tinne Holly.

All that frustration released. The irritation that Draeg couldn't get a handle on whether the Yews were involved in the fanatical edge of the Traditionalist Stance targeting young Nobles.

Another lie. It wasn't annoyance at the lack of clues that had led to his frustration. Man, his mind flung up rationalizations even as he plowed into the other men, rolled, turned, and began pummeling more.

He was sexually frustrated. He hadn't had a woman for a month before he'd come to this undercover spy job. And once he'd watched Loridana D'Yew's innocently swaying hips as she escaped her estate to ramble in Druida City, he hadn't wanted anyone else.

Why, he didn't know. Why was puzzling and something he didn't want to analyze.

So he welcomed the fights he got into as he trailed her—this wasn't the first—and as he cut down on the night crime in the city.

When he looked around after teaching the thugs that there was always someone better and more intimidating than you, the alley was completely deserted of all life.

His mind still tumbled with gleeful roughness and he couldn't get a fix on the quiet, innocent woman or the pompous, scholarly Fam, both of whom might be a whole lot more nice-minded and less cynical than Draeg himself.

He was sure that the woman had heard only the first couple of blows and short grunts. Sucking on his bloody knuckles that he should really send some Healing Flair to, not that that was easy for him, Draeg realized Baccat had looked at him from D'Yew's arms.

Baccat had *smirked* at him.

Draeg heard, with sensation that tangled inside him, the tenor of D'Yew's voice several blocks away, talking matter-of-factly to her Fam. She must have thought the fight just a scuffle. Not that she would recognize scuffle or fight.

Tonight Draeg had already tugged on the hook he'd set in the FamCat a couple of times. He hesitated to pull on it more since he'd met the cat today and the aura-hook was new. Baccat was definitely aware of Draeg and that he'd followed woman and Fam but probably thought Draeg had kept them in sight. If Baccat discovered the hook and trace, he could remove them more easily now than if a week or so passed.

So Draeg sucked in a few breaths to calm down, cocked his head to hear their voices again, and those floated to him from the southwest. And why the hell were they interested in southwest Druida? A question he couldn't ask her right now for sure, though he hoped to slide into her confidence enough for her to trust him with . . . with everything.

He heard a few groans that meant the first guys he'd laid out might be regaining consciousness, so he teleported the individuals to a local guardhouse . . . easy to do since he'd gone looking for trouble in the streets of Druida a couple of years back and found it readily for months. He knew his way around.

Then he stood panting with effort and strained to hear or sense D'Yew and Baccat again, and got nothing. He understood he'd lost them, and understood the real downside to his fighting.

If D'Yew got in trouble, Draeg would have to use the line to Baccat to teleport to the couple and help out. Then the Fam would understand he'd been tagged by Draeg. The cat would probably not like that and tell D'Yew everything he might know or guess about Draeg, which could be damn unfortunate and might put this undercover job at risk. He could only pray woman and cat would be more careful tonight.

Keeping his senses open to try to find them again, Draeg began the slow walk to D'Yew estate, grumbling all the way.

Lori kept a firm grip on Baccat and breathed quickly as they alit in an alley between buildings that only showed slight light from Celta's starbright night in the center. She and her Fam had worked together to 'port to a street, paused for a few breaths, then headed to this place as soon as they'd heard fighting in the other alley.

She'd heard flesh hitting flesh and bitten-off moans. At least two blows, she thought, though she didn't have the experience to visualize the actions. Yet even before the sounds, the hair on the back of her neck had risen, warning her of trouble. "I should have trusted my instincts," she muttered, beginning to think that she had better instincts for danger than her cat who'd lived on the streets of Druida.

Standing and petting Baccat, she frowned, trying to sort the sensations within her. Yes, she'd sensed . . . danger as soon as they'd stepped from the narrow way between the buildings into the smelly alley. Her Flair had surged. Her *newly* released Flair, her not-quite-known main psi power.

You hold Me too steadfastly, and for too long! huffed Baccat. He wiggled, pushed against her, and jumped down.

"Baccat!"

Tail high and twitching, he strolled toward some crates, discarded since the last time they'd traveled this way.

Horrible hissing, more than one screech.

Danger to her Fam!

She flung out her arms in alarm, Flair streaming from her to Baccat. She saw the light around her Fam waver. Lori choked with fear as a huge rat jumped *over* a crate, all claws stiff and ready to scourge Baccat.

No! She blinked and her eyes widened as she saw a bubble curve around Baccat.

The rat hit the shield—it was a personal shield!—and squealed as it slid around the bubble. When the rodent landed, it scurried away into darkness.

Baccat grunted as the bubble contracted, then shaped closely around him. Lori widened her eyes to see better and stared. No forcefield, no barely visible armor, no iridescence or follicle-tipping light showed. But she'd done it! She'd made a bubble around Baccat, then formed it to his shape! He *was* protected.

The cat stopped and turned around, put his nose on his shoulder to sniff. *It surrounds Me.* He paused, lifted one paw, then each of the others in turn. Twitching his whiskers, he said, *It coats my whiskers, each and every one!* He angled them. *The sensation is extremely peculiar.* He scowled up at Lori. *It is beneath Me, too, so I do not feel the earth, but it has no odor. It does no damage to My pads or paws.*

"It's my main Flair," she whispered in awe, knowing she spoke truly. "Personal spellshields. I'm sure."

Ah, Baccat said, sitting and holding a forepaw in front of his eyes as if trying to see what he could feel. Then he put his paw down, shifted his sitting position. *To reiterate, the personal spellshield feels quite odd, but I believe I can easily become accustomed to it.*

"That's good," Lori murmured, keeping an eye out for more

rats. She'd been bitten by one when she'd started cleaning up the stables as a child, and not only had it hurt, but she'd almost lost her freedom to be with her animals.

I do not like rats, either, Baccat said. *I have had to fight them for food before and they Do Not Fight Fair.*

Lori figured Baccat didn't fight fair, either, but would think losing to a creature of such minimal intelligence an affront. She wondered how many rats nested and lurked here ready to run out over her feet. This had been part of the best route. She'd have to scout the alternatives again. Being in the city remained fascinating, but time pressed upon her. She didn't know how long she could remain meek and mild with the Residence and her Family.

She could *taste* freedom.

Tilting his head, Baccat looked at each forepaw once more, then rose and shook himself. Lori still saw no hint of the shield.

It is quite an interesting phenomenon, Baccat said, ears rotating, then stepping forward.

"What?"

That two of the young women who have lived at Yew Residence have developed Flair encompassing security and shields.

"I never heard that," she paused. "Just that the person who made the estate shieldspell was unfriendly and wouldn't update ours." Lori had had to strengthen the spells on the estate's walls, gates, and doors quarterly herself, and she simply added to the spells already embedded.

Baccat instructed, *Your MotherSire's second wife, she who is now Lahsin Holly, is the premier person to build and maintain estate spellshields. Now you, Loridana Itha Valerian D'Yew, are mistress of personal spellshields. I have never experienced anything like this. Indeed, I have not heard of such excellent individual shields.*

"Oh." Her knees went a little weak, and if there hadn't been rats in the alley, she'd have sat down on a two-stack of crates. So she gulped and stiffened her knees and spine.

I wonder . . . Baccat said, just before he jumped into the darkness and attacked a rat!

Terrible, awful noises from the pair had Lori shuddering, wanting to put her hands over her ears. This was a fight to the death.

Then the bloody rat shot from the shrouded shadows, across her feet, and she clapped her hands to her mouth to suppress a shriek. The rodent staggered a couple of steps and fell over.

Ha! Baccat strutted from the darkness and spit out rat flesh, and Lori hurriedly looked away. He stopped in front of her. *Look at ME!*

She did. He actually appeared sleeker, more well groomed than usual.

Not a scratch on Me. He sniffed. *Not a bite, though the rat tried both. I am unharmed, nay, untouched, even.*

Lori gulped again. "Oh. That's good." She could have done without the demonstration.

I can fight and kill and prey cannot hurt Me, and I will be NO PREY to others.

"Very good." She angled a little so she didn't have to see the defunct rodent.

It is EXCELLENT. What we have here, My dear FamWoman, is an exponential development in defense. He hopped on the crates and stared at her until she met his reflective eyes. *How do you feel? Do you feel as if this shield continues to drain you because We are in close proximity and your Flair is being cycled to My shield?*

"Oh." She lifted her hair with the fingers of both hands; perspiration had dampened her scalp, more from the fight than the spell itself. She took stock of herself, then replied slowly, "No, I placed the bubble that contracted into a shield on you, but it does not continue to pull Flair from me."

Then We may treat this as a regular spell. No doubt it has a time limit and will wear off, Baccat said. His whiskers twitched. *My shield does not seem to be deteriorating incrementally. Therefore I would postulate that when the Flair you invested into the spell is gone, the protection will simply vanish. It will be well to note the duration.*

"Yes," Lori agreed.

How do you feel, in general? Baccat asked.

"Good."

Not too depleted from the magnitude of the spell?

Lori sank into her balance and stretched out her arms, then each leg. "No, I'm fine, no more tired than if I did a medium house-keeping spell."

Baccat's upper muzzle lifted as if in a smile, and Lori looked away from his bloody fangs. *Very well done, FamWoman! This MUST be your primary Flair.*

"Yes." Lori nodded, bit her bottom lip, let out a small sigh. "I used regular, daily Flair so often that my primary Flair has been slow to appear—"

Sluggish, Baccat said, a growl in his mental voice. *Sluggish to come because of all the demands of the Residence and your Family.* Another cat sniff. *I could stay in the Residence with such a shield now.*

"No!"

No, We do not want to reveal this new Flair of yours.

"Absolutely not."

Ears flicked back and forth. *I think We should call this Flair of yours "personal armor." Yes.* He groomed his whiskers.

"I suppose." A large shaft of twinmoonslight speared into the alley, skimming some damp puddles with silver. She looked into the sky and saw the edge of Cymru moon peeking over the building. "It's getting late, and it's been an eventful night."

"Yesss," Baccat vocalized. He hopped down from the crates. *We must consider the new twist in our situation. You could make a great deal of gilt providing personal armor spells, particularly if We can develop some that will last several specific durations, or if We can imbue an object, say an amulet, with the spell and have the armor triggered as needed. We could stay here in Druida City . . .*

She'd been listening and smiling at Baccat's business schemes, but this wiped the humor from her. "Ab-so-*lutely* not!" Lori said aloud, then to emphasize it, sent the words and *feeling* of denial telepathically to her Fam. *I am NOT staying in Druida City. My stridebeasts and horses and I are all traveling to MY Valerian estate.* She sliced a hand in the air. *That is definite.*

"Grrr," Baccat said. *I am a Civilized Cat and prefer Druida.*

She frowned at him, and then he said, *Oh, very well. I suppose I can attempt to bring culture to the hinterlands.* He waved a paw.

Setting her hands on her hips, Lori scanned the alley. "I think we must not use this passage again. There is too much stuff in it that might spook my animals."

Her Fam strolled into the next business street, empty and moonlit. *I do not like the rats. They might be a distraction to me when we leave town. I will advise the owners of the shops regarding the rats in the alley, and that the crates give them shelter.*

Lori didn't quite believe that the store owners would listen to Baccat but didn't say so.

As usual, they decided to do short teleporting hops and walk home, to continue to acquaint Lori with Noble Country and the area she must know well so she could lead her stridebeasts—no, the stridebeasts and horses, *her* animals—through the city safely. The stridebeasts liked her to lead instead of ride one of them, and she preferred to keep that lower profile.

And, after all, she couldn't teleport directly home, because her pulse still beat hard through her veins; she still radiated excitement from Baccat's fight with the rat, her trip outside, and the revelation of her true Flair.

How amazing that she had such *interesting* Flair! She'd have to practice personal armor shields in private, figure out if she could put one around herself, too. And whether she could shield the whole group of them during their escape and their trip.

Though her body felt tired, her mind still hummed with discovery and delight.

The Residence would definitely notice that. Especially since she was supposed to be working on the boathouse, and refurbishing some of the boats—which she couldn't care less about.

Not to mention that she couldn't bring Baccat into the Residence with her. The one time she had had been horrible for everyone but especially her Fam. Even though she *could* shield him now, she didn't know how long his personal armor spell would last. It would take experimentation for her to find out, and better that was done when not in a dangerous place or under threat.

She daren't fall into the Family fault of Yew hubris and arrogance. If the Family and the Residence learned of her plans, all could be ruined.

She swung open the gate . . . and faced Draeg Hedgenettle.

Six

Lori caught her breath at the sight of the stableman. Her heart pumped hard and felt like it surged into her throat.

He was beautiful. No, not beautiful, just exactly how a man should look. And what a man! Again she was struck that he was nothing at all like the thin, elegant builds of her male relatives, like her cuz Zus. Not much at all like the men she'd seen in her short forays outside the estate at night. He looked as if strength and masculine grace had been bred into his line . . . as she'd bred special qualities into the best of her stridebeasts.

Yes, his body was gorgeous, his face attractive, or it could be if he didn't aim such a dark scowl at her.

Solidly standing in the doorway, he blocked her entrance and crossed his arms. "It's about time you got back."

She swallowed and lifted her chin. Despite his glowering expression, she felt no danger as she had earlier that night, that had activated the use of her new primary Flair. He wouldn't physically hurt her. "Please move."

"I'm surprised you didn't just teleport into the Residence," he said.

"I can't do that," she answered automatically, "but if you don't move, I *will* teleport farther into the estate." She tilted her head. "And it seems as if you wish to speak to me?" She paused. "Not that I intend to tell you anything." But her heart beat harder. Would he report her to Cuspid, the maître de maison; Folia, the housekeeper; or the Residence itself?

If he did so . . . she'd have to leave. Now. As soon as possible, taking her animals whether it was good for them or not. Figure out some way to protect them from the freezing weather on the trip. She *couldn't* leave them as objects for any revenge the Family might inflict.

Draeg caught the door by the curved latch handle and swung it wider, stepped out of her way, and flourished a bow along with a sweeping gesture that she enter.

Baccat sashayed through, tail flicking. *Greetyou, Draeg HEDGENETTLE.*

As he straightened, the man's frown changed subtly into an expression of wariness. "Greetyou, FamCat." Draeg drew in an audible breath. "You smell odd."

"Odd, how?" demanded Lori. She hadn't noticed any odor other than remnants of rat-fight, so if her Flair held a scent, she needed to know about that.

Draeg shifted his gaze to her. One of his shoulders hunched. "Some herb I don't recognize."

Lori wanted to press further but didn't dare. She could be in enough trouble as it was.

I prefer to sleep in herb gardens, Baccat stated. *And I enjoy rolling in them, wherever I find them.* He inhaled with gusto. *I do not smell any unattractive aroma upon Myself.*

"Just saying," Draeg offered.

I believe I WILL take offense at your discourtesy, Baccat said. *Good night and sweet dreams, FamWoman; I will see you at breakfast tomorrow. Good night, Hedgenettle. I will see you tomorrow, too. Perhaps before I visit My friends at the Turquoise House, perhaps not.*

With a final swish of his tail, her Fam disappeared. She received the impression that he wished to hunt on the grounds, and test his new personal armor.

Draeg closed the gate after her, made sure the lock caught and the estate spellshields had engaged before piercing her with his stare. "What do you mean you can't teleport into the Residence? I'd have thought you'd have plenty of Flair for that." And the more he scrutinized her, the more she thought she sensed him scanning her for psi power. She pulled her mental shields tight and his brows came down.

Should she answer him or not? Earlier she'd treated him honestly, had made the determination to do so. Now she decided to continue that policy.

As far as she knew he hadn't lied to her, as her Family had, as the Residence had, so she would meet truth with truth, trust with trust. Her hands went to her sleeves, to tuck inside, but she wasn't wearing a tunic or gown with traditional sleeves, so she let her arms drop to her sides and walked ahead of the stableman on the path.

"Are you going to answer me, Lady?" he asked gruffly.

Now she felt tingles on her neck, but not alarm, no. More like . . . sensuality? Awareness that she was a woman and a man followed her closely, within her personal space. A man looked at her as she walked. Yes, her heartbeat remained elevated. "Am I going to answer you?" she asked lightly, then threw a glance over her shoulder and found him within an arm's length of touching. "To satisfy your curiosity?"

"That's right. I'm curious why you don't teleport into the Residence, why you sneak into the estate by a gate."

It was best to learn the path in the dark, know every footstep . . . every potential hoof step. "Don't you wonder where I'm going outside?" she asked, keeping a sharp eye on the small dirt trail that she and Baccat had beaten down over the last month.

He grunted. "You're out exploring Druida City, of course, nothing else beyond the gate. Unless you're meeting a gallant, a Nobleman, at his home in Noble Country."

"No!" The very idea scandalized. "I never even thought of that!"

The ends of Draeg's lips lifted. "Good. So why the gate?"

"Because the house is a Residence, of course."

His head angled. "So?"

"So it can sense my excitement, the beats of my heart, the heat of my skin." She halted at the top of the trail where it joined a wider dirt track she used when riding her stridebeasts. Draeg stopped short, his mouth hanging open.

"It would do that?"

Using a bit of the last of her Flair, she gestured at the bushes framing the path they'd come up to huddle closer together, moved leaves to cover the trail.

"It would do that?" Draeg repeated with some intensity.

She stared at him. "Of course. D'Yew Residence continually monitors me."

"That doesn't seem right."

He took a few strides until he walked beside her. "So that's why you don't 'port directly to your rooms."

She felt his gaze.

"You still look a little flushed and excited to me," he said. She thought he stared at where her pulse might show in her throat.

"I am. And the Family and Residence think I'm restoring boats and the boathouse. Which I mostly did two months ago. No one will want to use the boats in the river for another month or two, depending upon the weather."

"Instead you're exploring Druida City."

"That's right." She turned to face him. "I'm supposed to stay on the estate, always." She raised her brows. "Are you going to tell my Family or the Residence that I'm slipping away?"

Another grunt and a minute of silence. "This is a good job. I like it." He nodded once. "And I don't like to lie." A longer pause. "I will lie, if need be, for a good cause, and you remember that, but I don't like to. If they ask me, I'll tell them I saw you go in and out of the gate."

She laughed in relief. "I doubt they'll ask you."

"That's my reading of the situation. So, since you're still excited, what are you going to do? It's late."

"Not quite my bedtime, and probably no one but the Residence will check on me tonight." She sighed; that was a huge boon. "Everyone will be occupied with their own affairs."

Draeg snorted.

"What?" she asked.

He waved a hand. "Nothing. So you've covered yourself." He cleared his throat. "Covered your tracks with the boathouse thing. You're a crafty lady." He paused. "That was a compliment."

"Thank you." Instead of taking the graveled path wide enough for a glider toward the house, she kept straight on a bridle path that accommodated two stridebeasts.

"Where are we going and what are you gonna do?" he asked.

"I'm going to a grove to calm myself and meditate."

"Meditate!"

She smiled and slanted him a glance. He seemed so vital she didn't think he often sat still. "That's right. It works for me." After several more meters, she angled off the track to another path, this one kept intentionally grassy. She slowed her steps and began breathing rhythmically, first five breaths in and out, then six, until she came to a small, young yew grove, the most minor grove on the estate of trees that were of the Family name. Like most everything else she prized, it was ignored by her Family.

Her eyes dampened at the thought of leaving this place and the other spiritual groves that welcomed her. Inhale. Exhale. Remind herself of the future, of cuttings she'd take of these trees and those from the main grove of Yews four centuries old.

Hold the thought of the future, but calmly. Keep her intentions foremost, good solid plans she could carry out. That would ground her, stabilize her emotions.

At the end of her meditation session, when she'd teleport to her rooms, she'd remember how she'd restored the boats, and let those images lift to the forefront of her mind, where any Family member in passing, any sly spy, could sense them.

Draeg cleared his throat, and she jolted a bit; she'd almost forgotten he'd accompanied her. At least her mind and her emotions had been focused on doing what she must, on *being* what she must. Her body had continued to sense—and react with a warm flush under her skin—to the man who'd remained near.

She really had to school her body. Take charge of the emotions and the bodily functions would follow. Or still the body and the emotions would follow. Either way would work, but it had to be done, and rather quickly.

She could do it.

Head lifted, gliding the way she'd been taught that a lady did, Lori went to the middle of the small clearing, with sufficient space for two people, white and silver in the twinmoonslight and starlight. The next air she breathed in had a taint of midnight freezing, the last traces of the warmer evening air gone. Saving only enough Flair for a final teleportation, she set up a small weathershield over the clearing. Big enough for two.

Without looking at Draeg, she slid one leg down to the ground, body following in an easy movement, and crossed her legs.

Draeg watched the woman and yearned. Made sure to angle his body so his stiffening arousal wouldn't show. If he sat on the ground he'd be cold enough to discipline his body before it warmed under the weathershield.

Dipping his head at her, his voice gruff, he asked, "You permit me to join you in your meditation, Lady?"

"It's been a while since you meditated, hasn't it?" she asked quietly, but a small tint of inflection told him that she didn't believe he'd ever meditated, and certainly not in a semiformal ritual, or with others.

She was so wrong. He'd spent septhours meditating. Had done so daily with his mentor, Tab Holly, for years. Until Tab had died . . . just two months after Draeg had lost his natural parents, when he was seventeen. Tab had been old, and his parents had died of a sickness and were HeartMates so they'd gone together as HeartMates often did. They'd all abandoned him for the Wheel of Stars and their next lives. He'd taken it very personally.

Now, of course, Draeg realized that Tab would be disappointed in him, since Draeg couldn't remember the last time he'd simply sat and meditated by himself—four years? Five? He'd even struggled during the quiet times of Family rituals, when linked to the rest of the Blackthorns.

But GrandLady D'Yew had given him permission to join her, so he did, also sliding into the tailor position. Best that he sat next to her, though separate a good half meter, instead of in front of her. Less temptation to look at her. And, yeah, the frozen ground chilled his ass, a good thing, too.

She stared at him for a moment, and then, on a long sigh, she relaxed her muscles. He saw it happen, and more drastically than the fighters in such sessions in The Green Knight Fencing and Fighting Salon. Still looking at him, her lashes slowly dropped, and at the sight he got a little jolt.

Here she was, near midnight, sitting in a dark grove with a stranger, and she *trusted* him. Him, Draeg Betony-Blackthorn, after no more than a septhour of real time spent together.

What if he'd been a villain? At the notion, alarm surged through him. In the distance, a cat yowled. Baccat, the Fam, linked to D'Yew and himself. The noise relieved and reassured him. Her wary Fam would have alerted her to a villain.

D'Yew sat quietly, true, but she'd be aware of everything around her, of the scents and the sounds, if she'd reached a mindful trance state, and this estate was *hers*. If she wanted to, she could pound him to mush with tree limbs or rocks, call the horses to kill him, or any intruder, with their hooves. Raise up any and all of the feral animals that lived here against him, and probably the domesticated ones as well.

"Draaay-eeggk." She elongated his name like other exasperated females in his life. "You're not meditating."

He grunted. "You're right, it's been a while," he mumbled.

"Oh." Her eyelids opened, pupils wide. "Of course."

He kept from rolling his own eyes at her obvious naiveté. She didn't think he'd ever meditated, but every noble did. She didn't seem to realize how expensive his clothes were. His tough leathers had been treated at every step of their creation with top preservative and weather spells, and tailored specifically for him. He deduced that none of her folk wore leathers, and, as he'd suspected, the Family had no designated guards. Luck for him, but he disapproved strongly of a FirstFamily having no guards.

She stared into his eyes, her lips quirked up in an encouraging smile. "Let's try again."

"Yeah, sure." He lifted his butt and swept out the rock and a damn solid branchlet from under him.

With a nod, her lashes lowered. Within seconds she'd calmed, descended into a slower brainwave pattern. She obviously had a great deal of experience of relaxing into serenity . . . to control her emotions so the Residence couldn't read her well.

Draeg believed that a Residence always observing a person's vital statistics was just wrong, and next time he was in T'Blackthorn Residence, he'd ask it. He was pretty sure the Residences had rules like that.

D'Yew's breathing became regular, then hitched once, just before she said, "I yet feel your tension, Draeg Hedgenettle, and your breathing isn't rhythmic . . . or as slow and deep as it should be, considering your chest area."

He stared at her chest area, breasts limned by the twinmoons-light falling on her clothing.

Yep, his breath caught, too. Her thick, well-made, but old winter tunic didn't show even the hint of her nipples in the cold, but he could imagine them.

The warmth of the spring day had long since vanished and the night was becoming decidedly frosty. Better get this done.

He lowered his eyelids but kept them open a crack, and his gaze fixed on her, his head turned instead of ahead. She had the straightest spine he'd ever seen. As he watched, her breath became deeper and slower.

He picked up the pattern of her breathing—steady and to the count of eight. When she paused on the last of her exhale, began with the inhale, he joined her, matched her.

After a moment of seeing her sink further into a trance and breathing with her, he let his mind flow.

For tonight, and figuring he'd track D'Yew in the future and share more time with her, he went back to basics. He did what had worked for him as an awkward teen when he'd begun training. He hummed a quiet note only audible to himself. Yeah, he was a physical guy, and the feeling of the vibration in his chest and throat and mouth helped him center and focus.

He continued for minutes, lashes drifting closed, until the sounds of her rustling, and dropping the weathershield, brought him to the surface. Her serene face and gleaming eyes showed her even temper, a woman ready to have her being evaluated by a nosy Residence. Hiding nothing, but hiding everything. A clever young woman.

Draeg wasn't quite ready to finish, but they'd be better off inside. The cold had turned from a nip to a toothy bite.

Though his body stayed loose, his mind knotted at the idea of the so-far-as-he'd-seen uptight Yew Family teaching this D'Yew, Loridana Itha, meditation so well.

"You are very practiced, Lady," he said, his voice rough with disuse and the chill air. He coughed. "And you look . . . happy."

She nodded. "The old stableman . . . long, long before you, taught me how to meditate." Her brow creased a bit. "Like my nurse, I don't think he belonged to the Yew Family." Her chin raised. "But he was a good man."

"I'm sure."

"He said if a person worked with animals, he or she should have complete inner calm."

"So you learned meditation."

"Yes. And he said that a person's natural state is peaceful and joyful." She grinned, the first true lighthearted smile he'd seen, undimmed by any *thought* or feelings of responsibility. Spreading her arms, she said, "I feel happy and serene, and I spread that through the estate and my animal friends and they gave it back to me. They give me support so that I can face with equanimity the Residence and any Family member who might check up on me." A tiny sigh. "In truth, though everyone is outwardly calm in the Residence, they are not very joyful, and my delight rubs away." Again she smiled, this one like she had a secret.

The peace of the grove and the meditation swept through his blood. He rose in a smooth movement and took the long pace to her, then offered his hand. She stared up at him, eyes shadowed, but with the twinmoonslight softly falling on her face, her innocent expression.

Unexpected passion surged and he wanted to kiss her . . . more, take her back to his rooms over the stable and show her the intimacy between a man and a woman.

But he knew to his bones that he would be *showing* her, and for the first time, how a man and a woman came together.

Though with every passing moment he learned who Loridana Itha Valerian D'Yew was, and she was certainly appealing, they had only met that afternoon. He might be recklessly ready to explore this young woman, even reveal portions of himself; she was not.

Then she set her fingers into his, and his jaw flexed at the sizzle down his nerves, making him aware of all the long months since the last time he'd had sex with a woman.

"Thank you," she said as she stood.

"Thank *you*." Without thought, he pulled her smoothly to him, bent his head slightly for a sweet kiss, brushed her lips with his. More than a jolt this time, a throbbing anguished *need* as her plush mouth trembled under his. He yanked her against his hot and hard body, one hand on her upper back, the other curved around her small, tight butt, and Lord and Lady, she felt *fine* next to his favorite muscle. His hard erection.

Angling his head, he swept his tongue across the seam of her lips, teasing her mouth open, taking her warm and panting breath into his own, finally hearing little mews from her that twined desire tightly through him. Her arms wrapped around him and her hips tilted, caressing his cock, and his mind nearly exploded and the hand not clamping her butt insinuated between them and covered her breast.

She gasped and her mouth left his as she pulled away, gasped again. "I . . ."

He sucked in cold air that chilled down his throat to his lungs. What was he doing? This woman was an innocent.

She opened her mouth, closed it, gave him a wild look, and winked away.

Again he stood, stunned, wondering what had happened. Twice in a day . . . a day and a night . . . this young woman had dazed him.

Seven

*L*ori *had just enough presence of mind to teleport just outside a door* that the Residence didn't much watch—the secondary southern door closest to the river and the boathouse she was supposed to have been restoring.

No problem with energy and Flair, she trembled from it—from the passion Draeg Hedgenettle had ignited inside her. He'd kissed her. He'd touched her, her bottom and her . . . her breast. He'd kissed her. *His tongue had been in her mouth!*

Oh, Lady and Lord, Lord and Lady. The firestorm of . . . *lust* . . . seemed to warm the air around her and her breath came too fast, and perhaps too hot, too.

She'd never enjoyed anything as much as kissing Draeg. So *invigorating.* She might, now, understand some books she'd read. Her cheeks felt hot and she put her hands on them. Warm to her fingers. Warmer than her fingers. And the air she drew in with each short and choppy breath frosted her throat.

Her body pulsed with heat and . . . desire for the man's touch, the man's lips, the man's tongue. Her scattered emotions bubbled, her thoughts fragmented.

Except one. She'd teleported away without a word, had stared at him with her mouth hanging open and just *gone*. He must think her a foolish girl.

Next time—yes, there *would* be a next time—she'd be more sophisticated. She could hardly be less. Anyway, she'd be ready to participate and . . . and not let fear of the unknown scare her away.

One deep breath, harder to keep steady than any she'd taken all day, far from the calm ones she'd drawn during the meditation. Such energy now, buzzing through her!

She daren't go into the Residence in such a state. Over the centuries, that entity would have become exceedingly familiar with human sexual arousal and sex acts.

Biting her lower lip, she accepted the small pain and let it ground her in the here and now and not in imaginings of Draeg Hedgenettle, what he'd done to her and she to him and what they might do next—

Stop!

Another breath, considering her options. She stealthily crept away from the door and any viz or audio sensors the Residence had there and to the kitchen garden, yet bare. Tiptoeing to the center of the rectangle, she positioned her feet and once more connected with the land of the estate. Beneath her she felt the earth of Celta and in the garden, the faint stirring of seeds, ready to unfurl when the dirt warmed to sprout and thrust upward to the sun—and freedom.

As she wanted freedom, and the light of the sun shining on her and warming her at a different home where she could truly be Lori Valerian.

Draeg Hedgenettle would be a great distraction—even at his name her heart pumped harder, her thoughts misted, and she heated and sent more energy into the land until her knees wavered. Then she walked with slumped shoulders, hunched back, and her thoughts on restoring boats, to the door and into the Residence, dragged herself up to her rooms, undressed, and fell into bed.

* * *

*D*raeg *didn't leave the grove but sat right down again on the cold, cold* ground. Time to master himself—his raging arousal and his intense desire for a deep connection with Loridana Itha D'Yew. Steady his breathing, steady his body, and this unseasonable desire would dissipate. He hadn't been done with his meditation, so he'd practice more, and stay until the chill vanquished the heat enveloping him from the inside out, recapture the meditation experience.

Finally he rose, not quite stiff. A remnant of passion coursed through his blood, but also a sense of completeness, of calmness, within his being. The solid results of the meditation.

As he headed back to the path to the stables, he heard an echo of D'Yew's sleepy voice. *Good night, Baccat!*

The Fam replied. *Good night, FamWoman.*

More relaxed and integrated than he'd been in a long time, Draeg walked through the night, appreciating the ungroomed nature of this part of the estate: the tall trees silhouetted darkly against the starbright sky, buds beginning to show, the twiggy hedges, a tiny whiff of an upcoming green spring.

This quietude in his emotions enveloped him, balm on the restlessness that had haunted him for years. The recent memory of the benefit of sitting and letting his mind go blank, experiencing and embracing the current moment, flowed through him, and the last of his arousal faded. All this thanks to the help and serene presence of D'Yew.

She had reminded him of a practice he'd neglected, and in doing so had harmed himself because he hadn't had the calm reserves to call on when he'd needed them. Not three years ago, and not earlier that evening.

He'd disrobed and taken a waterfall, pulled back the bedsponge linens, when his perscry—his personal scry pebble—sounded in the quick blazer hum Draeg had programmed for Tinne Holly.

Now he grabbed a long tunic and pulled it on, stroking his thumb on the scry pebble and saying, "Here."

The holographic image showed the head and shoulders of Tinne, who seemed to have extra lines in his face compared to the last time Draeg had seen him.

"Greetyou, Draeg."

"Greetyou, Tinne. News?"

"Yes, and of the worst sort."

Sucking in a breath through his teeth, Draeg said, "Murder?"

"Attempted, and did include death." Tinne rubbed his temples with forefinger and thumb.

"Who?" demanded Draeg.

"A workman in the new GuildHall." Tinne's mouth twisted. "It appears that he brought in a celtaroon snake to let loose. Probably bespelled to find and bite a particular person. But celtaroons are notoriously stupid and difficult to control. The guy got bitten himself."

"Good luck for our side," Draeg said.

"Yes."

"Target?" asked Draeg asked.

"The man was scheduled to be working on the office of the new Captain of AllCouncils."

"Walker Clover," Draeg said harshly, "a former Commoner raised to Noble."

"Walker Clover." Tinne matched Draeg's tone. A few seconds' hesitation on Tinne's part when the lines in his face deepened, then he added. "As usual, Walker had brought a couple of his children with him today and would probably have done so tomorrow."

"Cave of the Dark Goddess. Still after the kids?"

Tinne rolled his shoulders as if shifting a burden. "Who knows? Getting rid of Walker would be . . . a great blow on behalf of the Traditionalist Stance."

Draeg followed his logic. "Because Walker is the first born Commoner to rise so high politically on his own merits."

"That is correct. And the Traditionalist Stance doesn't want any more Commoners to be ennobled, despite the strength and potency of their Flair."

"Yeah. What went on?" Draeg asked.

"Zanth and Felonherb FamCats happened to be in the Guild-Hall." The ends of Tinne's lips curved upward. "They *sensed* prey, found and tore the celtaroon snake to pieces. Apparently they considered destroying the thing a competition."

Draeg considered that. "Just as well."

Tinne snorted. "I suppose, though if there was any spell evidence on the creature, it was demolished. Neither our chief investigator in this matter, Garrett Primross, nor the Clover head of security, nor the Captain of the Druida City Guards has been able to determine anything from the shreds of the celtaroon."

"FamCats who 'help' can be a pain in the ass."

"Also correct," said Tinne, who had one of his own.

"So the workman got killed himself. Can't say I'm too surprised. Staging 'accidents' is problematic. When did all this happen?"

"At the change of shifts in the GuildHall from day to evening, WorkEnd Bell. A lot of people coming and going."

"I understand," Draeg said. As far as he knew, all the Yews had been at one of their formal dinners. Tired of standing, he went over to the bedsponge and settled in against two hard, thick pillows that no longer puffed out dust when he leaned against them. "What about the dead guy? Do we have any info about him?"

"He is a known member of the Traditionalist Stance, a minor relative of the Equisetum Family in the north who had their estate confiscated two years ago when their previous crimes were uncovered."

Draeg grunted, frowned, and shifted his gaze to the beamed ceiling instead of Tinne's expression that seemed to age before his eyes.

"What about the Yews?" Tinne asked.

Draeg raised his eyebrows. "I'm sure that you and the others realized that when I hired on as a stableman I would be *living near the stables*. I am, three rooms over the stables. I am not allowed in the Residence. However, I saw no glider leave the estate tonight."

"They *must* be embroiled in this. I think those of the Traditionalist Stance care about mixing Noble and Commoner blood. And I think the Traditionalist Stance has fanatics, like this workman today who targeted Walker Clover or his children."

"You're sure the workman was involved."

"He was found in an empty room with a celtaroon snake. A hole in the wall had been drilled for the beastie to be placed, for it to nest. Signs in his workbox showed he'd stashed a celtaroon in it and brought it in."

Draeg kept his voice even and stared Tinne in his cold pewter eyes. "I can and will assure you that the current D'Yew is not involved in hurting your woman or any other target."

Eight

You're sure *D'Yew isn't involved in any of the accidents or with the* bloody Traditionalist Stance fanatics," Tinne Holly snapped, holographic gaze on Draeg blazer intense.

Draeg shot back, "All of D'Yew's energies are going into her Household—"

Tinne's mouth twisted. "And that doesn't clue you in that something is twisted in that Family, that they should demand such and drain her so?"

"—and in loving and caring for her animals. Her stridebeasts, new horses, and FamCat."

"She has a Fam?"

"That's right, one called Baccat."

Tinne grunted. "Fams usually don't hang around people who aren't loving to them." But his face set again. "Doesn't mean the rest of the Yews aren't up to something." Finally he hesitated, then said, "And I'm sure that the Yews are deep in the Traditionalist Stance."

Draeg said, "I need the button you found under the balcony that broke."

"The button is our only evidence that the Yews might be involved!" the man protested.

"The Druida City Guards don't think it's evidence. Translocate the button to me and I'll ask D'Yew about it, casually."

"You're sure she's not part of this?"

"She's more naive than your daughter Aurea, and I haven't seen any buttons on her at all."

"All right. Give me the cache coordinates for your apartment."

Draeg did and a moment later, he heard a ping. He opened the box and plucked out the button engraved with a Yew sprig. He'd recalled it correctly.

"What do you feel?" Tinne Holly asked as Draeg closed his fingers over the object.

"You, I feel your vibrations." Draeg smiled. "Sense Holly Family."

"Great. Later." The scry bowl went dark.

Lori woke up and stretched luxuriously, then glanced at the wall timer. She'd awoken early and had a full septhour before she needed to be in the study with the Residence. How she loved the earlier sunrises, the days stretching ever longer, getting ever warmer.

She felt so good! And *then* she recalled the dreams in the night that had trailed from that passionate kiss she'd shared with Draeg Hedgenettle. He'd really kissed her! And his fingers squeezed her rump. And put his hand on her left breast! She could still feel the tingles.

She'd felt them in her dreams, too. An imaginary lover's gentle hands on her body that had stroked her to core tightening increments and ecstasy. That had never happened before. Before her sexy dreams had fallen far short of the sense of hard hands on her body. She chuckled to herself.

"You are awake and in a good mood," the Residence stated.

"Thank you for the horses, Residence," she enthused.

"You are welcome."

Yes, part of her cheer this morning was having horses, no doubt. But she didn't hide from herself that much of her new delight was meeting and interacting with Draeg Hedgenettle.

And, she'd discovered her primary Flair! What a wonderful day yesterday had been, only diminished by the standard Family tussles.

But today was a brand-new day. She bounded from her bed-sponge, waved a hand to tidy the covers in the precise way the house-keeper insisted upon, and headed into the waterfall room.

Rrrowww, came a purring voice in her mind, and she sensed her Fam yawning, stretching, and sharpening his claws on the inside planks of the small garden shed she'd fixed up for him. *You are up, FamWoman? I am HUNGRY.*

As always, she sent. *I will be down in good time.*

It takes you, on an average, eighteen minutes before you arrive in Our garden with My food. You do not teleport.

You are aware of eighteen minutes?

I am unique and special. I can count passing minutes with a twitch of my whiskers, he boasted.

You know I have rules to follow. I must groom and dress appropriately before I leave my room.

Rrow! This time *he* sent irritation. *I do not consider those rules to be efficient or cost effective in terms of energy or Flair, particularly with regard to Me. They are stupid rules. When We have Our own house WE will make the rules.*

Yes, she said mentally, though she kept her amusement to herself, sure that Baccat thought he'd impose his notion of rules on her, which wasn't going to happen.

You could translocate My food to Me, he said slyly.

She put hurt in her voice. *You don't want to see me?*

Of course I do, but I want My food, first.

The Residence likes to keep track of the food in the no-time storage units and has locked them down, which means I have to take portions out by hand. You know this.

But it's MY food. You let them boss you around!

Like you're trying to? If you want food now, go to the stables, Draeg should be up. The whole conversation began to rub away her good mood. *I've tried fighting*, she replied tersely. *Several times in my life. It doesn't work. The Family outnumbers me and*

*the Residence can lock doors and windows against me or gas me
with sleep powder.*

Baccat growled. *It is definitely time to leave this backward estate.*

*I agree. I'm done with my waterfall and dressing, and I will be
out there shortly with your food.*

*That's very good to hear. Thank you, FamWoman. I love you.
I love you, too.*

She pulled a weathershield around her as she left the house
with ground furrabeast steak for Baccat. To her dismay, a hard
frost had returned to edge the twigs of the bushes with rime.

Still not warm enough to leave. Not if the stridebeasts, and now
the more delicate horses, had to spend the nights outside on the trail
for weeks until she arrived at her very own estate, set aside for her
father's child or children upon his marriage to D'Yew.

One of his memory spheres that Lori had found and hidden from
destruction had described the property, and Lori knew it would suit
her needs perfectly. Or, rather, she'd determined she'd suit it.

At twelve, when she'd begun studying with the Residence and
the maître de maison, who stewarded the Yew properties and invest-
ments and bank assets, she'd seen the condition had been noted as
"acceptable." Since then, she'd managed to allocate a bit more gilt
toward the upkeep. She knew the house contained five bedrooms
and the land parcel was equally large. To the Yews the estate seemed
tiny and barely adequate for a Noble lifestyle. For her, perfect.

She walked through two kitchen gardens and took a right
before she entered the small herb garden that she'd claimed for
herself and Baccat, so insignificant that no one else disputed her
wish. The old, silvered, once-warped door to the shed creaked
open and Baccat stuck his head out, then greeted her with a cat
smile and rolling purr.

She set his pottery plate with steaming furrabeast on the stool
chin-high to him that he preferred to eat from. While he munched,
she went into the tiny shed, as warm as all the rooms in the Residence, and got a rake to move around the wind-disturbed mulch
to protect plants . . . plants she wouldn't see in full bloom. But

since the time when Baccat had moved from the stables closer to
the Residence, she'd tended the garden with an eye that it would
be healthy and hardy without human aid.

Baccat belched. *We must speak seriously a moment.* He eyed
a spot on the gray garden wall where the sun had melted away the
frost and warmed the stone. Then he jumped atop it to stare down
at her and gave a tiny cough. *We must talk about how the Yews
are perceived outside this estate.*

"Oh?"

*Neither Cuspid Yew nor Folia Yew, who are joint regents for you
as an unconfirmed FirstFamily Head of Household, have participated in the required rituals for FirstFamilies in GreatCircle Temple.*

Lori blinked. "I didn't know there were required rituals." Was
there any way she could leverage that knowledge to wrest control
from the older Yews? She pondered a moment, but didn't think
so. As far as she was concerned, she'd explored all other viable
options than leaving and was ready to hit the road.

If she brought outsiders in on a Family struggle, she'd never be
forgiven by all the rest of the Yews—about forty—who worked
on the estate. And as she didn't think she'd respect a person who
went outside the Family for help, she didn't believe others would
respect her.

Also, those outsiders so much more sophisticated than she
could take advantage of her and leave the Family worse off. It was
all too possible that the elder Yews, the ones in control now and
who'd been in control since her mother had died, and whose
power was backed by the Residence, would claim Lori was mad
or too stupid to handle the Family.

The simple fact was that she didn't dare lose such an important fight—as she'd always lost fights—with her Family. She had a
deep suspicion that she wouldn't be treated well for years, and her
animals might pay the price of a lost battle.

Meanwhile her Fam had lain down on the wall, paws tucked
under him, and stared at her with a superior look. *Are you finished pondering?*

"I was considering whether this changed our circumstances. I don't think so. We're still leaving. They'll forget us after we're gone."

I agree. His paws came out as he kneaded the wall, and the brick crumbled a bit. Lori frowned and sent a little Flair to reinforce it. Baccat sniffed. *I like dust from a FirstFamily estate on My paws.*

She sensed that it gave him some sort of status—that other beings, other Fams, could sense the age of the brick or the resonance of the energy that imbued the estate. She said mentally, *You are not allowed to harm OUR estate. Not our current estate nor OUR new one.*

He grumbled, looked away. *This dust helps and it is not a significant amount. The harm to your wall was infinitesimal. I like being a FirstFamily FamCat. I like being YOUR FamCat and others knowing that.*

We will discuss how to show you are a Fam of status later.

His eyes narrowed. *Tonight. When we go out. There is something I wish to show you. A tradition between FamPeople and their non-thumbed companions.*

As usual, the notion of being in the big city—the forbidden and the new—drew her. *A tradition? Very well.* Her brows drew down as a thought occurred. *What about your new personal armor? Other Fams would not have that.*

Baccat sniffed. *My new personal armor is amazing, but it is not readily perceptible to dull senses—cannot be seen or smelled well.*

Lori grinned. *That is a GOOD thing.*

Yes. Baccat sat up. *My personal armor lasted another three septhours, for a total of four septhours. Good for a FamCat, or perhaps smaller Fams, but I believe limiting for a human, who has more mass.*

Sighing, Lori said aloud, "For now."

For now.

She sensed the stridebeasts and the horses in the stables stirring, looked over the frost-white trees fading to brown, sent love-warmth to them, began speaking with Baccat telepathically again. *I am tired of the cold snaps this spring! I want to get going.* Though a little voice in her head stated that she also wanted to get to know Draeg Hedgenettle better. In fact, when she thought of him, a warmth emanated from between her legs and spread throughout her body.

Yes, he could be a major distraction, and her plans to leave were so far along that she shouldn't hesitate once the night temperature rose above freezing. *Maybe my personal armor spell doesn't last long now, but if I practice, it could get better.* She set her chin.

After a deep breath, she continued mentally, *Though I probably wouldn't be able to give all my animals personal armor on the trip, I might be able to give them weathershields some nights. It would be draining, but I would not have any household responsibilities.* Her mouth tightened. *Better if we could find out how long the weather will hold, how warm it will be during the days when we travel, how cold at night. The grass that my beasts could eat on the trip is slow in growing this year.*

I do not know any Weather Mages, Baccat replied. *But I may be able to ask my contacts to discover a person who is good at forecasting weather patterns. Weather here in Druida and along our path to the Valerian estate in the south.* His whiskers flicked and he looked slyly at her. *Or We could visit the starship* Nuada's Sword *and ask it.*

Lori shook her head. *I don't want to attract attention before we leave by going to places we might be seen and commented upon, so no* Nuada's Sword. *As for the weather forecasting mages—or spells—I doubt we could afford that.* She had very limited personal funds and needed to hoard what she had for the trip.

I know the Sallows, and the Sallows' stables, Baccat rumbled. *I could, perhaps, speak to one of the ferals who live there to extrapolate about a three-week trip for horses and stridebeasts, beginning, say, next week?*

Her gaze focused on her cat once more. *Yes, perhaps the end of next week.* Again she glanced at the stables. *Draeg Hedgenettle might know better than we of horses' stamina and needs, but I hesitate to ask.*

Baccat sat up straight. *You have Me to find out information for you.*

"Yes." She bit her lip, murmured, "It would be so much better if I had gilt, or if I could move about the city as myself, ask questions as myself instead of some shabby shadow." Then she tossed her head. "It doesn't matter. I will make my own life, and in under a decade my stridebeasts and my breeding program will be well known." Yet a decade seemed like forever to her. She set her jaw. She'd worked on the breeding program, beginning with two stridebeasts, since she'd been ten, but she was allowed to keep only six animals. That would change.

Baccat coughed, and the unusual sound had her stilling. "What?"

It is GOOD that you are not known as D'Yew outside this estate.

"Really? Why?" She'd thought a FirstFamily GrandLady in charge of her household, which she'd never been, would have been able easily to find out what she wanted, would have people happy to help her for her gilt or favors or influence. At least, when the twins came back from their outings, they always looked smug as if their egos had been stroked.

The Yews are not universally liked.

She snorted and went back to mind-speaking with her Fam. *They wouldn't be if they treat everyone like they do me.*

They DO treat everyone like they do US. Your MotherSire was NOT a good man.

So my father said in his record spheres.

Your MotherSire bought a young bride, just as your mother bought your father.

Knees weak, Lori stumbled to the nearby pitted stone bench and plopped down. "He never said that," she protested aloud. "Not in his record spheres. And in the memory spheres that he made and I experienced, he didn't *feel* bought . . . or unhappy."

It was a very good marriage for a SecondSon of an old Grand-Lord Family. He got gilt of his own, a couple of minor estates of his own from both the Valerians and the Yews, and a relatively independent lifestyle. Your mother was not . . . demanding of him.

Lori steadied her nerves. "If you mean that she used herbs and

Healers to get pregnant fast, I know. I saw the accounting for such in the ledgers."

She did not deserve You, for You are a wonderful person.

"Thank you." She stood. "I must get inside. The sooner I finish my work with the Family and the Residence, the sooner I can go to the stables and learn to ride my horses." And see Draeg Hedgenettle. She didn't want to think of her father or her birth now. All that was past and she had her eyes on the future.

One more thing, Baccat said.

"Yes?"

Neither your cuzes nor the maître de maison, nor your house-keeper, spend much time in the city.

"I don't care."

The other FirstFamilies are curious people and no Yews have been in their society for a long, long time. They do not know what is happening on this estate.

"I don't care about that, either. I am nothing to them, to any outsider except that shabby shadow, and no outsider is anything to me." Except, perhaps, Draeg Hedgenettle.

Baccat stood and his back rippled in a catlike shrug. *I am done with breakfast, and it is fun in the city. I will go speak with Fams of the Sallows or the ferals who frequent their stable complex. Perhaps I will renew My acquaintance with the PublicLibrary Fams. Though they are not interesting, they can sometimes be persuaded to ask the librarians questions.*

"All right." Lori suppressed a sigh. Baccat's morning sounded a great deal better than her own of taking inventory of all the food and items in the no-times on the estate and ensuring they were properly stocked.

I will see you tonight, Baccat grinned.

"Yes!" And the slight smudge of downheartedness vanished under fizzing anticipation. Exploring the city again, and Baccat would show her a Fam tradition! "Now we must play." She took a string from her pocket, slithered it along the ground. "So that I can hide my anticipation and excitement at leaving this place from the Residence."

The cloth mouse at the end of the string bumped and hopped with her gestures and the tiniest of Flair.

Eyes gleaming wild, Baccat leapt, caught the cloth on his claws. With a tiny rip, Lori whisked the fake prey away, turned, and trotted around pathways at the edge of the garden until Baccat rushed from under a bare bush, pouncing and yanking the cloth from the string.

He looked up at her holding the mouse in his mouth, showing his fangs in a smile that also reflected in his eyes.

I got it! I am the triumphant CAT king of D'YEW Residence.

She didn't know why he'd fashioned the title for himself, but it became all too obvious that status mattered to her Fam. She should probably count it as a blessing that he'd agreed to come with her to a small, unimportant estate.

"Hooray," she shouted.

"Are you finished amusing the animal?" asked Folia, the housekeeper. A tall, curvaceous blond woman no more than fifteen years older than Lori, Folia wore a coat that appeared new and of a different fashion than Lori's.

With a flatulent pop, Baccat teleported from the garden. Folia's mouth turned down. "Disgusting animal."

"He's my Fam."

"Cuspid requested that I speak with you about some document." Folia shrugged. "I have it in the small dining room for you to peruse during breakfast." She turned and led the way back to the Residence, expecting Lori to follow, which she did.

Nine

If Lori was eating in the small dining room, that meant no one else would be at the table with her, and loneliness warred with relief that she'd be solitary. Pitiful that she could be lonely while surrounded by Family.

She followed Folia to the back door set in the stone as gray as the sky. Perhaps that was why she'd had a brief wish that her Family were . . . different. Different like Draeg's must be, since he treasured his.

When they entered the room, Lori saw a long papyrus titled *Allocation of Funds to Allies*. She picked it up and handed it to Folia with a smile. "No business during meals." Lori repeated one of the rules she lived by; occasionally she could make them work for her instead of against her.

Folia scowled.

"Bad for the digestion. Furthermore, Cuspid and I and the Residence worked on the accounts already this month. This will have to wait until next month. The Residence is not flexible in matters of gilt." She pulled out a heavy wooden chair and sat. "What's for breakfast?"

"Oatmeal with currants," Folia nearly snarled.

Lori kept her smile. She loathed oatmeal, and no doubt if she'd studied the papyrus she'd have gotten eggs and porcine strips. There was always a cost for not going along with Folia, or Cuspid, or the twins, or the Residence.

"Good!" she said cheerfully, fully determined to pull a few spices from the pantry to make it taste better, maybe some dried porcine bits. Small rebellions the staff understood and would expect.

But as she ate her meal alone in a dim room with the windows closed on the grassyard sloping toward the river, she was *glad* she didn't like her Family. So much easier to leave them, all of them.

Draeg had awakened hot and sweaty and trembling with the effort to restrain himself during dream loving, to be tender when he wanted to ravish. Scrubbing his hands over his face at the complete feeling of *reality* of the dream instead of a regular, simple sex-and-release experience, he shook his head. That kiss with D'Yew had even more impact than he'd thought.

He grumbled to himself through his waterfall and large but mostly tasteless breakfast, wondering how long he'd be able to keep his hands off the woman and how to explain to Tinne Holly that he intended to sleep with the man's main suspect.

Time to head to work.

After tending to the animals' morning needs, Draeg rolled his shoulders to stretch them, looked around and sent his senses out to check if he was being observed, found he wasn't. Then he flowed into a fighting drill developed by Tinne Holly, one of the two people the Yews hated the most.

Though the more Draeg *didn't* interact with the Yews, the more he believed they wouldn't know a Holly fighting kata—any Holly pattern—if it came up and bit them on the ass. Draeg wasn't the best household guard in the world, but if he'd been committing crimes and a new person showed up on his estate, he'd be down in person to check him or her out. Draeg had met only the dried-up stick of a maître de maison, Cuspid Yew; the housekeeper; and D'Yew herself.

If this had been his estate . . . the words, the *feeling* snagged in his brain. Sometimes the stables and the land around it felt like his own, since he worked by himself, had barely seen anyone since he'd arrived two eightdays ago.

Somehow this particular place felt . . . good, almost familiar, or as if he'd been waiting to find it, stupid as that sounded.

He let his workout carry him from the courtyard and behind the stables, facing the thick woodland that separated D'Yew's land from lesser Nobles' estates and, farther east, the more crowded middle class neighborhoods of Druida City. Tall evergreens as a backdrop for the reaching branches of bare-limbed trees and thick brush added a solid, living green to the gray day.

He finished the exercise and breathed deeply, letting the pleasing smells of Yew estate suck into his nostrils and lungs. Stables and stridebeasts and horses first, of course, then the scent of the land itself. Bushes and ancient trees and grasses, more tangled around the stables than the smooth yard surrounding the Residence. The fragrance of the sea.

Yew estate didn't border the Great Platte Ocean like those across the avenue and to the west of it. Fine with Draeg; that huge body of water made him deeply uneasy. He'd never known how his mentor, Tab Holly, could have actually sailed on a ship *on top* of it.

So he started another long and traveling training pattern that would take him back to the corral and the horse pen, concentrating on the perfection of each move.

A bird cawed raucously overhead and Draeg glanced up to see it circling. *You are too close to my horses, man, step away*, came clear and astringent to Draeg's mind. He followed through too hard on a foot sweep and was forced into fancy footwork to keep from falling on his butt.

Yes, his kata had taken him near the horses' pen. He'd moved it close to the stridebeasts so the animals could get used to each other. The horses knew about stridebeasts—the Sallows had picked up three from the lost estate—but the Yew stridebeasts thought the horses were funny-looking creatures.

Quickly finishing his drill, Draeg withdrew a couple of paces but kept moving in the cool air. As a man of supposedly little Flair, he hesitated to pull a weathershield around himself.

The raven sounded a last caw and settled on Smyrna's croup, glittering black eyes fixed on Draeg.

I have been with these horses many twinmoons. They are mine more than yours or the woman's. His beak clicked as if in scorn.

Draeg bowed to the bird, though he kept his eyes on this new player in the intimate little game going on.

"May I ask your name, GentleSir Bird?"

Another beak clack. *I am called Corax.*

"Greetyou, Corax. I am Draeg Hedgenettle."

You lie, the bird stated.

With a swift look around the area, Draeg muttered. "You may call me Draeg Hedgenettle. My birth name is Draeg Betony-Blackthorn."

You have too many names, the bird grumbled. He strutted up Smyrna's back and she blew out a breath. Though her muscles flexed, she made no move to rid herself of the bird, not even when he flew to the top of her head between her ears. Draeg got the impression that the horse had missed the raven. Ragan, whose neck had been stretched over the pen toward the stridebeasts, turned and trotted toward Smyrna and Corax, whickering in welcome.

Corax lifted and circled over both horses, then touched down on Ragan's back. Smyrna slapped her tail against her butt in irritation, especially when Corax tilted his head and focused on Draeg again. *I think I would like a FamMan who would provide regular and easy meals as you do for the horses. I have missed my suet and my oatmeal and apples and my raw clucker. I think you would do.*

Draeg's adoptive father and several of his siblings had Fams, but he'd never felt the need for one.

But now . . . he was alone on this quest, with only occasional contact with anyone outside the Yew estate. And his decisions as to how to handle this particular situation, how much and when to interact with the Yews, Family and estate, were his own. His great responsibility. He could use a friend inside the walls.

A *friend.* The sizzle of his blood when he thought of Loridana Itha D'Yew tempted him to take her as a lover . . . but whether she could be a friend as well, something rarer and more important to Draeg, still needed to be seen. The woman was so damn naive, innocent even.

The black raven studied him, appearing streetwise, and as dark as all Draeg's cynical thoughts made solid. "Deal," he said.

At the word, the bird—his *FamBird*—flew to his shoulder. Draeg tensed at having the sharp beak so close to his eyes.

Corax cackled. *You trust me, FamMan, Draeg-of-the-many-names.*

"Maybe." Draeg spit the word through clenched teeth, but the raven lifted his wings and sidestepped back and forth on his shoulder with scratchy steps from twiglike feet.

This perch is broad enough. I like, Corax said. Coming even closer, he stopped near enough that Draeg could smell spring dirt dust on his feathers, and those feathers actually brushed Draeg's neck in a soft caress that prickled his skin. Slowly he lifted his hand and stroked the bird with the back of his hand.

Harsh, simple images of a bowl of mush with fresh fruit bits and a side of raw clucker flooded his mind.

I like that meal best.

"Uh-huh. I'll see what I can do," Draeg said, but a small warmth coated his insides and he couldn't stop smiling. He had a Fam. Clearing his throat to loosen it, he said, "How many raven Fams are there?"

Corax lifted his wings slightly and Draeg felt disinterest from his new FamBird. *Don't know. There is a hawkcel flying around the city, but he thinks muchly muchly of himself, and does not speak or pay attention to me.*

"So I may have one of two known FamBirds." Yeah, his smile

stretched wider into a grin. Wasn't often in his life that he was unique. In fact, never. Well, never until he took this job as an undercover stableman; these particular circumstances were unique for sure. Before that he'd just been an angry young man, ex-merchant-guard, looking for trouble.

D'Yew's Fam, Baccat, jumped onto one of the thin posts of the temporary pen, a pole too small for his fat rump, so he was forced to dance around the top as he strove for balance. The horses shied back and Corax took flight.

So there is a new Fam, a Feathered Fam; most interesting, the cat said, gaze following Corax as he circled, then returned to Draeg's shoulder, cawing in irritation.

"Do you mind that I have a Fam, cat?" Draeg challenged.

Why should I mind? Baccat raised his nose.

"Another Fam in your territory?" Draeg said.

This time Baccat snorted before replying, *I do not consider this My territory, or, rather, I only consider My particular herb garden My territory.* He fixed big yellow cat eyes on the raven huffing in Draeg's ear. *THAT individual had better not leave droppings in MY garden, or look to eat MY furrabeast leavings.*

Corax whistled. *Furrabeast?*

Draeg thought he heard the bird swallow. *You had furrabeast this morning? I had desiccated mouse.* Beak turning, he pulled at Draeg's hair. *I am hungry. I have had nothing I have not caught or found myself for many, many, many days.*

Baccat licked his forepaw, groomed his whiskers. *I deduce from your mind that your many, many, many days is three. You scared away other birds eating the Sallows' suet three days ago.*

Long time.

"We'll see what I have in the stable's no-time." It had been stocked by the Yews, and not, he thought, by D'Yew herself. He'd taken some extremely basic meals from it. *I can get food when I am out this evening*—Draeg jutted his chin toward Baccat—*you and your lady go out this evening?*

Perhaps, the cat said, and Draeg took that for confirmation. He suppressed a gleeful smile of his own. *He* had a Fam who could keep an eye on the wandering duo of D'Yew and Baccat.

Yes, Corax whispered sibilantly in Draeg's mind, on a private telepathic stream that had already formed between them. *That will be fun. I can SEE much more than cat. Observe more.*

You will be a great help to me, Draeg said, then amended that when he recalled watching Baccat and D'Yew, and others with their Fams. *WE will be a great TEAM.*

Yes.

Returning to the discussion of My territory here, Baccat nattered. *If anything, the rulers here are the older members of the Yew Family, she who calls herself the Housekeeper and he who is styled as the maître de maison, and the Residence, of course, but he is not mobile.*

New information! "He?" questioned Draeg. "The Residence considers itself male?"

A lift of the nose and muzzle. *As I understand the situation, the persona modeled after My FamWoman's MotherSire remains in control.*

Draeg winced. "The T'Yew who was killed by Tinne Holly's HeartMate." He paused. "They treated her ill." Draeg had heard stories of DepressFlair bracelets put on a child bride, now Lahsin Holly, to control her. As soon as she'd reached adulthood at Second Passage, she'd run away. Tinne Holly went after her and found her.

That the arrogant T'Yew's persona still held sway was bad news. Though, on the whole, it might be better than a persona of his daughter, the madwoman who'd been Loridana D'Yew's mother.

Unless you are blood of the maître de maison, you are treated ill, the cat said. *They kicked Me.* The FamCat stared at Draeg, no doubt expecting some extreme reaction like he'd get from his FamWoman. When none came, Baccat switched his gaze to Corax. *I strongly suggest, bird, that you do not enter the Residence through any open window. That being is sufficiently vile to drop a sill right on you and kill your feathered self.*

Baccat snapped his teeth once and loudly as if in punctuation, and Corax screeched in Draeg's ear, just as a shiver passed through his blood.

Then the FamCat jumped down and swaggered away from the pens. *I will go talk to My friends, the feral cats of the Turquoise House—*

Uh-oh; well, if Baccat didn't know who Draeg was now, the cat would learn soon. Draeg's brother Antenn Moss-Blackthorn lived in the Turquoise House, and the House itself chatted to Fams.

Then I will talk to the Sallows. The cat looked at Corax. *Perhaps check your references, bird.* Flicking his tail, he scrutinized the horses. *And speak with the Sallows about these beasts.* He paused, sniffed. *They are looking better since My FamWoman has visited them.*

All the animals reacted with cheerful snuffles when Baccat sent the image of D'Yew to them.

Without another word, tail waving, the FamCat strolled away. He could have teleported, but that wouldn't show his disdain of Draeg and Corax and all the other lowly beasts as much; Draeg got that.

I could divebomb him, Corax said.

Draeg lifted his hand and gently swept fingertips down the bird. *Not yet.*

After lunch, Lori received permission to work with the horses for a couple of septhours. Those who formally oversaw the estate, Cuspid and Folia, seemed happy that she'd expressed the wish to concentrate on breeding stridebeasts and horses as a career, which would leave them in power.

The Residence considered her very young and yet in training.

Lori herself must determine whether to continue with her breeding program course or make it secondary to offering personal armor spells for sale, but plenty of time to consider that.

Testing her connection with her stridebeasts *and* her horses and finding the link with Ragan and Smyrna thin but strong, Lori ran to the area of the paddock and temporary corral. And stopped, gasping.

Before her, in the horse pen, stood Draeg Hedgenettle, with a big, black bird on his head.

Ten

*B*oth man and bird turned their heads to stare at her, the bird lifting his wings.

Draeg smiled and Lori felt it deep inside, sending warmth to parts of her that she didn't think about too much—or hadn't before she'd seen him yesterday, kissed him last night, and the hot dream in the dark. Wisps of that dream slid through her mind, and she flushed. Perhaps he'd think she took on color because of the run.

Raising his elbow, Draeg held it out. "Please sit on my arm, Corax. I don't think this perching on my head works well for us."

The bird clicked its beak. As Lori drew closer, she figured that the thing must be a raven, an Earthan bird, and a good seventy centimeters long. It looked healthy, and the sun that finally broke through the clouds shone on its blue-black feathers.

"Apparently this raven is a friend of Smyrna's and Ragan's." Draeg nodded to the horses. "He lived and bonded with them on the Alexanders' estate and flew here to be with the horses."

Lori spread her senses wide and felt the affection between the horses and the bird, a bond. "Of course," she said softly. "Welcome, ah, GentleSir Raven."

Clearing his throat, and with a wary look in his eye, Draeg said, "He, Corax, says he'd like to be my Fam, too."

At that, Lori's eyes widened. Draeg appeared stoic. Cuspid, the maître de maison, had told her the stableman had little Flair, which meant it could be a real strain to bond with a Fam companion. That, in turn, meant that Draeg had more psi power than he might have revealed to Cuspid. Lori was sure the rest of the Yews would prefer an outsider working for them to have minimal Flair.

They shared a glance and Lori recalled that he already knew a couple of her secrets. It would be good to have one of his. Tacitly agreeing to keep this knowledge to herself, she nodded and said lightly, "Greetyou, Corax."

Greet, said the raven, hopping onto Draeg's lifted elbow, then walking up to a shoulder that Lori noted was broad enough to easily accommodate the bird.

Baccat couldn't perch on her shoulders unless she made an invisible shelf extending from one.

Though she wanted to touch her horses again, spend time with the new and fascinating beasts she'd wished to have for years, she went into the stridebeasts' corral and said hello to each one of her animals by name, feeding each a small fruit treat. From the tenor of their minds, she sensed that they'd accept the horses into their herd. She let out a sigh of relief. It would be so much easier to travel with the animals if they thought they were one herd.

Then, finally, she could leave her stridebeasts. She walked from the paddock and into the pen, and the horses moved fast, crowding her, knocking her off her feet.

She fell backward and strong arms caught her, held her against an equally strong body. Corax screeched and flew to a fence rail as Draeg lifted her and paced away from the horses toward the corral gate.

Wonderful! She *smelled* him, Draeg. He smelled . . . a lot like the land around her, to be honest, surprising her. Cool and earthy, with promise of a quickening spring and hot summer. She swallowed. She couldn't recall the last time she'd been held other than the night before, but that included passion and this didn't, really.

Perhaps the old stableman, long dead, had been the last to hold her when she'd been a child.

She'd never been held, or carried, by a man who thought of her as a woman. Heat radiated between them and she flushed.

He kept her against his chest, arms under her legs and behind her back, and didn't seem to notice her height or her weight. He certainly didn't use any Flair as they moved to an edge of the large circular pen.

Sensations flooded her, the solid muscle next to her side and in the arms that carried her, the close view of his square jaw and the slight bristles of his shaven face, darker than his regular skin. His nose appeared to have a slight bump in it she hadn't noticed before, and she saw a white scarred knot just below his temple. His chest went up and down steadily; she seemed to pant, herself.

Every step he took caused heat to rise in her, and because she wanted to squirm, she stayed very still. Yes, she felt his warmth, hers, mingling with the sun to heat them both and radiate out into the day. She smelled him, and some of that earthiness must have come from a slight odor of sweat, and she got the idea that he'd been doing those training moves again, and the aroma of that exertion lingered. It certainly had a great effect on her.

She wanted to taste him again. This time do more than inhale the fragrance that had her mind reeling. This time she'd remember what he tasted like. This time she'd explore the texture of the skin on his cheek, his jaw, his neck with her tongue.

Her arms had naturally gone around his neck, and their balance together good. They fit.

Most incredible of all was the feeling of utter security in his arms. That seeped in even under the lust flickering inside her.

Finally the disturbed thoughts of the horses impinged on her brain. She looked to see that they'd fled to the far side of the pen and huddled together.

She stopped enjoying Draeg's arms around her and stared at the mares. "They're afraid."

"Wha—?" asked Draeg. His voice sounded low, husky, and she

naturally tightened her grip on him, and then the moment broke when the stridebeasts rustled in their corral, coming close to the pen and watching the horses. More, Lori's nose twitched at an unfamiliar tinge in the air that she puzzled at, then identified as horse fear.

Reluctantly she shifted in Draeg's arms, and he let her go slowly. Her body brushed against his as her legs lowered, and he groaned and her breath came short. All of him was so solid!

She stayed within the circle of his arms for long seconds, until a questioning sound came from one of the horses. Then she turned toward the animals, who appeared calmer. Ragan's ears angled as if curious.

"They were afraid," Lori repeated. "Perhaps because they thought they'd be hurt since they knocked me over. Do you think they were abused?" She swallowed. She didn't like to think of abuse, because it dredged up too many feelings within her. She *couldn't* allow herself to imagine animals being hurt. It could break something in her.

"I think they're just skittish because they haven't been around people lately. Their owner was old and I don't believe she could attend to them well."

"Oh." Taking another pace away from Draeg, Lori focused on the horses. She clicked her tongue and patted a bag at her side. In a coaxing tone, she said, "Come here, ladies, I have treats for you, too." Lori blinked when Draeg shuddered beside her.

Ragan and Smyrna paced toward her, were more delicate as they nudged her, their minds swimming with the images of apples, of pieces of raw sugar.

"Aarrrghkk!" Corax the raven whisked in front of her and landed on Smyrna's head. *I want a treat, too! I am a NEW Fam!*

Lori chuckled. "Oh, a treat to welcome the new Hedgenettle Fam?"

"Forrr surrre," the bird croaked aloud.

"I didn't know ravens could talk."

The bird just lifted his wings.

"I didn't, either," Draeg said. She'd felt him come up beside her, and now he stood nearer to her than she was accustomed to any human standing.

Apple, Corax said mentally. *You have apple, FamWoman of snotty cat. I would like some.* A pause and a snick of a beak. *Please.*

Lori hesitated. "Baccat was snotty to you?"

Draeg snorted. "Baccat's feline, of course he's snotty. I—" He stopped before he finished the sentence that had nearly poured from his mouth: *I live with the Queen of Snotty.* No, couldn't say that about his stepfather GrandLord T'Blackthorn's Fam, Drina. Instead Draeg said, "And, despite what Baccat denies, he's territorial."

"Not to mention that this beautiful Fam is a bird, and cats and birds . . ." Lori held out a piece of apple for the Fam.

Thanks, said Corax as he took the apple, then ate it.

"You're welcome."

Draeg said, "We will get you raw meat in a little bit."

Thanks. I can hunt, but it is good to have a FamMan, maybe.

"I am sure it is."

Lori blinked. "Now that Baccat is no longer staying at the stables, there may be rodents in there. I stocked the no-times in the stables and your apartment according to a list given to me, and I think there is raw meat in them." She frowned, remembering. She'd worked with the Residence and Folia this morning on inventorying all the no-times in the house, renewing their spell energy, and her recollection of the stables storage units was foggy. "I'm sure I was allowed to put uncooked clucker, and perhaps furrabeast, in the no-times, in case another feral cat showed up to take care of any rodents."

Draeg nodded. He smiled at Corax with affection and Lori's chest tightened. No one smiled at her like that. A surprising need for such a smile shot through her. With a small, sighing breath, she set the want aside and turned back to the horses. "Now to say good morning to my beauties." She walked toward the animals even as they stepped toward her, quietly, no jostling. Whatever the reason they might be wary of humans, she interested them. She sent more soothing energy. She *had* been surprised when she'd fallen, anxious about them stepping on her, but none of that had happened. In any event, with her and Draeg's care, the horses would feel soon that they'd found safe haven.

For now, she fed them, stroked them, and as she did so, she let the stridebeasts know the reason the horses got extra attention was that they were new and scared. She checked the mares and saw that their minor sores had healed, and they looked better cared for, well groomed.

"You ride and train horses?" she asked Draeg.

"I've ridden more than trained, but yeah," he replied. "Smyrna and Ragan, at one time, were well trained."

Lori wondered how long ago that might be. Unlike native Celtan species, like stridebeasts, Earthan humans and animals had a longer life—and slower birthrate and more sensitivity to sickness. "Do you know how old they are?"

Draeg took halters that had been lying over the stridebeasts' fence in the sun and put one on Smyrna, the other on Ragan. "The Sallows thought they were about forty. Still plenty of vim and vigor." He patted Ragan's withers, then went back to stroke Smyrna's neck. Lori got the idea that he preferred Smyrna.

She'd have loved them if they'd been at the end of their lives, but knowing she'd have plenty of time with them pleased her. "That's good."

"Yes." Then he projected an image of the horses saddled and in full harness. The beasts seemed to perk up.

His mental image had been quite clear. No, this was not a minor-Flaired man.

They worked with the horses on lunge lines in the temporary paddock, until Lori believed all four of them—humans and animals—had settled and felt well in tune. She'd followed Draeg's instructions and actions and had had a good first lesson she wouldn't forget.

Then Draeg said, "Let's ride."

Pleasure surged from all of them—the two horses and Lori. Draeg grinned and her heart lifted further. Even though he didn't smile solely at her, but at the horses, too, she still got a portion of that smile and it sank into her . . . more deeply than it should, perhaps. She swung onto Ragan's saddle, and though it wasn't as intimate as the ride she and the horse had had the afternoon before, it seemed safer for them both.

Good to see my mare friends happy, said Corax the raven. He stretched his wings wide and Lori stared at the length of them and the big bird. *I need more airtime in this new place*, the bird commented, and launched himself into the sky. Lori sensed the mixture of wild and groomed areas on the estate pleased him, and that he might visit the farm and see what leftovers he might find. *Later, my FamMan.*

Later, Corax.

Fare well, Corax, Lori sent.

I will.

Then the four of them, horses with riders, walked around the stables. Anticipation humming in her, Lori set them on the wide graveled way to the east and the back gate toward the strip of forested shared land between FirstFamily estates.

The main route was fine until they reached the dirt path she'd been using to the small northeast gate in the wall. She *had* kept the trail overgrown with bushes, but now she saw she'd have to either use Flair when she left with her animal Family, or clear the way with physical effort or Flair a few septhours before.

She'd thought the trail would be fine for a stridebeast one at a time, but even with her discreet trimming, it was too narrow. Good for her and Baccat, but not for a horse or stridebeast. She must revise her plans. Once more. She set her teeth and straightened her shoulders. She would *not* let anyone stop her.

Lori felt Draeg's sideways glance even as the horses had slowed, then passed the small gap in the bushes that led to the old service gate that no one else used that she'd oiled and prepared. She knew what she had to do, and would do it.

"Hard to see that particular path," Draeg said, and she tensed. She'd actually forgotten he'd found her out last night. How foolish and shortsighted! Short-memoried. His touch and his kiss had occupied a much more predominant place in her thoughts.

He'd caught her staring too long. "We shouldn't take the horses through as it is," he said gently.

As if she hadn't already determined that on her own.

One of his brows had lifted. "Do you think to leave the estate and ride in Noble Country or the busier parts of Druida City?"

Her mouth dried. Why did he ask? Again she considered whether, somehow, her Family suspected she might leave, and have hired him to observe her. But no. Not one of her relatives would consider leaving the Residence, the stronghold of the estate, the civilized Druida City. She believed every one of them prized the status of belonging to a FirstFamily.

"Would you like me to trim the bushes back for you?" Draeg pushed.

For an instant her breath caught at the thought that he could be an ally instead of an opponent . . . or a distraction.

No. She didn't know him well enough to trust him, and probably wouldn't learn enough about him in the next week or two to trust him. Or let herself be open and vulnerable and reveal her plans to him. "Thank you, no."

"There *are* horse riders in Druida City, you know. Not many, but some."

She hadn't seen any and she didn't want to call attention to herself. Just tuck the thought away that she needed to think about and alter her plans for her and her animals leaving. She shouldn't have gone to CityCenter with Baccat last night and sampled food from someplace other than her own kitchens. She should have reviewed the route more—all the way from her gate to the portal in the southeast corner of the city.

And it didn't sound as if tonight she'd be tracing the route, either. Baccat had other plans. Soon, though, she'd have to quit amusing herself in the city and double-check her route. Perhaps tomorrow night.

Glancing at Draeg, she found him sitting easily in the saddle, as if he'd spent a long time in one. She experienced a twinge of envy as she smiled at him. "No, I don't think I will take the horses into the city proper." She leaned forward and stroked Ragan's neck, liking the feel of the horse's hair bristling against her palm. "They need to feel safe here before they leave."

They needed to trust her, so when they all *did* leave, they wouldn't be frightened of following her. But she'd learned that most animals trusted more easily than humans.

The realization that she didn't trust any human wrenched through her, and she swallowed hard. Sad and pitiable.

She blinked back sudden tears and straightened in her saddle. The fact that she didn't trust anyone might be sad and pitiable, but *she* wasn't.

Draeg still watched her, appearing not to be affected by her silences. He met her eyes and inclined his head. "Taking time to accustom your horses here before riding them outside the estate is a good strategy, and shows concern for your horses."

She only hoped her main strategy was as good. She knew it would be good for her when she left, and firmly believed it would be good for her animals. But she *couldn't* leave them behind, not if there was the least chance her Family would harm them for her actions.

A bird cawed, dove down and flew between the trees on each side of the road, swooped around them. *Nice place,* Corax sent. *I will look more. And no folk with arrows or blazers.*

Lori didn't think that her cuzes who putatively ran the farm, Vi and Zus, had arisen yet, and they didn't own such weapons. The regular Family workers wouldn't care about a scavenger bird.

Draeg's attention moved away from her to his Fam. Good.

She looked at the raven, then into Draeg's sapphire eyes. Perhaps she could determine whether he could be trusted, whether he might be a . . . an acquaintance favorable to her instead of a neutral party or an unfriend. Anyway, since she'd be spending some time with him, she should be friendly herself—as she'd decided yesterday. And when she left . . . after she got out of the walled Druida City . . . she'd send him a telepathic communication that he should escape Yew estate and the wrath of her Family himself. And if she hadn't developed enough of a bond to speak to him mentally, she'd send Baccat, or warn Draeg's own Fam, Corax.

Studying him, she said, "Tell me about yourself. Where do you come from and what did you do before you came here?"

Eleven

D'Yew's fragrance—like young spring shoots—drifted to him as Draeg pulled in a breath, deciding how to phrase his story. He could reveal a good part of the truth—and an ache of guilt bruised inside him that he lied to her—but he must definitely watch his words. Be detailed enough about some things that she wouldn't think of any omissions.

"I was born here in Druida, but from four until nine I grew up in the country, south of Druida."

She turned her head and her eyes blazed into his. "In the south? Where in the south?"

"A little northeast of Gael City."

"Oh." Her body tensed again and he got the idea that he'd answered the question wrong, but how and why?

"When I was nine, I was apprenticed to a Noble household guard here in Druida." Truth. Tab Holly, who'd owned The Green Knight Fencing and Fighting Salon, was a Holly guard. The preeminent Holly guard.

Draeg had shown an aptitude for fighting, and his First Passage that revealed his Flair had confirmed that he had fast reflexes, a sense for danger, an ability to stay cool in a fight. It was only later, when he'd lived with his adoptive father, Straif T'Blackthorn, that Draeg had begun to develop a portion of the legendary Blackthorn Flair for tracking. "I trained here until I was seventeen—" And suddenly he was breathless. He hadn't meant to say anything about the worst time in his life.

She looked at him and her pretty dark blond brows arched in question. Inhale, exhale, and her gaze went to his chest and that glance stirred his libido and that, in turn, eased the emotions crowding and tumbling inside him so he could finish the sentence. "—when my mentor and my natural parents died."

A little gasp from her. "Oh." Her mouth turned down as if in sympathy. "I can feel how much that grieved you; I'm sorry it still hurts."

He jerked a nod, and *he* could sense her sympathy, but it felt . . . intimate in that it was in response to him and aimed at him, and distant . . . because she radiated sympathy, not empathy. She didn't recall how it was to grieve for a parent. Or she didn't think she would grieve for any of her relatives. He got the idea that if she'd thought of a death of one of her animals, though, she'd be devastated.

No, the woman hadn't been brought up like him. Didn't value Family. And she was young.

"How old are you?" he found himself asking, though he knew.

"Eighteen."

He nodded. "You got your Second Passage."

"Yes." Her mouth flattened as if she didn't want to talk about the event. Well, it was never a conversational priority for him, either.

She cleared her throat and, with a sideways gaze, asked the rude question of him. "How old are you?"

"Twenty-four. A millennium baby, born in 400."

"I've been told that was a particularly auspicious year," she said in a serious tone. When they took the fork *not* leading toward the Residence, her shoulders relaxed. Interesting.

She slid him a glance. "So you trained as a guard. Did you hire on with any Noble estate? Did you work with any FirstFamily Noble before the Yews?"

He didn't know if she'd seen his references, but he kept to them. "I didn't hire on with any FirstFamilies." He'd been a proud lieutenant of the Blackthorn Family guards but hadn't gone through any hiring process. His allowance had been upped by his adoptive father. Before that he'd worked at The Green Knight Fencing and Fighting Salon with his mentor, not employed at T'Holly Residence. The Holly guards were all Family. Yeah, he minced his truths.

"I worked as a merchant guard for a while, along the southern routes to Gael City and back, even went as far as the Plano Strait that separates the southern continent from us. Then returned." That had been a bad time in his life, too, a dark gray time of no color and muffled emotions. "I was offered a job to accompany the folks excavating the lost starship *Lugh's Spear* east across the continent to the crash site." He shrugged. "I didn't go." The offer had been by people who cared about him and would have insisted on meddling in his life and talking to him all the time on the road, and there'd be no escaping them.

"Why didn't you go?" D'Yew's eyes had rounded, her pupils getting larger as she hung on his every word.

"Too damn far, too dangerous to come back alone, and I'd be stuck there—digging on the Ship or exploring it in bad air or something—for the whole summer." Instead he'd stayed home at T'Blackthorn Residence and stonewalled his adoptive parents and his older siblings when they expressed concern. He'd prowled the streets of Druida seeking trouble and finding it and delivering guys badder than him to the guardhouses.

"You didn't travel to *Lugh's Spear*. What an adventure that would have been." She sounded enthralled with the notion. Since the horses continued to walk, she patted Ragan's neck.

Draeg read the gesture. "Ragan would never have survived that trip."

D'Yew straightened, the sparkle in her eyes turning to horror. "Oh."

"Now I'm here," Draeg said, and urged Smyrna into a faster

pace, one of the special ones the mare had been trained in but was out of practice with.

D'Yew and Ragan kept up, with the horse moving better than his own mount. Draeg thought that was because D'Yew's bond with the animal had already grown strong. She seemed to have no problems opening herself to animal bonds while blocking most from humans . . . He tested the slight one developing between him and the young woman. Satisfaction glimmered within him. Yeah, he sensed the link and he'd be sure to encourage it. She trusted him on some level, probably because he took care of her animals and they liked him fine enough.

Hoof falls and breathing and birdsong filled the wordless quiet between them. Draeg felt comfortable. More comfortable with D'Yew than he had with anyone else lately. But she had fewer, easier expectations of him. Ones he could fulfill.

And he didn't have to pretend to be anyone he wasn't—like a responsible Noble of the Blackthorn FirstFamily who might be T'Blackthorn himself should Straif name Draeg as his heir. He didn't have to see worry in his female relatives' eyes when he left at night to hunt in—*clean up*—Druida City, torn inside because he knew he worried them, but still needed to prove himself.

As they rode, he figured that D'Yew cherished these moments away from the Residence and her Family, too, if Baccat had told the truth about her relatives. Like him, she was expected to fulfill great responsibilities. In fact, from how she acted, and what she said—he sure didn't like the idea that the Residence monitored her—she had to conform to more rules and manners and listen to more strictures than he.

Here, he lived free of Familial concern, which lay like a burden on his shoulders when at home. Despite that, he believed in duty and responsibility and Family; that's why he'd come here in the first place. Here where he had a job, which he should be doing.

He opened his fingers to show the brass button gleaming on his palm. "Did you drop this? I found it near the back door when I came to check on you."

She glanced at it. "No. I don't care for buttons. They catch on things." She fingered the frayed cuff around her wrist showing embroidered long Yew leaves. "I like the standard tabs and spells along the seams."

"You don't wear buttons at all?" He tilted the thing back and forth, but she didn't look at it again.

She grimaced. "I have some on stiff formal ritual robes, more for appearance than useful. Gold with rubies." She rolled her shoulders, but he figured she couldn't shift the burden of being D'Yew and she felt it bowing her back all the time.

"Whose might it be?"

"Ah, probably Cuspid or Folia or the twins, upper staff and inhabitants of the Residence. The cook or maids sure wouldn't wear anything like those." Lori's horse picked up pace and he rode to match her.

"Nobody'll miss it? You recall seeing anyone with a lost button?"

She looked at him, frowned in consideration, shrugged. "No, I don't, though I suppose I might have noticed if one *was* missing. The Residence has dress standards. If you want to give it to me, I'll send it to the button bowl."

"Button bowl," he repeated.

"Yes, in the sewing room."

"Sewing room!"

"We do make our clothes here, you know, and that's the ancient name for a place to keep fabrics and thread and buttons and whatnot. All of our clothes, though, use Flair." She looked down at her own scruffy and stained but clean work tunic and trous. "Even these, and, naturally, we are expected to use them until they are worn out." She smiled. "And these are comfortable. That matters to me."

"You want the button?" he asked.

"No. It's not important. Do what you want with it." But she tilted her head and her eyes narrowed.

He tucked it into his trous pocket. "You know how Corax loves shiny things."

Her face cleared and she chuckled. "Oh. Yes."

Dipping his hand in his pocket, he translocated the button to a drawer in the dresser in his apartment.

Then he deliberately guided the horses down a good path he knew led to the Residence and not the stables. He must bring up the topic of her relatives. Just a little preliminary probing, gentle questions, nothing to make her feel that he spied on her or her Family, or that he asked *her* to tell Family secrets.

When the trail branched toward the stables, he ignored the fork, and she followed after him, though he sensed reluctance. Soon they'd cleared the last of the thick trees that buffered the manor from one of the main avenues of Noble Country and looked at the front of the Residence straight on. It stood a good four stories in dull gray stone, with a long main block and two short arms facing them, both ending in stubby octagonal towers. A small walkway, complete with square crenellated walls, rimmed the roof of the whole building. Though the stone looked forbidding, there were a lot of windows, even two circular ones on either side of the front doors.

"A pretty place. A solid home," he commented.

She shifted in her saddle. "Yes, the Residence is quite strong."

"Handsome," he said, trying to draw her out.

D'Yew shrugged. "I suppose."

"Do you have a room in one of the towers?" A young, romantic girl would like that, and a tower could be well defended, so the MasterSuite or MistrysSuite could be there.

She gave a ladylike snort. "No. My rooms are on the second floor in the middle of the wall of the Residence, looking northward." She paused. "For a long time, I wanted a sitting room and bedroom on the top floor that looked out on the river, or in the back where I could see the forest and then the city lights of Druida. But now I like that in the winter I can see the lights of the starship *Nuada's Sword* through the leafless trees."

Rooms? Not a suite? And not on a corner with more space and windows and light? And on a middle floor where she could hear people above her and next to her and below her?

Draeg scowled. This didn't sound good—appropriate—for

her, the head of a FirstFamily Noble House. It irritated him on her behalf.

Sliding his eyes toward her, he continued, "I like it better than pictures of T'Blackthorn Residence, which is supposed to be the most beautiful Residence in Druida City." His adopted home was very elegant, and though the place had homey areas, it also hosted entertainments for the FirstFamilies too often for Draeg's peace of mind.

"I've never seen T'Blackthorn Residence," D'Yew said, like she didn't care about Noble society at all. She leaned forward and petted Ragan, then glanced up at Draeg. "But across the road from us in the west, on a bluff, is D'Marigold Residence. It's easily seen from the river banks. *That* Residence is pretty."

Draeg called up an image of the place, sort of a pale pink-yellow color, with layers and arches that reminded him of a wedding cake. He made a noncommittal noise.

"I haven't been down to the river," he said.

"It's not too high yet; the big spring runoff from the mountains upstream hasn't started." D'Yew urged Ragan forward, passing him and Smyrna, moving down the path and taking the next left toward the stables. That way was wide enough for both horses, and he caught up with her.

He gestured off toward the left and the small cottage of the gate house. Clearing his throat, he said, "I guess you know that I interviewed there, didn't get into the main Residence." He kept his voice matter-of-fact. "I'd have liked to step into such a place as D'Yew Residence." Not a lie; he was doing his damnedest to state only the truth, even if his whole life here was a lie. "Talked to a guy calling himself the maître de maison, and your housekeeper." From what they said, he'd deduced that a man who worked with animals and would live over the stables and not in the Residence wasn't at all important . . . and the Residence had no interest in meeting him, so they'd used the gatehouse for their interview.

During that interview, he hadn't been able to set a tracking hook in either Cuspid Yew, the maître de maison, or Folia Yew, the housekeeper. He *had* noticed at the time that they both wore buttons.

An antique-style vest had wrapped Cuspid's skinny torso, four silver buttons marching down his flat abdomen, slightly straining over a small paunch.

The housekeeper, a woman perhaps only a decade older than he, midthirties and attractive in a cold, elegant way, seemed to have whisked into the gatehouse just to study him, then left without a word. She, too, had had buttons, this time on the cuffs of her tunic sleeves and ankle cuffs that nipped in bloused fabric. Her buttons were smaller and looked to be carved of mother-of-pearl.

Here and now D'Yew inclined her head, and her neck, her whole posture didn't seem as supple. Because she'd been reminded of the starchy Residence and older members of her Family? Well, Draeg didn't know too much about the Residence—the only one he knew who did was the former D'Yew, now Lahsin Holly—and she'd had nothing good to say about that being. Baccat had called the Residence "mean." And from what D'Yew had let drop, the house was more demanding than supporting or sympathetic. In that it would match what Draeg had seen of the Family.

"Yes, Cuspid, the maître de maison, and Folia, the house-keeper, run the estate," D'Yew acknowledged in a colorless voice. She tossed a look at him and her eyes appeared greener. "I doubt you would have enjoyed being in the Residence."

If the person had been Draeg's stepmother, or another First-Family Lady, they might have looked him up and down, evaluating his work clothes. D'Yew didn't do that, but he couldn't quite read her.

"I am sure you are correct, D'Yew," he said.

Her spine straightened, her expression caught between a haughty Noble mask and the casual openness her face had relaxed into during the ride. She sent him a glance, let out a long breath. "I truly meant that the Residence would make you uncomfortable." She paused, said stiltedly, "Please call me Lori—Loridana."

Their eyes met, her pale green gaze steady.

So her first words about the Residence had been sincere. She didn't think the Residence would please *him*.

He inclined his head, said gruffly, "Thank you, Loridana."

The line of her shoulders sagged a bit; she smiled, and though it didn't approach a carefree smile, it caused him to smile back. "Tell me about the trips down south, to Gael City and beyond," she said.

Taking her conversational lead, he described the trips and in more detail than he'd anticipated. As well as the scenery and the landscape, she wanted to know of the waystations and the road conditions and the weather in all seasons. And this question-and-answer session—or him talking about the trips—lasted all the way back to the stables.

Since thick gray clouds blocked the sun once more and a bitter wind had picked up, they led the horses into the short eastern block of stables to groom and feed them. This wing held only eight stalls, enough for the six stridebeasts and the two horses. Right now the stridebeasts were happy in their corral. The weather didn't bother them as much as it did the horses.

Draeg wondered if Lori would open up the main, and larger, northern stables. He slid his hand down Smyrna's neck and back as he exited the stall into the stable corridor, and bumped into Loridana . . . He steadied her again with hands around her upper arms. And her body felt so good against his that he just kept on going, moving her against the brick wall of the stables. Yeah, moving in on her.

Something clattered, brush and curry comb from Loridana's hands, he thought. He'd already translocated his tools to the tack room.

Then they stood in the shadows, her body caged by his, soft next to his. Lord and Lady, how well she cradled him! Not much shorter than he, his cock lay against her flat belly. He could feel her breasts on his chest.

Her head had tilted back and he could see the excited gleam in her eyes but not the color. Despite the open door to the stable's courtyard, warmth wreathed them, pulsed from them. Heat fired through his blood, for sure. His mind misted with red passion as his groin grew heavier, his cock bigger. Ready for her.

He blinked to focus on her once more, saw her parted lips, her darker tongue sweep them, leaving gloss, and he was undone. He had to have her mouth under his, his tongue inside it.

So he kissed her. Her lips were plusher than they looked. She gasped a little and their breath mingled and his tongue probed the dimensions of her mouth; her tongue rubbed along his and they moaned together.

Immense need coiled through him, tightening every muscle, and his hands dropped from her biceps to brace against the wall on either side of her so he could lean solidly against her. Woman. Curving under him, wrapping her arms around him.

He lifted her leg, hitching it on his hip so they were center to center. Loridana ground against him with small whimpers, causing sizzling explosions in his brain.

Woman. And she smelled righter than anything, anyone, the scent digging claws deep into him, setting inside the marrow of his bones, maybe.

Or her fragrance sinking into the chambers of his heart.

Her taste coated his mouth as her tongue explored him.

He snatched one hand from the wall, stuck it under her muscular butt, and angled her . . . just . . . *right*. Soon, soon, he'd open these damn leathers and take her and make her his and—

Stop! *Young* woman. *Virgin* woman. Stop.

Stop while he could.

Lord and Lady, he wanted her, his erection harder than he ever recalled. Hard enough that the ache of need trembled through every nerve, set in every strand of every muscle. But he knew damn well that she hadn't met any other man.

She learned fast, for sure, and her tongue twined around his and she sucked it and he thought the top of his head just blew off, sending his mind scattered to the stars. No sense whatever.

When he had to come up for air, he managed to untangle their bodies, set her leg down. He took a step away from her, broke her hold around his shoulders, and his shaft was damn unhappy about feeling the cool air around them instead of being pressed against her warmth.

Panting, he sucked in enough breath to say, "We shouldn't be doing this. You're too young."

Twelve

That had D'Yew standing tall, drawing around her that First Fam-
ily GrandLady manner that had been trained into her, cooling her
expression . . . but her eyes showed different. Big and sad and
older than her years. "I am an adult. I can make my own decisions whether to kiss or not."

Her voice did waver with whatever wild emotions coursed
through her, and he knew they did, but he also sensed when she
slammed those feelings away and locked them down.

"Fligger." He tugged on his ear. "Yeah, I bet you've told your
Family that in just that tone, right?"

Her brows, as elegantly Noble as the rest of her, arched. "Cursing
at me is rude. But you are correct. Since the start of my Second Passage that legally made me an adult, I have continually informed my
Family that my status has changed." She drew in a deep breath and
inclined her head. "Like you, they haven't paid attention to me, either."

She inclined her head, but he saw the quiver of her lips indicating hurt feelings. Gritting his teeth, he took her hand and put it
against his groin. Hissed out a breath at the great sensation. "I
know you're an adult. All of me." He took away his hand, but she
kept hers on his erection.

He blew out a breath, held up both palms. "All right, then I'll be fliggering crude. You've never flig—" But he found he couldn't be that rude. The word wouldn't come out of his mouth. "You've never been with a man."

In the weak gray sunlight, he saw a darker tint come to her pale cheeks. Her lips compressed, then she said, "I think the word you are looking for is *virgin*. Yes, I am a virgin."

His shaft throbbed, and this time his shudder of need wasn't inward. He croaked, "That's a powerful thing, when a woman moves from woman to a sexual person."

Now her nostrils pinched. "Indeed. Then I suppose my Family has been deleterious in not recognizing that power in me and harnessing it."

He made a half-choke, half-laugh noise he couldn't figure out himself, flung a hand out. "I'm the first man you've kissed."

She tilted her head. Her lips parted and he thought she took a couple of those meditation breaths she'd talked about. "Despite this conversation, I found the action . . . good."

That stung his pride, and pure male instinct had him stepping forward. She didn't back up.

"Just good?" he growled, then stopped himself from leaning into her space, made a cutting gesture. "Forget it. Don't need a critique." A deep breath. "It was great for me and you should've figured that straight out."

Her gaze went to the front of his trous and he suppressed a smirk.

"Yeah, sure I think you're an adult. But you're still too youn—" He stopped, matching the tilt of her head while he stared into her eyes. "Too inexperienced."

"Are there some other men you'd like to introduce me to?" she asked.

Fury flashed his vision red. "Hell, no!"

"Good." She snagged the front of his tunic and pulled him in close, rose a little so their mouths matched, opened hers, and her tongue swept the seam of his lips. He groaned and scented her again and his mind shut off. His arms clamped around her and he took a couple of steps to steady her against the wall.

She brought up both legs, encircled him, put her sex close to his, separated only by clothing, and when they moved together, pleasuring themselves and each other, she gasped.

He. Should. Not. Be. Doing. This. One thought wisping through his mind and gone.

Lord and Lady, she felt good, better than any woman . . . he couldn't recall the feel of any other woman and that should give him pause, but his hands cupped under her tight butt, and he ravished her mouth, like he'd ravish her. Soon.

The kiss thrilled Lori. She panted, breathed with Draeg, took his breath into her, his tongue into her mouth, ached to take his body into her. Yes, a little scary. But if she shoved aside thought, let her body rule, go *wild*—what a notion!—she could ignore the fear-of-the-unknown part.

A yowl came, outside from a bench near the stables and inside her mind. *Your noxious twin cuzes come!* he added.

Nooo! No interruptions!

Lori! Lisssten! Baccat hissed.

Her Fam would continue talking to her. Her core throbbed, pulsed. She wanted sex.

Loridana! Another yowling demand, louder, more insistent.

She pulled her head away from Draeg's lips nibbling at her mouth, sucking on her bottom lip. Puffed out a breath and answered her Fam. *But the twins never come here!* she shot back.

They are not pleased at walking from the Residence.

The twins in a bad mood, tracking her down, coming to a place on the estate they disdained.

Fear jolted her cold and sane. What would they do to her if they caught her with Draeg? What would they do to *him*? Their teasing held a mean edge, and she felt so totally vulnerable this moment.

She must draw on her emotional armor.

Draeg's subvocal groan vibrated between them. He drew back, too, stared at her. Frowned, then swallowed. "Good thing you have some control."

She simply stared at him.

"What is it?"

"My cuzes come."

"That's what Baccat's whining about?" But now he sucked in air instead of her skin, shook his head, then took her by her biceps and lifted her away from him. So hot! Blood rushed under her skin. Blinking, she saw his gritted teeth. His chest heaved as if he'd exercised vigorously, and glancing lower . . . his sex looked thick and hard . . . and huge.

Her own sex clenched.

"Loridana Itha!" warbled her cuz Vi.

"Loridana!" Zus's voice sounded flat, more demanding.

She *wouldn't* have them coming into *her* private area. Especially not with Draeg here.

He moved away, and she flung out a hand. "Let me take care of this."

His intense gaze seared her and she couldn't guess what he might be thinking. But she must put him from her mind and concentrate on her relatives. Such a touchy situation all around.

Reaching out, she took his hand. "Please."

"I'm coming," she called, amplifying her voice slightly, heading down the hallway to the end of the stalls, through the door to the office at the open end of the block, then out of the office door, the one closest to the Residence.

Several meters away from the stables, her cuzes walked toward her, careful of each step since no gravel path twined between the main house and here, only a wide, slightly muddy animal trail they ignored in favor of dead grass.

Both looked sophisticated, elegant, dressed far too elaborately for the stables in fashionably cut silkeen, fancily embroidered. Abruptly reminded of her worn tunic and trous, Lori brushed at them, then clenched her jaw at the revealing gesture.

At least she didn't turn back to look at Draeg, whom she heard sweeping the hard-packed gravel courtyard with a push broom—that would attract more attention than her standard lack of confidence.

Her cuzes—children of Cuspid, who'd been cuz to Loridana's MotherSire—moved in step with languorous ease, their features more beautiful than her own in their narrow faces. But then their long-dead mother had been a distant Yew cuz working on the estate. So they had Yew blood on both sides of their line. Their hair showed a pale wheat color, when her own tinted more toward yellow-brown. No freckles dotted their faces.

"What brings you here?" Lori asked, every millimeter of her skin still sensitized. Between her legs she throbbed with needy desire for Draeg, and the air around her felt rough.

Arm tucked into her brother's elbow, Vi minced to the pristine square of flagstones outside the stable office door, then stopped a meter from Lori.

The stridebeasts had crowded to the far edge of their circular enclosure, all observing. The horses kept their heads inside their stalls, but watched.

Vi wrinkled her nose. "What's that smell?"

Zus laughed shortly, lifted his foot, and shook a clump of mud and grass off his polished boot. "I believe it is *horse*."

Vi made a disgusted moue with her mouth. "More animals." With a whisk of her hand downward to her expensive boots, she set a spell to protect her footwear. Lori thought her cuz drew the energy for the spell from the land. Good thing Lori naturally invested the stable area with a lot of Flair—and she used enough here that ambient Flair remained in earth and air.

"More pets," Zus said at nearly the same time. "Our little cuz remains childish and predictable."

Lori didn't react, her body straight but not stiff. She *was* shorter by some centimeters than both her cuzes, but Cuspid's children were eighteen months older than she.

"We thought you should reconsider signing that document Cuspid and Folia presented to you at breakfast," Zus said.

Lori shook her head slowly. "We have dealt with—" She saw Draeg come a little closer, so she changed the word *finances* to "that area of my responsibilities this month." And since they were so interested in the papyrus, the *Allocation of Funds to Allies*, they must be the ones in charge of dispersing the gilt. Money always interested the twins.

Vi actually hopped back when the horses thinned the top of the doors with a hint of psi power and stuck their heads out to look at her and Zus.

She sniffed, jutted her chin up. "Well, I suppose the horses don't look as *common* as stridebeasts." Her narrowed lips curled up at the corners. "But they were bred from excellent Earthan stock that our ancestors brought from our home planet and are therefore superior."

As always, Lori's face had frozen into the mask she wore for her relatives, and she didn't think they could get past that to read her emotions even if they wished.

Reading her cuzes was easy. They rarely hid their reactions, saw no reason to.

Her ears caught a tuneless hum from Zus, and she whipped her head around to see his sly smile as he glanced at the stridebeasts, then the horses.

"Ah. Look at that. Eight animals. When you are only allowed to have six." His smile broadened. "I think we must bring that up to the Residence and our father."

"Oh." Lori tried to infuse the sound with cheer, though she'd felt the blood drain from her face. "I was sure that you all took that into consideration when you purchased Rag—the horses for me. Didn't you?"

"We weren't part—" Vi began, her voice only to be overridden by Zus's.

"Of course. But it is a decision that should be revisited, I believe."

He gave Lori a charming smile that curved his lips but didn't reflect in his cold green eyes, the same shade as her own. Like a frost-covered spring leaf that had emerged too early. He scanned the shabby courtyard, the unused west and north stable blocks. Then he swung on his heel to look out over the land, much more wild in this area than the groomed grassyards around the Residence and the centuries-old tidiness and efficiency of the farm in the north of the estate. The farm he and Vi "supervised" for their Family income.

"Yes, our lands look a little—shaggy—around here, and you obviously haven't restored the stables to the shape they should be in if you want a true breeding program."

"Tsk, tsk." Vi clicked her tongue, then nodded. "Yes, we should speak to Cuspid and the Residence about culling two of your stridebeasts."

Lori couldn't, simply couldn't, glance at her small pack huddled in their corral as far away from the twins as possible. They didn't know what was going on, of course, but they knew the word *stridebeast* and sensed her turmoil. She hid her swallow. She wouldn't put it past Zus to kill two of her animals, not just sell them.

"Unless—" Zus studied his manicured fingernails.

"Unless—" Vi took up the notion with relish. "You *review* that document once more."

They didn't mean *review*. They meant *sign*.

"I hear you." Lori inclined her head in a slow nod, but she thought she could finesse this situation herself. The Residence didn't like modifying its plans. "Perhaps you are right. I should look at the papyrus again."

"We are always right," Zus said. He returned her nod, but as one of superior status.

Draeg grunted, stood with broom straight. Something about his body indicated fighting tension.

The twins turned toward him.

"May I introduce—" Lori began.

"No. Not at all." Vi sniffed.

Baccat hopped down from a bench on the far side of the stables, trotted over, and stropped Draeg's ankles, purring so it echoed.

"Commoners," Vi said.

Zus laughed, then turned his back on them all. "We have accomplished our purpose. Let's go do something interesting."

"Absolutely."

"We *will* see you within a quarter septhour, won't we, cuz?" Zus looked over his shoulder. He'd kept his smile and it remained hard.

Lori nodded.

Vi lifted her brows, meaning Lori had to answer with words.

"Yes. I'll be back at the Residence within a quarter septhour."

Without another word, they teleported away. Lori waited until she sensed they'd returned to the house before glancing at Draeg, who studied her with a serious expression.

He jerked his head toward the stridebeasts. "Your cuzes hold your animals hostage to manipulate your behavior and keep you under their thumb. Because you love your stridebeasts and they don't give a damn about the animals, or much of anything other than themselves, right?"

Lori shrugged. A huge ball of feeling had stuck in her throat, stung her eyes. Her imagination worked at what could happen to her beloved animals, her Fam, even to Draeg if she refused to fall into line.

And . . . what would it be like to share her fears with Draeg? To unload *everything* on him? Wonderful. But she still couldn't do it because she didn't trust him enough, couldn't find that in her for him, yet. Despite the fact that she lusted after him, even respected him.

When she didn't answer, because she couldn't without sobbing, and she wouldn't be so weak before him—she wanted to be *equals* with him—he nodded and said, "I understand how Family loyalty is."

She had little loyalty to her Family, especially for Vi and Zus, and it diminished every day, but her voice remained clogged.

"They, uh, wear fancy clothes," he said. "Are their duties tending the Residence?" His forehead furrowed. "I know I met the maître de maison." He grunted. "Is young Zus the butler, maybe, and Vi the cook?"

That had Lori swallowing a near hysterical laugh, glancing at her own worn clothes again. "No. They supervise the farm."

"Huh," Draeg said. "I've known some farmers in my time—" He stopped, held out one of his hands, and looked at it.

Lori followed his gaze. His big, strong hands, and her own smaller ones, appeared like they did manual labor. The twins' hands didn't.

Baccat sauntered away from the man, head up, ears slightly flat, tail waving. *The real people who run the farm don't like to have Zus and Vi around. They are malicious.*

"Got that," Draeg said. He looked as if he wanted to say more, but Lori translocated the brush and curry comb that she'd been holding before Draeg had kissed her and hurried to the far corner where the north and eastern blocks met, went through the open door to the tack room, cleaned the implements, and put them away.

When she came out, she had better control and walked up to where he leaned on the corral, looking at the stridebeasts who competed for his pets. She watched his hands, shivered at the thought of them stroking her. Oh, yes, she truly wanted that.

"So, you think we should, uh, take some measures to protect these friends?" he asked.

She didn't have the experience or knowledge to encase even one in personal armor, let alone two or all six. Nor did she wish to demonstrate her new primary Flair to Draeg.

"I have a few options." Large changes of plans as well as minor shading into minute modifications of each scheme. She'd been thinking of escape all winter long.

Drawing in a breath, she let it out, walling up her fear as she petted the stridebeasts chivvying for her touch. "I have a pen and lean-to, large enough for two stridebeasts, on the southern edge of the property, between a grove and the river. There's a shed there, too. You could take Semper and Cana there . . . this eve-

ning. They are the two who will accept separation from the rest
of the herd the best."

"You think that's necessary?" he asked.

Lori hesitated. "I don't know. I think it would be wise to . . ."

"Be proactive," Draeg finished for her.

She liked that word, rolled it in her mind and silently in her
mouth before letting her lips form it. "Proactive." She nodded.

"I'll take Semper and Cana there this evening after their last
feeding, then." His shoulders straightened. "I'll bunk in the shed
attached to the lean-to." He sounded as if he'd explored the estate
enough that he knew of the place. Eyeing the stables, he continued,
"There's a general danger alarm spell here that can be heard
throughout the estate and in the Residence, if I need to tele—hurry
back here."

"Yes," she said.

A fleeting smile crossed his face. "Better men than me have
lived in garden sheds."

She stared at him.

"You really don't know much of your history, do you? T'Ash
lived in a garden shed for a while."

"Oh." With a roll of her shoulder and another nod, this one as
equal to equal, she said, "I'll see you later." She hesitated, puffed
a small sigh. "Probably tomorrow." Then she teleported to outside one of the back doors of the Residence.

She scraped the soles of her boots, took them off before she
went inside, her mind still buzzing, her nervous system jittery
with renewed fear. She walked a very narrow cliff edge that crumbled under her feet. The twins would not expect her to simply go
along with their demands without a protest. Everyone knew her
animals meant too much to her for her to do that. So she had to
make *some* sort of objection, yet not irritate the twins enough
that her animals would disappear or she'd arrive at the stables to
find two dead.

The disappearing had happened before, more than once, and the
Residence had assured her that her stridebeasts had been sold by

Cuspid and Folia. She'd been inclined to believe the reports those two had given the Residence, since Lori had seen the income—quite a bit of income—from the sale of the beasts to GreatLord T'Ivy.

At one time she had thought to discuss those sales with T'Ivy, when she'd been confirmed as D'Yew, but that would not happen now.

As she'd told Draeg, she had options. Sometime soon she'd have to try to coat herself and Baccat in personal armor, a good experiment. Perhaps test very thin, strong shields that were hopefully near invisible to more senses than sight.

"Loridana Itha, what disturbs you?" The Residence sounded disapproving.

Thirteen

*S*he cleared her throat. *"Please provide me with the document that* Cuspid and Folia wished for me to sign this morning."

Silence. And she'd learned to sense the shades of the Residence's silence, too—now surprise lived in the atmosphere, curiosity, and more censure before he responded. "Which document is that?"

"I believe it was an allocation of funds to allies."

The twins appeared before her in the mudroom, both shouting her name. "Lori!"

Lori hunched instinctively, and then, thinking the snottier Yews would scold her for posture, she straightened and donned a confused manner. "I don't understand. I need the document to review, as you came to the stables to request." She cleared her throat. "I know we've gone through the financials this month, Residence, but the twins want—"

"Never mind," Zus snarled.

She hadn't anticipated such capitulation. She'd misjudged and now felt herself falling off that cliff edge she walked with regard to her cuzes.

Lori rushed into speech. "Oh, Residence, Zus and Vi stated that the acquisition of the horses means I can't have all my stridebeasts.

I'm sorry that is so, since I thought the horses were a gift from you all." To keep her content with the status quo of not being acknowledged as GrandLady D'Yew either here at the estate or to Druidan society. She snuffled as if her feelings were hurt, let tears come. Inside the Residence, summoning tears was easy. "I mistook your—"

Zus teleported away with another snarl, Vi with a hiss. Lori would have to be very, very careful and prepare for the worst since she'd thwarted their plans.

The Residence intoned, "As I recall, the east stable block, which I gave you permission to restore several years ago, contains eight original stalls, is that not true?"

After swallowing, Lori nodded, the Residence had a scrystone in the wall it could observe her with, though she didn't know how that worked. "Yes. The east stable block contains a tack room at the corner with the northern main stables, then eight stalls, a small office, and, of course, apartments above to house staff," she recited in equally formal tones.

The Residence continued, "It is as we detailed previously in our conversations?"

"Yes."

"Since we have eight stalls and each of your animals can have inside shelter—though I do not think stridebeasts *need* such pampering and a lean-to, at the most, should be acceptable for them—I believe we can allow you eight animals."

"Oh!" She let her relieved sigh puff audibly from her chest. "Thank you *so* much! It's lovely that you or Cuspid or Folia or the twins won't be selling the beasts to T'Ivy."

"That process had not been discussed or begun."

"I must have misunderstood the twins." She coughed, then lifted her voice and magnified the spell of it so it would resound throughout the Residence and the twins would hear her and the Residence. "I must have misunderstood the twins all around, about their request for more gilt for our allies, and divesting ourselves of two expensive stridebeasts and—"

"No doubt," the Residence interrupted her. "And since we

have not spoken of our allies lately, perhaps we should review *that*. I will give you a quarter septhour to cleanse, then come to the ResidenceDen."

"Yes, Residence." Obviously her training with the horses had ended for the day. And her groping with Draeg.

Though she remained unsettled. As she moved through the house to her rooms, she spurted a mental comment to Baccat. *I do not think we should leave the estate tonight.*

But you PROMISED, he whined. Then fell back into his scholarly lilt. *This expedition tonight is extremely important to me, Loridana.*

She sighed as she hurried into the waterfall room. *I will reconsider.*

Excellent! I also promise, on My part, to trace the route I believe will be the most efficient and timely for Our escape, even if you cannot do that. I will do so tonight or tomorrow.

I really need that weather information, too, she stated.

I will make that a priority. She sensed him rising from his bench, stretching. *Neither the Sallow ferals nor the PublicLibrary Cats had acceptable information.* He hummed to himself and she *felt* it, furry in her mind. *I have thought of a brilliant notion.*

Just a small exchange with her Fam had Lori relaxing and smiling, recovering her optimism. *Yes?* she asked telepathically.

I will go to the Mercenary Guild and speak with the Cats there. They do not know Me, nor that I am your Fam—

That's good, Lori said.

But They might overhear comments about weather predictions for the next week or two.

Lori gritted her teeth. *We may have to leave within the next few days. I cannot allow my Family to harm my animals.*

Of course not. Baccat coughed up a hairball and Lori grimaced, wishing she hadn't been so closely tied to him. *I may need a token of good intentions for the Mercenary Guild Cats.*

With a sigh, Lori translocated a large batch of dried jerky she'd stored in the stillroom to Baccat's location in the stable courtyard. Then heard hissy feline outrage. *That evil bird, he swooped down and stole one of My pieces of jerky! MINE! That greedy raven Corax, that* . . . More sputtering and hissing and finally, *You had better speak with Me instead of laughing at Me, Draeg HEDGENETTLE. I require recompense!*

D'Yew? the Residence prompted silkily. She couldn't spare any more attention to her Fam and his problems, and answered the Residence quickly. "Yes, yes. My humblest apologies for keeping you waiting." She teleported into her waterfall room and scrubbed fast and thoroughly, thinking hard.

One option was to leave, within this very week. An itchiness under her skin, a clenching of her stomach, or maybe the continual rising of the hair on the nape of her neck prodded her to escape. As fast as she could. Weather or no weather. Perfect route selected or not.

Just. Go.

That felt right.

Except she'd be leaving Draeg Hedgenettle and all the wonderful sensations he roused in her. Who knew when she'd have time to take a lover again?

So she should have sex with him before she left.

Oh, yes, yes, *yes. That* felt right.

Modify another plan . . . but this time her smile turned into a grin.

*T*en minutes later she and the Residence looked at the extremely short list of formal alliances. The air pressure in the room changed in what sounded close to a human sigh. "When your MotherSire lived, we Yews had great power and influence."

Lori kept her mind from drifting off toward Draeg and what he'd made her feel. The Residence would definitely notice her squirming or elevated pulse, and that would clue it in that she didn't pay attention.

"The Ivys and the Willows are the only FirstFamilies we are

allied with, since when we signed those contracts, the term was for three generations."

"My generation," she said.

"Correct," the Residence stated. He paused and the silence became slightly awkward. Was he expecting her to press, once more, to be recognized as D'Yew?

In that moment she realized she'd truly given up on her former life, was now in stasis before she made a new life. Something that hadn't been true even yesterday.

The horses had come into her life. She'd met Draeg. She'd come into her primary Flair. All those events had widened her perspective, her horizon. She would never be happy here.

Glancing down at the papyrus listing the contractual allies, she said, "Some of the rest of these Nobles on the list seem to be of ancient lineage, ah, important, and, perhaps, well connected."

"It's not enough." A click of a window shutting tighter. "But we will remedy that in the future."

Lori figured his "future" was her "far future," like when she was twenty or twenty-five or some such. Far later than she intended to wait.

She inclined her head. "As you wish."

"Yes." Another long pause. "You are dismissed."

"That is all?" she asked. "Our whole discussion about our allies?"

"For the moment," the Residence said, more sadly than repressively. Almost she felt a twinge of pity for the sentient house. But he—it—and her Family had brought all this on themselves with their isolation. They were not considered part of the human herd of the FirstFamily Nobles.

Almost, she wanted to announce to the Residence to let one of the twins have her title. But that would be too revealing—and revolutionary to the poor thing.

"I believe I will work in the stillroom."

"You do not return to the stables?"

"Not right now." She yet walked the narrow ledge, and here in the Residence, she could sense her cuzes' energy. Besides, she had need of a new potion she must craft. Rising, she turned to a large mirror and gave a formal curtsey to the Residence. "Thank you for meeting with me." Then she let a small rush of words come. "And thank you for the horses, once more, and for allowing me eight animals. I'm grateful."

"You are welcome," the Residence said absently, as if it had moved on to thinking—or brooding—about other issues.

She slipped into the stillroom and let her hands reach for ingredients in cupboards and on shelves, began mixing herbs, adding liquids. Not *quite* acknowledging what she did . . . until the smell wafted to her nostrils and her nose twitched and she swallowed and had to brace her hands against the counter. She was brewing an anticonception potion she'd take every day.

Because she was going to take Draeg Hedgenettle as a lover. Her *first* lover. And, yes, she panted a little at the scariness of that, and the anticipation, and the excitement. Leaning harder against the counter, letting the square edges poke into her—and what rational person would make a counter with square edges, anyway—she let her mind whirl with the huge *change* coming in her life.

Even more important than leaving the estate. That had been planned in as much detail as she could. Everything about that— except for when nights stopped freezing—was under her control. But she believed that engaging in sex with a man like Draeg Hedgenettle would strip the control she had over her emotions. Gulping, she nodded acceptance that she'd willingly *share* control with him, give up some of her precious need to regulate herself and her emotions to him.

"Your heart is racing more than is generally acceptable, Loridana Itha," said the Residence, causing her to flinch.

Pushing away from the counter to stand solidly on her feet, she said, "I'm making potions for the horses! So exciting!" Her voice sounded high to her ears, and her words slightly childish. But since that was how the Residence thought of her, maybe it would believe her. Clearing her throat, she tried a steadier tone. "You know, the horses did not come to us in excellent health."

"What! No, I did *not* know that! Someone dared to cheat *us*? The Sallows?"

Uh-oh. She didn't want the Residence corresponding with the Sallows, or Cuspid or Folia or the twins contacting that Family, either. "I think the horses had run wild a bit before they were found at an estate where the last of the Family had died."

A harsh rattle of the window as if from a winter blizzard, but truly from the Residence itself. "Another Family has died out? Which? Was the house a Residence?"

"The Alexanderses, the last of which was a GraceLady," Lori replied. "I don't know whether D'Alexanders had a Residence." She gave a tiny cough. "But didn't you teach me that the, uh, councils of Celta would care for a Residence, put another Family in place so the house would not be harmed?"

The air in the room sighed from a draft that shouldn't be there, with the potential to hurt delicate herbs.

"You know little of what you speak," the Residence snapped.

Irritation rose in Lori and she quashed it, as always, stopped her teeth from grinding. Patience. She'd be gone within three weeks. Instead, she said mildly. "I only know what you have told me."

"I do not think the Alexanders' house had become a Residence. After all, their GraceHouse was only established less than a century ago."

"I'm sure another Family will be . . . ah . . . will live on the estate and cherish it," Lori said.

Indifferently, Yew Residence said, "It does not matter. No one outside of *us* matters. Remember that, Loridana Itha."

"Yes, Residence." She stirred the potion but strained to sense the Residence's attention and that of others in her Family who wouldn't mind interrupting her. The twins' energy seemed active and focused, and she could only hope it wasn't on how to punish her.

As she continued, the work in the stillroom helped her concentrate on something other than her body's clamoring need for Draeg. Her mind spun with alterations to her plans, options, and fear—fear of reprisal by her cuzes, fear of discovery of her need to escape.

She only had to get through Druida and outside the city walls a few kilometers, she was sure. Just beyond the reach of her Family, Cuspid and Folia and the twins and the Residence who'd imprison her on this estate more than she already was.

No doubt people would see her, even deep in the night, and she couldn't pass as a shepherdess now that she'd be traveling with the horses, too. When she'd only had six stridebeasts she could have been considered a herder. Yes, others might have thought her a trainer as she moved through the city. The additional two horses made that problematic, because of the mixed herd and the number of animals.

Still, she'd be breaking no laws, and if a guard came to ask her of her business, she could reply truthfully that the animals belonged to the FirstFamily Yew and she was responsible for them, and hope he or she wouldn't check at that time of night with the Family.

All she had to do was escape her Family's clutches. Make sure they wouldn't grab her and label her insane and pen her up again. No one else would care what she did.

She kept repeating that as she worked on the potion.

Finally, she'd sipped the liquid, yet warm with heat and Flair, and licked her lips. It didn't taste too bad. She wouldn't mind taking the contraceptive daily.

In truth, conception didn't occur as easily with humans here as she'd read about on old Earth, but she would not take any chances. Caring for eight animals was sufficient, and she knew how to do that, but a tiny baby? No.

Pouring the distillation into vials that held a week's worth of medicine, she stoppered them and slipped one each in her trous pockets, set four more far back in a deep overhead cabinet. A thought occurred that perhaps, just perhaps, she might ask Draeg to accompany her. If so, she'd need the extra.

As she untied her apron and placed it in the stillroom cleanser, the Residence creaked—an action like a human clearing his throat.

"Yes, Residence?"

Fourteen

*GrandSir Zus Yew and GrandMistrys Vi Yew have requested ad*ditional funds for the farm budget. They wish to purchase a new porcine breeding pair."

Lori's head went light and dizzy and she leaned against the counter next to the door. If she handled this correctly, she might forestall any harm to her animals, to her, to her plans. If the twins thought they'd won a skirmish over her—yes, they'd be too cheerfully spending the gilt to think of penalizing her. She swallowed, closing her eyes.

Once again the timing of her leaving wobbled back and forth in a balance. Exhausting, to revise and revise and revise her scheme again. Tears leaked from under her lashes. She used the faintest touch of Flair to make her voice sound normal—Flair the Residence would have noticed if she'd been in the main chambers or corridors, but not in the stillroom since she worked with Flair there.

"What is your recommendation?" she asked lightly.

"Though we have allocated our budget this month, this is a standard request, and I believe we should give them the amount they need to procure the porcines."

"What is that amount?"

Of course, when the Residence named a figure, it was half again as much as Cuspid and the twins had wanted for their "allies." Lori suppressed a snort. "That sounds reasonable to me." Actually, it didn't. It sounded far too high, but the Residence had a bias against mobile sentient humans and Fams, and considered animals far beneath it. Whoever had pinched the pennies on the horses, it hadn't been the Residence.

"I will authorize the expenditure, then," Yew Residence rumbled.

"Fine." But Lori touched a vial in her pocket. She might not be leaving as soon as she'd anticipated a couple of septhours ago, but she yet intended to seduce Draeg. Perhaps she'd have enough time— they'd have enough time together—for her to begin to trust him.

"I believe I will read a little," she said. "I'm teleporting to my rooms."

The Residence said nothing.

Once she'd arrived in her rooms, she let her whole body relax, stumbled to the nearest easy chair and slumped into it. With a little luck the Residence would be too busy with Cuspid and Folia and the twins and whatever else to spy on her.

So tired of being spied upon!

She picked up an antique book on Earthan history, opened it to the marked page, and bent her head, but did not focus on the words.

Tentatively she *reached* out to Draeg, thought she sensed that a real bond had formed between them, strong with the beginnings of friendship and definite mutual attraction. *Draeg?* she sent mentally.

From him she felt slight surprise, and that he'd gone to survey the area where he would move two of the stridebeasts; she almost seemed to see the filtered sunlight and feel a slight, chill breeze.

I hear you, he said, perhaps a little shortly. Should she have continued to pretend that he didn't have much Flair? Rebellion at that idea flashed through her. Such a lot of her life now involved pretense; she wanted to be open and true and real with him. She wanted the same from him. And she treasured the small thread spinning between them.

Yet she kept her own words quick and on the shade of formal. *I believe I have forestalled any harm to my animals and any change to my herd.*

A pause from him—consideration? *Did you give the twins what they wanted?*

She let out a little sigh, thought he sensed it. *We engaged in the standard maneuvering. They got more than what they wanted, so they are pleased and believe they won this battle, which is fine.*

She felt a surge of fury from him, then calm as if he'd stuffed that away. *Why did you let them win? Why didn't you fight?*

Those two questions brought her to the brink of her own anger, made her nearly spew a defensive speech . . . and she wasn't ready to be so vulnerable to him as to reveal her plans. So she replied with equally forced serenity. *I must choose my battles carefully. Please respect that I know the ones I must fight.*

Of course, he shot back.

Frowning, she considered bits of emotions flowing between them. At her words, she thought he *did* believe that she'd handled her Family correctly, *did* respect her.

He accepted that she knew her Family best. She blinked and swallowed sudden, unexpected tears. He'd gone against his own instincts to fight, to push her to fight, took what she said as true without proof. When had anyone other than her Fam given her that grace?

Huge warmth suffused her, centered in her heart; she saw a tiny spark flow down the whisker-width link between them and smiled. *Thank you.* A pause for a nontrembly breath. *I'll talk to you later*, she said, and closed down her side of the private mental channel running between them. The Residence could monitor her physically but couldn't hear all her telepathic conversations. In the privacy of her waterfall room, she hugged herself at the thrill of having a friend she could speak with secretly.

*D*raeg *closed his eyes and leaned against the shed he'd finished* cleaning—this time triggering the housekeeping Flair spell embedded in its walls with a nudge of his own psi power. No physical labor necessary. He hadn't sensed any other person in the shed for several months, but he didn't have the same strong tracking Flair as his distant-cuz-adoptive-father.

Now he studied the one-fiber bond strung between himself and Loridana D'Yew.

In no way was the bond between him and Loridana, between himself and any of his friends, family, or Fam, like a tracking hook he could set in a person's—entity's—aura. A personal link predominantly carried emotions . . . and a new and fragile bond such as his with Loridana would leak sensations from one to the other. He wondered briefly what she'd felt from him.

But he couldn't find her by just their bond. Well, maybe if he traced it step by step like following a string. With a hook, he could just mentally check the location, and since he'd practiced his craft and knew Druida City well, he often knew exactly where his target was.

The hook in Baccat had challenged him a bit since the cat could slither into places where humans wouldn't go.

And now he had hooks in three individual Yews—Baccat and the twins, Zus and Vi. He'd managed to set the new ones this morning when the pair had visited the stables to whine at Loridana.

He rubbed his hands and that shifted the new bond a bit, and he twitched.

Nope, a hook didn't operate like a true bond. If the link was strong enough, and a person was reckless enough, trusting enough of the bond, one might be able to teleport to where the other was. But no one forgot that just a few years ago some guy had teleported *into* a piece of furniture. End of guy and wardrobe.

When Loridana had first touched him mentally, instead of the bond going from center to center, it had felt like her fingers brushing his cock. He'd managed to suppress his swell of lust, though it had blurred any logical thought and loosened the hold he had on himself, affected their conversation.

But by the time she'd finished the dialogue, the tie between them had settled firmly in his heart, a fact that scared him.

*   *   *

For Lori, the rest of the day and the evening meal passed in blissful insignificance. After dinner, she dressed in her old clothes and stated she'd be working in the boathouse. She actually teleported there, moved things around from the night before and got rid of several layers of dirt on the refinished floor, making it look like she'd put in more septhours of work.

Then she met Baccat at the northwest gate, and a few minutes later they strolled along a street in CityCenter. Though spellglobes lit it brightly, and a few people walked in the cold like she and her Fam, no one paid any attention to her.

Just looking in the shop windows at all the myriad and strange things for sale and that people might buy amazed her.

I spoke to a mercenary guard who has often traveled south and she said that the weather remains uncertain for about three eightdays, three weeks, with alternating warmth and cold. The temperatures she stated would be close to the tolerances of the horses.

Lori set her teeth and replied mentally. *Below the tolerances of the animals if I did not protect them from freezing at night.* Her hands opened and closed and she wiggled her shoulders. *The longer we string out this planning portion, the more the risk of being caught due to our impatience or differing behavior.*

Baccat sniffed. *I am a fabulous actor. I will not inadvertently reveal Our plans in any aspect.*

His response made Lori smile before sighing, then stiffening her spine. *The constant revising of our escape strategy wears on me.* She cleared her throat, then spoke quietly and aloud. "And the twins remain volatile enough that I'm not sure of their moods or what actions they might take against me. If they keep pushing, I will be expected to take a stance, and I believe I would yet lose in any power struggle—not that I care about power struggles and conniving in the Family and Residence." She shrugged. "Let them have it. I do not want to live that way all my life. But because of those circumstances we must be ready to leave at any moment."

Her Fam stopped in front of her and placed himself in the middle of the sidewalk, forcing a few laughing pedestrians to walk around him. He stared up at her. *You have gathered enough gilt for all our food and have bags of My catnip?*

She inclined her head and said, "Yes." She'd made cuttings from the estate plants and kept them in bespelled flasks in a tiny makeshift greenhouse on the roof, accessible by the parapet, the crenellated walk around the top of the Residence.

Then I am ready to leave if disaster strikes. We will do this, FamWoman.

With a nod of his head, Baccat rose to his paws once more and sauntered, tail high, down the street. *I have been a very good Fam.* Baccat lifted his nose. Lori bent down and petted him, murmuring compliments and scratching him behind his ears for a good three minutes.

He rubbed his head against her hand, then gave her fingers a tiny cat lick, an unusual sign of great affection. His rumbling purr vibrated in the air and against her hand, and her smile widened.

I have been a Very Good Fam, Baccat repeated.

Lori felt she'd missed a cue. She gave a small self-deprecating cough. *You have indeed been a GREAT Fam.* She sent the thought because she could be louder, more fervent, than if she whispered. Even walking on a bright, wide, lowly populated thoroughfare hadn't diminished her caution, or her awe, at being in the big city outside the Yew environs.

Baccat stopped their progress once more by sitting down on his large rump, raising his forepaw, and licking it, meeting her eyes. *It is traditional for the FamPerson to give the Fam FurPerson*—he paused—*and perhaps the Fam FeatheredPerson . . .*

She could feel her eyes enlarge even more at the reminder, then stepped close to a store and sent her glance questing through the sky. "I don't see Corax." She grimaced. "The lights along the street dull my night vision so I can't see if he's blocking out stars as he flies and watches us."

I can sense the bird. He is with his FamMan and not near.

Baccat flicked his tail. *I should have not have distracted you from the main discussion.*

Lori chuffed another cough, this one more amused. *The main discussion is?*

Lifting his head in a regal manner, Baccat said, *It is the custom for the FamPerson to give the FamFur-or-Feathered Person a collar—a token of his or her affection.* He paused. *That is YOU. You are supposed to give ME a collar since I have been a GREAT Fam for MONTHS.*

With a tilt of her head, Lori studied her Fam. She'd tucked in her lower lip to bite it to keep from laughing at her pompous Fam. Mentally, she asked, *How many months is usual?*

Yet keeping his gaze on hers, Baccat blinked slowly. *We have been together a sufficient amount of time. I have not disappointed you in Any Way, have I?* He scowled. *What happened in Yew Residence when I attempted to join you and was rebuffed was Not My Fault.*

Lori shook her head, all amusement fading, as usual, at the thought of her Family and the Residence. *You made a real mess.* Torn drapes and carpet in her rooms and scratched hands of Folia and her cuzes as people tried to teleport his "filthy" self away and outside and . . . to whoever knew where. Cat urine flying and puddling. She shuddered at the mess.

I was provoked.

Yes, you were.

You had brought Me in and put Me on Our bed.

That's right. Lori lifted her own chin. *And I took care of the cleanup, too. No one except me was inconvenienced.*

I am glad you rescued me from the dungeon room, Baccat said politely. *Thank you.*

You're welcome. Now Lori shuddered. Foolish her, to not have anticipated that she wouldn't be allowed to keep him inside.

She straightened her spine, donned her FirstFamily Grand-Lady attitude for just an instant before the surroundings impinged on her awareness again and she let her body relax. She nodded decidedly. *We WILL get you a collar.*

With a huge cat smile, Baccat hopped to his feet and began running down the street of shops faster than she'd ever seen him move before when not endangered.

She took a moment to stretch, then fell into the long stride she'd developed when walking over the Yew estate, a pace she hoped would serve her and her animals well on the road.

Baccat stopped in front of a glass door with huge glass windows on either side. The wares inside—incredible jewelry—dazzled Lori's eyes. Her breath simply stuck in her lungs.

Smiling ingratiatingly, Baccat said, *T'Ash is the BEST.*

Lori swallowed. "I can see that." In fact, she'd never seen such jewels, such *art*, in all of her life. She managed to wrench her stare away from the main piece, a long waterfall necklace of glisten metal and jewels that she couldn't imagine wearing. Having it in her room to look at—or even hanging it in a window so the sunlight could dance on it—just wonderful. But it had to cost more than . . . maybe the shop it sat in.

You are not looking at the Fam collars, Baccat said. *They are here, in this corner.*

Yes, the lower corner next to where you'd pull the door open, where Fams could see them and admire them, and no doubt nag their person to purchase them. T'Ash's cleverness surprised a short laugh from Lori.

I like THIS one. Baccat tapped the window with unsheathed claws. In the pyramidical display of Fam collars, he'd chosen a rich gold one set with large square yellow topazes. Lori eyed it and then her Fam. He was a big cat, but she didn't think he was so big as to carry off that collar with panache.

It will look good against My fur.

It would certainly contrast against shades of gray with black.

Business hours had passed, but Lori was sure that Baccat would want her—them—to look at the collars in person. Did she dare, absolutely *dare*, go into a shop run by a FirstFamily Lord with such a formidable reputation?

Baccat had said that many Families didn't like the Yews. That the Yews had hurt them. Would T'Ash, or other FirstFamily Nobles . . . penalize her for being who she was? Take her as a hostage for good behavior from her Family? She made a tssking sound. Her imagination carried her away.

I prefer the gold and topaz one.

She weighed the need of her Fam for something expensive and sparkly versus food for the trip, refurbishment of the small Valerian property at the end of the road, care for her beasts along the way. Lori gulped, winced, loosened her stomach that had tightened, and let her breath sift out.

Of course other shops would carry Fam collars, jewelers like T'Ash or Fam outfitters or whatnot; Lori just didn't know of them, had no idea where they might be found. And surely she wasn't the only person who didn't want to spend outrageous sums on a FamCat collar that might break . . .

T'Ash's collars are bespelled to return home. Sometimes they are bespelled to return the Fam home, if injured. Though Baccat stated the words evenly, the angle of his ears and the slight ruffle of his fur showed his offense that she didn't immediately commit to purchasing the collar.

"Wonderful," Lori breathed. "Ah, you *do* want to eat on the way to the trip, don't you?" She inhaled a breath. "It is too expensive."

Fifteen

*B*iting *her lip, Lori said to Baccat, "I have only a couple of pieces of* jewelry of my very own. A baby ring, and I was given a necklace for completing my First Passage by the Family." She visualized it, sent the image to Baccat. The piece contained silver links, not gold, but included six small oval rubies and one ruby drop. "It is *mine*," she said, and her emphasis echoed against the glass window, sounded down the now-empty street, so she switched to mind-speaking again. *I can give it to you, if I wish, unlike any of the ancestral jewels.* Which she'd seen at one time, a huge cabinet made especially to house them in the MasterSuite, though she hadn't been permitted to touch them.

She didn't want them anyway. Not one of the pieces—mostly rubies because of the redness of yew berries—looked as pretty as . . . that pair of copper marriage bands studded with sapphires and amethysts in a simple Celtic knot pattern sitting on a velvet stand before her. She shook her head at the uncurling desire for the beautiful objects. *Marriage bands* of all things. The last thing she wanted was marriage. The Family would have no hesitation arranging a husband and a marriage for her, one that would benefit them. They'd done it often enough through the past centuries.

My collar? prompted Baccat, purring. *Yes, I would like that First Passage necklace. YOUR necklace for Me.* He paused. *The Family did not give you a Second Passage necklace last year upon your attainment of your majority?*

"No," she said shortly and aloud, jerking her stare from the marriage bands and turning away. Telepathically, she said, *It's late. Let's walk to the area south of here that will be our route and check that street for a few blocks before we return home.* She strode away and Baccat kept up with her, radiating satisfaction.

I get My collar!

Yes. A thought snagged her mind. *Did your old scholar give you a collar?*

Baccat gave a little hop, didn't look at her but picked up his pace as if embarrassed, then answered, *He did a braid spell on a string with some paper scraps of old notes when I pointed out I needed a collar. He laughed.*

That man had hurt his Fam's feelings. Even though she learned more every day about Fams—like this business with the collar that she didn't know yesterday—she knew enough about animals, and about herself, to understand when feelings got bruised.

My First Passage ruby necklace is in the HouseHeart, she said. She kept it there with her other treasures—the few memory spheres and record spheres she'd discovered of her father's—in a box no one else could open. Even Cuspid and Folia could only enter the HouseHeart three days a month at the most if *she'd* ordered so, and she had. The HouseHeart, who was not the same persona as the Residence, listened to her as long as she remained reasonable in her requests. *I'll get the necklace for you.*

Baccat whirled and raced back to her and jumped for her shoulder. She hastily formed the invisible shelf support for him. When he landed, he leaned against her and purred loudly.

Though that comforted her, she realized her mind felt tired, her whole body did . . . and that she'd been using too much Flair what with the standard spells she did every day with the Residence, and working with the horses to get them ready for the trip, mixing herbs in the stillroom today, and these after-dark excursions.

She'd have to cut back on something—the Flair she used in these adventures. Not a pleasant thought. She found her jaw ached from gritted teeth.

LET'S CELEBRATE! Baccat's shout filled her head and jolted her from her doldrums. She forced a smile. "What did you have in mind?"

He nuzzled her ear and tickled her with his fur, and she wished it weren't her cat, but Draeg's tongue. A little shiver went through her at the thought—and because the temperature had turned freezing.

Slyly, Baccat said, *I went to the food carts earlier this evening and destroyed a humongous spider. The vendor lady expressed her gratitude with two tubes of an acceptable Pinot Noir and marinated clucker cubes. They are quite extraordinary clucker cubes.* She felt the touch of her Fam's rough tongue, but more in passing as he licked his paw and groomed his whiskers. *I hid them in a cache; they are waiting for us.*

"All right."

After retrieving the very good clucker cubes and eating them by hand, Lori felt slightly more optimistic. The lights on the streets had dimmed and the fabulous star-studded Celtan sky sparkled like her renewed spirits. She'd always looked to the abundant stars in the night sky, accepted their shine in the darkness as inspiration. They'd be even more brilliant at her new home.

And some night, before she left, she'd ensure that she and Draeg made love with the stars sending light through a private pavilion's windows. She hoped.

Yes, her Fam, the food, the stars helped. She burped discreetly and began walking along the start of the smallest of the three streets that led back into Noble Country.

A humming attracted her attention. She stared, mouth open, at the sleekly modern gliders zooming toward her on the narrow street. She hadn't thought such vehicles could go that fast.

Side by side, they raced, like in a competition. She stared.

Look out! shrieked Baccat mentally. Then he hopped on her shoulder, bounded somewhere else. *Jump up and back, to Me in this doorway!*

Gasping, Lori did, and her fear triggered her Flair, she felt it pulse—but it didn't encase her soon enough. The edge of the bumper struck her shin and she heard the break as well as felt it, hideous pain shocking through her, stopping her breath. *Then* her personal armor formed around her. She hit the wall, bounced away, back into the air behind the glider that had passed.

She panicked. *Home!* Not the Residence, but the estate. One bright thought sliding under the nauseating pain—where she'd told people she would be. *Boathouse.* One last clear idea. *Path to river!* That should cover her explorations. She teleported before she hit the ground . . . of the street. Instead she landed in the bushes close to the steps to the river. Steps that, if she'd fallen, could have broken her leg.

The bushes and her personal armor cushioned her and she had just enough strength to roll onto the steep stone staircase. She drained the Flair powering her armor to relieve the pain.

It didn't do much. She'd never broken a bone, never been so physically injured. Tears running down her face, she called, for the first time in years, to her Family.

Cuspid! Folia! Not to the twins, never the twins, who would mock her. *I have fallen.*

Where? snapped both voices in unison.

She sent them an image, then as pain made sickness crawl up her throat, she turned her head, vomiting in the dirt, curving her fingers into claws to scratch soil and leaves over the regurgitated clucker cubes that she hadn't eaten here.

Seconds seemed like minutes as the chill of the night mixed with the cold sweat coating her body, her face. Her mouth tasted nasty.

Baccat appeared and meowed plaintively, licked the side of her face where tears dribbled down, then walked to her uninjured side and began purring. She concentrated on the warm vibration against her body, steadying her breathing.

She heard Folia's steps first, quick light footfalls descending the stairs. Then Lori looked up into the housekeeper's beautiful face and knew she'd interrupted the woman, who must have been with a lover in her rooms. Folia's silkeen gown scandalously clung to her elegant figure; her face had been enhanced for intimacy. Her red-slicked mouth pouted. "You stupid, clumsy girl." Her voice almost lilted. She smiled, unpleasantly, grooving a couple of lines in her pale forehead, accented by the twinmoonslight.

Leaping to his paws, Baccat arched and hissed.

"That filthy animal!"

"My. Fam," Lori said weakly. Moving her arm to pat him sent crisp waves of pain radiating through her, and she had to focus to control her bladder from emptying. She had no Flair to protect her Fam. Had no Flair at all. Weak and vulnerable as she'd rarely been since her Second Passage. Her panting came rough to her ears.

"Hey!" Two voices shouted and loud thuds pounded toward her, slaps of hard and soft leather, she thought, but her mind had grown odd and fuzzy.

Cuspid showed up first, then, right behind him, Draeg Hedgenettle.

The sight of him turned on her sobs; she didn't know why. Perhaps because it appeared like he cared she was hurt? Perhaps because he might not be a friend, but he didn't seem as hostile as the others.

"Let's see, let's see." Cuspid spoke more gently than she'd heard in years—at least to her. He used his tender voice with his children, the twins Vi and Zus. The maître de maison went around Folia, and Lori found herself lifted from the stairs, slid over on a gliding cushion of air to a grassy part of the incline a meter away. Everyone followed.

Baccat hissed again.

"Enough of that, cat," Cuspid said. "Go to your garden shed, or I will 'port you to the dungeon again."

She is MY FamWoman. I must protect her!

"She is a daughter of the house of Yew. We will care for her. Prepare her room," he ordered Folia. "And any medical necessities."

"She broke her leg," Folia said.

"Obviously," Cuspid said.

Draeg tramped around the steps, in the dirt runoff and up to her. "I c'n carry her," he said.

The other two turned to him and as they did, he slouched round-shouldered, his posture matching his lower-class accent.

"Or ya got an anti-grav stretcher?"

"We can teleport to her bedroom," Cuspid said with cold arrogance. That indicated to Lori that he continued to check on her rooms when she wasn't there, since he knew the light well enough to 'port there.

Draeg stared at them, his eyes appearing dull. "Ain't ya gonna take her to a Healin'Hall?"

"That is not necessary," Cuspid said at the same time as Folia said, "No. It's a simple break."

"'Kay. Which one-a ya gonna hold her? Best if ya lie down beside her, I'm guessin'." He scratched his head. "I don' know everythin' I should 'bout 'portin'."

Not a lie, Lori figured, her thoughts distant. Who did know everything they should about teleporting?

Folia retreated up the stairs to the boathouse deck. "I'm teleporting to the stillroom for supplies." Lori sensed her disappearing from the scene.

"Cat, you *must* move," Cuspid demanded.

Snorting, Baccat sent mentally, *You promise on your word of honor you will not hurt her more?*

"Cave of the Dark Goddess," Cuspid muttered. "Swearing on my word of honor not to hurt Loridana! Stup."

Draeg squatted down beside her, took a softleaf from his trous pocket, and wiped her eyes and nose. It smelled of him, and that soothed, helped her steady her chest from heaving sobs. Then he pushed her hair away from her forehead. Clearing his throat, Draeg said, "I promise on my word of honor I will not harm Loridana Itha Valerian D'Yew."

A bird cawed from a nearby tree branch. Corax, she supposed, though she didn't really feel him and sure didn't want to move her head to look for a black shadow against the night sky.

"Cave of the Dark Goddess," Cuspid repeated. "All right. I swear on my word of honor I will not hurt Loridana Itha Yew any more than is medically necessary when treating her wound."

Baccat growled, but lifted his head. *I accept your word of honor, maître de maison. I will monitor My link with My FamWoman.* He walked to her cheek and licked it again and she received a private message. *The stableman will look after you. You are in good hands, there.* Then, with a last brush of fur against her face, the cat winked out of sight but had started Lori thinking less about pain and more about Draeg's hands and the future of those hands on her body. Not tomorrow—or later today, as she'd anticipated. But in the next several days, she hoped. She swallowed.

Draeg stroked her head again, dabbing up sweat, she thought.

"Since you ain't takin' her ta no Healin' Hall, uh, do you all have a Healer on staff—"

"Not a full Healer," Cuspid snapped. "I have enough standard Flair with a touch of Healing to handle this."

"All righty," Draeg said. "Though a real Healer in a Healin'Hall could fix this break tonight." He coughed. "I got some experience, too. I c'n set that there bone right here, but it's gonna hurt."

Lori blocked a whimper from escaping, swallowed bile, and nodded, tensing.

"I can help, and place a Flaired splint on it," Cuspid said.

"You got pain relief–type spells in your Flair?" Draeg asked.

"Of course."

"Then I think ya should be doin' that." His voice sounded rough and his body moved with unusual jerkiness.

"I beg your pardon?" Cuspid huffed.

"Lady is in pain. You care about that?" Again Draeg shifted. "Temp's movin' ta freezin' and she's goin' into shock. Let's set this now, afore you *have* ta call fer a Healer ta help her out."

"That won't—"

"By the Lady and Lord!" Lori cried out. "I can—" She started to sit up and suddenly Cuspid held her shoulders and pressed her back down to the glacial cold and hard ground. The movement caused her stomach to lurch unpleasantly in her body and she subsided. Pain ebbed and flowed like waves. She thought she might even hear the ocean. Perhaps it was only air rushing in her ears. Or perhaps it was words her brain could no longer distinguish.

Then a last, wrenching, sickening yank of pain sucked her into the dark.

Sixteen

Draeg stared at a far too pale Loridana D'Yew, whose pearly skin in the moonlight showed other pearls—translucent ones of pain sweat.

He and the maître de maison, Cuspid Yew, had straightened the woman's leg and she'd passed out. Then the guy had translocated splints and bandages. Draeg had lifted and held Loridana while the man had fussily sent the excess materials away, then turned back and efficiently splinted the leg.

Reluctance along with wariness had Draeg drawing Loridana close. Not at all the fuss that would have happened at his home if one of his sisters had broken a bone. No mistress of the house taking charge and giving orders, no gathering of siblings to help in any way they could. No calling of a FirstLevel Healer to their home—or taking their injured Family member to Primary HealingHall. Just one old and unsympathetic man working on an ill-lit slope with a grudgingly lit spellglobe. As a supposedly poorly Flaired person, Draeg didn't want to chance providing light or anything else except main strength.

He wished he could see to her. He'd have had her to T'Blackthorn Residence in an instant.

He didn't want to let her go. Not to the Residence, the little caring of this one man, the unknown others who populated the great house and hadn't been bothered to help. Even whatever Draeg could manage in his apartments in the stables with medications and supplies for the animals felt like it would be better than her Family's help in the intelligent Residence.

Yep. Wanted to keep her, take care of her *himself.* None of the Yews he'd seen had impressed him, and he didn't trust them. He'd trust Loridana's FamCat, but there were limits to what some Fams could do, and he didn't know the power of Baccat's Flair, whether the Fam could teleport Loridana as well as himself. And Baccat had been banished to his garden shed.

Cuspid Yew heaved a sigh and braced outthrust arms. "Give her to me and I'll teleport with her to her bedsponge. I had hoped she'd outgrown her clumsiness." He sniffed.

Draeg felt his jaw flexing. He'd only seen Loridana move with grace, especially when riding.

His own Fam cawed and sent a short burst of telepathy to Draeg. *I think I can sense woman of much Flair. I will fly past the windows to find her. Maybe there will be a ledge where I can perch and watch.*

You didn't see what happened to her? Draeg asked. He'd thought the bird was keeping an eye on her and the cat.

No.

We will talk later, Draeg sent to his Fam as he set Loridana as gently as possible into the thin arms of the maître de maison. Aloud, Draeg said, "You sure she's gonna be all right?" He scrubbed a hand over beard bristles along his jaw.

Cuspid Yew gave him a contemptuous look. "With the resources we have in our FirstFamily Residence, a break like this should be Healed within three days."

Grunting, Draeg hunched back into a servile position. "Huh. I dunno. Thought that a reg'lar Healer could do that bone in a night." A Healer could mend a clean break in a septhour, more like, but Draeg kept that comment to himself, and just said, "I'll keep the beasts fine for her then, an' won't expect her down at the stables fer a while." He cleared his throat. "Pretty clear she likes riding, though, and is an active wo—girl."

After only another sniff as punctuation, the man disappeared. Corax launched himself from the tree and flew toward the Residence. Draeg walked down the steps to the boathouse and back up, looking for any sign of blood, and found nothing.

Questions buzzed in his mind that he'd ask Corax, and Baccat, and, when he could, Loridana. Meanwhile the edgy energy cycling through his nerves demanded he *move*, so he ran to the secondary shed he'd begun to clean out and prepare for two of the animals, then back to the stables. Around him, the night breeze whispered secrets he couldn't catch, but the hard earth under his feet felt good and right.

*M*urmurs *and shifting shadows and just plain distress, physical* and emotional, pulled Lori from bad dreams.

A drifting scent, a stroking hand along her arm outside the covers—and what was her arm doing outside her covers in the cold?—slid hard nails along her skin. Someone was in her room, a Family member, even! Watching her. She *hated* that.

Gasping, she yanked her arm away, strove to see in the darkness, tried to sit up, and pain shot through her from her leg. Broken, newly set, and slightly Healed. Pushing up on her elbows, she panted the order,

"Light-spell!"

But when it came on, she saw only the closing door.

"Residence, who was in my room?"

The house didn't answer, so she knew someone with more status had ordered it to be silent. Might have even ordered its scrystones and listening off. Pure crap, the way she was treated.

She deserved more respect for all the Flair she sent to the Residence and the work she did for the Family. And that was a new thought. Her emotions had turned the corner from repudiating the restrictions the Family put on her and yearning for freedom. Now she felt irritation at the lack of respect, more of a self-worth issue. She knew why: because of her association with Draeg. Just *his* manner when they discussed the Family and the Residence, what she did for them and the animals, concepts that remained unspoken between them, but that she'd felt.

A creak came from outside her door. Flinging up a hand, she focused on her Flair, about halfway recharged through sleep, and a stingy sharing of power that had been returned to her in the form of Healing.

In no mood to put up with her Family's passive aggression, she flung off the covers and teleported away—to the HouseHeart—and hung suspended in air a few centimeters above the thick cushiony grass in the warm and comforting air before settling gently on her good side.

Sweat had coated her body at the effort. Or maybe it was from the flush of anger. Breathlessly, she ordered, "Maximum privacy for Healing and meditation, HouseHeart, please." She bit her lip, waiting to see if it would grant her that.

"You are injured!" the female voice stated, sounding a little shocked.

"Yes. I fell against hard stones." Her words weren't quite a lie. She wouldn't lie to this entity, this Yew persona, who'd treated her better than anyone else in the Residence. Though Lori knew this core of the Yew Residence wouldn't go against the main, the strong, masculine character based on Lori's MotherSire.

"Very well, I accept that you should have full privacy. You are allowed two fully private sessions a month."

Lori hadn't known that, but if the Residence kept track of the amount of privacy time and told the Family, better to use it as sparingly as she had.

Clicking of small pebbles simulated a human tongue's tsk. Blinking, Lori lifted onto her elbow to see if she could pinpoint the sound. The only pebbles she knew of coated the trough bottom of the low fountain running along the entire circular rock wall of the chamber.

"Lie back down, D'Yew, so I can Heal your leg fully."

So Lori rolled to her back and let the scent of grass and wild-flowers come to her, closing her eyes against the sunlike spellglobe that flickered on at the top of the rounded dome of the ceiling. The HouseHeart always lived in summer—at least when Lori came to it. How it handled its plants for the seasons, the fading of autumn, the hibernation of winter, the regrowth of spring, she didn't know.

But here and now she was safe. Heat radiated around her, moved from the ground under her leg into her body, as if every blade of grass released a droplet of Flair from the top to wash her free of pain, fill her with Healing energy. Her lungs compressed in an involuntary sigh.

"Sleep," crooned the HouseHeart, and she did.

*D*raeg paced his quarters, and the horses' and stridebeasts' anxiety impinged on his thoughts. They, like he, had felt the blow to Loridana. And it had been a blow, not a fall. All the animals had shrieked in his mind, even his raven, and Draeg himself had fallen against the animal pen he'd finished erecting. He'd recognized the pain of a broken leg, had taken a few seconds to send calm to the beasts, assure them that Loridana would be fine, before teleporting to the place her mind had projected.

After he'd set her leg, he'd returned to the animals and tried to soothe them. He'd done a pretty good job, focused on them and their emotions rather than on himself—until he'd left the beasts for his own rooms. Then he couldn't settle.

What the fligger had happened?

And why wasn't he with Loridana, helping her? Where he needed to be.

Because the Yew Family and Residence wouldn't let him stay with her, didn't recognize their link of friendship.

So he paced.

A tapping came at the window glass, and he saw the black shape of his bird. With a gesture he thinned the window to air, watched with brooding gaze as his new Fam zoomed into the room, circled, and perched on the top of a wooden dining chair. Since the gouges Corax left with his claws just showed newer than the rest of the scratches on the battered piece of furniture, Draeg said nothing.

But he stared into the bird's dark eyes. "What happened?" Corax clicked his beak. *I was not watching.*

"I thought you were going to," Draeg said through clenched teeth.

I followed them all night, but they went to a place with many shinys. And I saw some scattered shinys on the street. Shinys that humans like, too. He clicked his beak. *I found them. I took some.* He lifted his wings, opened his beak, and spit out a jewel. It was certainly shiny, especially from Corax's spit. Draeg raised his brows. The diamond appeared as if it had been set in a necklace.

Corax cawed. *For YOU.* Draeg got the impression the raven felt a little guilty for not watching Loridana and Baccat as he and Draeg had agreed. *Woman and cat were on the street that leads to these big lands. Walking back here.* The raven lifted one foot, set it down, raised the other, like a person's nervous shifting. *I did not see the kind woman hurt.*

Reaching out with his forefinger, Draeg stroked his Fam's head. *I understand.* Every being had certain natural urges difficult to deny. Good to know Corax would focus on shiny items.

That left one last informant. Draeg grunted. *Baccat!*

The Fam didn't answer, but Draeg knew the cat remained in his shed, a place Draeg had not visited before. Since the animals continued to be affected by his emotions, he took the stairs down and stepped back into the night. Corax joined him.

Draeg's breath frosted white in the air. With a grumbled couplet, he initiated a weathershield spell. Corax alit on his shoulder, nudged against Draeg's ear. *Warm FamMan. Thanks.* And Draeg understood that the raven thanked him for his understanding, too, though he had to squelch his disappointment in his Fam hard, to hide it from the bird.

"'Welcome, Corax." He left the stableyard and tromped on

the path leading toward the series of gardens behind the Residence. Would the cat ignore him if he showed up?

Easily following the hook he'd placed in the cat's aura—that he should have checked on more often this evening, dammit!—he walked through the gardens prepared for growing. Not many early spring flowers since the Yews kept their estate self-sufficient and used their land and Flair efficiently.

He came to a walled garden with a vividly blue door and smiled. It seemed to be a symbol of Loridana's hope—that she'd soon come into her own as FirstFamily GrandLady D'Yew.

From his experience with the powerful Flair of the old First-Families, and his observation of how much she already contributed to her estate, this very fine estate, no one in her Family would be able to deny her. Her particular bloodline straight from the original colonists was as strong as Draeg's own adoptive father's. Lord and Lady knew that a natural son of Straif T'Blackthorn would have twice or maybe triple the strength of Flair that Draeg and his brothers had. They came from a diluted offshoot of that Family line.

The Flaired lock on the door stymied him a moment, so wrapped up in Loridana's Flair. But with a little figuring out, he got through it. Another indication that a bond had begun to form between the woman and himself. That night Draeg had sensed a few of her emotions: love for her Fam, determination, nothing of true fear. Thanks to his hook in Baccat's aura, he knew they'd stayed on the well-lit main streets of Druida, no alleys this time.

"So what the fligger happened?" he asked as he yanked open another door, the one to Baccat's garden shed.

A small lightglobe illuminated, and the cat, lying on an overstuffed golden velvet pillow, blinked at him and hissed, his gaze going to Corax first. *Bird, My instincts and My ravenous stomach signal that you would taste good. I suggest you stay outside My home, into which you were NOT invited.*

Corax clicked his beak and made a disgusted noise. *I beat you in a fight, CAT.*

The feline sniffed. *Unlikely.* His whiskers quivered and his tongue came out and gave his muzzle a lingering swipe.

I will wait outside. On the scarecrow.

Draeg touched his Fam's feathers and set a small weathershield around the bird.

Thank you. You are a good FamMan, Corax said, flying away to settle on the head of a stuffed mannequin that appeared to be dressed in Loridana's old clothes. Older than the ones she usually wore. Looked like an insult to both her and her Fam—showing that the person who set the thing up didn't believe Baccat would earn his keep by keeping vermin from the garden.

I am getting a collar from My FamWoman, Baccat gloated with one last comment.

Cats demand such things, Corax shot back.

Baccat snapped at Draeg, *Close the door!*

Draeg stepped into the small, luxurious space and did. The light-spell brightened. "Stop playing the weak tom. I ask again, what the fligger happened to Loridana tonight?"

Ignorant man. The cat's side went up and down. *Surely you must realize that I am involved in helping my My FamWoman Heal!*

"Sorry, but I need to know what occurred tonight in the city."

Two gliders were racing; one of the speeding vehicles hit us.

"What! That's not an accident. Not at that time of night."

Baccat rolled over on his side and lifted a weak paw. *I cannot discuss the incident with you at the present moment.*

"Too bad, I insist."

The FamCat's eyes glared. *I do not accept your insistence. GrandSir Draeg Betony-Blackthorn.* He rose slowly to his paws, arched, and ruffled his fur. *I do not accept this psi-object you snared in My aura.* With a huge shake, Draeg's hook went flying. The minute it left the cat's aura, it vanished.

Draeg's hands fisted, but he'd get Corax to watch better, bribe the bird with tastier and more food. He'd also develop a stronger bond with Loridana so he could sense it.

"The glider hit wasn't an accident," he said. "Who wants to hurt Loridana?"

Lifting his upper muzzle to show pointy teeth, Baccat said, *Look to your allies, FirstFamily Son. They are prejudiced against My FamWoman.*

"No one on my side would do that!" He took a stride forward. Baccat hissed.

So, we have "sides" in this matter, as I hypothesized, Baccat sneered mentally. *You postulate that your "side" is so pure they would not wish to scare or harm Loridana?*

"Yes." Draeg met the cat's hard stare. "They wouldn't hurt her."

You seem assured of that. I am not. Baccat angled his head away in an arrogant move. *However, if it is not your side, then look to the other Yews' allies. It would be to their benefit to have someone other than Loridana as the head of the Yew household.*

"Which Yews? And which allies?" Draeg demanded.

Go away. I will speak with you no more. The cat lowered his eyelids.

Seventeen

Gritting his teeth at the sudden fury sweeping through him, Draeg stalked out of the garden shed. After two strides he realized how nearly out of control he was and stopped to shake out his limbs, settle into his balance, then suck in and puff out a few calming breaths. Just that had him returning to normal, especially since he'd continued to meditate a few minutes every day, so he had a recent basis for clearing his emotions.

Odd, though, how angry he'd gotten at the thought that Loridana had been targeted and deliberately hurt. Killing hot. And such a lapse of control shook him. In his world, his social strata, a man was measured by his control.

He found Corax sitting on the scarecrow's head, pulling a piece of straw from a rip in the top of the noggin that looked new. The dummy's hat lay on the ground.

Since Draeg figured Loridana would have to repair it, he snapped, "Stop that, Corax!"

Something shiny inside! Corax flung out a huge hunk of straw, dipped his long beak all the way into the head, and rustled around, pushing inside the face of the mannequin in a way that made Draeg a little queasy. The bird's chirrup sounded muffled before he pulled out a thin broken chain that looked like brass. Of little value. Some links really shone, enough of the . . . bracelet . . . that it attracted Corax's attention.

Mine! the raven crowed, great pleasure wafting to Draeg through their strengthening bond.

"Good enough," Draeg muttered, picking up the straw and the hat, jamming it back into the head. He sent his senses out into the night. The twins had returned home and, he thought, had retired to their . . . suites. If their areas were side by side, they had significant space for themselves. Better than the bedroom, small sitting room, and tiny waterfall room Loridana D'Yew had. And the rooms of the twins were on the third floor of the Residence with views of the river.

No, didn't feel like anyone watched Draeg, so he ran a finger across the open seam, melding it shut—unevenly—then stuck the battered hat back on the scarecrow's head.

MY FamWoman is giving me a ruby jeweled collar, came the thought from Baccat, still inside the shed.

Corax screeched, flew to the eaves of the shed, and banged on the window with his beak. *You rude to MY FamMan. NOT talking to you.*

If only that were a true statement, Baccat sneered mentally.

NOT listening to you, neither! You shut up!

"Come along, Corax, let's check out the gliders' garage." He lifted his upper arm to attract his Fam.

Will join you in minutes. Must put my shiny in cache. Corax flew away in the direction of the stables.

Baccat's voice sounded in Draeg's head once more. *You will not find the two gliders who drove at us in that garage.* Yep, still sounded arrogant.

No? Draeg questioned.

No. They were modern, not like the antique gliders in the Yew garage. Only one of those vehicles has been renovated, but it remains an old model.

That gave Draeg an opening. *Have they been used?*

A cat snort. *The twins used the polished one in the winter and earlier this month. Before you arrived. You will find nothing of importance with regard to those gliders.*

Nevertheless, I will check them out for the sake of thoroughness. Then Draeg pinched shut the small bond and mental stream he might have with the cat. All right, he admitted to himself that he felt a sting that the Fam had been canny enough to find his hook and fling it away.

Keeping his footsteps gliding and quiet, his senses sharp to anyone who might observe him walking through the back gardens in the night, Draeg traversed herb, vegetable, medicinal gardens with a reluctant kernel of admiration that the Yews had managed to be self-sufficient for so long. All the Noble estates he knew of had that capability, but the Yews had actually done that.

Not that he, nor anyone he knew, thought that withdrawing into one's estate with minimal contact with others was healthy.

And he'd reached the garage, a blocky building of the same gray stone as the Residence. Pausing for a moment, he leaned against the wall and checked on his bond with Loridana D'Yew, and found she slept peacefully, more comfortably than he'd anticipated, and with no anxiety. Stretching that particular link as far as he could, he caught the comfort of softness beneath her, not of a bedsponge, and a whiff of four elements.

She'd retreated into the HouseHeart; good. Rubbing his face because the depth of her sleep had him recalling that he hadn't had any this night, he straightened and pulled open the garage door.

It creaked, and Draeg froze.

None of the stable doors creaked. Obviously someone other than Loridana dealt with the garage.

The back of his neck prickled as he stepped inside, slowly pushed the door until the creak began again, and stopped. He murmured the most common light couplet and a dim overhead lightglobe shone yellow.

As he stalked around the two gliders, renewed anger simmered at the thought that Loridana had been hurt. The two Yew gliders

sat on their stands. He checked out the fronts, but from his calcu-
lations, if either of these had struck Loridana, the break would
have been in the upper bone of her leg, the femur. The blow would
have caught her higher.

He circled them a couple of more times but didn't lift the doors,
in case they were alarmed. He wished he could have, though. He
might have been able to discover something regarding the twins, or
the Family, or the nav might have some info as to where and when
the gliders were last driven.

After no more than fifteen minutes, he left the building, this time
murmuring a spell to muffle the sound of the door as he shut it, then
flicked his fingers to remove any trace of his presence on the handle.

Once again he checked Loridana and found she yet slept.

He couldn't; too restless. So he ran, pushing speed and agility,
hurdling over obstacles, back to the stables. He slowed when he realized he'd awakened the animals, who were all tucked into the stalls.

Naturally he counted noses, with all eight present. Neither the
twins nor any servers they might have had bothered the beasts
that night.

But Draeg couldn't settle, even after a waterfall.

When he scried Tinne Holly, the man's sleepy voice came.
"Here. Draeg?" A quick inhalation as the warrior came immediately to his senses. "What's wrong?"

"Loridana D'Yew—"

"You found proof of her guilt!"

"No." Draeg's own voice clipped fast and hard from him. "She
suffered a mysterious glider accident."

"Dead?" The dark pebble lightened to show Tinne leaning
against the soft cushions of a couch. His silver-blond hair stuck out.

"No. Broken leg. I don't have a good description of the gliders—"

"More than one?"

"Yep. Two. But I think they're modern. No Family clunkers
for this." He stared into Tinne's gray gaze. "We need to investi-
gate this. It could be retaliation."

Tinne narrowed his eyes. "No one on our side of this situation would have stooped so low, been so dishonorable."

Draeg raised his brows. "You're absolutely sure? As far as I can determine, the 'accident' occurred a septhour before midnight." He'd backtracked from the time he'd teleported to Loridana, calculating the few minutes before when he'd experienced her hurt.

Nearly snarling, Tinne said, "Are you asking me where I was at that time?"

Draeg shrugged.

Face flushed with anger, Tinne's tones came precise and cold. "I was here in T'Holly Residence, with my wife and my children, training for defense in our personal sparring room. You can ask the Residence if you don't believe me. It wouldn't lie to cover any dishonorable actions."

Oh, yeah, the man's temper steamed. If Tinne hadn't been a cuz to Draeg's adoptive father, feud might have been called on Draeg.

Relief wound through him. He loved Tinne like a brother. Draeg rubbed his head where his hair itched from sweat and from growing out of the short cut he preferred. "Sorry. This whole situation has skewed my head. I'm not nearly as good a spy as I'd thought." He let one side of his mouth kick up in an ironic smile. "It's harder than it looks, pretending to be lower class, without Flair, and not being who I really am."

Tinne's expression softened marginally. He inclined his head. "I accept your apology."

Draeg hadn't really figured it was an apology, just a polite word, *sorry*, but let Tinne think what he wanted. Especially if the guy would give Draeg what he needed. He scratched his head some more, kept his voice mild. "Still, be best to make sure everyone on our side—" And bitterness coated his mouth at that phrase. He didn't like being on an opposite "side" from Loridana. Guilt began to seriously gnaw at him.

He cleared his throat and continued, "Everyone on our side— T'Clover, T'Ash, T'Willow, and my Family"—whom he'd have to speak with, or ask T'Blackthorn Residence and the Turquoise House about—"are covered for not causing the accident." More bitterness seeped into his words. "Lord and Lady know, I'm sure our opponents are providing themselves with alibis."

Looking thoughtful, Tinne nodded, this time in a more casual manner. "You may be right."

"And I guarantee you that T'Yew Residence would lie about the whereabouts of its Family."

Tinne's stare sharpened. "You think so?'

"Yes."

Draeg drew in a sure and steady breath. "And I think it's time we take our suspicions to the Captain of the Druida City Guards."

"Winterberry," Tinne said, his mouth twisting. "We have no proof."

"No, but if this whole situation becomes messy and a scandal everyone in the city talks about, we want to be more aboveboard, show we've acted honorably."

Tinne's expression shadowed again. "We have no proof."

"Winterberry must already be thinking about the 'accidents': the broken balcony that almost hurt your wife and daughter, the celtaroon incident at the GuildHall."

Tinne grunted, not sounding as if he agreed.

"I'll talk to him," Draeg stated. "Since I know both sides."

"*Both sides?*" Tinne snapped.

"Since I know our group, and I've had some experience with the Yews. Which no one else in the whole city has, including the guards."

Swiping a hand, Tinne said, "Very well." He sank back into the couch.

"And I want a jeweled collar from T'Ash," he stated.

That caused Tinne's eyes to open wide. "What! What for?"

"D'Yew's Fam has sloughed off my hook. He's the arrogant kind—"

"Like most cats," Tinne interrupted, glancing at his own hunting cat lying on the couch at the edge of the perscry vision.

Draeg continued, "And I want to put a strong tracking spell on it. The thing doesn't have to look new. In fact, better if it appears old."

He'd keep back the fact that he had a small bond with Loridana.

Another grunt from Tinne. "I'll arrange it. Can probably get it to you later this morning. How are you going to ensure D'Yew's cat gets it?"

A laugh escaped Draeg. "That's easy. There's a rivalry between my Fam and Baccat."

Tinne blinked, grinned. "You have a Fam? Congratulations!"

"Thanks," Draeg smiled himself. It was *good* talking to someone who wasn't a Yew, a man he knew well and liked. Someone who had known him since Draeg's boyhood, someone who didn't think he was a damn stableman. "My Fam is a raven. I can have him drop the collar by mistake"—Draeg didn't want to say *accident* again—"while Baccat is around; no doubt the FamCat will claim it."

"Good tactic," Tinne said. He glanced toward a wall where Draeg knew a timer hung. "I think I'll take myself and my wife off to bed." Standing, he stepped over some toys to another couch, becoming smaller in the perscry as the view followed him toward another long couch. He picked up his ten-year-old sleeping son, soothed his wife awake with soft words and an equally tender smile, took her hand and kissed it, and then they all vanished, teleporting away.

Draeg was left with a yearning in his gut for what his cuz had.

A new, envious feeling. Very unwelcome.

Eighteen

Straightening the line of his shoulders from too high and tight, Draeg swiped his thumb over the perscry pebble and visualized Ilex Winterberry, Captain of the Druida City Guards. Draeg grunted. Circles within circles within circles, that's what the Nobles were. Winterberry was a cuz a couple of steps away from Tinne Holly, or Tinne's older brother. And the guy had handled most of the problems the FirstFamilies had over the years that involved investigations.

Yeah, circles. Draeg continued to stare at the foggy perscry. His Flair had connected with a perscry or scry bowl in Winterberry's quarters, but the man hadn't answered yet.

When Straif T'Blackthorn, Draeg's adoptive father, had acknowledged the Betony Family as true Blackthorns and had taken them into his Family of three, Draeg's parents had been raised from the lowest Noble circle to the greatest, and so had Draeg and his two natural brothers.

Draeg had been four, but he still vaguely recalled the earlier lifestyle, never really considered himself a FirstFamily son despite all that—though he'd kill or die for his Family, Betony and Blackthorn alike.

"Here," said Winterberry's rough and slightly panting voice, and embarrassment flooded Draeg at the knowledge he'd interrupted—or hurried—sex between the man and his wife.

Draeg cleared his throat. "I guess you're not as accustomed to being awakened in the middle of the night as you were when you were a regular guard."

The mist shrouding the perscry cleared, showing Winterberry's supremely satisfied expression. One of his white brows quirked up. "Draeg Betony-Blackthorn. I've noticed that your depredations on the criminal life of Druida City have diminished."

"Sorry about that?" Draeg questioned, rolling tightness that had settled between his shoulders again. On the whole, he'd been feeling significantly better since he'd come to the Yews, worked with animals on the isolated estate. He'd only fought those who might have harmed D'Yew on her midnight rambles.

Winterberry shrugged easily, "Your nightly fights removed some problems, caused others. Glad you found something else to do with your time." He smiled—a smile that disappeared as soon as Draeg began telling his story of the group of younger Nobles sending him to T'Yew's undercover.

At the end of his recital, Draeg heard Winterberry's teeth click together as if biting into something not to his taste. "We of the guard *have* been taking into account all the so-called accidents going on. We have also been observing the Traditionalist Stance. Tinne Holly should have spoken to me long before this. Or T'Clover." Winterberry paused, his expression turning impassive, his eyelids lowering over a glinting gaze. "You're at D'Yew's, eh?"

"She has nothing to do with this." He paused, trying to give his next words extra weight. "I have never met a more innocent woman."

Both Winterberry's eyebrows climbed high. He inclined his head, and Draeg released a quiet breath in hopes that the Captain of the Guards might actually respect his opinion.

"I will take your conclusion under consideration." Winterberry paused. "You believe this glider accident is one with the rest."

"It feels like it's a part of the puzzle."

Winterberry didn't hide his own massive sigh. "Tinne Holly is correct that we have no evidence . . . *yet*, to tie radical members of the Traditionalist Stance to the events. What have you learned of the Yews?"

"I am at the stables. What I've learned comes from speaking with the FamCat Baccat, my particular observations of the Residence, the maître de maison, Zus and Vi Yew, and what I've been able to glean from D'Yew herself in casual conversation."

Now Winterberry appeared thoughtful. "D'Yew exploring Druida City at night. What is she up to?"

"I thought rebellion against the tough strictures of her Family," Draeg said.

"Think some more. You set hooks in the twins?"

"Yes, yesterday morning. They *were* off the estate at the time of the glider accident, but not in the area where D'Yew was. I didn't see them take a Family glider, so they must have teleported."

"That means they know the place where they are going, how the light falls, et cetera." Winterberry grunted, cast a glance at Draeg. "Could you think back and pinpoint their location?"

"Probably."

"Do that." Then Winterberry said, "I suppose I should thank you for this mess you've handed me. At least I know more about what is going on and can deploy my forces accordingly, anticipate some matters." He showed his teeth in a smile. "I will grill Tinne Holly about all his suspicions tomorrow."

*W*hen *Lori awoke, feeling better and whole, if not as full of energy* as usual, her mind went first, as always, to her plans to escape and when.

Stay or go now, tonight?

How she disliked this wavering back and forth on a decision, always trying to figure out what would be best for her animals, and her, and the Family and Residence with each new event!

Her first thought every morning, her last each night.

Not last night when she'd fainted from pain. Echoes of fear reverberated through her. There'd been moving shadows in and outside her room in the deep of the night. Worse was the bright and flashing memory of those two racing gliders heading toward her, the white light bars across the front of the vehicles seeming to trap her. She shivered.

Danger she hadn't sensed until too late. The hair on her nape rose at the thought of any more threats when she roved the city, even simply to confirm the best route through it and out of the walled place to the southeast. Yes, another shiver rippled again.

Since she'd been dilatory, she didn't know the streets well enough—now she wouldn't want any narrow byways, not with eight animals instead of six, and two horses. She didn't know if the pavement on the route would be acceptable for horses' hooves.

Reluctantly, she decided she didn't know the horses well enough, either. Would they follow her through the city with no problems? They hadn't bonded with her stridebeasts or her as deeply as she wanted yet. And they'd lived on a Noble estate for years; had they ever been in the city? A lot to spook them even if they traveled in the wee septhours of the morning.

Leading eight animals through the city would be harder than ever. As for the horses, to prepare them, she'd have to touch their minds, send pictures of the city and the path to them. Just as she had been doing with her stridebeasts to get them accustomed to the idea of a trip.

She definitely had to build up more trust with Ragan and Smyrna.

Druida City had become scarier to Lori.

What with the Flair drain, and now this frightening accident, perhaps she should curtail her nightly excursions outside into Druida City proper. Calculating exactly what she must do—no more shopping or food carts, a pity—she thought she'd only need to scout two more times. Walk the full course from the northeast gate of Yew estate through the shared greenway, to a street through the big estates called Noble Country, into the city and south to the newish southeast gate.

Yes, she'd enjoyed her expeditions discovering the city, but that wasn't why she'd gone into the busy town in the first place. Ignore any more temptation. She could do that, though she mourned a little.

Unless an imminent threat appeared, she couldn't leave for her own new estate tonight.

Letting out a shuddering sigh, she accepted the relief flowing through her. Because she didn't want to leave Draeg. Not before she had sex with him, though that would complicate her life, too.

She recalled the night before and Draeg's hands on her as he set her leg and the pain that spun her into unconsciousness.

And before that, the hot kiss in the stables, the one in the grove. She squirmed as liquid heat swam through her from between her legs to suffuse her whole body. So much better to feel this than fear and pain.

Having Draeg here pleased her, and becoming lovers with him was a huge reason to stay—for the moment.

But Draeg also eroded her self-control in more than the sexual area, by treating her well, like a strongly Flaired woman.

Just leaving would be so much simpler.

No, she didn't think she could walk away without feeling Draeg's hands on her as a lover. Stay, then, until the weather remained warm enough that nights out on the road wouldn't harm her animals, until she bonded well with her horses and her animals would follow her anywhere.

Not to mention the fact that once she and her animals arrived at her own estate there'd be a lot to do and no time for a lover. And she had no notion if there *were* any attractive men on estates nearby. So if she wanted to experience sex with a man who stirred her, she had to grab the chance *right now*.

The decision reaffirmed, to stay for a week, or two, three at the most.

When she went, she'd be on her own. She'd be leaving behind Draeg, but taking her animals and her Fam with her.

Focusing on her Fam, she recalled that Baccat wanted a collar, the necklace she'd received for surviving her First Passage and showing an excellent amount of Flair.

If she pulled her necklace from her treasure box here in the HouseHeart, she'd have to hide it in one of her caches until they left, but she didn't know if she'd be back in the HouseHeart before she went away. Best she get the necklace-collar now.

As long as she'd be taking the piece for Baccat, she should remove her father's spheres, too. All would go into the cache in the pantry and into the large saddlebags holding the most important items she'd be taking with her.

Of course the Residence knew of that cache, if not exactly what was inside the old saddlebags. But the house believed her hidey-hole held little of value and was an unfortunate emotional response to being bullied by her Family. She'd tinkered with the cupboard and the old no-time within it subtly and discreetly until she didn't believe the Residence could keep her from accessing it. Her main objective remained to leave without alerting the Residence and Family.

With a big breath, she rose, and her leg felt whole but her stance, and her walk, a little shaky. She crossed to one of the elaborately carved cabinets, opened a top drawer, and took out her personal box—also carved wood—and lifted the lid. Lightly she trailed her fingers over the viz and memory spheres—four, cool to her touch. The velvet jewelry case with her necklace and an old ring felt contrastingly warm. Shutting the box, she translocated it into the saddlebag in the pantry that she'd lined for that very use. Yes, another step toward leaving.

Since she still felt a little weak and stiff, she did some stretches, recalled Draeg and his patterns, and regretted that she'd have no time to learn any of those.

"Is there anything you need, D'Yew?" asked the HouseHeart.

Lori shrugged away her scheming, concentrated on the now, let out a slow breath, and said, "I love you, HouseHeart."

"I love you, too, D'Yew."

Yes, just hearing the title that wasn't officially hers yet rubbed

Lori raw. She had to swallow hard before she spoke again. "You know I haven't been confirmed as D'Yew. There has been no loyalty ceremony for me to vow to honor and protect my Family and for them to vow to be loyal to me. Nor has Cuspid or Folia introduced me to the FirstFamilies of Celta as D'Yew, ah, acknowledged me, even informally as D'Yew." Yes, that definitely rankled, and more each day. She had to leave before her control slipped.

But just as no one was bound to her by vows of loyalty, so she remained unbound to stay and do her very best by her Family. Of course, with that ceremony and the vows of loyalty, she wouldn't have left. Because she would have the authority to enforce her orders, not only with Flair, and with the stated backing of the Residence, but because of the vows. She didn't exactly know the weight of the authority and Flair that came with the vows, but there must be some.

"I *have* been ready for that loyalty ceremony for over a year." She kept her tone light.

"I know, dear," said the HouseHeart. "Patience. It will come all in good time." A pause. "Change is not easy for us."

Lori didn't know whether the HouseHeart referred to itself and the Residence or the Family or all of those entities.

She found her teeth aching since she'd gritted them. She'd just have to dig for patience, practice all her control with her Family and the Residence. She didn't think she'd last to the Vernal Equinox.

No. She couldn't stand around in major celebration of the wheel of the year and not be D'Yew. Her endurance as well as her temper had shortened. Let those who ruled this place, who would lead that circle, as always, care for the estate and the Residence since they had no intention of letting her be D'Yew in anything other than the empty title. She had her own estate, her own life to live.

Lori walked around the room, did a few exercises, and asked a question that had often come to mind but she'd never spoken aloud. "How many personalities do you have?"

"Hmmm," the HouseHeart hummed with a vibration that went clear to Lori's bones and resonated in her marrow. "Four, dear."

Easy, keep the questions easy like casual conversation. "I like yours better than my MotherSire's that the main Residence uses."

The HouseHeart chuckled. "What you call your MotherSire's persona is actually from the T'Yew two generations before him. *His* FatherSire's."

"Oh, um, about change. Is it possible for the Residence's main character to change?"

"If the whole entity wishes, the Residence and the HouseHeart and the HeartStones who control the personas, it can be done relatively simply." Now the voice took on layers, became a multivoice, and Lori heard a definite tinge of the Residence she knew all too well.

"And otherwise?" she asked.

"With the request and Flaired insistence of the Family, or the head of the household." The HouseHeart's tone held warning. Lori knew what that meant—she'd have to challenge the Residence, an entity built three and a half centuries ago.

She'd lived eighteen years.

She wasn't sure of their respective Flair, but she thought that one chandelier dropped on her would finish her off. And she didn't know if the Residence would do that. More likely, she'd be fitted with DepressFlair bracelets and stuck in a storage chamber and go mad. Lori thought either Vi or Zus would love to be D'Yew or T'Yew instead of her.

Her lip curled. *They* had no self-control. The Residence had drilled into her that a FirstFamily GrandLady *must* be in charge of her emotions, and Lori had learned. The spoilt twins hadn't.

And, truly, with regard to replacing the main Residence's persona, how would Lori feel if that happened to her? She shuddered. Would she remain herself? No, it wasn't right to insist that someone else change to meet her needs; better to change herself. Even though she believed change to be good, a Residence that had lived so long probably couldn't change easily, certainly not as easily as she. Perhaps it had fossilized.

"Do you know if any other Residences have changed personas?"

A throbbing silence. "I believe some are flexible enough to do so when a new head of household is installed, especially if the gender of that head changes." Another pause. "We haven't been in contact with the other Residences, the FirstFamily circle of Residences since before you were born."

"Oh. That's sad." Lori paused herself. "Not to have friends the same as you."

"We are unique and we have *our* Family." Again with the multivoice. "That is sufficient," it intoned, and then the HouseHeart said in its female voice, "D'Yew, you *must* eat."

"Oh, yes."

"I recommend a high-protein meal." The HouseHeart tinkled one of the four wind chimes in the chamber, and Lori turned toward that area and the no-time there. The outer door had opened, and when she approached, the inner door slid aside and the scent of steak wrapped in porcine strips and creamy orange taters made her salivate.

"Thank you, HouseHeart." Lori translocated the hot plate to a tray with legs, took it, flatware, and a softleaf to sit near the firepit.

"My, pleasure, dear."

As soon as Lori picked up her fork, ravenous hunger struck and she shoveled in the food with little savoring. She finished quickly, cleansed her plate and utensils, went to her favorite stack of huge pillows, and leaned back on them. All of her felt better, stronger, though her leg ached a bit. Despite the Flair the HouseHeart and the Residence and Cuspid had given her, only Cuspid had a minor Healing gift. She'd Heal faster, but it would still be her own body working on the injury, sapping her strength. So she'd have to take it easy for a few days.

She shouldn't have even considered embarking on her trip, though if her animals were endangered she'd leave if she had to flop sideways over one of them to ride and sneak away.

Then she remembered Baccat, and that she hadn't checked on him. Closing her eyes, she visualized the thin but steely thread between them. He slept, and she sensed his well-being and sighed with relief.

Very quietly, the HouseHeart said, "We Residences do have standards and rules."

Lori blinked; she'd been sliding into sleep and hadn't noticed how many minutes had passed. "Yes?" she prompted, equally softly.

"Your FamCat should be allowed in here, with you." A click like that of a tongue. "But the primary Residence character does not care for animals—in any way—not even those with some sentience.

"And . . ."

"And," Lori asked.

"You should have been proclaimed as D'Yew as soon as you finished your Second Passage last summer." A sigh of air and tinkle of chimes. "Like humans, Residences may decide not to follow the rules and standards."

Surprise flicked through Lori. Residences had rules, and Yew Residence might not be following them! Her mind boggled. Lady and Lord forfend if *she* didn't follow any of the Residence's or the Family's rules. Nonchalantly, she said, "Ah, I hear you, House-Heart. Surely a situation like mine has come up before in our history when someone lost his or her parents too young."

The fire flamed and crackled in response to the HouseHeart's surge of Flair. The HouseHeart said, "Yes. Such circumstances have occurred twice before."

Nineteen

"What *happened before when a person too young to take the title* inherited?" Lori asked.

Murmuring, the HouseHeart said, "One individual was confirmed as the FirstFamily GrandLady after her Second Passage at seventeen."

"And the other heir?" Lori asked.

Another flare of fire shot up orange from the pit. "Once the regent was dilatory in handing over the management of the estate. That was a difficult time of turmoil in the Residence as the Family took sides and fought internally." The HouseHeart's voice quavered, then turned into a whisper. "For over three years there was constant strife. Finally *outsiders*, the others in the FirstFamily Council, named him and recognized him as T'Yew. *Outsiders* messing in our business. A great disgrace for us all. Not ever to be tolerated again. And one of the reasons we don't trust others; they usurped our personal authority."

Lori's spine stiffened as she sat up straight, feeling the sting to her Family pride herself, even flushing with embarrassment at the visualization of the loss of privacy and honor to the name she carried. No, it was not well done to go outside the Family for anything, even if she'd contemplated such. Her reaction of gut revulsion would be mirrored by every one of her Family members.

Infighting. She'd wanted to avoid that and she had. Mostly because she believed she'd lose in any battle with anyone else. Now she set her lifted chin. She might be leaving, but she wouldn't be tearing the Family apart—just letting them decide who would be a better head of the household than she. Since, despite all that she'd done, they didn't believe she was old enough, acceptable enough to be GrandLady, inasmuch as they hadn't scheduled a ceremony to recognize her.

Then the light dimmed as if the HouseHeart sighed. "Situations and events linger in our memory and we make decisions based on the past instead of looking forward to the future. We, as a full Residential being, are like that. You are our hope, D'Yew, young enough to disregard the very heavy weight of past mistakes and make decisions on your view of the future. Always remember that."

Lori gulped and nodded but didn't answer aloud. She was abandoning her Family and the Residence. It didn't matter that she deeply felt—and thought—that they'd abandoned her first, and when she'd tried to make those decisions that the House-Heart just referred to, she'd been overruled. She still was selfishly leaving the Family and the Residence to their own decisions based on the past, or whatever.

She arranged the large pillows into a nest, settled into them, and closed her eyes. When she did, she became aware of all the aches in her body, and especially her leg, which now felt fragile.

Guilt followed Lori into dreams. She thrashed until the gray bleakness faded . . . and transmuted to warmth and tenderness, and not from her animals.

No, this time she felt the heat of a man, a lover in bed with her, his hands on her, as she'd imagined.

As she wanted, and soon.

As she needed *now*! She awoke with desire churning inside her.

*   *   *

$\mathcal{D}$raeg *checked on his bond with* $\mathcal{L}$*oridana midmorning and found* her sleeping again, still in the HouseHeart. Continuing to worry about threats to her, and with her injury the night before as an excuse, Draeg made sure the animals could spare him for a while and walked up to the Residence.

He planned on speaking with the house, trying to gauge the personality of the structure himself instead of relying on comments from Baccat and Loridana.

As soon as he reached a point where someone could see him from the roof walk or the windows, he hunched his shoulders and modified his stride to a slower walk that a common guard who'd spent a lot of time mounted would use. The path transformed from a small beaten-earth trail to wide stone set in smooth ground that would be surrounded by a centuries-old lush grassyard in the summer. The area became groomed to a near perfection that itched at him.

He'd considered which door to head for and decided on the side door nearest to the stables, though at other times he'd gone to the back door near the kitchen, the one at which a low-status person would present himself. When he reached the entrance, he took off a battered soft hat he'd worn and screwed up his face so the incipient lines on it would groove a bit and added anxiety to his expression.

Shifting from foot to foot, he noted the two scrystones on either side of the door embrasure. He lifted the iron knocker and let it fall, waited for a couple of minutes. No one opened the polished wooden door. Hand on the iron latch, he pressed the tongue of it and pushed the door inward, then followed it to stand in a small mudroom set with the same gray stone as the building.

"Uh, hmm," he said, then cleared his throat and ducked his head as if addressing a person of great status, keeping an eye on a faceted clear crystal inset in the ceiling. "Ah, FirstFamily Grand-Lord T'Yew Residence?" he mumbled.

"I hear you," it replied in haughty tones.

"Uh, hmm, uh, I come ta check on the wo—the girlie who fell last night, see how she's a-doin', whether her leg is Healed and when she might—"

"GrandLady D'Yew will come to the stables when she is completely well and after her duties to me and her Family are fulfilled. Begone."

"Well—"

"You let in cold air! Impossible creature." The door handle beneath his fingers gave him a jolt of electricity, and Draeg yanked his hand from it, jumped, and swore. Then the door swung shut, hard, sweeping him with it, and slammed, sending him flying a meter and landing on his butt, falling to his back, his head hitting hard ground. He lay gasping for a good minute, began to instinctively teleport home and summon the Blackthorn Family Healer, and recalled himself in time.

FAMMAN! Corax screeched in his mind, and Draeg thought he might also have done so aloud, but he couldn't hear him with his ears. Of course his ears buzzed with shock and pain and the tough rush of his own breathing.

Meet me at the big yew between the Residence and the stables, Draeg instructed.

Yes, FamMan. Don't like you hurt.

I don't, either. Allowing himself awkward movements—he wasn't in The Green Knight Fencing and Fighting Salon *now*—he rolled over, head down, rocked to hands and knees and then to his feet, to stagger back down the path to the stables. From the heat on the back of his neck, and a wariness that suffused his whole body, he believed that some of the Family members in the Residence watched him limp away.

What happened? Corax's tone was as dark as his feathers.

The Residence hurt me.

Bad house. Draeg sensed his FamBird snicking his beak.

Yeah. When the trees masked him from the Residence, he leaned against the yew and shuddered in and out a few breaths, gingerly stretched, and heard a couple of tendons twang and joints crack as he settled his body. His vision seemed fine though his head throbbed—but his gritted teeth and anger at the Residence didn't help that headache.

Corax hopped from a low branch to Draeg's shoulder, and he flinched. "Sorry," he said.

The bird tugged at a hank of his hair. *Sorry, too.*

Stiffness from the fall seeped into his muscles, and he knew he had to move. Though it hurt, once again he checked on each of the animals.

"Let me hold you while I teleport to T'Blackthorn Residence." He reached and took the bird from his shoulder to cradle Corax against his chest. The Fam fluttered a little, then settled.

We go?

"Yeah, my head doesn't feel quite right. Going now, and not counting down." On a sigh, he teleported home to his bedroom. Once there, he sent out a mental call for their Healer, opened his arms to free Corax, then took a couple of steps to fall facedown on the bedsponge, and that hurt.

Trapped! Trapped inside! Thin window, FamMan!

Without opening his eyes or turning his head toward the long window that looked out on the first-story roof terrace, Draeg said the Word to thin the window to air and heard a whoosh as his Fam exited the room. A minute later, feathers tickled his nose along with the pungent dust smell of bird.

Thanks, FamMan. Good to know I can get in and out and in and out and in—

"Welcome," Draeg mumbled.

Since Draeg's adoptive father and distant cuz had been the last of the colonist's direct line, the Blackthorns didn't have a huge Family who worked in the Residence. The current SecondLevel Healer had contracted with them for a few years. The guy arrived at Draeg's second-floor suite quickly enough, knocked, and entered when Draeg yelled at him to come in.

After a brief and nearly sickening examination, punctuated by mental comments and beak clicks by Corax, along with admiring compliments about the FamBird by the Healer, the man went to work on the crack in Draeg's skull and his bruised butt and back. Then the guy left with an admonition to be more careful and a last remark that he'd thought Draeg had quit his looking-for-trouble-and-finding-it ways.

Draeg had grunted in answer, then just continued to lie face-down on his bedsponge—he'd forgotten how wonderful a good bedsponge felt.

Corax flew in and out of the room and Draeg learned the sound of his Fam's flight. Vaguely, Draeg kept the mental and emotional links he had with the Yew animals open. All was well, so he could spare a little time for questions.

Projecting his voice, he said, "T'Blackthorn Residence, I have some questions about Residences."

"Because you are working and staying at D'Yew Residence," the deep male voice of T'Blackthorn Residence stated.

"That's right." Draeg rolled over and stuffed a couple of fat pillows behind his head. Even though he hadn't been hurt for long, he welcomed the smooth movement of muscle, bone, and sinew gratefully.

Corax glided through the window and perched on the wooden headboard of Draeg's bed. Good thing it was battered from tussles with his siblings already.

He cleared his throat. "My injuries were due to sustaining an electrical shock from my fingers on the iron door latch, and then the door flung me back and away as it slammed shut."

Bad house! Corax yelled.

"What!" The remaining closed window in his bedroom rattled, and some of the tension in Draeg's shoulders eased that *his* home sounded as angry as Draeg had felt at the unexpected and uncalled-for violence.

"I'd knocked and opened the door, stepped in, but kept my hand on the latch." He still didn't know whether that was a mistake. Odds were, the Residence could have hurt him worse if he'd closed the door behind him and stayed inside.

"If D'Yew Residence still remained connected to our circle, we would have sanctioned him," T'Blackthorn Residence stated in a flintlike tone. A pause. "But that entity withdrew from our company." Another few heartbeats of silence—human heartbeats; Draeg wondered how the Residences ticked away the time, marking the passing of minutes, or years. Finally, T'Blackthorn Residence said heavily, "It is not good for those of us who are centuries old to be isolated. We depend on the contact with other like beings for support, as well as our Families."

"I understand," Draeg said quietly. "People in your Families come and go."

"Mine die," T'Blackthorn Residence said bleakly. "Four times I've seen my Blackthorns succumb to an illness that other Families have survived. Four times the Blackthorns have been reduced to a single member."

"I'm sorry," Draeg said.

Corax made a sympathetic noise.

The Residence continued, "And Straif grieved hard and went away, leaving me. It was good that I had others of my ilk to communicate with."

"Good."

Good! Corax echoed.

"Thank you, FamBird. I am pleased to see that Draeg has finally found his Fam."

The house heard me! Corax sounded thrilled.

"Indeed," the Residence said.

Preening, Corax straightened a feather and said, *My FamMan waited for me. I am best for him.*

"Indeed," the Residence agreed. "And it is good that you three brothers of the Betony-Blackthorn bloodline have been adopted into the Blackthorn Family. Through the marriages over the years with more Commoner people, your ancestry has strengthened the original strain and made it sturdier."

Draeg finally found the courage to ask the Residence a question he'd thought about since he'd been a child. "Then you're all right with the title and the fortune and . . . and *yourself* passing to us? Or to one of Straif's and Mitchella's adopted children?" His breath hitched. "Or, I should say, *we* will be passing to you, because you are the constant of the Blackthorn Family."

A ripple of wood sounded, windowsills or the floor or the door-jambs or something, the Residence chuckling. "My thanks, Draeg. That is, of course, my point of view. It has been four hundred twenty-four years since the Earthan colonists stepped upon this planet, and my walls were built within the first decade with the settlers' machines. I do not remember that, but I have seen people of the FirstFamilies come and grace my halls in gatherings, and felt the energies of each person as they contributed to rituals that helped me and this estate throughout the years. The FirstFamilies who are the strongest are those whose members have wed HeartMates, no matter what station their spouses were, or how much Flair the individual had. The next most important quality was marriages with diverse individuals, people not necessarily of the FirstFamilies, but from the lower Noble or Commoner classes. If we are to build a thriving civilization, we must continue to make our bloodlines strong."

"I understand, but what of the Blackthorn tracking Flair? It's an important skill."

Corax sniffed. *I like the smell of tracking Flair. Makes you smell RIGHT.*

"Uh-huh," Draeg said, but waited for the Residence to respond.

Another chuckle, not as deep or prolonged, which pleased Draeg because the creaks were just creepy. He worried about the house doing damage to itself.

"You say the skill is important because it is one you also have," the Residence said.

Tracking IS important, Corax put in.

"I don't have tracking Flair as strongly as Straif." A hint of the hero worship Draeg had for his adoptive father came out, surprising him.

"Both you and your younger brother have *a* tracking ability, if not the same as Straif's or as potent as his." The Residence's words grew softer. "We must trust in the Lady and Lord that the skills we sentient beings of Celta need will be developed." Then the Residence turned brisk. "Genetic mutation of you humans and animals will adapt you better to the planet. And as you adapt and change, you will help us, the immobile intelligent people, change."

"Ah. Right. That's one way of looking at it." A very long view of the whole thing, and the Residence seemed to discount the great Flaired skills that every member of a FirstFamily prized.

Birds are getting smarter all the time. Corax added a small, self-satisfied caw.

"I'm sure," Draeg said. He could only spare a few more moments before returning to the Yew estate, but additional questions pressed upon him. "Did you—do you have any observations about the Yews?"

"Naturally I have not met the current D'Yew. Her mother, the previous D'Yew, yes, she came through my halls a couple of times as she matured. As did her father, the MotherSire of the current D'Yew, and *his* father and FatherSire. I have seen that particular Family become more conservative. We, the Residences, have speculated as to why, but we have no solid conclusions. There are some entities, human and non, who become more conservative, perhaps more selfish of what they have and more fearful of change that might take away what they have, as they age."

"Yeah, I've seen that." All right, he'd experienced that himself, more particularly in the last month. He'd been fighting in the streets and that had satisfied his wild side, but being with the animals had made him aware of the pleasure in caring for others, and the love animals could give him. Not to mention having his Fam, Corax, just for a little over a day, had made him feel special, unique.

And spending time with Loridana . . . *that* fulfilled him like nothing else. He thought his very heart and being had expanded.

He wouldn't give any of that up and he'd fight anyone who'd try to take the animals, Corax, or Loridana from him.

Whoa. That had him opening his eyes wide.

"We, the Residences, are also unsure why the Yew Residence withdrew from us, and what went wrong with that Family. The Hollys, most particularly, spoke to us of the trials the current wife of Tinne Holly, the former wife of old T'Yew, went through when living there. That the Residence is conservative is completely understandable. That it might be violent is disturbing."

A cool draft whirled through the room. "I strongly suggest that you have no more contact with D'Yew Residence, Draeg. I care for you."

That had a lump closing his throat. He coughed. "I care for you, too, Residence."

"I want none of my Family to perish in any untimely way again!"

"Understood." He'd agitated his home. Good job. Grimacing, he sat up, then stood, shaking out his limbs. "Feeling fine."

"Very good. But I will speak to my fellow Residences about how one of us harmed you."

"Do as you think best."

"And you should eat. Should I call the Family to come and keep you company?"

Food is always good, thanks, Rez! Corax enthused.

"I can't spend the time to talk with the Family." A septhour or two would drain away with all the questions they'd want answered, all the speculation from various members.

Corax made a noise in his throat; disappointment emanated from him. "But, Corax, feel free to explore T'Blackthorn estate." Draeg frowned. "I think I can make one of the windows thin in only one part so you can come and go into these rooms."

"I am in contact with the PublicLibrary, whose people have a hawkcel Fam. I will ask what is necessary to provide for a bird Fam, such as a perch and food and water dishes for Corax's use here. He can supervise."

As long as Draeg could recall, Fams liked to supervise. "Sounds good. Think I'll take a waterfall, dress in some more of the old clothes I got for this mission, and return. Take care, Corax, and be aware of the cats."

I will broadcast that I am the new Blackthorn Fam!

"I'm sure most of the Fams already know," the Residence murmured.

"Yeah, gossip travels fast in this Family." Which meant his parents and siblings might be showing up at any minute. He stripped fast and hustled his ass into the waterfall.

When he came out, Corax had left and glass covered most of the window the raven had been using, but still allowed entry for his Fam, who had taken to the air, exploring the estate.

Draeg would have liked for Corax to come with him back to the Yews, but he sensed the bird enjoyed the pleasant and loving atmosphere of the Blackthorns . . . and maybe teasing the cat and fox Fams with his flight.

As for him, though his home comforted, Yew estate seemed more challenging, more his. And Loridana . . . he liked being in her company, and he wanted to see her.

He welcomed that heat continuing to surge between them.

Draeg had just finished dressing, and stretching to make sure the clothes fit all right, when a warmth flowed down the link between himself and Loridana D'Yew.

Draeg? she sent mentally.

He wondered if she knew that her Residence had hurt him. *He* knew that she wouldn't be surprised.

I will be there shortly, he sent back.

She also seemed unsurprised that he might be teleporting back to the estate.

I want you, Draeg.

The sensuality behind that statement slammed into him, and his trous tightened as arousal flashed. His wits scattered as he wondered exactly what she meant, what *she* felt beyond those words. What his own reactions and actions should be.

Because, by the Lord and Lady, he *ached* for her.

I'll meet you in the southeast corner of the stables. Where they'd kissed, where dim light filtered through high windows, where the air smelled of grain and hay and beasts. And love.

Love. Not a word he'd applied to any female other than his relatives, certainly not to any of his casual bed partners.

His body throbbed, ready for sex. Love he didn't know about and shut out of his mind.

But this time when he touched Loridana, he didn't think he'd be able to stop.

Twenty

❤

*W*hen *he reached the southwest corner of the stables, she was already* there. She looked fabulous, and whole, her broken leg Healed. Beautiful woman. The light shining through a clean window spun her hair to gold, deepened her eyes to emerald, outlined the subtle curves of her body.

Her fragrance came to him, the light floral of spring flowers, a touch of summer grass. Female desire? Yeah, he thought he could smell that, too, and seeing her, scenting her made his shaft grow thick and as hard as iron. No way could he slide open the front tab of his trous, not without disgracing himself.

"Loridana," he said, and his voice sounded urgent and rough to his own ears, even as he reminded himself again and again that she was untouched, he had to go slow.

He swallowed hard and when he could propel his voice past dry lips, he said, "Are you sure?" He cleared his throat, fisted hands that wanted to reach for her, forced himself to think with his *head*, not his groin. "You've gotta be sure, Loridana D'Yew. What . . . what we are about to do can't be, you know, undone."

Her eyes lit and she laughed, freely. "I'm Lori. Call me Lori."

She laughed again. "I've had standard Healer examinations. I don't have a maidenhead."

That was a really old-fashioned word for the hymen, but in line with all the antique rules and beliefs around here. He managed to nod, then felt himself flushing. "But a woman before she's had a man and afterward . . . there's always a difference." He knew that from seeing his adopted sisters mature.

Loridana's, Lori's—and he really liked thinking of her as that, the way she thought of herself—pupils dilated further. Her wide smile faded and her shoulders straightened. "Do you . . . do you want me?"

The insecurity in her voice pulled him from his balanced stance to take a step toward her. Within reaching distance, taking distance, and her aroma wafted to him again, more pungent like she was nervous, sweating a little. He inhaled, needing her even more.

"Perhaps I should leave—" she began, and he realized he'd taken too long to answer her.

"No!" he nearly shouted, but toned it down. "No, please." Meeting her gaze, he felt his blood heat and his erection enlarge. All of him so hot. So needy for her, just the trail of her fingers on his cheek, even. "You should know, should have felt the attraction between us, that's real and true." An inward flinch of mind and heart that other things about him in relation to her weren't real or true. Push that *away*. Not time to think of that. Not when this incredible woman stood before him. And again he felt he lagged behind her, and with fraying control.

He sank once more into his balance, so he wouldn't move when he wanted to pounce. Then, still with his stare locked on hers, he shut his eyes. "We have a bond," he said, now more aware of the atmosphere around him, and how his lips felt fuller, warmer, needing her kiss. Not only her scent, but that of a close bed of straw where they might lie—*Stop that thought, too! Talk to her, the inexperienced lady.* "We have a bond," he repeated. "Thin but strong. One made of . . . friendship as well as that attraction." Gruffly, he added, "It is open on my side. *Feel*—" He stopped before he begged her to put her hands on him, stroke him.

So he closed his eyes. "I want you. But you must want me, too." He *must* please her. If he didn't it would be disastrous to his feelings, to their growing friendship, to . . . his whole life. Standing here in the gray shade that painted the inside of his eyelids, he realized he hadn't wanted something as much as he wanted Lori Yew for a long, long time, certainly no woman.

Had she touched him? That feathery slide across his chest, a brush on his shoulders? He swayed, had to bend his knees to keep his balance solid. And found that his whole body trembled.

His aura felt as if she moved into it, close to him. He thought he could hear the faint susurration of her breathing. Inhaling, he tried to find her breath, take it into himself.

Then she kissed him. Little nibbles on the angle of his jaw. He nearly jumped when her tongue slid along his skin.

The sound of his heavy breathing seemed to echo in the stables. All the animals were outside in the corral together, mingling, getting to know each other.

Lord and Lady, he *did* want to get to know Lori more, deeper, *intimately*. And soon. She moved so damn slowly. But he was determined to let her proceed as she wished, and in her own time frame, even if he did feel like he might explode into tiny bits and never be whole again.

He already was sure he, like Lori, would never be the same again.

There, her lips touched his! He strained forward as she withdrew, trying to keep that slight contact. Sweeping his tongue over his lips, he tried to taste her. A drop of sweetness only.

His lashes fluttered.

"Don't," she whispered. "I'm liking this very much." He heard a lilt of amusement in her voice, other layers like an undertone of rich, breathy lust, sheer wonder. Subtleties that he would have missed, must often had missed, if he'd been looking at her instead of concentrating on her words and everything else about her, instead of drinking in the sight of her beauty, watching expressions cross her face.

Her fingers trailed across his face from temple to chin, ear to jaw. For a moment she framed his face, kissed him lightly again, though when he opened his mouth, to his disappointment, she didn't accept his invitation to deepen the kiss.

"Pretty Draeg," she said.

That had him rearing back. He'd heard that tone before, those words before. She called each and every one of her animals "pretty."

"I'm not," he growled, and had to squeeze his eyelids shut so he wouldn't glare at her.

"Draeg, you are the most gorgeous man I've ever seen."

"You haven't seen that many. Especially men who aren't related to you and don't look like your Family."

"You have a fabulous body."

He gave that a small thought. "I train, uh, exercise. Stay fit."

A tiny, ladylike snort. "You're a fighter, admit it. And"—challenge laced her tones—"let's stop the pretense that you're a lower-class Commoner—"

His heart thudded hard. How much did she guess? Had that damned FamCat revealed his true identity to Lori?

But she continued to speak and he nearly missed her next words. "I know you have good Flair and can teleport, which, again, makes you at least middle class."

"I wanted to work on a FirstFamily estate with horses," he mumbled, not able to think much past his passion. "And I'll agree to anything if you just stop talking and get on with making love to me . . . with me."

"Yes," she whispered again. "Yes."

He felt her hands on his shoulders, her fingers separating the tabs.

"Shirt off," he ordered, and the thick cloth fell away. The air around him cooled his heated skin.

"Oh, yes," Lori said, her voice uneven with little pants, as unsteady as his own ragged breath. "So very beautiful you are, your body is . . ." She traced the muscles on his chest, touched a scar or two.

"I am not the beautiful one of the two of us," he muttered.

He heard her small gasp. When she spoke her voice sounded high. "You truly think I'm beautiful?"

"Yes. Absolutely." She stepped close until her soft breasts under equally soft cloth pressed against him, her flat stomach against his shaft; her arms went around him in a hug. "Lori." Her name grated out of a dry throat. "I am ready, *past* ready to . . . to seek pleasure with you. You test my control"—his voice cracked at that, something he'd usually be embarrassed about, but now he couldn't care less—"and I want this first time of yours to be good. To be right. Please." He sifted air in and out of his lungs. "Take me."

"Oh!"

Pure desire thrilled through her, her blood, her nerves, like nothing she'd known. Not at all like love or tenderness. This emotion wrenched at her, unexpectedly fierce and fiery. Made her bolder than she'd ever been.

Draeg made her freer than she'd ever been. All her emotions seemed to have expanded, enlarged, until cramming them back into Lori-the-Responsible-and-Unacknowledged seemed impossible.

She'd worry about that later. Difficult to even think when she touched Draeg. Rational thought seemed to evaporate. She released him and stepped back. He rolled forward onto the balls of his feet, then subsided back with such grace, such control of his body, that she stared at him for a moment in pure admiration. Every muscle of his chest and of his abdomen was clearly defined. They looked hard.

She swallowed, unable to take her stare from his chest to look at his face that had tightened, too. Since his lashes remained down she wouldn't be distracted by his blue eyes. She had noticed that his pupils had darkened from blue to nearly black.

"Lori?" Draeg leaned forward. "I didn't frighten you, did I?"

"No." But he'd broken the moment, and her stare slid away from his chest hair and down toward his trous, and the obvious bulge in the front, evidence of his arousal. She'd never seen a human male's penis, erect or otherwise.

"Ah," she gulped. "Aren't your trous too tight?"

"You have no idea," he said. "Um, can I open my eyes now?"

Insecurity zipped through her. "I'm enjoying myself." And she still had her clothes on; he wouldn't think her so beautiful with her clothes off, would he?

He grunted. "Going slow is difficult."

"I thought human mating took more time, perhaps had a little more . . ."

"Tenderness? Affection? Finesse?"

"Ah, yes, I suppose."

"Trying very hard for that, Loridana."

"Lori."

"Lori, my lo—" He stopped; his chest rose as he drew in air, and she saw now that a slight sheen of sweat showed. That made him all the sexier. "I want this to be good for you," he repeated. "Right for you; go ahead with whatever you want to do to me."

Lori thought her mouth dropped open at that offer; several conflicting ideas, along with images, clashed in her mind. As she watched, Draeg backed up to a stall and braced himself against it, his fingers curled into fists. That emphasized his physique, too. Her mouth literally watered; her nostrils widened instinctively to pull his scent of man—aroused man—and spice into her lungs, let it settle into her. But the aroma swirled in her head, causing all sorts of interesting reactions in her body.

Delicately, she stepped toward him, this virile man who gave her the freedom of his body, who stirred her own.

She set her hands on the hard curves of his biceps and discovered a fine tension imbued his entire body. Was that sexual arousal, too? She didn't know. So much to learn, and how lucky she was that a gorgeous man such as this would be her teacher! Enjoying the sensation of supple skin over developed muscle, she trailed her fingers down to his hands, and his fingers locked on hers.

"Lori," he said. "Lo-ri-dan-a." He weighted each syllable of her name with thick emotion she didn't quite understand.

But with that connection, that clasp of fingers intertwined with fingers, for an instant, she felt less the clamoring of her body for sex, and more of the link between them.

His overwhelming need, also ignited the fire of her own until she breathed—panted—with him. Her whole world turned red with lust, with greed for mating. All her instincts flamed and she found herself fighting for control, too, just so she would not throw herself at him.

Bite him.

The thrill turned a little savage and she welcomed the gleeful, wild feeling. Something like this was what her stridebeasts must feel when they mated.

"Lori, I'm begging you."

She put her hands on his shoulders and ordered, "Clothes off!" The seams opened and they fell away from him, even his boots, so they must have been made of quality cloth along with excellent Flair. As well put together as any of the Yew Family tailors and seamstresses could do. Though the spell wouldn't have worked if Draeg hadn't wanted it to.

One glance at his nude body and Lori could sure tell he wanted to be undressed and having sex with her.

She hadn't thought that his penis would be quite that large, or thick, or, ah, rigid. She retreated a step.

"Lori?"

Glancing up, she saw his lashes open, his eyes that brilliant blue again. She took another step back at the intensity of his gaze, his total focus on her.

"Lori?" he asked once more, holding out a hand, one that trembled.

"I just want to see all of you," she whispered. "All the hard muscles and lines that aren't . . . aren't like mine."

And all those muscles became harder before her eyes; arms and thighs looked as if perspiration gilded them as well as his chest. "No, Draeg, you are not beautiful," she mumbled, staring at the part of him that would forge into her body, her own sex dampening and her thighs clenching. Yes, her body prepared herself for him, her breasts swelling as did her tissues below. "You are magnificent."

His other hand joined the first in supplication. "Lori." His jaw clenched, and then he closed his eyes again, and when he spoke he whispered, "Touch me."

"Your, um, your penis?" she asked doubtfully, though her core heated and the blood throbbed to a hard beat through her veins; her skin seemed sensitive to the very motes of air in the stable.

A crack of laughter ripped from him. "My cock, Lori."

"Oh." She supposed an earthy man like him would prefer a word like that. She sidled back to his thrusting . . . cock and curled her fingers around it. He shuddered; his hands lifted higher, then dropped with a smack to her own shoulders and the shoulder tabs of her shirt.

"Lord and Lady. So good. So very, very good." His voice sounded deeper and more guttural than she'd heard from him before. Once again her breathing became unsteady, then matched his.

Shuddering, he put his own hand around hers that curved around his penis-cock. The contrast of ultrasoft skin under the palm of her hand and his callused fingers enveloping the back of her hand, two textures of the same man, sent lightning down her nerves. She intended to take this *man* who had aspects she hadn't discovered into her body.

Have him change, with her, her life from isolated girl to a true woman with a lover. For a few instants she quailed at the thought, and then Draeg pulled her hand away from his sex and swung her up into his arms.

Roaring filled her, her ears, her mind, and she realized it came from the link between them, from Draeg.

Twenty-one

A moment later she was in the sun-bright bedroom of the apartment over the stables, plunked on her feet. Draeg had teleported them. He tapped her shoulder, growling, "Clothes off!" And Lori stood naked before him, all the freckles on her body so very pronounced, brown spots on milk-pale skin.

Another grunt and he lifted her and tossed her onto the bed-sponge and she felt the softness of well-worn fabric beneath her. The next second she had hard male atop her and his erect penis between her thighs, pressing at the entrance of her body.

She gasped and he jerked against her; the blue eyes that had been blurry focused in on her. He grimaced, and she understood that it was supposed to be a smile.

"Sorry, little control. Lori, you unman me."

"That is obviously not true," she said, surprised she could say anything at all in this intimate situation.

His laugh sounded gruff. "In my circles, a man is measured by his control. How he controls his body, his emotions, his circum-stances."

Her body was becoming rapidly accustomed to having a man's skin against her own, his hair rubbing against her, especially how her nipples felt so good and her dampening core really ready for him, for a man, for a male. For penetration. She shivered herself and said, "You are managing this situation very well."

"You think so?" His whisper was raw.

"Yes."

"I think," he panted, "I can go a little slower." He lifted up and the head of his cock moved into her. Then he stopped. She felt stretched and yet the great *need* intensified.

He looked at her breasts. "Pretty, Lori. Such pale pink nipples. Pretty color."

"Thank you." Now that he'd gotten her tucked under him where she couldn't escape unless she wanted to teleport them both somewhere naked, he seemed slightly easier. He probably did feel more in control. But looking at him with her own narrowed gaze, she thought he used some meditation techniques, measured breathing, a small distancing of the mind from the body.

And she thought she knew how to break those—break that control of his. After all, she'd worked with animals most of her life, had observed her stridebeasts, even helped them with mating—the pairs she'd chosen. If they were anything right now, she and Draeg, they were male and female, mating.

So she herself drew in a long, smooth breath, considered his cock with regard to the depths of her body she wanted him in . . . Augmenting her physical strength with Flair, she lifted her hips, aimed herself at him, and slid onto him, savoring the shock in his eyes and how his gaze went foggy again.

"Neither of us holds back," she said. "We're both in this together."

He blinked and she thought she saw a touch of sadness and something else, but then he nodded shortly and said, "Slow or quick?"

"Slow."

"You got it."

A chuckle bubbled from her throat. "I've got *you*." She tightened her arms around him.

Then he surged fully into her, more stretching, more compression of her inner flesh, and such utterly delicious sensations that all thought evaporated and she let her body arch and writhe and *move* for maximum pleasure.

Stroke after stroke, they rose and fell together and her moans and whimpers matched his groans and a curse or two and his *cock* plunged into her sheath, and great and fabulous tension coiled, wound tight throughout her, almost, almost, and *there!*

Deep and shocking, the transcendent pleasure of orgasm struck her, shattered her, spinning fragments of her away into the world and space.

"Lori! Mine!" Draeg yelled, and grabbed her tight. He shuddered and his seed spurted inside her.

Even coalescing from her explosive, glorious experience, she'd heard the word, didn't want to confront him with it, though it alarmed her a little, didn't want to deal with any sort of conversation about . . . claiming. Just a male's possessiveness of a female with whom he'd had sex, she assured herself.

He collapsed on her and she had to use some of her Flair to inflate her lungs under the weight of him so she could breathe.

Large tenderness filled her, as much as the man, *for* the man. She couldn't imagine how her first experience with sex could have been better. So gorgeous, the man and the event! Cherish this particular man.

Lady bless her, Draeg smelled good. Sweat and the essence of himself, a male animal. Just as Lori herself was a female animal, though she'd never felt so much so until this moment. The Family and, of course, the Residence, didn't place much value on physicality.

"Thank you," she murmured.

Draeg grunted; as she smiled and began to laugh, he rolled with her until she lay atop him, a feat since the bedsponge was meant for one person. And now that she thought of it, her bedsponge was the same size. Neither would let them sleep comfortably together on it.

Did she want to sleep with Draeg? As opposed to simply have sex with him?

A resounding yes sounded within her, from her heart or her gut she didn't know, but the instinctive feeling informed her mind that she very much wanted more than sex from Draeg. And he was leaning on his elbow, scanning her face with that intense gaze of his. He touched her lips. "What are you smiling about?"

"I like you."

His chest sank with a little whoosh and he smiled back at her. "I like you, too."

Should she reveal where her thoughts trailed in and out with regard to that? Why not? Continue on as she'd always been, open with him. Reaching up, she stroked his face, noting the change of sensation from his cheek above his beard to the roughness of sprouting hair. "I was thinking how wonderful this has been."

He winced and trapped her hand. "I tried, but I didn't do so well. I definitely lost control several times during the process."

"Only after I lost control, which doesn't matter. Does it? At least during sex?"

"I didn't want to hurt you."

"And you didn't," she said, though she was becoming aware of some aches and strains and a certain rawness here and there. "You gave me . . . shared with me, a glorious experience." She grinned, her mouth curving more than it had, perhaps, ever.

"That's good, then."

She bobbed her head. "Very good." She continued her line of thought. "It would have *not* been a good or acceptable experience with anyone else but you."

He looked surprised and grinned himself. "Ha!"

"Like having sex with anyone the Family would have approved as a lover for me"—now her mouth pulled down—"say, anyone Zus or Vi might consider appealing."

She was yanked against him, her legs tangling with his, her breasts squashed against the slab of his chest, his arm like iron behind her. "No," he said. "Nobody else but me." He paused a few seconds. "For now."

His skin yet smelled good—*her lover's scent*—but her nose

and her whole face was mushed against him. She wiggled a little and his grip loosened enough for her to angle her head and meet his eyes and say completely seriously, "No, no one else for me except you for now."

He inclined his head. "I haven't had any more than occasional lovers for a long, long time. About three years."

She supposed that sounded like a long, long time to him, but it had taken her years to find a lover, while she knew the twins had been sexually active for some time. Or had it taken her so long? The moment she'd *seen* Draeg—

He pulled away, his arm, his body, putting wide centimeters between them. "I know you haven't had any choice of men," he said roughly, his face drawn into a scowl.

"I chose you."

He shifted as if uncomfortable. "How many men of your own age did you even see before me?"

"The Family is relatively diverse—"

"Relatively diverse. Ha, ha." He didn't sound amused.

With dignity, she replied, "I am the last of the direct line of the Yews, at least from my MotherSire, though he had a younger brother from whom Cuspid and the twins are descended. The other strains of the Yews are even less closely related to me, and there are a few boys my age. As I said before, I like you. Better than any of those boys, who didn't know or care to understand what I did in the Residence, my situation here, how I was trained, being trained." Yes, she liked him better than any of her relatives at all.

"What of you?" she asked, a little daring. "And your Family?" She understood from their previous conversations that he valued Family.

"My parents were HeartMates, and they went together when sickness struck them. My father failed first, but my mother didn't care to live without him, so they died within minutes of each other. HeartMates often do." Just from the way he slipped the words into the quiet told her that he'd loved them.

She nodded. She'd heard that but had no personal knowledge

of HeartMates. She reached up and stroked his face. This was a man, not a boy, not like any of those other boys who were her own age and had stared warily at her as D'Yew over the years. For them she'd been but a formal stranger from the Residence.

She was a person, an individual, to Draeg. And she thought that he'd have seen behind her manner had she put the formal attitude on along with the formal clothes, seen *her*.

With a few movements, Draeg arranged them so she could stare into his blue eyes and talk easily. His arm cradled her head, and she'd put her hand near his torso where she could trace the indentations of muscles when she wanted. She noticed that he appeared to be getting interested in sex again, but she definitely liked that the bond between them had grown, and the emotions flowing back and forth between them spoke of like minds. The more time she spent with him, the better friends they were becoming, and she couldn't think of anything more important than a true and open lover who was a good friend.

"What I don't understand," Draeg said, "is why all you Yews are isolated from the rest of Druida City. And the FirstFamilies, too."

Lori tensed a little. "My mother made the decision before I was born. It had something to do with the death of her father, my MotherSire, who was T'Yew at the time. I haven't been told all the details." Rather, she'd been told several different versions of the story, all changing in details, and she hadn't been able to deduce the truth. In the vizes he'd left, her father hadn't said anything about that particular matter.

"You keep everyone cooped up here?"

She shrugged. "Most of the Family enjoy living here rather self-sufficiently. We have had people who became restless and left, six, I believe. Those of the Yews who have left have been disinherited. They aren't ever allowed back. Our business is our business and we want no interference from outside. We need no bad influences."

He shook his head. "I don't understand it. There's a wide, wide world out there, just beyond this estate. Starting with Druida City. No wonder you sneak out every night."

Her stomach tightened a bit. Should she tell him what she intended to do? That they were alike on this, too, that she wanted to see much, much more of the world and would not be staying here and that, like other Yews who left, she'd be disinherited.

No, not yet, she didn't trust him yet, but she might come to that. A quick dizzying vision flickered into her mind, then gone: Draeg accompanying her to her new home.

That notion was far too scary. She could barely believe she would trust him *that* much.

Her calendar sphere dinged and appeared, flashing a notice of her quarterly appointment with the head fisherman in fifteen minutes. The river fishers were a small but important part of the Family. "I must go."

He caught her hand as she rose from the bed to her feet, and, yes, her legs wobbled. "You'll be back this afternoon at your regular time to work with the horses?"

She smiled at him, squeezed her fingers, and then shifted from foot to foot. "I'll be here, of course—"

"Not only just because of the animals. Because you want to spend time with me, too."

"Yes. I do. But perhaps not to ride. I have some unusual aches and pains."

He grinned, narrowed his eyes. "Your leg looks good." His brows went up and down. "Great legs." Then his amusement faded. "Where do you go? Will your Residence and or your Family question you?" His mouth firmed into a straight line. "Will you have to be careful? Your Family won't like that you've taken a lover, especially someone like me."

Her own expression hardened. "I will have to hide this from them." She tossed her head. "It's *my* secret." Lady and Lord knew that Vi, Zus, Folia, Cuspid, and even the Residence probably kept secrets from her. The twins and their excursions to their new friends, for instance, and those new outside-the-Family friends.

He sat up, then stood, all economy of effort and masculine grace. "What of tonight, Loridana?"

"What do you mean?"

"Will we be together tonight?"

"For more sex?" She rolled her shoulders, which felt a little tight, and smiled. "I don't think I could give up such pleasure with you."

He heaved a dramatic sigh. "Good, because I want to get my hands, and all the rest of my body, on you again."

She smiled. "You can be my teacher in this as well as showing me how to train the horses."

That thought seemed to strike him. "Oh, yeah!" He rubbed his hands. "Can do. We will explore what we have together."

Serious now, she held up her index finger. "Two things. I will not slight my animals in having sex with you instead of caring for them. We must find other times to be together."

"Agreed."

She sighed. "I'd planned on cutting back on my nightly excursions in Druida City anyway, as they seem to be more draining than, ah, profitable."

"I can't think of anything in life better to do than loving throughout the evening. And your second stipulation?"

"The Residence and the Family believe I am refinishing the boathouse, which I did last winter. I've been anticipating the projects they've been giving me and am ahead on them."

"So we will meet in the boathouse? Or is there some other project you want me to help you with?"

"I believe I'll finally get permission to refurbish the north side of the stables."

"Great! Glad to help with that."

She nodded. "I do want to keep our affair secret from my Family; that is easier all around, and they won't interfere if we do so."

"You mean the maître de maison won't fire me."

"Or the twins won't torment you."

He jerked his chin. "Let them try."

He might be a match for the twins, and that might be another reason he attracted her so. "But the Residence will expect me to sleep in my own bed every night."

Stepping up to her, he put his arms around her in a simple hug. "Much as I'd enjoy the contentment of sleeping with you all night long, I understand that it can't be so. We will explore other satisfactory pleasures, I promise you."

"All right." One last scent of him, and she pulled away. As it was, she'd have to do a Whirlwind Spell to cleanse and dress for her meeting. "Later."

He lifted her hand to his lips and kissed her fingers, a gesture that unfurled warmth and tenderness within her. "Later, my lady, my lover."

Twenty-two

*A*s soon as *Lori teleported away, Draeg collapsed on his bed, the* cheerful optimism he'd had with her, when all he thought was of the moment and loving her, drained from him. Guilt bit hard and gnawed. At one point, he'd started to tell her the truth, but he knew everything about her would close up and shut down if he revealed his lies, the pretense of his life here.

She might even throw him out of her life, be hurt enough to tell her Family about his mission.

He couldn't take that chance.

But, no, that last wasn't the real reason he said nothing.

He simply couldn't bear the thought of hurting her. Somehow, when they knew each other better, he'd be able to ease her into the truth of what was going on—his gut told him that at least one Yew was involved in this whole mess, but who?

With that thought he checked on the hook he had in Zus. The man—the *boy*—sauntered in the direction of the stables. Draeg couldn't tell if the guy's twin, Vi, was with him, but he should figure she was. From the images he'd picked up from the stride-beasts' minds, and those from the more knowledgeable Baccat, the twins stayed together.

And he had to look as if he had been working for the last sept-hour instead of making love to the daughter of the house. Reaching out with his Flair, he opened the gate to the paddock so all the animals could roam free. Yesterday neither the twins nor the beasts had been happy to see each other, and there might be enough milling confusion to cover his lack of work and his absence for a few minutes. He could trust the horses to stay close to the stables, where they felt safe. The stridebeasts would probably stay in the area, too, but if a couple took off, he had bonds enough with them all to find them.

Racing to the tiny waterfall, he washed, used a drying spell, then pulled his well-Flaired clothes around him.

"Hello, the stables," called a female voice, Vi.

Draeg swore, then teleported to the tack room, picked up a piece of harness that needed mending, and strode out the open door.

Both twins were in the U-shaped courtyard of the stables; Draeg glanced at the corral to his right and saw it empty but sensed all the animals close and providing the distraction that he'd hoped.

Zus, the male, appeared bored, but his sharp gaze took in the nearly derelict west stable block, the run-down north stables that looked worse on the outside than inside since he'd been doing some work on those, and the shabby but sturdy east block.

Vi smiled at him. "Greetyou . . ." But she hadn't wanted to be introduced yesterday and apparently she hadn't asked her father, Cuspid, Draeg's name, so she couldn't use it. Instead she revved up her all-lips-no-eyes smile that left Draeg cold. "Greetyou, stableman. Is Loridana Itha here?" she asked.

Draeg donned his most dull expression. She must really think he was stupid. Even here and now, if he tried, he could determine exactly where every one of his siblings and cuzes were through his links with them. He stared into her eyes, a different shade of green not as pretty as Lori's. Yes, Vi thought he was stupid and Commoner and poorly Flaired. He got the feeling that just one of those attributes would have made him beneath her notice, and all three made him only of interest if she had a use for him.

"FirstFamily GrandLady D'Yew?" he asked.

A cloud passed over her expression and Zus aimed that sharp gaze in Draeg's direction, gave him another once-over and dismissal.

"Yes, FirstFamily GrandLady D'Yew, Loridana Itha Yew," Vi said. "Always the first thing she checks on, her animals."

Draeg retreated to the tack room and, still in full sight of the twins, glanced down the east stable block. "Not here." He meandered to where he could see the corral and the animals, all keeping that structure between them and the twins. "Don't see her here. I guess not. We're working with the horses later at our regular time," he said. "Do you need her?"

"No, no," Vi said. "We haven't seen her this morning and wanted to make sure she was well after that accident last night."

Blinking slowly, Draeg said, "She broke her leg."

"We know that!"

For a moment he wondered if he handled this correctly, being a slow stup. Would he learn more from these two if he adopted a servile, willing-to-please manner? Or should he be confrontational? He didn't know enough about them, nor enough about the Family in general, to gauge those options.

Right now his gut feeling said that they wouldn't treat him any better if he bowed and scraped to them the way he thought they preferred folk to do. They'd take that for granted and wouldn't tell him anything. If they were involved in the "accidents," he didn't see them doing anything themselves; they'd already have somewhat trusted sycophants for that.

He stared at them. "You're FirstFamily GrandLady D'Yew's cuzes."

"That's right."

Furrowing his forehead, he said, "But you haven't seen her today, like at breakfast and lunch?"

"No," Zus nearly snarled. "She took her meals in the House-Heart."

Draeg looked toward the unseen Residence. "HouseHeart, huh. Thought you gotta Healer for her, big important Family like yours."

Zus snorted. "We did our best for her."

Sounded like a lie to Draeg, one that Zus didn't care if Draeg heard as a lie.

Accompanied by his twin, Zus stalked out of the courtyard and around the southern end of the stables toward the paddock. Draeg followed slowly and touched the bond, still strong and steady, between himself and Loridana, sensed her usual serenity and that her meeting was ending. In a quick burst, he sent mentally, *Your cuzes are looking for you.*

Irritation flowed back from her. *They're at the stables?*

Right.

In his mind she snorted, a lot like her cuz had done. Her tone dismissive, she said, *They probably want to see for themselves how Healed my leg is. Perhaps check out my energy and Flair levels. Watch out for the animals.*

Of course, Lori. He lilted her name with affection, felt the return of that emotion to him.

Draeg. His own name came from Lori on a wash of tenderness. Then a quick pinching of their bond, a sigh. *The Residence summons me.*

Later, he whispered back, but didn't know if she heard him. He'd caught up with the twins and observed Zus staring at the animals.

Only four stridebeasts stood on the far side of the corral. The animals watched the humans and drifted farther toward the back of the stables.

"Only four; where are the other two?" Zus asked.

And Draeg realized that in addition to checking out Loridana, and maybe him, these two continued to want a blackmail hammer against Lori.

"Around," Draeg replied, gesturing vaguely. "Do you wanna ride? I can get ya saddles and pressure halters for two. Which ones ya want?" He didn't think the pair knew the animals' names.

"Ride?" Vi's laugh was brittle. "No."

But the twins now circled the corral and all but the two largest male stridebeasts galloped away. Those two watched the humans just as intently as the twins stared at them.

"Be careful a'them, they spit and bite," Draeg said, then cursed himself for revealing that. Who knew what Flair the twins had, whether one or both could send a killing blow to the animals instead of trying to take them physically.

Zus stopped, slanted Draeg a look. "Is that so?"

"Yup. GrandLady D'Yew's been a little spooked 'bout their health lately an' asked that I remind them'a their natural defenses. They's smart beasts, they can unnerstand mind images real well if ya go slow and think hard at them."

"Really?" Vi dragged the word out in a sarcastic way.

"Yup." Draeg rocked back and forth on his heels. "So Grand-Lady D'Yew and I have been a-workin' with the beasts, and the horses, too."

"I don't see the horses," Zus said. "Are they well?"

"Yup, a little shy, though. We're keeping them in a pen on the opposite side of the stables away from the stridebeasts." He could lie, too.

"And you're caring for those animals well, too? Talking to them in mental images?" Zus continued.

"Yup, though they ain't used ta humans and are shy around us, too." Draeg didn't think these two had observed either Lori or him riding the horses, and riding them well. "The horses are a little nervy so they's already on alert like when folk come around." He looked at them, showing his doubt. "I s'pose I could get you two on the back of them and walk you around the paddock."

"Not necessary today," Vi said.

"Good." Draeg nodded. "The horses need to settle more. We— GrandLady D'Yew and me—are protective of them. No offense."

Zus showed his teeth in a fake smile. "None taken."

"Not to mention the Sallows," Draeg said casually, but keeping a narrowed glance on the twins, noted their expressions hardened so they resembled each other even more closely.

"What about the Sallows?" asked Zus.

Draeg wished he'd had a soft hat he could have taken off and crumpled nervously in his hands. A hat would have been an excellent prop for this little acting exercise. Instead he ducked his head and looked up from under his brows at the young man. Younger than he in years as well as experience, and too arrogant to realize that even a lower-class man Draeg's age could be wiser than he. Draeg couldn't actually bring himself to shift from foot to foot, be even a little off balance in front of these two.

"Well, ya know. Caprea Sallow, he tol' me that these horses I be lookin' after, well, you folk ain't had none for a long time and they—the horses—is only here on, like, loan until you Yews show that you take care of them good."

"What!" Zus's pale face flushed. "The gall of the man. His Family is barely a secondary GrandHouse."

Gritting his teeth, Draeg did it, shifted from foot to foot, twice. "Well, I'm s'posed to tell him if anything goes wrong with the horses." Then he set his balance and rushed into speech. "But everythin's goin' really, really good. You don' have to think about no, no repercussions like from the Sallows."

"And just exactly what do the Sallows think they could do to us?" Vi hissed.

Draeg glanced aside, then back to meet Vi's haughty gaze. "Them Sallows," Draeg shook his head. "They take the well-bein' of animals right seriously. I wouldn't put it past them ta come right onto your land here and take them horses if they ain't been treated right."

The spring air around them shimmered with danger. Threat from people unused to being thwarted. Anger—no, fury—seethed through the twins standing before him.

And a moment of pure clarity enveloped Draeg. He could see how this whole situation could escalate to FirstFamily against FirstFamily, dragging Druida City back into terrible feuding and duels. Worse than the Holly-Hawthorn feud decades ago. At least the then-T'Hawthorn had come to his senses. He couldn't see much other than pride and hubris standing before him. But there were others who would be making such a decision to cry war and call up their allies.

"As a Family, we will never let outsiders dictate to us again," Vi stated with complete implacability.

So Draeg had to be very careful from now on, more than he had been, and he had to get Loridana on the side of reason. Somehow.

Right now he shrugged. "Well, everyone here and them Sallows know that them horses are here for a probationary period. I'm sure all you'd have ta do is give them Sallows the horses. Not like they're in bad shape or nothin'," he said in a soothing tone. He hoped he wasn't dooming the stridebeasts. He'd have to be careful to keep a wary eye out for their well-being, too. And he and Lori had thought the dangers to the stridebeasts were over. He wasn't looking forward to telling her of this conversation.

"Loridana has had the stridebeasts longer," Vi murmured. "She must love them more."

Just as if the length of time were an aspect of love. Draeg set his teeth. He was tired of the twins; definitely time to send them on their way. He scratched his head. "Really not sure why you are here if it ain't to ride, and since FirstFamily GrandLady D'Yew ain't here."

That drew their attention off the animals—who took the opportunity to run away—and focused the twins' malice back on Draeg. He chilled from the sensation but stood his ground in the long flat silence.

Then he widened his eyes and gave them a grin. "Oh, I got it! I know what yer here for! You're here to apologize for that there Residence a-bein' rude to me."

He let his smile fade under their disbelieving and icy glares.

"No?"

"No."

Hands open and out, Draeg shrugged his hunched shoulders. "Whatcha here for, then? I got work ta be doin'." He frowned. "And now I gotta beat the woody areas for them beasts."

"Do not speak to us in that tone," Vi snapped.

"Do not question *us* or our actions," Zus added.

"We will not stand for that," they said in unison, then teleported away. Draeg followed the line of the hook he had in the twins' auras to the Residence.

He whistled but none of the animals came running back toward him.

Expanding his senses and Flair, he knew that Lori was in the Residence, but not with the twins. And no one of the Family, neither those who lived in the Residence nor those in cottages on the rest of the estate, watched him. So he used Flair to gather the stridebeast and horse droppings into a bin that would be translocated to the farm—not, of course, by either Zus or Vi. He sped a quick Whirlwind dusting spell through the stables, tack room, and over the packed gravel courtyard, tidying them all.

Corax cawed and glided down to perch on Draeg's shoulder. *I saw and heard. But I did not come to you. I don't like those pale people.*

"You're not alone," Draeg muttered. "And I felt you near." Now that he thought of it, he knew that his Fam had roosted on the ridgepole of the stable roof. With the back of his hand, Draeg stroked his bird's feathers. "I felt your support." Subtle, but it had been there. "Thank you."

Corax tugged on Draeg's shirt collar, and he realized it had been crooked under his tunic. He smiled. Another signal to the twins that he was what he seemed. "I would rather you stay safe and away from any danger." And he knew to his bones the male and female were dangerous. Anyone who had such an ego that it couldn't be flouted, such a self-image that couldn't take even a sliver of tarnish, would do a great deal to preserve that ego and image.

I support you, FamMan, said Corax. *And I will stay safe. I am not stupid.*

"No," Draeg said aloud.

I am not stupid, either. Baccat swaggered close to Draeg as they entered the stableyard. *Draeg Betony-Blackthorn, who has mated with My FamWoman. You had better be good to her or you will suffer My wrath.*

The word *mated* caused a little ruction in Draeg's gut, but he said mildly. "So far, cat, I think that I have treated her better than you."

That is because you do not know Me, or what is between Lori and Me. You did not even perceive that she thinks of herself as Lori and not Loridana. There is much for you to learn about Us, if you manage to stay with Us long enough. The cat made the sound of that circumstance extremely doubtful. *I will wait here until Lori arrives to school the horses.* Baccat found a spot in the sun in the center of the courtyard entry where he'd be in the way of any coming or going and settled in to wash.

It took no more than a minute or two to discover the animals. The horses had retreated to the stables and a couple of open stalls. To Draeg's surprise, he found all the stridebeasts huddled by the northeast gate that Lori and Baccat used to exit the estate. They'd broken bushes and bracken, forcing a larger path. He walked them back to the main way one by one, paused, then disguised the path, and led the animals back to the stables.

After that he actually mended the piece of harness he'd dropped sometime during his discussion with the twins, and frowned that he hadn't noticed when that had happened.

He couldn't afford to be the least bit sloppy any more.

Twenty-three

*A*t the boathouse, *Lori* had the worst time concentrating on her duties. By ruthlessly focusing on the fisherman himself, how he looked sturdier than the Yews who lived in the Residence, on *his* responsibilities and needs, she kept away any imaginings of Draeg and the intimacy they'd shared. In the end, she'd approved more gilt to be disbursed from the household funds to the man than he'd asked. A slightly reckless move, but *she* felt happy and optimistic and knew in her blood and bones and core that her beckoning future would be wonderful. She wanted him to feel some of that optimism, too. He left the boathouse with a spring in his step.

And, of course, she could and did justify the additional funds when reporting to the Residence. That slight altercation that she won also satisfied her.

For a moment, she hesitated, pondered. She'd thought of contacting the farmers, the fishers, other relatives here on the estate and telling them of her abuse. But they'd think her a whining teenager, a weak adult. And she didn't see them going against the house folk who'd run the estate for so many years, when it had prospered. They wouldn't confront the Residence itself.

After she met with the Residence, Cuspid insisted on examining her leg and testing her general energy and Flair. The former had Healed well due to the ministrations of the HouseHeart, but the maître de maison clucked over the weakness in the latter. Mostly because in the few minutes after she'd been notified of the exam and before meeting with Cuspid in the Healing chamber, Lori had used some inner reserve to ease the hurts from her first bout of sex. She hadn't been sure Cuspid, not a Healer, would notice those, but she couldn't take the chance.

Then it was time to see Draeg again, and despite her own words, she found it difficult *not* to short her animals the attention they deserved when she wanted to stay in her lover's company, even if he was only a paddock away.

She noticed the animals seemed a little skittish and, since she overbrimmed with love and affection, had no problems soothing them with an excess of emotion. And in the giving, she also received love and affection and Flair from her animals.

Draeg and she rode a pair of stridebeasts that needed a bit of special treatment, and Baccat insisted on being in a carrier basket behind her saddle. Corax flew along with them.

Draeg set a pace of a walk and headed toward the north wall of the estate. "I thought we could go through your main eastern gate and ride along the shared greenway."

Lori tensed, all of her good cheer vanishing in an instant. "That's against the rules."

Baccat hissed. *Do you WANT us to be eviscerated, stable-man? We should not be taunting the Powers of the Family and the Residence at this time. Especially with regard to that visit by the twins earlier.* Her Fam turned his head to stare at her with glinting eyes, whiskers quivering. *You must know they threatened ME.*

"You weren't even here," Draeg said.

Just because you did not observe me does not mean that I was not present. Baccat sniffed. *I will admit you gave an excellent performance as a dimwitted guard, and that subtle threat of the Sallows, quite masterful.* Baccat lifted his nose.

"Threat?" Lori squeaked. Anxiety, even fear swirled within her, her palms sweating on the reins.

Draeg glanced at her sharply. "Why are you so concerned?"

"I don't want to irritate the twins at this time." Not when her trip was upcoming, not when she might have to run when the weather remained too cold. Not when she'd discovered the pleasure of a lover.

Stopping, Draeg reached out and took her hand. "Lori, you must begin to fight for your rights."

"You think I haven't been doing that?" she spit out, his words flicking her on the open wound. "I've been doing that since I finished my Second Passage last year. There is a balance in managing Family politics, Draeg Hedgenettle, or don't you know that?"

Baccat snorted. *You know nothing of what you speak, you who have only been here two and a half eightdays! Perhaps you are more dimwitted than I believed. Action isn't always the solution to thorny problems.*

Not looking at the cat, the man shrugged before answering Lori's question. "Give and take, compromise."

She heard the ugliness in her own laugh. "Those are concepts that the Residence, who has lived two and a half centuries; my elders, who raised and trained me to be D'Yew with all those responsibilities; and my cuzes, who are spoilt, do not recognize." Too long, her words flowed too long, were too fussy to impact him. He preferred simple, effective sentences. A tinge of despair wound around her thoughts, but everyone from the Residence to Baccat spoke and *thought* more formally than Draeg. Perhaps another reason why she was attracted to him.

On their private mental channel, Baccat said, *He has much to recommend him, which is why I have not sent him away already, but I know his type. He is stubborn.*

With fast blinking, she rid herself of incipient tears and looked at Draeg, who frowned in confusion. Dear, he was so dear already.

And could upset her equilibrium, cause her to upset the fragile dance she did with her Family. After a long inhalation, she addressed both Draeg and Baccat. "The twins issued threats." No wonder the animals had been upset.

"I got the idea that they haven't given up the idea of using your animals as a hammer to blackmail you into doing what they want."

She gave him a short nod. "I should have considered that, but in the last negotiation I had with them yesterday, I lost and they won. That their victory didn't satisfy them for even a day isn't a good sign."

"What do they want?" he asked.

She raised her brows. "Gilt, money, fortune." And they would not be pleased that she'd talked the Residence into giving more gilt to the fishers instead of the farm.

More power than they have now, Baccat added.

As she straightened in her saddle, she withdrew her hand from Draeg's. "Please, Draeg, let me handle my Family in my own way." She heard the pleading in her tone, didn't care for it, but her other option would have been to pull a haughty manner around her, and she could guess that that particular pathway would have strained their budding relationship. And she did want a relationship with this man.

His jaw flexed. "It irritates me that you are not given your due. That your cuzes don't respect you."

And how much do you respect her, Draeg Hedgenettle? Baccat stared at him. *Enough to put her wishes above yours? Her experience above yours?*

"Yes," Draeg answered the cat.

She sighed with weariness, made an abortive gesture. "I am accustomed to little respect from my Family. They still consider me a child, especially the Residence."

"Maybe we can discuss this later, draft a plan. A plan of simple, incremental steps for you to come into your own."

Baccat snorted again, turned around in the basket so he didn't face out and toward Draeg but looked over the withers of the stridebeast. Her Fam said privately, *This man of action doesn't know what we've done. Thinks Us dilatory in solving Our problems. I am weary of speaking with him.*

Lori had tried to implement small changes all last summer, most of the autumn, and had given up when she realized it could take *years* to become D'Yew in truth as well as in name. Years of patience she found herself desperately short on.

So she'd made new plans, refined them with Baccat's input. Now she had good plans in place to deal with the whole matter. Not the way Draeg might, but she knew the Residence and her Family better than he. And now that she calmed, she felt the flowing concern from him. Meeting his dark blue eyes, she said, "Will you let me deal with this in my own way?"

He raised his own brows and said gruffly, "You seem to be giving me some power here."

"You do have power. We're lovers; of course you can influence me."

His gaze warmed. "All right. I get that you walk a line—"

"Yes."

"And, it seems, going outside to ride stridebeasts on the common greenway would upset that balance."

She nodded. "For no good reason. I must choose the battles I fight."

"I don't like this whole situation. But the cat is right. I've been here two and a half eightdays and you've lived here your whole life. You know the players better than I."

Finally a valid assessment, Baccat said, still not looking at Draeg. *I suggest we continue with our ride. The reassuring of the less sentient species took some time.*

Lori kneed her stridebeast to begin moving again. "I do need additional information from you."

"Yes?" Draeg asked as he urged more speed from his mount and Lori's picked up pace, too.

"What's this threat of the Sallows?"

The twins wished to see how healthy the horses were, Baccat said. *Not good.*

Draeg reminded the twins that the Sallows have only given us the horses for a probationary period of a month.

Gasping, Lori said, "What? I didn't know that!" Once again her plans seemed to fall into ruins around her.

"They must be well treated for a month before they become the Yews'," Draeg said.

Of COURSE they are well treated NOW, Baccat stated. *Lori has Healed them and welcomed them into Our herd.* Baccat sniffed. *And so I have told Caprea Sallow. I have recorded memory spheres of My interactions with Draeg and Smyrna and Ragan for the Sallows.*

"I didn't know this," Lori said, her mind buzzing with how to fit this into her plans. "The Family, those who bought Ragan and Smyrna for me, agreed to this stipulation?"

Draeg lifted a brow. "So I was informed by the Sallows."

Yes, said Baccat. *But your Family knows you, Lori. They knew that you would care for your animals well.* He dipped under the lip of the basket as he rearranged himself. *But, of course, they may have prevaricated. An actual contract was not executed.*

"Oh." She glanced over at Draeg and spoke to him mentally, since the stridebeasts were running down a wide bridle path. *Have you reported to the Sallows?*

He answered her telepathically, *Not yet. If you wish me to, I certainly will. The horses' health is significantly improved since arriving here—*

You helped with that, she said, giving credit where it was due.

You gave them love that sped up their Healing, and they return that love.

She let out a relieved breath.

They are well settled here, Draeg added, and that didn't ease her dilemma. *And so I will tell Caprea Sallow, and all will be well. You do not have to worry about the Sallows.*

The salient point of this conversation, and the confrontation with the twins, Baccat said, *is that neither Zus nor Vi knew of this particular condition, either.* She sensed that he kneaded the bottom of the basket as he thought.

A half minute later, he said, *It is my considered opinion that the twins will not move against the horses at this time. Nor will they try to intimidate or buy off Draeg.* They will have checked with *Cuspid and Folia and the Residence by now and confirmed that the stipulation regarding the horses was, indeed, made. And, in their requesting information of their elders, they will have indicated an interest in the horses that is suspect, especially in light of your confrontation yesterday. They will drop any plan to hurt the horses, and perhaps the stridebeasts also, since it might not bring the results they want.*

Cause them too much trouble. Not be worth the effort, Draeg said. *Not that I would be intimidated or bought off. But I agree with your analysis, cat.*

I am so glad, Baccat replied. His ears twitched in the wind. *I am becoming accustomed to this manner of travel. I like it. Especially when the stridebeasts STRIDE.*

That had Lori smiling.

Her Fam glanced at her, then at Draeg, then finished his assertion. *And it may be that the twins studied the stables for unknown reasons, or to evaluate the stableman and his character, or, in fact, simply to scare and irritate you, Loridana.*

To mess with Lori's head, INTIMIDATE her.

Manipulate me, Lori added. *That may be true.* They turned at the end of the path near the north wall and cantered back toward the stables.

I have listened. A more staccato mental voice sounded in Lori's head, along with sense of rustling that she comprehended to be wind in feathers, Corax's voice. *I can guard.*

At what price? Baccat shot back.

For shiny stuff, like this.

Flying overhead, it dropped an object into the path.

What is that? demanded Baccat. *Halt, stridebeast!*

Lori signaled her mount to a walk and circled back to the fallen item.

It is a piece of trash I found on the streets of Druida City. But it has shiny bits on it.

Baccat scratched a hole in his basket, getting out, then leapt down and trotted over to sniff what looked like a thin piece of leather with a buckle on the end. *It is a collar! MINE!*

The bird swooped, but Baccat didn't flinch. Lori wondered if his personal armor made him less cautious and more foolhardy.

Foolish raven, Baccat sneered. *This collar cannot fit you.*

"That's true," Draeg said. "As a collar, it's too big for you, Corax."

Taking it in his teeth, the cat leapt up in front of Lori. The stridebeast's ears twitched, but she didn't move. Baccat grinned around the piece. *Look what fate has sent Us.*

Lori rather thought it had been Corax's scavenging skills that had dropped the collar in their laps.

Looking at her from sly eyes, Baccat dropped the drool-bedewed leather on her thigh. *FATE,* her Fam insisted. *Until I can wear My OTHER collar.*

Corax cawed protest from a nearby branch and flapped his wings. *I FOUND that! It's—*

MINE! Baccat shouted. *Mine, mine, mine, MINE!*

Twenty-four

❦

Six "mines" in all. *Lori knew that meant the cat would not give the* thing up without a fight, and she didn't want to reveal the personal armor yet. She hadn't perfected it. Sighing, she picked up the collar, a leather strip with small diamond-shaped bits of metal fashioned to catch the light. Her fingers tingled. "It is imbued with Flair."

Baccat stretched out his neck. *Because it is solid and if I catch it on some protruding object, the collar will fall away. As it no doubt did for its previous owner. Who obviously did not deserve such a piece.* He sniffed. *I smell low-class Cat, not a Fam.*

Corax screeched. Lori heard a stifled laugh and saw Draeg suppressing his amusement.

"Very well, I will pay Corax for the collar." She had two pouches of silver, one of them nearly flat, for the journey. "And for watching my herd."

It is an old collar, well worn, with tooth marks of a small canine as well as the scent of a different Cat. We should not pay much for it, Baccat launched into bargaining.

It has shiny bits! Corax countered.

After a few more rapid exchanges a price was set, much lower than Lori had anticipated.

Corax landed on Draeg's shoulder and stared at her, head tilted, neck feathers ruffled, with beady eyes. *And you will pay me for watching*, he confirmed.

"Silver slivers," Lori murmured. "I can spare some silver slivers." A couple of months ago, she had given Baccat an old bill to change and he'd come back with new silver slivers. She, too, had been charmed at the gleam of new coinage she'd never seen.

She sent a thought to the RavenFam: *Would you accept a silver sliver for every night you watch?* Not much payment, but what she personally could afford from the small stash of her father's that she'd found.

Yes! enthused the raven. *Deal!*

Good. Thank you, Corax.

You are welcome.

I will translocate some slivers, say enough for a full week, when we get back to the stables.

Draeg's Fam didn't say anything further, but she sensed the warmth of gratitude, and more, burgeoning affection for her, and that touched her. It didn't seem as if the raven had enough shiny stuff in his life, and she would help with that. So little to please that particular Fam.

She leaned over and stroked Cana's neck, sending the female stridebeast love and gratitude for the ride and a resurgence of her happiness. Lori had been blessed that the little physical items she could afford to give were sufficient for those she cherished.

This collar, and My Fam collar when We get to Our new home, is enough for Me, Baccat replied to her thoughts. *You give Us all an abundance of nonmaterial gifts, which We treasure. In the final measure, those are more important than pretty jewels and shiny objects.*

Though you still want your ruby necklace, she said.

Though I still want My ruby necklace, he agreed.

Yes, she began to reassemble her plan to leave.

She did know one thing. She loved the horses, too. She dared not leave them behind at the mercy of the twins and the Family, with or without the threat of the Sallows. She didn't know much but couldn't believe a lesser Noble Family would challenge a First-Family GrandHouse, especially not for a couple of horses. Lori would take them with her. If worse came to worst, once she and the animals were settled in her Valerian estate, she'd invite one of the Sallows to come and check out the animals at her cost.

She glanced at Draeg, believed he'd been following the emotions of her Fam conversations even if he didn't know the exact words, since she and Baccat spoke on a private telepathic channel. He smiled at her and her insides squeezed, her sex from the slight heat in his eyes, her heart and the rest of her from the tenderness in the curve of his lips.

As soon as they'd stopped in the stableyard, Draeg leapt from his stridebeast and offered his arms for her to slide down into. Smiling and placing her hands on his shoulders, she let him lift her down and draw her close to his aroused body. She leaned against him, listening to his steady but rapid heartbeat, feeling the strength and muscularity of his body. The sun broke through the clouds to shine brightly on them and give her this perfect moment.

Ragan whinnied and broke the quiet atmosphere and Lori stepped away from Draeg, turning to the paddock that held the rest of her animals. Both groups, stridebeasts and horses, had merged well with each other and considered themselves part of the same herd.

And that was due to Draeg's efforts as well as her own, and the fact that the stridebeasts were loved and loving and welcoming and the horses had been lonely and abandoned.

A dark shadow crossed her eyes: Corax flying to the ridgepole of the stables and reminding her of their bargain. Closing her eyelids, she visualized the saddlebag and the leather pouch that held her traveling funds. Then she lost the image she needed to translocate the little sack when she realized what she was doing, showing Draeg all her gilt, packed and ready to go. She didn't think she could separate eight silver slivers from the rest—

Baccat snorted in her mind. *Just translocate the pouch.*

Yes? she asked privately, and doubtfully.

Trust Me on this, Loridana Itha. That shabby pouch of gilt you have is less than what a regular mercenary guard keeps on his person, let alone takes south to Gael City, and much less than Draeg has. Her Fam hopped down from his basket and trotted to sit on her feet and look up at her with a cat grin on his face. *I could go up and find HIS pouch in his rooms and see how much he has.*

Absolutely not!

"Is your cat making fun and laughing at me?" Draeg asked. He had the reins of both stridebeasts in his hands and was leading them to their stalls.

"I think you're very good at figuring out what's going on through our link."

Draeg stilled, his expression going impassive, eyes wary. "Is that a problem for you?"

"No, I like our connection," she said immediately, then thought of the drawbacks, of her private plans that began to feel like secrets she was keeping from him.

His smile flashed and he ducked his head in respect. "I think I might have had more practice than you with bonds."

He was probably right; she kept her own Familial bonds as narrow as humanly possible, her personal shields up. So she might not be as observant as he, either, but she couldn't live with open links or revealing the true self—the real woman—she longed to be. Only her animals and Fam had wide bonds with her. With that thought, she held out her hand, visualized the pouch in her saddlebags, and brought it to her. Opening the drawstrings, she pulled out a handful of silver slivers and counted them out on the gravel for Corax.

Draeg didn't even glance at the bag.

I'm sure all your gilt is pocket change for Draeg, Baccat sneered.

Shiny! Pretty! Corax trilled. He came by and walked up and down the line pecking at them, lifting his wings and cackling, appearing supremely pleased. Then, one by one, he took a coin in his beak, flew away to stash it somewhere, and returned.

"Tell me about the twins," Draeg asked. "What are your cuzes' Flair psi powers?"

She frowned. "I don't know."

"They do have Flair?"

"I'm sure." She shook her head. "They went through their Second Passages within a couple of weeks of each other, with Vi first, I think. No doubt hers triggered Zus's, or maybe the other way around." She shrugged. "I wasn't allowed in their rooms because I might disturb them. I haven't really seen either one of them practice their Flair—I mean, use any Flair they have."

"You practice *your* Flair," Draeg commented quietly. "How strong is Zus's and Vi's Flair?"

"I don't know. Substantial, probably, since they are Cuspid's children and he has a good amount."

"Can't you tell when you are in a circle with them?"

She hunched a shoulder in disdain. "They are lazy, always. They only contribute the minimum amount of Flair and energy necessary in any circle."

His eyes fired. "They disrespect you."

"Always."

He opened his mouth, looked away, then shut it and said nothing more.

As a precaution, Draeg and she put the stridebeasts and the horses in the stalls of the east block, more secure than leaving them in the open. Lori checked on the store of Flair needed for a loud alarm that would be heard throughout the estate and began to top it off when Draeg shook his head and did it for her.

Without words but with a flow of images and feelings, she and Draeg and the Fams had organized their evening; Baccat would explore Druida as usual, Draeg and she would make love in the boathouse while Corax kept watch on the stables, later she and Draeg would meditate in the grove, and then they'd retire to their separate beds.

A very simple and homey evening, but she found herself antic-ipating it more than any exotic excursions in the city.

Her calendar sphere popped into the air, chiming to remind

her of dinner, and suddenly the air constricted in her lungs. She shook herself out and began the cycling of gratitude, love, and joy that she felt for her animals and Draeg. With a last blessing, she ended the daily ritual, more at peace.

Until Draeg yanked her into his arms and kissed her. This was a kiss like no other. A kiss as intense as the man. The kiss of a real lover. One that involved his tongue sliding along her mouth, dampening it with his taste, causing her lips to feel fuller. The arm around her back squeezed her close, until his erection pressed against her stomach.

Her mind began to spin, thoughts draining from her, only desire flowing in her veins, lust sizzling along her nerves. His tongue thrust against her teeth and she opened her mouth and discovered a whole new range of sensations as she rubbed her own tongue against his, played with him, dueled with him, then daringly darted her own tongue into this mouth.

Her knees went weak and his arm held her up, held her tight. The taste of him was like nothing she could ever imagine.

Wildness held under a thin layer of control, but deep earth ready for roots, winter herbs, an explosion of tastes that flashed memories or sensations or images that went straight to the core of her and tugged her close to orgasm.

Corax screeched, interspersing his cries with the alarm sounding on her calendar sphere.

Mushy stuff, cawed Corax. *I will go eat, then come back to watch the animals.*

"Ouch, dammit, cat!" Draeg jumped back, leaving Lori wobbling on unsteady feet. Blood welled from his cheek.

Lori must depart NOW or all might be lost! Baccat yowled.

Not enough time for her to cleanse in a waterfall and dress for dinner. She'd have to suffer through another Whirlwind scouring spell and the scolding during dinner at not managing her time.

You have the excuse that everything You did today took longer because of Your injury last night, Baccat snapped. *Now GO!*

Without another word to her lover, she teleported away.

* * *

*D*raeg ran lightly down the steps to the boathouse. Once there, he touched his hooks. Zus was off the estate but in a different part of town than he had been the night before. Wherever he was, he'd teleported there because after Draeg had settled the animals in the stables, he'd checked the garage, where both gliders sat, accounted for.

Zus's twin was with him, but if good and proper Loridana Itha Valerian D'Yew found this place boring and needed excitement in her life, Draeg would bet the whole magnificent T'Blackthorn land and fortune that those twins also considered Yew estate deadly dull. However it didn't appear that *they* were much hampered by the rules that surrounded Lori.

Draeg opened the door to the boathouse and paced, waiting for Lori. He'd done as many drills and exercises as he could to tamp down his lust, moderate his anticipation of seeing his woman again.

The interior of the place appeared half-finished, but he thought that under a cover of dust, the wooden floor would gleam, and if cleansed, the walls would be a lot less rough. A tarp lay over a section of built-in cabinets.

He searched for a bedsponge. Nothing. This would be a party place, a meeting place, a place for picnics and gatherings and embarking onto the boats in the dock a story below. He wondered if any of the boats were river cruisers, maybe as old-fashioned as the gliders. With beds.

Standing in the middle of the room, simmering with sexual frustration, he squeezed his eyes shut, visualized one of the storage rooms in T'Blackthorn Residence, and with a mighty grunt translocated a bedsponge big enough for two, then realized as he panted that sweat covered his body from the effort.

The door opened and Lori walked in.

He pounced.

Twenty-five

Lord and Lady, she felt good in his arms, like no other. All other women's faces, bodies, had vanished from his mind. Only perfect Loridana. Perfect for him.

They were much of a height, but she was so slender, her curves so subtle, that he felt strong and manly, and just simply wide.

But her flexible body showed lean muscles, often used, under soft and smooth skin.

He couldn't wait to get her out of her clothes. Hauling her over to the bedsponge, he dropped her on it, stripped off his shirt that stuck a little to him.

Bouncing a little on the thick bedsponge and laughing, Lori said, "What's this?"

"I got it."

"I can see that. From where?"

He shrugged. "Home."

"It's dusty."

He grunted.

With an exhalation of breath, she raised her arms and said a simple housekeeping spell of a few lines. One he should have thought of, if he'd been capable of thought, but he had all the mind and finesse of a stallion in heat. He thought his cock would pretty much look like a stallion's, too, released from loincloth and trous.

Before she had lowered her arms, he'd whisked off her tunic and thrown it atop his shirt, staring at her small breasts outlined by her breastband. Like the stained work tunic, her breastband was a simple horizontal piece of cloth in white. The kind of underwear a virgin would wear.

And she'd been a virgin before him. Before just this early afternoon.

The idea drove him crazy. He'd been her first lover, and he'd barely touched her. They hadn't had time. Tonight, maybe, they'd have about three septhours. Hardly enough time to explore her the way he wanted.

He had to go slow. He'd thought of that during their first lovemaking, and he'd tried hard to do it, but the whole thing blurred in his mind.

She was here, and looking at him with desire in her eyes, so maybe he hadn't bungled too badly. Her nipples tightened into hard little nubs and he groaned.

"Clothes of—"

"Wait!" Lori said, hopping up from the bedsponge where he'd put her, needed her.

With a sweeping gesture from her, the mattress disappeared. Draeg felt wetness sting his eyes. He thought he growled. Until she took his hand, tugged.

Naturally, he followed, to a small room in the back. There lay the bedsponge, fully covered with linens, a comforter at the bottom, four pillows at the top. Atop a small cabinet was his shirt and her tunic, folded. A spellglobe glowed softly in the corner, adding romance.

The room smelled of Lori, fresh springtime, the promise of summer blooms.

Oh, yeah. Draeg inhaled deeply and his nerves dropped away, his mind cleared from lust. Better grab this moment.

He turned to her, grasped both hands in his own, stared into her wide eyes that showed a hint of that springtime green.

"Lori, Loridana, you honor me by joining with me." First he lifted one hand, then another to his lips. "I have never known anyone as valiant, as caring as you."

She pinkened and the blush flowed from her cheeks to the top of her breastband. "Surely you have," she whispered.

"I don't recall. I don't recall any woman other than you." *Not romantic, dammit!* He reddened. "You eclipse everyone, like . . . like the sun rising at dawn outshines the twinmoons." *Better.*

"I don't think so—"

"Say, 'Thank you, Draeg, for the true compliment.'"

Her expression, her manner, lost the insecurity he'd seen, that being with her Family in the Yew Residence had put in her since he and she had been apart. No, he didn't like the effect her folk had on her. Something to think of *later.*

Not daring to touch her yet, he bent forward, angled his head, and placed a soft kiss on her pink lips. Lips as pale as he recollected her nipples to be. He lingered, tracing her lips with his tongue to get a hint of her taste, as subtle as her scent, as potent.

She opened her mouth, and he didn't thrust his tongue quick and hard into the depths like he wanted. Control, control, control. He slipped his tongue along hers and groaned, opened his eyes to see that she'd closed hers, and he pulled back, rocking back on his heels to put a little distance between them. "A very beautiful woman."

"I don't—" She stopped herself. "Thank you, Draeg."

"A very beautiful woman I want to undress slowly, to see and savor every view of her."

She wetted her lips and the sheen of it nearly did him in. He released her hands and placed his palms on her shoulders, smoothing them down her arms to her wrists, letting himself feel the soft and throbbing bond between them, see the effect of his touch in her eyes, the way her lips curved, the relaxation of her shoulders.

Under his hands, her skin was warm and he understood that she'd heated the full boathouse since he'd come in. The Flair this woman had mastered!

Another turn-on for him, that her power might be more than his own, that she outstripped him in that as he did with her physically.

Power and control and responsibility and caring. Qualities to be prized. Qualities he couldn't live without.

Her pulse beat fast and steady; their breathing had synchronized and he swallowed, fighting down the rising tide of desire.

He rested his hands on the faint flare of her hips and the unfashionable narrow-legged work trous as stained as her tunic, yet beneath his fingers, the weave of the cloth was tight and fine.

"Trous off," he said, smiling as the trous folded around her workboots, then fell away from those. Yes, she wore white pantlettes of a cut his sisters had worn when children. The heat in him ratcheted up another couple of degrees and he had to swallow, then clear his throat. He took another step back, two, to let his gaze linger on her. He scanned her from her hair pulled back and braided to keep it from her face, straight shoulders, slender torso still girlish, flat stomach. Her arms and legs were well toned from riding; he'd felt that, under his hands, as her body moved against his. Now he appreciated her lines as a whole.

He smiled and glanced into her eyes again, discovering that her own gaze lingered on his chest. He glanced down. His nipples were tight, too, of course. Not too many scars, and none from stupidity to be ashamed of.

She strode toward him, her lips parted over perfect teeth, her lips moist again. Had he missed her tongue swiping them? Too bad. But better, right now, not to think of her tongue or mouth.

His thick leather belt didn't prevent her from hooking her thumbs under his trous and loincloth. Their flesh met flesh and he shuddered.

"Trous off," she said, and the cloth fell away from his legs and feet as well. He stood only in his loincloth, his erect cock prominently pushing against his underwear.

"You're wearing a blue loincloth." She blinked. "And it's not like those I see in the laundry."

"It's a fighter's breechclout," he explained, but felt his cheeks redden. He felt overdeveloped—the thickness of his thighs, his shoulders, his neck. Did he appear brutish to her as well as her cuzes? He sincerely and desperately hoped not.

He cleared his throat again. "I'm a fighter, a mercenary guard. I've trained since age seven. I consider my body my greatest tool."

She nodded.

"You find my body . . . pleasing?"

Her brows went up and her smile grew wider. "Draeg, I told you this morning you were gorgeous. Say, 'Thank you, Lori, for the true compliment.'"

"Thank you, Lori, for the true compliment. And I thought you were complimenting my eyes, earlier," he teased.

"They are a beautiful blue, but your body is . . . exceptional." She laughed. "I stopped in our library a few minutes to peruse anatomical art books, and I can tell you that you compare very well to the male studies. I like your shape."

"I like yours, too, and will like it better when I can see all of it. But I must confess that I don't recall much about this morning. I wasn't thinking much. And I can pretty well guarantee that shortly I won't be thinking again, so you, uh, must take that into consideration when I fall short in the memory department."

"Oh." She looked thoughtful.

"What?" he asked.

"So you were running mostly on emotions this morning?"

"Mostly basic animal instinct."

"Oh. Me, too. It's a wonderful thing, animal instinct." She dropped her gaze and stared at his crotch. He hadn't thought he could get any more aroused, but he'd been wrong.

"Thought is fading even as we speak," he said, panting.

Her smile was slower, completely amused, and lit her eyes. "Good." She sucked in her bottom lip and his shaft twitched. Keeping her gaze on him, she said, "Pantlettes off."

His stare zoomed to between her legs and the blond hair there. She held out a hand. "Let's go have sex."

"Make love," he corrected, his words coming from a dry mouth. He drank in the aroma of her once more. "Loincloth off." The cloth constricting his erection fell away, and Lord and Lady, did he feel good, really ready to touch this lady, sink into her. *Slow down!* He grasped her fingers and circled around her in a dance pattern in the two strides it took to reach the welcoming bedsponge. She pivoted with him, matched his steps.

"You dance."

"I was taught. We have big parties for all the Family on Mid-Summer's and Mid-Winter's Days. I dance then."

"But not with your cuz Zus."

Her expression soured. "Do you want to spoil the mood?"

"Sorry, really don't." He locked his arm around her waist and spun fast, gauged the angle of the bedsponge, and took them down. They landed side by side and laughing, and the beauty of her laughter hit him so hard that he lifted her leg over his hip and plunged into her, watching the surprise in her eyes. Liking how she closed her lashes and moaned a little. Maybe liking that too much.

He closed his own eyelids, just to savor the moment. Not moving. Thankfully, she'd been wet enough for him. Now heat and dampness closed around his cock and being inside her was the most important thing in the entire universe. He could feel her tight nipples against his chest, the softness of her breasts. One of her arms had gone around his neck, and he moved his hand on her hip along her sweet spine to the nape of her neck where her thick braid tangled. "Undo," he whispered rawly.

When the tresses slid across his fingers, caressing them, he couldn't prevent thrusting into her body, once, twice, stopped before a third stroke would have him pounding into her. She didn't need that, more fast loving.

So he slid his fingers through her hair, straightening the strands, enjoying the different textures of Lori. All of her was soft, but her hair waved more than he'd noticed, she'd braided it so tight. Again and again he slipped his hand through it, found it came to her midback . . . and he rocked inside her and listened to her quiet whimpers.

He was pleasing her, stoking her slowly to orgasm, exactly as he wanted. He listened intently to her little breaths, how they hitched, paid attention to how her hand on his biceps clutched.

Control, with control he could make this exquisite pleasure on the knife edge of pain last and last. Move slowly, thrusting just a little deeper every few strokes. So. Damned. Good. Just. Plain. Perfect.

She began to rock, as if needing more of his cock, and harder thrusting in particular places. Her eyes had closed, a woman caught in primal instinct, focused on herself and her impending climax. Her lips had flushed, as had her hard nipples and her skin. Beautiful.

Her head tilted back, her mouth opened, and he couldn't resist; he kissed her, thrusting his tongue like he plunged with his shaft, and she screamed into his mouth as she trembled with her orgasm.

He kept moving, knowing he skated on the edge of his self-mastery; soon it would unravel.

"Wonderful," she murmured. "But it's better when you're with me."

His heart slammed against his chest at that great sentiment and broke his control. He rolled her under him and surged hard as far his cock would go. Basic instinct to mate ruled and he withdrew to his tip at her entrance, giving himself maximum pleasure. Her rolling chuckle of delight came to his ears, her legs wrapped around his waist giving him better access, but now it was all about wringing the most ecstasy out of him during the best sex he'd ever had in a fast, pounding course to soaring orgasm.

She gasped and convulsed around him, clamping around his cock.

Utter rapture blasted through him and he arced, back bowing, his hands under her ass and taking Lori with him as he exploded into motes of light and life and the spiral of fabulous sensation spun him out, going on and on and on.

When he came back to himself, he lay on her, felt every indentation of her body. With supreme effort, he rolled over, but she escaped his limp grasp and lay on her side while his vision fixed on the ceiling. "Sorry. I'll be able to look at you. Someday. Sometime soon, maybe."

She giggled, and a weightless joy filled his chest, through his being, flushing the burden of guilt away.

He'd made love to her, given her satisfaction, pleasure, orgasm. And made her giggle.

They stayed in silence for a while, and their breathing kept rhythm.

Lori couldn't take her gaze from her lover. He lay on his back, his chest pumping up and down, lightly sheened with sweat. She stared at his penis, flaccid but yet thick and long. Nearly as beautiful as his defined muscles. She didn't think she'd ever get tired of looking at his body.

A low chuckle rolled from him and her gaze traveled from his sex up his abdomen to that nice, wide chest, then his face and smug expression. "Like what you see?"

Impish humor tingled through her. She moved her hand to his shaft, curled her fingers around it. "Studly."

He jerked. "What?"

"I know studly when I see it. You're very virile, Draeg." She leaned close and kissed him on his lips, which appeared plump from sex and arousal and kissing. He tasted different, more earthy, after sex. She liked it, found herself humming a purr as if she were Baccat.

Experimentally, she moved her hand up and down his penis and his whole body stiffened—such an effect on his entire body from touching his cock. "Excellent reflexes there, GentleSir Hedgenettle," she teased.

He stiffened even more, shaft and body, but she sensed it wasn't due to the same emotion, so she checked their bond and found some kind of distress.

She could banish that. Head tilted to watch his penis grow erect under her stroking, she moved her hand up and down from base to tip, saw his small nipples tighten to hard beads, his skin flinch and his teeth clench as he sought control.

She loved seeing the changes in him, *feeling* his arousal under her hand, how he became erect, thickened. Her own pulse raced and she clenched her legs as the anticipation of pleasure dampened her inner core and the folds of her own sex.

"Too much," he gasped, and pushed her hand away from his fascinating shaft, pushed her to her back and put his mouth on her breast.

Glorious pleasure! Tugs that made her wet, her legs restless, created a *craving* in her for sex, more for Draeg and Draeg alone inside her, joining with her, experiencing shattering climax together.

Her nipple hardened under his swirling, darting tongue. Then he lifted his head enough for her to see his glinting sapphire eyes. He lowered his head and gently, gently rasped her skin with his beard as he moved over to her other breast. This time he kissed her breast, laving all around her nipple but not taking it into his mouth until she arched upward.

His hand trailed down between her thighs, and his fingers feathered over her, then dipped inside her entrance and a long, broken moan sifted from her. She could only feel. Physical sensation ruled her; only the quest for climax mattered.

One of his fingers penetrated her, and his thumb moved over the top of her sex and his lips played with her nipple, and waves of bliss washed through her, gaining strength and potency, collected into one massive tide of feeling ripping through her that crested, then broke, and she heard her own shrill cry before she subsided limply onto the bedsponge.

The minute she could catch her breath and open her eyes, she did, surprising a fiercely concentrated expression on his face.

He took her fingers and brought them to his shaft. "Show me you want me, put me into you." His voice was so low she could barely hear him, and rough.

She swallowed as another quiver—either aftermath or prefatory—fluttered through her. Lashes down, she regarded her pale hand around his darker sex, slid him between her legs, drew his erection into her. "Draeg," she whispered.

"Loridana," he lilted back, sliding into her. She closed her eyes and savored the friction and the joining, then moved her hands to his strong shoulders to feel him flex there as they made love.

A second later she thought she heard something and frowned. Then more noise that her mind insisted she notice. Then the clatter of feet on the boathouse deck, testing the door she'd locked. Imminent discovery! *Move!* "Eeek!" she cried out, bit that off and shook Draeg by the shoulders until he stopped moving. "Teleport now!"

Twenty-six

❦

*T*apping came at the door. Draeg tensed and nodded admission of the danger. "I can help—"

"Port!" she ordered in the command tone that she'd been taught but rarely used.

Scowling, he drew out of her, away from her, leaving a chill behind, and vanished. Her heart clutched as she realized he hadn't finished his orgasm. *Deal with that later, institute emergency measures now!* She scrambled off the bedsponge. It had to go! She translocated it *away*, to the first place she thought of: the rickety secondary summer pavilion.

"Whirlwind Spells, workclothes here, add recent stains and perspiration!" Good thing she'd memorized such a spell. The thing whisked her around, scrubbed her sex-sweat away, layered on physical-labor perspiration and the scent of wood varnish. She coughed.

Three Whirlwind Spells in one day, punishment enough for her breaking so many rules.

Quick, quick, quick, move onto the next step!

When she got her lungs working right again, she squeaked out a brand-new Flaired couplet she'd memorized that morning, a housekeeping spell to remove the odor of sex and replace it with a general herbal fragrance.

"Loridana?" called Zus.

Teleport to the main room, yank off the tarp over the cabinet, snap open a can of varnish, and pull liquid into a brush she'd translocated from a table, into the can, then into her hand. Brighten the light in this area! Turn on the music flexistrip player set to be unheard from outside.

Lord and Lady, the amount of Flair she was using!

She hurried to the door and yanked it open to see a surprised Vi and Zus with dropped mouths.

"Yes?" She tilted her head. "You didn't knock or call very loudly."

Zus raised his arm and ostentatiously looked at his wrist timer. "It took you long enough to open the door."

"Music," she said, then waved the dripping brush toward the corner where she supposedly worked. Droplets flicked from the brush to speckle Zus's trous suit; Vi jumped back in time.

"*Stup!*" Zus snarled.

"Are you sure you don't have an alarm on this place so it will tell you to return when the atmosphere is disturbed by other people?"

Lori stared at her, blinked, let her own mouth fall open. "What? What are you talking about?" She frowned as if examining Vi's words. "There's a spell for that?" Lori blinked again, then nodded. "Oh, yes, like the one I have on the stables to notify us of intruders. But that sounds a siren."

"Stup," Zus said again. He'd finished brushing at his clothes with a cleansing spell, then pushed her aside as they walked in. Vi wrinkled her nose at the stringent smell in the main room, and Lori hurried over to wipe the excess varnish off her brush and placed it across the open can, as if ready to resume work when her visitors left.

She caught up with them in the kitchen as they opened and closed cabinets—already refinished—and Vi checked idly on the no-time that held a moderate amount of snacks. She studied the dates the food was supplied, but Lori had been canny, there, too. She was good at planning and delayed gratification.

The twins stalked through the boathouse and Lori trailed after them. When they strolled through the small bedroom, she stuck her hands in her pockets, flexed her fingers. As far as she could tell, nothing seemed out of order. What might they sense, though?

Vi sniffed.

Lori fisted her hands, realized the telling gesture, and pulled them from her pockets and forced her fingers to relax by her side, stopping herself from speaking nervously.

"This room has not been rehabilitated."

Rolling a shoulder, Lori said, "The common areas for Family meetings and gatherings are prioritized."

"By whom?" Zus asked, striding back to the doorway and shoving her aside with his body when she didn't move fast enough to get out of his way.

"The Residence, of course," Lori answered, staying in the dim hallway until Vi exited the bedroom.

"Of course," Vi mocked.

Since she thought it would look odd if she returned to work right after they'd studied the bedroom, Lori continued to follow them. How small and ordinary the chamber had seemed without the vitality of Draeg filling it up. The place had zero ambience. That was twice she'd picked very unromantic spots to have sex with him—the stables, and here. Embarrassment twisted her insides.

Finally, she joined the twins where they stood in the lit corner of the main room, Zus sneering at her music. "We didn't even find the cat," Zus said disgustedly.

"Cat hair, varnish, and stain don't mix," Lori pointed out.

"Have you been here all night?" Zus's voice demanded an instant answer.

"Since I left the Residence after dinner," Lori responded, quickly and truthfully, her manner totally open.

Their annoyed expression emphasized the similarities of their features.

Then Vi said, "What a dull and lonely life you have." She raised perfect brows. "Or do you?"

Yes, the mocking note in Vi's voice told Lori that they were checking up on her, had thought to find the place empty and to report that to Cuspid, Folia, and the Residence. But Lori shrugged, cleaned off the brush by hand, and capped the varnish.

"You wanted to tour the boathouse? You have. Anything else?"

Vi aimed a haughty glance at Lori. "The Residence wishes to speak with you."

"What, now?"

"Would we be here if it weren't now?"

"No."

"You're right," Zus said. His lip curled as he scanned her up and down. "I suppose there is no time for you to change clothes."

"Except for a Whirlwind Spell," Vi said.

"You know the Residence disapproves of me using those," Lori said; *had* Vi sensed such Flair, or something else? Lori continued, "It means I didn't calculate my time and my schedule and events wisely." She lifted her chin. "If the Residence wants to see me now, then it will expect to find me in work clothes, won't it?" She spared them both a glance. "I'm surprised you're acting as messengers."

"You're right, I have more rewarding things to do." Zus snorted and teleported away.

"The house said to meet with it in the ResidenceDen," Vi instructed, and vanished, too.

Lori sagged, more from the aftereffects of the earlier adrenaline dump than relief, and sudden weariness. Checking that everything was in order, she banished the spellglobe, turned off the music player, left, and locked the door.

Walking through the night, she tried to appreciate the swath of bright stars in the infinite blackness of the Celtan sky, but the temperature had plummeted to freezing and she didn't have a coat. Something in the atmosphere felt a great deal like the night before. She passed the place by the steps where she'd landed with her broken leg, and understood that she'd never enjoy running up and down these stairs again.

So she concentrated on the warmth, the *heat*, she and Draeg had generated in the boathouse. She'd always associate the boathouse with him, and she smiled, felt a little warmer, and scrounged up enough Flair to surround herself with a weathershield.

She sent a mental call to him. *Draeg?*

I'm here. Anything I can do to help?

No. She smiled at the offer, and with no strings attached, no expectation of a favor in return, a nearly unique experience for her. *I've always had plans in place in case of discovery. But it was a near thing. If we hadn't been in the boathouse—*

I'd have thought of something to cover for you, he sent to her. *An emergency in the stables I needed you for.*

She opened her mouth in surprised relief, again at his help and cleverness. As if she weren't alone in conspiring against the Residence and the Family. Did she dare contemplate asking him for help with her *other* plans?

Lori?

The Residence needs to speak with me. I'm almost there. She paused, let appreciation and affection with a touch of sexual desire flow from her to him through their bond. *Thank you for being with me tonight.*

She received back what she'd sent: appreciation, affection, more than enough sexual desire to heat her up.

I should say that, too, Draeg said. *Thank you for being with me, Loridana.*

He lilted the syllables of her long name, and she liked hearing it; perhaps that's why he said it that way.

Good night, sleep well.

Take care, call for me if you need me. Solid determination shot through their bond from him.

Good night, she repeated, and gently pinched their bond shut, acknowledging that hearing from the Residence at this time of night when it thought she was in the middle of a project was not at all a good thing.

As she proceeded through the Residence, she touched her bond with Baccat. *I am speaking with the Residence shortly*, she stated. *Then I'll head to bed.*

Whose decision was this? Baccat went straight to the heart of the matter.

His, the Residence's.

I am at the southeast gate of the city. I will teleport to My shed. There's nothing you can do. Please continue scouting. Perhaps for streets that will allow three or four beasts across, so they feel comfortable.

I am aware of our requirements. I requested an up-to-date map from the PublicLibrary Cats. She sensed grooming of whiskers. *One of Them fancies Me. As soon as I obtain the map, I will return. I remind you that if necessary, you can teleport to the HouseHeart, who will shelter you.*

I am low on Flair, but thank you.

You are welcome. I will speak to you later. I am marking down a septhour to contact you. A pause. *Also if necessary, I can teleport to the stables and have the man run to the house with an emergency you must solve.*

Two minds, Draeg's and Baccat's, with nearly the same thought. Two accustomed to teamwork and sharing responsibilities. Rather sad that her brain hadn't been able to come up with that notion. *Thank you. Later.*

Later! Baccat said. She sensed his nose twitching at the scent of mouse—prey.

At the door to the ResidenceDen, she drew herself up into the posture the entity would expect—spine and shoulders straight, chin high—opened the door, and closed it behind her.

"You have kept me waiting," the Residence said.

"I was not informed of the specific time you wished to see me." She walked with dignity to her usual wing chair.

"I believe 'as soon as possible' speaks for itself." A window rattled, once, in punctuation.

"I'm sorry, the twins did not relay that particular information, nor that you wanted me to teleport. I wished to get out into the night after varnishing cabinets in the boathouse mainspace. It's a beautiful night, though cold."

A floorboard cracked like a human snort. "I have been informed you have been leaving the estate and wandering around Druida City itself."

Instant shock and fear, immediately suppressed, but the Residence would have sensed it. She couldn't hesitate too long, and if she lied, the Residence might catch her in lies, or she might trip herself up now, or forget her lies later.

Huge emotion was her only option, to cover all and any slight reactions with major ones. She jumped to her feet, threw up her arms, and stomped back and forth, letting the simmering resentment of her whole life flash into anger. "What? Who has told you that?"

But this rage, this fury could burn all her resolution to ash, could ruin all her plans if she continued the outburst. She *must* control her ire. Tamp it down, grab a different feeling. Confusion. Yes, confusion would work.

She collapsed back into her chair, huddled in it, face in her hands, discreetly wiping away angry tears, awaiting the Residence's answers. Though she knew.

Only two people who lived in the Residence visited Druida City openly.

When she lifted her face, she kept her expression bewildered. With all her might she projected hurt bewilderment.

"Why would my cuzes lie?" She uncurled from her hunch but kept her shoulders slumped and her arms in front of her body and turned her gaze to the Residence's scrystone. "Did they say they saw me?"

Making her gulp obvious, she whispered, "You know there have been more conflicts than usual between us, lately." She paused so her next words would carry weight. "About the gilt for allies, and how many animals I should be able to have." A big breath. "Why would they lie about me?" she wailed.

"Act like D'Yew," the Residence snapped. "Not a child.

Automatically her spine straightened, not touching the back of the chair; her knees and feet came together as she sat properly and folded her hands on her lap. Her chin lifted. Big emotions, yes, more anger could be released now. "I am not a child!"

"You are certainly acting like a child," said Cuspid as he stepped into the room, his lined face set in a disapproving frown. His children, Vi and Zus, followed him.

"That's right, Loridana, you're acting like a little girl." Vi glided into the room.

"Did you call in reinforcements, Residence?"

"He had no need," Cuspid said. "I could hear you well outside in the corridor."

"How interesting. I closed that door. We shall have to study your soundproofing capability for this chamber, Residence. I quite thought it was superior to what it is. As for lies." She faced the twins. "Why are you telling them about me? Saying I've been off the estate. Where and when did you see me?"

"How do you know we were the ones who told the Residence you were in Druida City?" Zus asked.

Lori suppressed her childish habit of rolling her eyes. "You are the two who are allowed out of the estate—"

"For political purposes and meetings with our allies!" Zus said.

"So you told your father"—she glanced at Cuspid—"and he told the Residence. So the Residence heard the story thirdhand and believed it?" She let her voice rise in shock and paused a good thirty seconds and watched as the twins shared a glance, then repeated herself. "Where and when did you see me outside the estate?" She hoped she had her emotions, her small physical reactions locked down and masked by now, and suffered through more silence as no one answered her.

"Perhaps we should drop this matter—" Cuspid began.

"So I can be brought from *my* work at any time to be asked about my conduct? Is that fair? Is that honorable? I have been taught to be fair and honorable all my life . . ." At least the Residence and Family had given lip service to those qualities, even though the old stableman and her nursemaid had instilled the basics. "So I would like that applied to me. Did you see me in Druida City, Zus?"

Twenty-seven

*A*nother *glance at his sister.* "No."

She aimed her gaze at Vi. "Did you see me, Vi?"

"No."

"Then why would you tell your father and the Residence that you did?"

"*We* didn't see you. A friend of ours did."

Lori let the gasp come. "Who?"

Zus shrugged. "You wouldn't know his name. The person who told us they saw you is quite reliable."

"This person who casts aspersions on me, lies about me. How does this person even know what I look like?"

The twins appeared startled. Vi pressed her lips together.

"Have you been passing out vizes of me?"

"Of course not," Zus said.

"Then how do they know it was me?" Lori hesitated. She'd have to burn some bridges, and that was her tentative controversial relationship with the twins to downright adversaries. Not a decision she liked, but she had to protect Draeg and her affair with him, and her plans to escape.

She stood and fixed her gaze on Zus, the more spoilt twin.

"Where was I supposed to have been? When? You don't give any of us details where I was supposed to be or when."

"Night, out at night, after dinner," Zus muttered.

Lori wanted to fling out her arms; she swallowed her anger instead. "Oh. When I'm refinishing the boathouse? You've already gone through the boathouse to check my progress." She met Cuspid's eyes. He was poker stiff, which meant he was uncomfortable, his children's manners reflecting upon him. Lori angled toward the Residence scrystone. "When they came to summon me to see you about this whole mess, they toured the boathouse. Did they report on my progress?"

"No," the Residence said.

"And I met with Fastig Yew, the fisher, this morning. He saw my work. You may ask him."

"Get a fisher involved in Residence inhabitant matters?" Vi snorted delicately. "No."

"He is a Yew. He is Family. And he wouldn't lie for me. You think he is less because he doesn't live here in the Residence?"

That statement lay heavy in the air because no one, not Residence or Cuspid or Vi or Zus, wanted to answer in the affirmative, though they all believed it was true.

Lori stood tall. "Your friend erred in thinking he saw me." She slid a glance toward Vi. "Since you weren't with him, perhaps he mistook you for me. We are somewhat similar."

Vi's mouth tightened.

"He couldn't have done that. Look at you and your clothes. My sister is fashionable and sophisticated," Zus sneered, flicking a hand up and down Lori.

"Yes, my clothes. My work clothes that I dress in every night after dinner. Would I look like D'Yew in Druida City in these stained and mended clothes? Did he describe these clothes?"

Zus's mouth fell open. "Ah—"

"Check all my good clothing to see if it's been used anywhere other than here."

"It has not," the Residence said heavily. "Loridana is correct, your friend must be mistaken. How would he know her? Cuspid, your children have wasted Loridana's time, and more importantly, my time, carrying outrageous tales to us. Perhaps *outsiders* hope to manipulate us; certainly association with *outsiders* is besmirching their characters. You and Folia and I should reconsider these outside meetings with so-called allies. I have not seen any benefit—"

"No!" Zus yowled. "You can't do that to us! Keep us here on this bor—"

"Zus," Vi warned.

He shut his mouth, but his pale face flushed with anger and his hands fisted.

"You gave us permission months ago to prepare the ground for the Yews' entrance into Druidan society again. That's what we've been doing, circulating in small gatherings. We should continue to do so," Vi said soothingly.

Lori's anger surged. Cuspid and the twins would flatter the Residence and smooth everything over, as usual. She clamped her mouth shut for a full minute as blocked fury pounded in her ears, and then she said, interrupting someone nattering about something, "This does not concern me. I am weary and wish to retire."

"Permission granted," the Residence said. "You need not go back to the boathouse to finish work."

She hadn't been asking, but she inclined her head. "I will see you all later." With gliding steps she went to her rooms.

$\mathcal{D}$*raeg had teleported away naked, his clothes in his hands, and cursed* under his breath as he landed in the bedroom of his stable apartment. The cold diminished his ardor, but Lord and Lady, he ached.

No way could he sleep.

After a quick waterfall he dressed in another set of work clothes and went down to check on the beasts. He found them calm and mostly sleeping.

He also kept his bond with Lori open, felt her emotions—fear and anger, confusion and impatience— sensed how she covered or exploited her feelings for the Residence and her Family. It occurred to him that she might be an excellent actress.

Was she pretending to him, just as he was to her?

No.

He'd experienced her open heart, seen her vulnerable expression when they'd first met. And he'd been with her often enough as she moved with her animals to know she hid nothing from them . . . and nothing from him, either. She didn't mask her emotions to him any more than anyone would with a stranger.

She didn't deliberately deceive him. He'd have perceived that.

He moved through the shorter east arm of the stables in use to the main north stable block that Lori worked on now and again. Draeg had done a bit, too. As far as he knew, it would be the next block rehabilitated.

He needed action. Creating a couple of lightglobes illuminated the front stones of a medium-sized entrance hall meant to impress at one time.

Rolling his shoulders, Draeg muttered a housekeeping spell he'd become all too acquainted with lately and watched it scour the floor. He rubbed his hands and translocated boxes of materials for his creative Flair from a storage room to land with clinking near him.

Greetyou, FamMan, what are you doing? Corax asked, perching on the top of a stall divider.

"Thank you for watching over the animals. I know you aren't nocturnal."

I love my horses and they are happy here. Stridebeasts are nice, too, but not as interesting as horses.

"Yeah," Draeg said.

Nobody threatened.

"That's good."

I do not like the feel of this place. Like Blackthorn's better.

Draeg opened his mouth to agree again, but shut it. He didn't know the Residence, but what he'd experienced, he didn't like it, nor the Yews of the Residence that he'd met. The other members of the Family that he'd run into while working seemed like regular people except for being a little insular.

But the land—the estate—something about the place satisfied him, and more than the Blackthorn estate. More variation in the landscape, ridges, and hollows. And Straif T'Blackthorn had worked hard on making his estate a gem, groomed as well as efficient. Yeah, if the Blackthorns had wanted to withdraw as the Yews had, they could do it. Most of the FirstFamilies could be self-sufficient, probably the very reason for the large estates in the first place. The First-Families were descended from the colonists of old Earth who funded the starships, people with psi power who'd been threatened back then. Security had been a big deal. Mostly still was, and part of that was being able to live off the land, if necessary.

What are you doing? repeated Corax.

Draeg grunted. Though his mind had run off in a different direction, he still had too much energy and unfulfilled lust. He'd use it.

Rubbing his hands, he said, "I'm going to practice my creative Flair."

Shinys! Corax flew down to one of the boxes, flipped open the top, and began poking into it with his beak.

"Careful, some of those small tiles are delicate."

Corax looked at him with a beady eye. *I will be careful.*

Draeg moved so the closed entrance doors were behind him, measuring the area by eye. Standing in the middle of the hall, he gathered his Flair, his psi, his energy and let it *sear* through him. He had no image in mind, but let the pattern groove into the stone beneath him, setting no bounds on it.

Flapping and squawking came from Corax, and when Draeg opened his eyelids, he saw the bird staring at him. His Fam opened and closed his beak. *Big Flair, smell of burning STONE.*

"Friction," Draeg said, and stepped away with a gesture that would clean up the ground stone dust of the meter-sized engraving.

He stared at the pattern. He'd thought of Lori and horses, and beneath where he'd been was a Celtic knot incision of two horse heads staring at each other—in a heart shape. Ready for him to set mosaic tiles into the grooves.

With a nod to himself and Corax, he decided the left horse would have Smyrna's gray and black coloring and the right Ragan's roan shade. The rest of the knot itself would be a dark brown.

He stretched and did a quick drill to loosen his muscles, then summoned his knee pad for the work. A lot could be done with Flair, but setting the small tiles in the stone could be as much a meditation as sitting in a grove. It freed the mind except for contemplation of color and the right tile, as well as the repetitive action of his hands.

Hooks and tracking were his primary Flair, his best Flair that he used to support himself. He expressed his creativity in mosaic making, and tonight he wanted to burn his energy and Flair here in the stables. And not worry about Lori in the great Residence.

Corax kept him company, commenting now and then as Draeg set the outline first, then the bird culled some tiles from Draeg's boxes and flew off to stow them in his cache, or nest, or whatever.

Draeg himself sank into a rhythm, moving dexterously and with Flair so that his hands blurred. A septhour passed, nearly two, before he inserted and glued the last tile into the dip where the two curves joined to make the top of the heart. He chanted a spell to clean it up, shine it, protect it.

When he finished and stood, scanning the beautiful work— perhaps his best mosaic—a streak of understanding nearly knocked him to his knees. He staggered the couple of paces to the side of a stall and leaned against it, hoping the wood was solid enough to take his weight.

He was falling in love with Lori. So quickly after meeting her.

And Loridana Itha Valerian D'Yew was his HeartMate.

Twenty-eight

If Draeg had made a HeartGift for his HeartMate during one of the Passages that freed his Flair, he could offer it to her and, when she accepted, wait a week or two and outright claim her as his Heart-Mate. Those were the laws of Celta and HeartMates.

But his Passages hadn't followed the standard model. None of the three had occurred to him at the usual age, and when they *had* inflicted him, it had been like his brain had exploded with Flair and he hung on to survive. He'd survived only because of his links and the physical presence of much of his Family in his bedroom, his bonds with them, and Straif T'Blackthorn holding on to him for septhours. So, no HeartGift for his Lori.

The laws also stated that he wasn't allowed to tell her that he was her HeartMate, because it took away her free will to choose someone else. His gut grabbed a quick clutch of fear at that thought, and anger, and the determination to win her at any cost. Though lying about his true identity wasn't the best position for wooing her. Somehow he'd manage, even though guilt at what he did seemed to coat his every vein.

* * *

$\mathcal{L}$ori huddled in her bed, thoughts spinning. She'd lied to the Residence, serious lies, not omissions, not little cover-ups, not pretending, all immoral in themselves, but out-and-out untruths. Well, she hadn't actually spoken words of denial. Guilt chomped on her, right in her stomach, clogged in her head like the tears she shed. The Residence monitored her, of course, and the stuffy nose from tears worked with the knowledge that she was being observed to act like a suffocating blanket.

She'd lied to the Residence and her Family to protect Draeg, because she wanted him unscathed, and here with her. And she'd lied to protect her plans. To abandon the Residence and the Family.

A sneaky feeling of glee whipped through her. She'd outmaneuvered the twins, as she had the day before. But yesterday she'd let them win. If she stayed she could erode their influence . . . but it wasn't worth it. They weren't worth bothering with.

The Residence would believe her, give her the benefit of the doubt. But the twins would know she'd lied. So she couldn't stay on the estate. If she was lucky, Vi and Zus thought she was rebelling against the restrictive life for fun, or simply exploring something different. But they'd keep a lookout for her, scrutinize her actions more. And Lady and Lord help her if they found her in the city. Somehow she'd have to figure out how to avoid them.

Straightening her legs, she murmured a little warming spell on the sheets and tried to quiet her mind, to stop thinking of what else she'd planned on doing tonight. She'd wanted to meditate with Draeg in the small grove after sex with him.

With a look at their bond, she found him asleep. Just as well, because speaking with him mentally would have stirred up all sorts of emotions again and had her disguising her reactions again, tiring her more.

She took long, deep breaths and her mouth turned down. She'd thought to end the night by trying her skill at personal armor on one of her stridebeasts. She certainly couldn't sneak out now. She *felt* the Residence actively observing her. No way would it allow her to leave the house.

FamWoman, your thoughts are restless and noisy in My head, Baccat said, obviously returned from his wanderings in Druida City.

I will have you know, I have NOT been wandering. She sensed his nose lifting, and he stopped from kneading his pillow in the shed. *I WALKED Our route from Our gate to the southeast city gate. And I obtained a map.*

Tiny excitement spurted through her. *Well done!*

If you will not accompany Me as I examine Our path, I suggest a memory sphere so I can record My observations.

She'd never heard of a Fam transcribing a memory sphere, but if anyone could do it, it would be Baccat. Lori let her admiration fill their bond. Baccat settled on his pillow and purred.

Then she ran through her confrontation with the twins, Cuspid, and the Residence.

Baccat sighed through a yawn. *This is not good news, Loridana.* No.

I will think on it.

As I have, she said. *But the twins may very well retaliate and try to hurt those I love. So I MUST experiment with my personal armor more. The armor helped me a little last night after I was hit by the glider. How is yours? Does your personal armor work well?*

Yes, I have tested it extensively.

She sighed, let tension and hurt, guilt and anxiety spiral from her as she concentrated on thinking instead of feeling. *I haven't missed any energy I use to power it.*

Good. You will start your practice with the stridebeasts?

Yes, with one, tomorrow night—ah, tonight, Cana, the smallest female. And see if my armor will protect her the whole night.

Draeg may notice that.

She bit her lip. *Then I will have to think on this.*

You are not ready to trust him.

With her body and with her animals, but this secret new to

her? Shouldn't she want to trust him with everything now they
were lovers? Probably.

*I want to cherish the secret of my primary Flair, and keep it
between us. It's special knowledge and a prize. Also, I have
known him for too short a time.* Yet she'd made him her lover.
Had great respect and affection for him.

He is trustworthy in matters of the care of the animals.

Lori wondered at Baccat's phrasing, then sank into a light
doze, though sharp and angular bits and pieces of the day poked
at her. *The stipulation,* she whispered down her continuing link
with her Fam. He purred and she could nearly feel the vibration
comforting her body as well as her mind.

Which stipulation? Baccat asked.

*The one the Sallows demanded of us, the Yew Family, that if we
do not treat the horses well for a month, they shall be returned to
the Sallows. I don't like breaking a promise that the Family gave. Is
it possible to stop by the Sallows' on the way out of town? Is their
estate anywhere on the way?*

*Call upon the Sallows when we leave in the middle of the
night? And would you trust them not to stop you?*

*Very good questions. I don't know. But it is troubling to me
that one of my last acts as a Yew will be breaking a promise.*

Or we can wait until the month is up and leave, Baccat said.

Something in his tone echoed in her mind. *I thought you wanted
to go to my Valerian estate with me.* She tried to keep her own tone
inflectionless.

*It is what is necessary. I realized, just as you did, that we can-
not stay here for the amount of time it would take for Cuspid and
Folia to release the reins of control of the Family into your hands
and care. They like their status and power. From what I have
observed, we would have to wait approximately two to three
years.*

Lori shuddered, fully awake now.

And I calculate that the Residence will be ready to acknowledge you in fact as D'Yew in a decade, perhaps a decade and a half, at least.

Now Lori swallowed. She hadn't thought everything was quite so bad, but she trusted her Fam's analysis more than her own. He was less invested in the Family.

BUT, continued Baccat, *were our circumstances different, naturally I would prefer to live in a civilized, cosmopolitan environment such as Druida City as opposed to the wild outback of somewhere south, a tiny estate far from any minuscule gathering of huts, let alone a town.*

"Oh. I'm sorry." But restlessness claimed her again, the need to take a step toward her ultimate goal. *Go to the main back door. I want to work with my personal armor on you—*

What!

Please, Baccat. She swallowed. *Also, I wish to see you.*

I am your Fam and your friend. I will stand by you and with you staunchly, he said, and teleported to the door.

She rose from bed, wrapped herself in her winter robe, and walked through the sitting room and out the door.

You are going somewhere, Loridana? the Residence asked mentally, as if he couldn't tell. Irritating.

My FamCat is at the back door. I want to pet him and say good night to him.

It is very late.

I have been working late for months. Absolute truth, though it had been on her own project, not the one approved by the Residence, Cuspid, and Folia.

This seems unwise to me, the Residence said, but didn't forbid her, as it might have last year. Was it, too, wondering about the limits between them? Who knew? It would never tell her.

I want to pet my Fam, she repeated, running lightly through the house, disabling the alarm on the main back door. Baccat leapt into her arms, big furry cat, and her face stuck a little to his fur, wet from her tears.

He licked her cheek and sent through their private telepathic bond, *I like the salt.*

That caused her to smile. *I want to coat you with the strongest armor I can, all right?*

He purred. *An excellent experiment. Ready!*

Stop me if you begin to feel uncomfortable.

I will not. So far, your personal armor is exquisite. Flexible, not interfering at all with any actions. Very tough. I have received no bites or clawings from dogs, hunting cats, raccoons, foxes, or celtaroons.

Good. Though she didn't like him testing her Flair so extensively.

And I have had a small rest. Perhaps I will stroll about on some of these other FirstFamily estates. No Fam can touch ME!

Baccat made her smile, and she encased him in the best personal armor with the strongest Flair she had.

Time will pass, situations will be resolved well, he said as he licked her cheek again.

He sounded hopeful. She wasn't. There didn't seem to be a way for her to get everything she wanted.

A hole ripped inside her.

*A*ll morning, Draeg fulfilled his duties, trained the horses and exercised the stridebeasts, even drilled himself in fighting patterns, waiting for Loridana with near breathless anticipation. Certainly a lot of sexual anticipation—he remained partially erect—and tenderness slopping around in his heart.

He told himself he must have mistaken his feelings. The use of his creative Flair, the construction of the mosaic and that trance-like state and its release, had made him believe Lori was his HeartMate. And he rationalized.

But when he saw her coming toward him at her regular time in the early afternoon, his heart thudded hard, and a glow emanated from her, the most beautiful woman in the world.

In this moment, he would do anything for her, and he knew he'd lied to himself. He and Lori were HeartMates.

As she came closer, under the glow that his love vision gave her, he noticed a layer of gray smudge. Easily determined to be an amateurish tracking spell.

When he took her hand and brought it to his lips, they tingled as they came in contact with the spell. Her cuzes, the twins Zus and Vi, had used joint Flair to set the tracer spell on Lori.

To leave it would be wrong, but to remove it might alert the twins that someone watched Lori and observed them, and endanger his mission here.

He struggled with the morality, then Baccat swaggered up and Draeg grinned. With a flick of his fingers, he transferred the spell from the woman to the cat. Let the twins try to figure out what had happened. Maybe think their inept spell had transferred to the Fam.

Baccat wrinkled his nose and spat at Draeg.

Lori chuckled, withdrew her hand from his, leaned forward, and brushed his lips with a kiss.

The moment dazzled him: the spring sun shining on her hair, her gaze soft and tender, the scent of horses and stridebeasts and trees budding and the land.

Nothing could be better.

And he spied on her. His whole life here was a pretense. She didn't know his true name.

No!

He would *not* think of that, spoil this moment, these days of falling in love and discovery. No, and no and no. Shove guilt and everything else aside and into a box and don't open it.

He deepened the kiss, tasted her lips, explored her mouth, ran out of air and stepped back, his chest rising and falling too rapidly. Then he stepped in and took her in his arms, against him, lifted her up and whirled around, listening to the joy in her laughter.

Later, much later, he'd fix this mess. Somehow. Now he held on to his lover.

* * *

*T*welve days passed. *Every moment stolen. Every moment glorious* for Draeg because he became more and more deeply involved with Lori. She spent more septhours at the stables, with him and her animals, appearing committed to bonding with her stridebeasts and the horses as strongly as possible. He found her forehead to forehead with each of them every day, communing with them.

And every day when she ended her work with the animals and before she teleported to the Residence for dinner, she did that little ritual of sharing her energy—enveloping all the beings, including him, with a calm and refreshing spirit. Along with love.

They all anticipated that moment. Wherever Baccat and Corax were, they'd show up a couple of minutes before then. The time for dinner at the Residence was set in iron.

Draeg himself, the Fams, the stridebeasts, the horses, and various small and wild animals would all bask in that energy and her benediction, her link with the land that she shared. He could almost taste the essence of the estate on his tongue. He wasn't sure how he'd learn to live without it.

So it went during the days.

The nights, he and Lori rolled over the bedsponge, or in a grove, a pavilion, a meadow, the boathouse, wild with sex.

As for his mission, he'd been able to trace his hooks in Zus and Vi to a couple of lower Noble houses, though they didn't go out so much, and Draeg reported the locations to Tinne Holly. That man told Draeg that the Nobles had hosted discreet gatherings with most of the attendees being members of the Traditionalist Stance political party. Tinne had put some observers in place.

No one left the Yew estate by glider at any time, and Tinne Holly had not discovered any damaged modern gliders.

The twins' tracing spell that Draeg had transferred from Lori to Baccat had unraveled throughout that day, gone when the Fam teleported away that night.

But Draeg was less concerned with his mission than with his

own feelings and his . . . HeartMate. His bond with Lori grew thick and strong; emotions flowed easily between them, open on both ends. He marveled that she let him see her so vulnerable, and he did the same. Taking life and love as they came, living in the moment, with no deep thought or logical analysis.

He hadn't been back to T'Blackthorn Residence, had stayed here on the estate, enjoying the budding of trees, the blooming early spring flowers, the blossoming of Loridana D'Yew. He cherished each second of this interlude, wondering—dreading—when this special bubble of time would shatter.

Twenty-nine

The past week and a half had thrilled Lori, made her laugh and cry and feel and *live* as never before, because of Draeg.

Naturally, she hid all her excessive emotions from her Family and Residence, an equally difficult acting exercise as her usual watchful tension.

Monitoring by the Residence increased, and not only on her, but its chambers and corridors, too. The house and Folia had asked fisher Fastig Yew to check her progress on the boathouse every morning after she "worked" the night before—a reluctant duty he did with thinned lips since it delayed his own day.

In this manner she spent at least a septhour a night in the boathouse refining what she'd done last winter . . . and restoring the bedroom that she'd neglected before. She had Draeg's help with that.

Yes, she studied the map, and Baccat's memory sphere when he delivered it, walking through the streets of Druida again and again, impressing the way on her animals.

She also experimented with her primary Flair of personal armor, renewing Baccat's to impenetrability every evening before he pranced off to enjoy the culture of Druida City. And she practiced until she could cover her whole herd, stridebeasts and horses, with a light weathershield and armor during the night, expanding one by one.

She didn't think Draeg really noticed that because he was preoccupied—with her, to her own soaring delight.

Lori set aside her immediate plans to leave.

After their confrontation with the Residence, the twins had been careful and subdued. They hadn't left the Residence as often, but they hadn't gotten in her way, either. They, too, knew about appeasing their elders for a while until the moment was right to press to get their own way.

Now was a time of waiting. For them. For Lori, it was a time of loving.

As the nights warmed into spring, instead of going into Druida City, she slipped into the stable apartments and learned all the angles and textures and tastes of a man.

She might be able to last out the probation the Sallows had stipulated for the horses. She would steel herself to participate in the Spring Equinox ritual, Ostara, letting Cuspid and Folia lead but this time contributing only what she must. No more would she provide more Flair than necessary. She wouldn't make up for the slacking of others, not even if it meant the ritual lasted three septhours instead of one because the energy had to build enough to be used.

So she enjoyed the hiatus, relished her lover and the bond strengthening between them . . . and dared to imagine that perhaps . . . perhaps . . . when the time was right for leaving, she might be able to ask him to come with her.

He wasn't a lowly Flaired man, and he valued Family, but he was here, with her on her estate. She observed how he interacted with her animals . . . caring, even loving. More than once she'd found pleasure on his face as he looked over the land, stopped to look at a particular view. He spent most of his time here, at least the days, and nights they spent together. So if he had Family, perhaps it wasn't here in Druida.

Dare she believe, even in the slightest, that he might come with her to her estate? She'd have to ask about that Family of his.

She sang with the spring. Until the morning she found Zus tormenting Baccat in the Fam's garden. She should have expected that. The twins were too spoilt and impatient to deny themselves their pleasures for long.

Her breath caught at the sight of Zus dangling Baccat by the scruff of his neck—holding the FamCat in one strong, vicious hand, a branchlet in the other. Lori froze for long heartbeats as she saw Baccat struggle to evade the jabbing pointed stick. Finally her feet came loose and she ran, yelling, "Halt!"

With a gleaming-toothed smile Zus let go of her Fam, and Baccat plummeted. Then Zus *kicked her cat.* Her horrified scream mixed with Baccat's shriek as he went flying over the garden wall toward a field. She stopped and flung her senses down their bond—managed a gasp when she understood the personal armor she'd encased him in last night still enveloped her beloved companion. She *knew* when Baccat bounced, sudden silence replacing his screech as he drew in air and tumbled down a ridge, surprised, dizzy, but unharmed.

More panting and her throat seemed to close in reaction to her terror. She bent over and braced her hands on her thighs, listening to Zus laugh.

Slowly, slowly, she straightened her spine one vertebra at a time, then pivoted to face Zus squarely, no more than two meters from him.

"What?" That one questioning word mixed mocking and sneer. "Did you think your miserable pet was the first animal I killed?" He tossed the stick end over end, caught it, then threw it away into the brush.

"You can't do that!" It squeaked from her tight throat.

"You have no power here, no say, little girl." His upper lip rose.

"That's what you think." She tried to stay cool, to steady her breath and her spinning mind. "I'm simply biding my time."

"What!"

But his ugly expression was too revolting. Barely aware of what she did or her surroundings, she stepped up to her cuz. And vomited her breakfast on him, chest, legs, feet.

He yelled and swung at her, and she pushed him back with her Flair, knocked him on his ass.

*D*raeg, *feeding the animals in the paddock, with Corax on his shoul*der, heard a terrible mental scream from Baccat, then Lori.

What happened? Draeg demanded, but for the first time since he'd known her, her thoughts had muddied and held hysteria.

Corax flapped into the air. *I go see. They are in the cat's garden.* Draeg blinked as his Fam flew, then disappeared as he teleported through air, then appeared again, a smaller spot.

Cat is in field. Mean man in garden with Lori, THREAT!

Teleport to me, Lori! he commanded.

She did, swaying, smelling of puke.

"Let's clean you off." With a fast couplet, the spell cleansed and refreshed her, and then she flung her arms around him, panting.

"What happened?" Let her get the hard emotions out, tell the story her own way.

"Zus tried to kill Baccat. He didn't, but he tried!"

Fury exploded inside Draeg, running fire down his veins, energizing his muscles. "You want me to beat him up?"

"What?" she mumbled, with her head on Draeg's shoulder.

"You want that I should find your fliggering cuz and teach him a lesson with my fists?"

"No." She hiccupped. "No." That sounded a little more steady. "But I can't stay here now. Zus thought he killed Baccat, but I saved him with—"

"What?" Draeg's turn to ask, though he felt the granite determination to *leave the estate* solidify in her aura. The resolve washed to him through their bond, settled in her body.

"What do you mean, 'leave'?"

She withdrew enough so they stood, eye to eye, hers dark green.

"I've been planning to leave since the winter," she said simply.
He stared. "Leave."

Nodding, she expanded her comment. "I have no place here.
What power I have I must use to finesse events and manipulate
others." Her lips twisted. "I am only used, my energy, my Flair."
She stepped away and he let her, surprise still immobilizing him
as he understood what that might mean for *them*.

She stalked back and forth, rubbing her arms; she wore no coat.
Draeg flicked the fingers of both hands at her, said, "Weathershield."

Another nod, this one of thanks aimed at him. "I am not respected."

"You're D'Yew."

She turned to look at him, a sneer on her face. "I am called that
so I will behave. I have been called that so I would behave since my
mother died." One shoulder lifted and fell. "It means *nothing*."
Standing tall, with fire in her eyes, she continued, "I was not formally named as D'Yew after my last Passage, nearly a year ago,
when I attained my adulthood at seventeen." She flung out her
arms, as if sweeping the past away and aside and gone. "No ceremony to vow loyalty to me as D'Yew has been done, *has even been
scheduled*. I am finished here!"

Realizations clunked into place in Draeg's brain. "The wandering through Druida City."

Her laugh cracked, once. "Not wandering, determining a route
away."

"The animals—" he began.

"We've been waiting for the weather, the nights to warm for
good travel." Her lips tightened briefly before she spoke again.
"Then we will leave Druida for a *Valerian* estate in the south that
is mine alone as the child of my father."

All those questions about his journeying south.

"Leave," he repeated.

She gazed at him, then beyond him to the land, then her survey must have focused on the animals. "There's nothing for me here. I'd hoped . . . but, no."

Striding back to him, she stopped no more than thirty centimeters away. Her direct stare matched his. "Will you come with me?

"I—" He actually flapped his hands in a confused gesture. "This is sudden."

Her jaw clenched and she glanced aside. Then her head tilted. "The Residence summons me to my duties." A harsh laugh ripped from her. "I will do as I have been trained, follow the schedule the Residence and my elders set. Do as they want." She met his eyes. "But not for long." She shook her head. "Zus will think that Baccat is dead. Can you hide my Fam in the stables and keep him safe?"

"Absolutely."

"Thank you. I must go."

Draeg held out his hand to her. "Lori, lover—"

"You'll try to talk me out of this, won't you?" Another shake of her head. "You can't." She made a cutting gesture. "It's done. I. Am. Done." Her lip curled. "Now I must go pretend to be the dutiful daughter of the house, as I have been for months." Her lashes shielded her eyes for an instant. "It has never been so hard."

"Lori—"

"Later, Draeg, I have my duties." She vanished.

And he let his knees simply give way and plunked onto the ground.

Corax circled overhead, spiraled down, then landed before Draeg.

The cat is unharmed. He teleported away. So did the man.

Automatically, Draeg checked his hook in Zus. The man strolled in CityCenter.

Wrath turned Draeg's vision red and he suffered it, then let it ebb naturally. Mostly anger for Lori, at her Family, her Residence, all those who'd hurt her and used her and hadn't supported her during her life.

And there was anger at fate. His tentative hopes and dreams

crashed. He had to get away from the estate—how foolish!—that
he realized he'd begun to think might be his someday. Stup!

Some anger he saved for himself. He couldn't see how he was
gong to manage not to hurt her, himself. He swallowed hard at
the guilt that ate him like an army of ants.

Draeg snapped out a telepathic thought to Tinne Holly to have
Zus followed, observed, his every action noted. Spied on.

The female cuz, Vi, remained in the Residence, her aura hook
solid. He'd alert watchers when she left, too.

Meanwhile, now that his life had taken this turn, he had to
reevaluate it, and plan.

*You should get away for a while. Been stuck in one place for
too long,* Corax said. *But I will stay with you.*

"Thanks. I appreciate it, but I'd rather you looked out for the
animals."

I will do that. No one will harm my horses!

"And the stridebeasts."

No one will harm stridebeasts or ME! Corax gave a wild,
fighting scream and flew to the stable ridgepole. Draeg hopped to
his feet, fulfilled his own responsibilities to the animals, then took
off walking.

Everything inside him roiled. He was falling in love with, and
sure enjoyed fabulous sex with, Lori D'Yew. She was his Heart-
Mate. And since that particular realization, he'd been scrutiniz-
ing the estate. Riding over it not just to exercise a stridebeast or a
horse, but with the simple knowledge that it could all belong to
them. Them as a couple, he'd assured himself, when the thought
that he'd presumed uncurled and twitched nastily in his gut. Never
had he thought of it as only *his.* Though, of course, he'd thought of
Lori as only his.

He'd begun to appreciate the estate, the elegant grassyards surrounding the Residence, the gardens, especially those places his
lover, his HeartMate had made hers. He liked the occasional roll of
the land, the bluff above the river, the paths, the Yew groves.

And Lori didn't want it.

He'd heard that in her voice, saw it in every taut line of muscle in her body.

She wouldn't even fight for it, which was beyond comprehension for him. Could. Not. Be. Scanned.

Of course, he'd fight for the respect and the title and the estate for her—for them. Face it, he'd fight for the land for himself, and not just because he liked it, loved it, but because in some niggly part of his mind he'd come to think of it as his. That he'd be T'Yew. Some selfish part of him that made him writhe in guilt, but had set roots so deep that with mere thought or hideous shame, he still couldn't uproot it.

He wanted the estate . . . and hadn't really known until a few minutes before. A selfishness whispered inside that he'd wanted the status, too.

Lori didn't. She was stubbornly determined to leave, and another tiny notion beat frantic wings inside his head, his heart, like a trapped flutterby. He wouldn't be able to talk her into staying, sex her into staying . . . *love* her into staying. She would carry out her long-term plans and he couldn't convince her not to.

If she had to choose between him and what she thought was her freedom, her estate, she would choose the animals she'd loved before him, the freedom she cherished more than their loving, her plans more than his wishes to fight for this land.

She'd choose that Valerian land she'd mentioned over his devout vows to fight for her deserved place at the head of the Family.

At least she'd choose that southern estate over her lover, since she didn't know they were HeartMates. He wasn't sure what she might do if she knew they were HeartMates, and he couldn't tell her.

She might give HeartMates and Draeg Hedgenettle a chance. Might accept him.

He fliggering doubted she'd give Draeg Betony-Blackthorn a chance after all the lies he'd told, the lie he'd lived. He wasn't at all the man she thought him to be.

Crap, his head ached. He stopped a moment to massage his

temples, stretch tension from his neck, hell, from all of his muscles, his entire stiff body that seemed to match the rigidity of his mind.

Then he bent over, rolled his spine up vertebra by vertebra, and felt a little better. He breathed in the long and deep pattern that matched Lori's when she meditated. And smelled sweet long grasses beginning to poke their tender blades above the ground, scented the large river.

He hadn't been all the way down to the river, seen that edge of the Yews' property.

Thirty

The Yews' property. Those words poked like a sword into his inflated ego, his own tender shoots of wishes to be master of this place.

To hide her plans, when she stayed out at night and away from her Family and the Residence, she'd done various refurbishing jobs. Now he understood why she'd hidden her work in the boathouse—not that he'd ever given that a thought before. Some detective he was.

Yeah, that hurt, how long she'd been planning and how little a possibility he had of turning her from those plans.

The boathouse deck overlooked the river, though he really didn't need any more amazing views seared in his imagination. Yet he stepped onto the deck of the boathouse and a spell fizzed against his skin. He blinked as the wood beneath him showed silvery gray, then polished brown. He swallowed. Lori finished the inside first, then the outside . . . the Family and the Residence thought she was working on this when all the while she explored the streets of Druida, or made love to him. She'd already done the work and set an illusion spell. One, he thought, that only a Yew would see, so he was exempt.

He *felt* that the spell would erode from showing old to revealing new, day by day. Probably she'd set a trigger in it to drop when she left the estate for good.

He descended the stone steps past the boathouse, until he reached a treated wooden fence a meter from the edge of the bluff that held a gate. No doubt the steps became steeper on the other side. Studying the fence, he saw it towered high enough and solid enough to keep the stridebeasts from jumping over it, though might not keep a horse—a stupid horse—out.

They'd have to add another half meter . . .

No, shuttle that thought aside.

He examined the sturdy gate that appeared no older than a couple of months, well cared for, the metal handle and latch not at all rusted and with preservation spells. When he touched it, he stilled. Only preservation spells imbued the gate . . . He sent his senses running down the fence in both directions, found not a hint of a spellshield. Shock clenched his gut. Nothing to keep out burglars. Or murderers.

Not that those sorts could breach the Residence walls, but to have perimeter walls with no spellshields shocked him.

Of course, the older Yews would consider *the* best wielder of spellshields in the world to be their worst enemy, old T'Yew's second wife, who had killed him in self-defense, and propelled—they'd think—Loridana's mother into madness. The woman now married to Tinne Holly. So when whatever spellshields had been on this fence, or the previous one, had failed, no new spellshields had been done.

No shields. Inconceivable. Lori would know that this fence was vulnerable, but did the other Yews who lived in the Residence? Did the Residence itself care? He didn't know. He didn't even know how much the Family would care. Perhaps they put all their faith in the bastion of the sentient Residence, though that building was more on the lines of a manor house than a castle in the scheme of FirstFamily Residences.

Draeg locked the gate carefully behind him. A good lock, one that he wouldn't have been able to open had his skin not tingled with the codes of Yew approval, and that Lori had made stout, but the fence itself . . . Draeg shook his head.

Studying the bluff edge, he noted she'd been careful to set the fence back from any ground threatening to crumble, a responsible caretaker, even when not happy in her duties. So showed the path, too, now no longer steps but well-defined and hard-packed ground and a layer of crushed white stone, solid, the incline not too great to ascend or descend and switching back twice. Everything tidy and well kept. As he walked down the path, the fresh scent of the river, of greening trees, drifted by him on a lazy spring breeze. Yes, everything about this place satisfied him . . . and Healed little aching pockets within his mind or heart that he didn't know he had.

And everything reminded him that Lori planned on leaving. That he'd have to wrestle with the decision to leave with her or stay. He had to stop and steady himself, tear his gaze from the view to his feet, until he'd calmed again. For some reason his body thought that if he hauled out a sword or a blazer and simply *acted*, everything could be solved.

Or if he loved her enough. She was his HeartMate; he *should* love her enough. But the dread threading through him made him all too aware that when she found out his deception, she wouldn't ask him to come with her.

He continued down the path, looking upstream at the wide river flowing through the end of Noble Country, then downstream past one last Noble estate where the water tumbled into the Great Platte Ocean. Pink and white, purple and beige and pale yellow blossoms floated on the deep green water that showed riffs and rills of white foam.

The odor of the water itself, cold and earthy with a touch of far-north mountain ice, now overwhelmed the lighter fragrance of spring blossoms. Water had not filled the banks and lapped at the fine dark brown sand turning into mud. Draeg strolled downstream until he reached the demarcation of the end of Moungala Street and across. He continued to walk, trespassing for a few meters on the D'Marigold estate, before the sun grew too warm and the taste of salt from the ocean touched his lips, reminding him he'd gone too far, so he turned back.

"I know you," a high, young voice said. "I like you!"

Draeg stopped in his tracks. He wanted to pivot and see who addressed him, but he also wanted to run away. He knew the boy he'd see if he turned.

He'd heard of the child. But the Hollys and the Blackthorns had made sure that he and the boy had never met, and Draeg finally understood why.

"I know you and I like you," the boy repeated.

Draeg's insides rippled in a long shudder.

This youngster could only be Cal Marigold, the reincarnation of Draeg's beloved teacher, Tab Holly.

Slowly Draeg inched his feet around, increment by increment. Until he stared down at the seven-year-old. Whose bright blond brows lowered. "I know you and I like you and I remember your walk."

The shudder spread from Draeg's inside outward, until his skin flinched in the breeze off the cool water. He trembled, sank slightly into his balance to remain stable through shock, just as the individual before him had taught him, kept his eyes on the source of the consternation.

Cal's gray eyes went distant, then seemed to glaze; when he spoke it was in the rough, deep tones that Draeg had not heard for so very long, and that sounded odd coming from a smaller chest. "You remember. You settle into your balance well, Draeg, and move better than the last time I saw you."

Which had been at Tab's deathbed.

A choked sound ripped all the way up from Draeg's gut and rasped across the dry tissues of his throat and out.

He swept the boy up in a hug. One he wanted tighter, but the bones were not the long, strong, thick bones of an older man, but the malleable, easily broken ones of a child. Draeg buried his face in the child's torso. "I have missed you," he mumbled gutturally. "Missed you." Words, too, tore from him. "So much."

He hadn't thought they were so close to the river, but it must have been spuming wetness because his face was covered in damp.

Small hands patted his head, and Draeg lifted it to meet a steady pewter gaze. The boy's soft mouth pursed, flattened. "I came back, you know."

"I heard."

Cal nodded. "Because I wanted a HeartMate." His expression simply brightened with an inner light. "And I have one this life." He grinned, showing a few missing teeth. "I've been granted that boon!"

"Yeah," Draeg agreed.

"My parents are HeartMates," the boy confided, then cocked his head in a gesture that sent another pang through Draeg, "Do you have a HeartMate?" he asked.

"Yeah," Draeg replied.

"That is the very most important thing in the world. You must treat it so, as the most important, your greatest priority."

"Yeah."

The youngster shook his head, gave Draeg's ear a tiny slap as reprimand. "*No.* You must think of your relationship with your HeartMate first and do what is right, *first*."

"Ah."

"I guess that was why we were supposed to meet. You think?"

"You think?" Draeg said at the same time.

"Yup," the kid said.

A roar came from the path above them. And the sound of winter-brittle uprooted bushes. Pebbles and larger rocks bounced down around them.

"That's my dad; you better put me down," Cal said.

Yeah, Draeg better, because Cratag Maytree T'Marigold was one of the few men who could wipe the polished fighting salon floor with Draeg's practice robes—and had. But Draeg's arms remained locked gently around the child.

"*Down!*" Cal ordered.

Draeg set him carefully on his feet.

"It was good meeting you, but we shouldn't see each other again for a while, I don't think," the child said seriously. "We were too close before and I have to forget before and remember now."

"Live in the moment, the eternal now," Draeg said rustily, as

Tab had once admonished, every time they settled down for a meditation session.

"Yes. I'm going to be an actor." The small chin—not at all like the features of one lost Tab Holly—set.

"An actor." Draeg let his appalled surprise show.

"That's. Right." Small shoulders straightened. "I am an *artist*."

"I—"

"Maybe you should go soak your head," the child said gruffly, again using close to Tab Holly's tones.

"Yeah?"

"I mean it." He gestured to the water. "Clear your head."

"In a cold river?" Draeg asked. And the boy had distracted him just enough to have a huge hand grab his shoulder and spin him around.

"Don't come near my son again. He must forget his past life." Cratag Maytree T'Marigold stopped all the words, all the questions in Draeg's mouth with a punch to the jaw that dropped a curtain of blackness upon him.

When Draeg awoke, the sun, Bel, hadn't crossed the sky in much of an arc. In fact, he thought he heard the words, "I'll see you later. Remember what I said," plop down in childish tones as he stared upward.

He'd said that a HeartMate should be *the* priority.

FamMan? questioned Corax.

I'm all right, he sent telepathically. He rubbed his jaw, wiggled it, then rolled to his feet and dusted himself off, brushed twigs and dead leaves off his clothes, shook off dried mud. *Returning from the river, slowly.*

Good. I watch the animals! Bo-ring.

Good. He repeated his Fam's words, then his mind spun back to his recent staggering encounter.

Tab Holly, Cal Marigold. Cave of the Dark Goddess. Yeah, like most people he believed in the Lord and Lady, in the Wheel of Stars and reincarnation . . . and like most people, *including* Cal himself and Cratag T'Marigold, Draeg had been totally freaked out to see rebirth in solid, unmistakable action.

A little comforting, maybe a lot comforting as he thought on it. But face to face. He rubbed his own face. Face to face, plain scary.

They'd been right, the Marigolds, the Hollys, his Family of Blackthorns.

Because seeing Cal had shredded Draeg.

Loridana went through the motions of her duties. *Today she inventoried* the same huge and crammed attic storeroom she did once every spring. She reported to the Residence the items in the trunks, the discarded furniture, the antique clothes hanging in several wardrobes. They were supposedly checking for stuff to discard, but, as usual, the Residence wanted to keep it all, so she renewed a lot of preservation spells. She didn't think anyone in the Family would care if moths ate the clothes, but she obeyed and kept quiet.

She didn't think Zus had told anyone—except maybe bragging to his sister—that he'd killed Baccat. No pretense of grief needed, though she didn't think the Residence would care if Baccat had died. The house must sense her love for her animals, for her Fam, but it wouldn't understand love. Love wasn't as important as appearances.

Mostly, Lori thought of Draeg. He didn't want to come with her. Perhaps he could be convinced. She *had* sprung the question on him; perhaps she should give him the benefit of the doubt. Their bond had narrowed considerably during their little conversation that morning, yet she still felt wave after wave of disturbance, hurt, coming from him. He didn't seem as flexible as she'd thought.

But *she* had no doubt that he'd try to talk her out of it first. Fight for her rights or something, despite what she'd already told him.

She didn't want that discussion. She wanted to revise her plans.

Get out of here no later than the night after next. Excitement fizzed through her and she quashed it ruthlessly before the Residence sensed it. Finally, finally, she'd *go!*

And her moods swung up and down, dread and incipient grief at telling Draeg good-bye. Freedom at last!

We are done, Loridana Itha, and since you are paying little attention to your training, I dismiss you, the Residence scolded.

"Thank you, Residence," she said humbly.

I suppose you wish to examine your horses. Have you any recommendations as to whether we should breed them?

"Ah, no. I'd like them to be in better health before discussing that matter with you."

Very well, you may go and continue their training and seeing to their care. Animated beings need a great deal of care, the Residence grumbled.

Lori believed she—and the Family—spent double the time and energy in a year caring for the Residence than she did for all her herd. "Thank you again, Residence." She hurried down to the ResidenceDen to file the inventory, then to her rooms to change into her riding clothes. Checking her link with Draeg, she frowned. Apparently he walked along the river, not quite within the estate boundaries.

Ah! He'd needed someplace else, somewhere not-so-familiar, to think. Her lips curved. They had that in common. He probably practiced some of those patterns, too. She thought she felt a physical ache as well as mental turmoil.

She sighed with relief, unready to talk to him again, simply too sensitive to subject herself to rejection.

Now she could go to the stables and prepare her animals for the journey, once more. Inform them that it would be one or two nights away. She wouldn't have to hide her excitement, and they would feel that, the excitement, and most of all, the love as they traveled together to freedom.

Her mouth set. And today she'd go into Druida, to look at the route, and perhaps to say farewell to the city she knew so little.

Thirty-one

Draeg had picked up a limp. His knee had hit a stone when Cratag had knocked him out, so he strode back to the Yew estate slower than he'd planned.

He must *convince* Lori to stay. He'd better damn well figure out what kind of legal rights she might have. Maybe convincing her to press those rights might sway her to stay.

He paused his walk by a small, eddying pool. Maybe he *should* soak his head. Rubbing his knee, he muttered a Healing spell. He hadn't wanted to because this day was shaping up to be a bad one and he might need the Flair. Healing spells needed more energy from him to work and weren't as effective. Not a skill of his.

Kneeling, he dipped his hands in the frigid water, splashed his face, wiped the back of his neck, and massaged his scalp to dry his fingers and promote thinking. It cleared his mind. A little.

What would make Lori stay? Beyond him and his loving, because from what she said, he figured she'd ask him to go with him, and Draeg Hedgenettle would have. Maybe even Draeg Betony-Blackthorn would. His shoulders tightened again. No. Draeg Betony-Blackthorn would always fight. Even a losing battle? Cave of the Dark Goddess, he hated so much damn thinking!

He could understand why she'd take her animals with her. From what he saw, she didn't dare leave the animals she loved behind to be slaughtered, to be tortured, if she left. Though that was another thing Draeg couldn't wrap his mind around.

She must have had to revise her plans when Smyrna and Ragan came so she could take them with her, too.

Lori loved animals . . . if he could get her one more, one perfect horse, one thoroughbred that she might want to breed, and here on this land instead of taking it away from civilization to the wilds of a small estate and village in the south . . . maybe she would stay.

It hurt to think she might stay for an animal and not him. Forget that.

A new horse, a thoroughbred, perhaps a stallion at the edge of her skill, could delay her trip once more.

Delay with the stallion, then convince her to fight for her rights. Draeg had a plan.

Despite his wash in the river, Draeg felt dirty.

He put his plan into effect immediately by teleporting to The Green Knight Fencing and Fighting Salon. He found Tinne Holly, the owner, at his desk in his office, grumbling at some accounting work.

"What?" asked Tinne, scowling up at Draeg.

"I need a stallion, an excellent, somewhat challenging horse. Immediately."

Tinne's gray eyes widened. "What?" This time he sounded surprised.

Draeg dropped into a client chair and, as his ass hit the cushion, he realized how lacking in comfort the chairs in his stable apartments were.

"That's what I said. What. Lori is planning on leaving the estate."

Tinne shrugged, fiddled with a writestick. "So?"

Draeg quit grinding his teeth. "*Abandon* her Family and her estate. Head for some puny Valerian estate in the south and take up living there. I need her here."

The writestick fell from Tinne's fingers. "Leave her Family?"

"Inconceivable to you, too," Draeg muttered.

Tinne kept shaking his head in denial.

"She's taking all her animals with her. Six stridebeasts and the two horses we introduced to the estate. Another horse—a fractious stallion—would keep her here longer while I figure out what else is going on."

"That's one option," Tinne said.

"You got any other?" Draeg shot at him.

"In the thirty seconds of thinking time you've given me? No." Leaning forward, Tinne locked his gaze on Draeg's own. "You truly believe this."

"Oh, yeah."

"I don't think—"

But Draeg cut him off. "Didn't your very own wife run away from T'Yew Residence? Didn't she plot and plan to leave and carry out her plans and succeed?"

"She wasn't the Head of the Household."

"Neither is Loridana. She has little power in the Residence, none with her Family." Draeg couldn't stay seated; he got up to pace. With a smoldering glance at Tinne, Draeg said, "Her Family isn't like ours. Isn't irritating but lovable, with bonds we can't break— don't want to break. She's ready to leave, has only been waiting for the weather to warm."

"So the arrival of the horses would have set her back."

"That's right. It did. Lord and Lady, we had luck there."

"I figured out a while ago she was your lover," Tinne said drily. "I understand why you're concerned about her."

"My HeartMate."

"Cave of the Dark Goddess," Tinne swore.

Draeg flicked a hand. "Yeah. I gotta figure out what I'm going to do."

"Especially since we both think something is rotten in the Yew Family, yes?"

"Yeah."

"And you don't want to leave your Family or the Yew estate or this mission or Druida, do you?"

Draeg hesitated. "I'd rather not."

Sucking air between his teeth, Tinne said, "You have problems."

"That's right, and I'm trying to solve them."

"Ah, you wouldn't ask her to stay here, with you?"

Draeg slanted him a disbelieving look. "What do I, a stableman, have to offer her?"

"She's asked you to come with her."

"Yes. I'm thinking on what I'll do." He ran his fingers through his hair. "How long I can keep up the pretense I'm a stableman? And when she finds out—"

"Doom," Tinne said.

Draeg swallowed. "Yes, I doubt she'd give me a chance to tell the whole story." He shook his head. "From her point of view, it's practical, having me on the trip, giving me a place on her estate."

"Cave of the Dark Goddess. No way you can talk her out of this?"

"I'll be thinking of things, but right now we need something solid and tangible to keep her here."

"Like a challenging stallion."

"Yes."

"We're going to have to come up with an excuse to give her an expensive horse."

"I've thought of that. An old debt, now being repaid. The man heard she liked horses, had purchased some from the Sallows, and wanted to give her one."

Tinne picked up the writestick again, tapped it. "That could work. None of her Family would confiscate the horse? Resell it?"

"Something so valuable? I don't know. They might want to placate her; she's restless and I'm sure they've noticed *that*. And if they sold the horse, they might think that could totally alienate her, and they don't want that, I don't believe."

"A lot you don't know."

"Tell me about it."

"All right," Tinne said. "Who's the man with the debt?"

"FirstFamily GreatLord Saille T'Willow. They should believe that. Old T'Yew wasn't happy with Willow's MotherDam's matchmaking. And Willow isn't known to be very political."

"He's on our side," Tinne said.

"Yes, he is, but *quietly* on our side."

"And he doesn't like the Yews."

"No. Like everyone else who dealt with them, they annoyed him." Draeg frowned, shifted his shoulders. "Might be something more there, but I don't know what it is."

"All right. I'll talk to the Sallows, and to the Ashes—"

"The Ashes?"

"Danith D'Ash and Gwydion Ash, the animal Healers, might have some horses. And I'll discuss this very expensive debt with Saille T'Willow."

Draeg stiffened. "I can purchase the horse. I have the gilt."

Tinne waved that away. "We'll figure that out later. Now we must find a horse." He raised his brows. "And you are here in the middle of the day."

"Yeah, my Fam is covering for me, but I gotta get back. I've been gone long enough." But he sure wasn't going to tell Tinne that he'd met Tinne's reincarnated G'Uncle and Cratag Marigold.

"I think I'll need today to set this up," Tinne said.

Draeg frowned, shrugging. "All right." With a nod to him and a grunt, Draeg returned to his rooms in the stable.

Corax flew in the window. *Lori here, then gone. At house now. All the animals excited.*

"Great." Disappointment mixed with relief.

*I*n *her bedroom after a late tea, Lori let herself pace her room . . .* twice.

Baccat had informed her that he couldn't be with her that day and evening, and she didn't press for a reason since he stated it was his private business. She had to admit a thrill had zipped up and down her spine at the thought of being by herself if she wanted to head into Druida City. And she did.

Since the ritual for Last Quarter moons that she would lead later that night occurred when the twinmoons rose in the middle of the night at FourBells, everyone had ostensibly gone to rest before dinner.

Lori couldn't, just couldn't, since excitement filled her at the thought of *going into the city just before the shops closed for the evening all by herself*!

Yes, she would trace the route, but after she looked around a bit. Heady freedom.

The Residence and the Family thought she took time to meditate in a pavilion at the far edge of the estate overlooking the river. She kept the building a little run-down on the outside and comfortable inside. Like most other places she used by herself, the rest of the Family left it alone as unimportant.

Her fingers trembled as she opened the secret compartment in the bedsponge frame. Unlike the massive and heavily carved generational frame in the MasterSuite, this simple one didn't look as if it contained a hidden niche. She thought even the Residence was unaware of it, but she had skimmed the house's awareness to determine whether it spied on her from the crystal in the room before sliding her fingers over the panel.

The bed frame had been her father's and she'd found his memory spheres in it. She *had* copied those and put them in the library. Maybe the Family wouldn't destroy the copies when they found them . . . ages after she left, she hoped. After all, he'd been a member of the Family even though she thought all the use they'd had for him was simply to impregnate her mother.

She fingered the few pieces of gilt inside the cubby hole, then pulled out one of the small pouches fat with silver slivers. She wasn't sure if or what she might buy, but wanted money, no matter how little, jingling in her pocket.

Thinking of which, she pulled out some old clothes that Vi had put in the deconstructor just this week but that she'd saved because she knew they'd only be a little big. From the few people she'd seen on the street, and in the vizes she watched, her garments would look like Noble hand-me-downs and out of fashion, but respectable. She *was* tired of wearing her own old casual garments with stains and frays that made her appear poor.

Quickly dressing in the clothes, then checking herself out in a mirror, she nodded. She stuck the little pouch into her upper trous pocket instead of her long, square tunic sleeves.

Good to go! And go she did, teleporting out of the Residence.

Cave of the Dark Goddess!" Draeg swore. Loridana had just left the estate, teleported away somewhere. Dammit. He hadn't even imagined she knew a place within the city that she'd feel comfortable teleporting to. You usually had to understand the light at all times of the day and night, all times of the year; how could she do that?

But she had, and he sensed through their bond that she'd arrived in an upscale Noble neighborhood and headed toward CityCenter.

Dammit.

He *couldn't* leave the animals half tended and fed, a couple of the stridebeasts and Smyrna unexercised. Cave of the fliggering Dark Goddess.

Baccat wouldn't be with her; the Fam was on a mission for Garrett Primross, who was handling the real investigation of the violent fringe of the Traditionalist Stance. He was probing the backgrounds of everyone at the gatherings Draeg had pinpointed that the Yews attended. As far as Draeg knew, those people were under observation. By humans and by Primross's feral animal informants.

Draeg's own Fam, Corax, was seriously working on his nest at T'Blackthorn estate, another Fam activity Draeg shouldn't intrude upon.

Draeg tested his bonds with his Family, trying to find someone free to help him—first the man he trusted the most, his adoptive

father, Straif T'Blackthorn. Who sat impatiently in some late
FirstFamilies council meeting. Draeg ran through his adopted
brothers—all busy. Then his sisters, equally occupied. Dammit,
he'd never realized until now how active his Family was!

Grimly, he cycled through his bonds with his friends. The one
best able to help—lounging in a park in CityCenter waiting for
his father to come out of that same FirstFamilies meeting—was
Nuin Ash, AshHeir.

Draeg winced, but the man four years younger than he was in
the right place at the right time. Though, really, the last person of
his friends he'd trust to be unobtrusive and reasonable was Nuin
Ash. Unlike all the other Ashes, especially his parents, Nuin was
a hothead.

Still, Draeg needed assistance in keeping an eye on D'Yew.

Nuin! Draeg sent a sharp thought, catching his friend's attention. He sensed the guy sitting straighter on the bench. Yeah, just
like someone had spoken to him mentally. Sure, a wonderful person to tail D'Yew. Not.

Yeah, Draeg? Nuin asked.

Unsure of how much Nuin knew about the attacks, Draeg
said, *I need someone to watch out for Loridana D'Yew.*

Thirty-two

*E*xcitement zoomed from Nuin. *What! Now?*

Sighing inwardly, Draeg replied, *Yes, now. She looks like this.* He sent Nuin a visualization of Loridana as he usually saw her, long blondish hair pulled back and falling beyond her shoulders.

Pretty girl, Nuin said. *I like the freckles. Hardly any girl shows her freckles.* He paused. *What IS she wearing?*

Stable clothes, Draeg answered.

Oh, Nuin said doubtfully.

You have horses and stridebeasts, Draeg replied.

I am not one of the animal Healers in my Family, Nuin returned.

Draeg sensed him shaking his head. *Terrible taste in clothes. Only to be expected in a Yew, I suppose.*

Not bothering to call Nuin on his anti-Yew sentiment, with a frown Draeg checked on Loridana. She moved more rapidly than at a walk; a public carrier, then. He set down a grid of the portion of the city where she was, fixed the image in his mind, and spurted the map to Nuin, who'd jumped to his feet.

I can see that! I know where that is, on the public carrier line between the Turquoise House and CityCenter.

Too bad Draeg's adopted brother wasn't at home at the Turquoise House. Draeg was a little surprised that Nuin even knew about public carrier routes; the guy had had a sports glider for three years, since his adulthood.

The image Nuin sent back to him looked different, not a flat map image but three-dimensional with buildings. Only to be expected; Nuin was one of the top Fire Mages in the city and worked with Air Mages to put out blazes. He'd be interested in the buildings.

I'm on it! Nuin enthused, jogging from the park to a public carrier plinth. Draeg got a quick visual from Nuin himself, and the bit he saw showed Nuin in latest extreme fashion of a young, wealthy FirstFamily Noble.

Like Loridana wouldn't notice *that* tailing her.

Draeg sighed, then shrugged; better she be safe and her whereabouts—if anything happened that could be blamed on the Yews—be known. Nobody would doubt Nuin Ash's word.

Still, the back of Draeg's neck tingled with warning, knotted. He rolled his head, then walked to the whickering horses. Now all he could do was pray.

The moment Lori teleported away, it felt like an oppressive cloud wrapping around her and a heap of stones hunching her over with their weight vanished. She straightened, not to the proud stance she'd been drilled in, but naturally, like when she was with her horses. Put aside everything that happened today, let pleasure flood her! Her first time alone in Druida City! In the *light*!

Moving easily, she stepped out of the tiny secondary teleportation closet in Apollopa Temple. She'd learned by experience that the Priest who manned the small jewel of a temple kept a light-spell burning all the time, and it never varied.

Neither he nor anyone else was evident, and she let out a little, happy breath. She only took a half minute to soak up the calm ambience, when usually she lingered.

Today, though, she had gilt and put some silver slivers in the donation urn for all the times she'd used the teleportation room.

That felt good, and she couldn't keep from smiling. Her steps nearly bounced with her enthusiasm to see the city by day . . . well, sunset would come within a septhour, but right now she walked in rich light.

She wanted to look in shops. The ones in CityCenter, where Baccat had taken her to see the jewelry store, T'Ash's Phoenix, were too expensive, so she flipped mentally through the areas she'd scouted. Southwest had a nice district, but she'd have to transfer to another public carrier line in CityCenter, another adventure.

Each new thing pleased her; she laughed as she hopped on the first carrier.

Getting off at CityCenter, she walked a block to the colored plinth of the glider bus line she wanted and waited with others, people who looked like they were heading home from work. Lori tried to imagine what it would be like to work all day at a shop or some other business, but she had no experience to base anything on. She bit her lip as she slid her eyes around at her companions. She *couldn't* empathize with anyone here because she had no notion of their lives.

That struck her as too sad all around. With a set chin, she determined that she wouldn't keep to her own property when she reached it. She'd visit the nearest town and become part of a community.

The very thought, the yearning it brought, simply made her ache.

Are you all right, FamWoman? Baccat asked, checking in with her.

Since he seemed distracted, it was easy to mask her thoughts a bit and pretend she remained at home. *Just the usual,* she said, hoping he wouldn't catch the lie.

We will be gone SOON. He gave her their mantra and sent a stream of love that had her relaxing her body. Then his mind distanced; good.

"I see a member of a FirstFamily is out," an older man said drily.

Lori froze. How had she been discovered?

"Oh, my," said a woman who appeared to be with him.

Incrementally, Lori angled her gaze to follow theirs, and goggled.

Hers wasn't the only gasp as she stared at the young man. A girl elbowed her and shared a cheeky grin. "Zow. Who's that?"

Everyone had turned to look at the Noble—surely no more than a couple of years older than Lori—in a yellow loungesuit made of slick silkeen. At least what she could see of him as he sat in the open-topped fire-red sports glider.

"His tunic has . . . things . . . on the shoulder," Lori said.

"Epaulettes, with buttons," said the girl next to her. "I'm in fashion and those are the *latest*."

Lori wondered a little what "in fashion" meant. The girl worked in an upscale clothing shop? For a tailor or dressmaker? *Designed* clothes? It could be any of those, she supposed. "He is a sight to be seen," she admitted. Long and lean, but with muscles under those fashionable clothes, black wavy hair and deep blue eyes, with even features.

"That's T'Ash's FirstSon and Heir, Nuin," said the older man. He cleared his throat. "Not much like his father."

"Looks much more amiable," said the older woman with approval.

"No marriage bands," said the girl next to Lori.

Lori shivered a little. She didn't want to get married, barely thought of men like that. Except Draeg Hedgenettle, rather. *That* man stirred feelings in her. Draeg wasn't as tall as the Ash Heir, and looked a lot stronger, in body at least. Though she thought a FirstFamily man would have a lot of Flair, at least as much as she did, and she had the most in the Family.

Because the Yews had bred for Flair.

Then the public carrier glider trundled up and they all entered in a line. The girl sat next to her, even as she smilingly shook her head at Lori. "You *aren't* in fashion."

Lori chuckled. "No." She paused. "What is your job?"

"I'm a journeywoman to a designer; what do you do?"

"I serve an estate."

"That explains it. Excellent-quality material . . ." Her fingers hovered close to Lori's sleeve, "May I feel the fabric?'

Lori nodded.

The girl did and sucked in a breath. "Ab-*so*-lutely *saturated* with Flair for spells."

"Really?" Lori asked. "They seem standard to me."

The girl gave her an odd look but said, "Not only will they wick away sweat and stay looking great, no wrinkles, they are tear resistant and able to tint several colors, change a bit of shape in the fullness, too."

How about that. But the Family would consider bespelled clothes as shortcuts to real grooming and care for one's possessions. At least for Lori.

*U*pdates *from Nuin Ash hadn't been sufficient. The guy had said* Loridana was *shopping* and had sounded bored. Draeg didn't quite trust Nuin to be observant or watchful.

No use for it. Draeg had to expend a good amount of Flair to finish his chores, and he shorted a couple of stridebeasts and Smyrna their run. The horse snorted angrily and sent a vague image of kicking Draeg the next time he approached. Draeg sent back a sense of immediate danger and the visualization of Lori cowering. Too much! He stirred anxiety in the whole herd and they rustled in their stalls.

"I'm going to take care of her," he stated in a loud voice, and though they settled a little, he still felt tension from them. In his apartment, Draeg changed into unremarkable middle-class clothes and stuck a slightly battered hat on his head, then checked the tele-portation pad in the Mercenaries' Guild Office in the southwest part of the city. Nuin had sent another three-dimensional map image to Draeg, and that was the nearest teleportation pad Draeg knew.

Just before he stepped into the corner of his mainspace that he kept clear for teleportation, he heard a screech from Baccat. *Draeg! Primross, come quick!*

Come where? Draeg demanded, and heard his words echoed from another mind, Garrett Primross, the private investigator.

Rotunda park. Grovestudy for Marin Holly!
Draeg's gut clenched. *On my way.*
Heading there transnow, Primross stated.

But the Fam wasn't listening to him; he fought big people, scratching, clawing, biting. Draeg sucked in a breath, took precious instants to make sure he knew the area, the closest teleportation pad. It was in use. Hopefully Primross. Three seconds of prepping for a fight, breathing, settling into the zone; the signal came that the pad was open, and he left.

Panting with caught sobbing breath and whimpering hit his ears. In the sunset he saw a limp and bloody cat, ten-year-old Marin Holly, and Primross with a blazer out, pivoting, checking out the area with flinty eyes.

Marin stared down at Baccat.

Horror jolted through Draeg at the sight of Baccat; his skull appeared dented, one of his eyes crusted with blood, broken ribs in his side. How could he—they—ever explain this to Loridana?

He'd put the strong tracking spell on the collar instead of the teleport-to-Healer-if-injured spell. Wrong call.

Draeg's breath whooshed out as he saw the Fam's side rise and fall, then realized the cat must be hiding his condition from Loridana.

Draeg spun himself, checking out the park, used more Flair and sent it sweeping over the area. No one hid in the dark and lengthening shadows. He checked his hooks in Zus's and Vi's auras. Sure enough, they were in Druida City, at a lower Noble's house. Then Draeg ran to Baccat.

"What happened?" Draeg demanded.

Primross holstered his blazer, then flipped a gold tag onto Baccat and the Fam disappeared.

"What the hell did you do?" Draeg demanded.

"Sent him to Danith D'Ash."

"Oh. Before we could question him?"

"Cat's nearly unconscious, no questioning," Primross said. His mouth thinned. "And he has a head injury, so he probably won't remember much."

Fligger! "Maybe you, and Marin"—Draeg bowed to the boy—"could inform me what's going on?"

The slightly trembling boy shuddered once, then went still, but he remained pale. He gulped and Draeg thought he swallowed tears.

Primross stated evenly, "Marin, here, convinced his Family that he didn't need a bodyguard."

This time Marin's swallow was audible.

"That he was old enough to defend himself," Primross continued.

Draeg winced, but the boy's obvious misery pushed him to say, "I don't see any villains around."

Marin wiped his nose on the back of his hand. "The Fam-Cat . . . helped—"

"*Saved*," Primross insisted.

"—me." The boy scowled. "I've had my First Passage. I have good Flair!"

Shaking his head, Draeg rolled his hand in a "hurry up" gesture.

"So I assigned Baccat as a feline guard today," Primross said.

"I'd put off weeding my grovestudy garden and our tutor scolded me so I stayed behind, just me and the friendly Fam. He likes jerky." Finally Marin pulled a softleaf from his trous pocket and wiped his face, blew his nose. "I forgot I wasn't supposed to be alone. I just forgot."

"And?" Draeg prompted.

"A pretty lady came by eating a flatsweet with cocoa chips." Another gulp from the boy. "It smelled hot and *good*, and I was hungry."

Draeg recalled always being hungry at ten, and having a faulty memory for parental orders, and temptation too much to ignore.

Standing straight, lips compressed before he answered, Marin said, "I took the flatsweet and I was gonna eat it, but the FamCat yelled and teleported onto my shoulder." He blinked rapidly as he looked down at Baccat's blood staining the grass. "He's a big kitty and I wasn't expecting him." Marin sucked in a breath or two, sank into his balance. "I . . . saw something from the corner of my eye, *sensed* someone, and whirled, and drew my blazer." He patted the small holstered pistol. Draeg was definitely impressed that a boy his age had qualified to carry one, but he belonged to the best warrior Family on Celta.

"The FamCat jumped at the lady with all claws and she screamed and *hit* him. She *hit a Fam*!" Marin's eyes went from gray to silver at the outrage. "And the guy lunged at me and I had to fire, and it hit and he yelled and I smelled singed skin." The child shuddered.

Draeg squatted before him. "First time you had to blaze a person instead of a simulacrum?"

Marin nodded. "Then they both teleported away, and left me with the FamCat and he was down and couldn't teleport and I can't, either, I'm too young."

"Baccat sent an alarm to me," Primross said. He rubbed Marin's shoulder. "On the whole, you did well, Marin."

"Not good enough to escape punishment." The boy's knees dipped even lower as he sank farther into his balance. Because he'd been trained not to shift his weight and risk being off balance.

"Primross is right. You did well. Your original decision may not have been wise, but your actions were correct, and you'll never make the same decision again, will you?" Draeg held out his arm to clasp, a courtesy of one man to another.

"No, sir."

"Where is this famous flatsweet?" Draeg asked.

Primross grunted. "Gone, along with the pair of humans, but we found a broken bit and I translocated it to the guards' laboratory. What did the woman look like?" asked Primross.

"Tall and blond with light green eyes. The man looked like a relative."

Draeg's chest tightened. Cave of the Dark Goddess.

Thirty-three

Carefully, carefully, masking the fear Marin's words had spurted through him, Draeg sent a request for information to Nuin Ash, Draeg's friend who also was a friend of Marin's older sister. *Anything to report?*

A huge, bored sigh. *D'Yew is walking with another girl, and they are hitting every shop on Woodruff Street.*

You see her?

Yes, yes, Draeg. You're like a clucker with one chick. I see her. I've SEEN her for the last septhour.

My thanks. He tried to send the thought lightly but something tipped Nuin off.

What happened?

Just keep an eye on D'Yew.

Draeg heard a growl in Nuin's mind, wondered if the man let it out of his throat.

You tell me what happened now!

Oh, yeah, that was FirstFamily arrogance. And concern. And protectiveness.

All is well here, except for a FamCat. You defend D'Yew. Because she'd be blamed if any other Yews had a choice in a scapegoat.

I will guard her with my life! Nuin vowed, then said, *Why is she at risk? None of OUR allies would harm her.*

She'll be blamed by everyone as the one holding the title for any of her Family members' evil actions.

WHAT ACTIONS? Nuin demanded.

I have your word that you'll stay there?

Yes, yes!

Marin Holly was targeted and attacked, Draeg said.

"What?" Nuin Ash demanded, arriving in person—recklessly teleporting to where he no doubt sensed Draeg to be, blessedly missing Primross and Marin and the trees around them.

"So much for your word to guard," Draeg said. Deliberately not adding Loridana's name or title.

"Are you all right?" Nuin took two strides and swept the boy up into his arms. Marin flushed and wiggled.

"Let this be a lesson to you, Marin, that even men of twenty make poor decisions," Draeg said. "Nuin, what of your word?"

"I'm all right," Marin said. He slanted a look at Draeg. "You *told* him." His fair skin flushed even darker. "Please put me down, Nuin."

"What of your word?" Draeg repeated.

With a harassed expression, Nuin set Marin on his feet. "I didn't think—"

"No, you didn't."

"Children," Primross said, obviously including all of them in a hard glance. "Draeg, take care of your own business. Nuin, please teleport to your mother's Animal Healing Office and check on Baccat, who guarded and saved Marin." The private investigator stepped up to Marin and put a long arm around the boy's shoulders. "I am teleporting with Marin to the GuildHall and the pad just outside the FirstFamily Council room. I will speak with members of the FirstFamilies and call in the Captain of the Guards, Ilex Winterberry." After a count of three, Primross and Marin vanished.

Feeling irritated, Draeg pivoted toward Nuin. "So much for believing in your word, thinking you're a responsible man."

"You think the Yews had something to do with this?" Nuin demanded.

"I don't know." Draeg jutted his chin. "But you watched Loridana D'Yew; do you think *she* is involved?"

Nuin flung up his hands. "I can't say."

"What you can say is that she was shopping when Marin was attacked, and I expect you to do that, if asked. In fact, you should make a memory sphere of the last couple of septhours, immediately, and translocate it to the FirstFamily Council chamber to where you occasionally sit. Now I must hope I can catch up with Lori . . . just in case the same person who targeted Marin decides she might make a good scapegoat. A good, *dead*, scapegoat. Finally we have witnesses in this case."

"Draeg—"

"Do as Primross ordered." Irritation sizzled down Draeg's nerves, and if he kept up this conversation he could ruin his friendship with the guy. Mentally he checked the teleportation pad in the courtyard of the Mercenaries' Southwest GuildHall, found it free, and 'ported away.

Once there, he got a bad feeling about missing whatever arguments—probably chaos—might be happening in the First-Family Council chamber or wherever. He hired a couple of guards he knew, one male and one female, to tail Lori *discreetly* and protect her if trouble found her.

He also checked on his hooks in the twins. Both of them had returned to the sanctuary of D'Yew Residence.

*W*hen the last of the sunlight disappeared behind the buildings and street light-spells flickered on, Lori's new friend, Anthema Mayweed, regretfully excused herself so she could eat with her current gallant.

Leaving Lori alone again. She'd enjoyed being with the other girl, listening to her talk about her life, so different than Lori's own, but didn't press her to keep in touch. After all, soon Lori would be gone.

And she'd bought something in a shop! She'd purchased a warm hat, knit on the outside, with a layer of batting, and felt on the inside. The Flaired thing only needed a tiny priming Word to work even in the worst weather! Such an efficient and minimal use of Flair awed Lori, used to funding everything in the Residence and on the estate.

Smells from local restaurants serving dinner teased her nose, but she didn't have the gilt to buy a meal, and worried at actually sitting down and having people look at her instead of being on the move. Unsure how eating in a public place actually worked, she ignored her growling stomach.

Daringly, she went into a shop, all by herself—the Fam accessories store that she'd eyed when with Anthema, but which that person had passed as if it didn't matter. Baccat had said that Fam animal companions remained scarce, and no one else in the Yew Family had such a friend, but the Family, in general, didn't like animals. They were essential to Lori.

Once inside, she perused the Fam carry bags, and distress welled through her. She shouldn't have bought the hat; now she didn't have enough gilt for even the most minimal bag, let alone for a bag to attach to a stridebeast or horse. Baccat would have to stick with his battered basket. Still, she walked around the shop, wanting a gift for her Fam.

Finally she settled on a small bag of catnip. She grew a patch of the herb in her small greenhouse plot, but perhaps Baccat would like a different taste. So she bought the nip and considered teleporting home for a snack, but the city lured her, and her plans to escape, as always.

Once outside, she walked to the nearest point of the route she'd studied and continued through the city toward the southeast gate at a pace her animals would walk—slightly faster than her own. She concentrated on the brightness of the streetlamps, experimented with spellglobes, and tried to gauge how much Flair she'd use to keep everyone calm and safe.

A whole lot more energy and Flair than if she had Draeg Hedgenettle with her, and her heart ached as she strode through the emptying streets.

*J*ust as *Draeg had suspected, the assault and suspected attempted* murder of Marin Holly created an uproar with threats of feuds—fighting Hollys and their allies versus the conservative Yews and whatever alliances remained in place with them.

Tinne insisted the only reason his wife or children would be targeted more than any other Family was due to the enmity the Yews had for his wife, the former T'Yew's child bride, nearly two decades ago. He reminded them all that the former D'Yew, Lori's mother, had made death threats against his wife and children. He brought up the fact that a Yew button had been found near the scene where the balcony gave way, nearly killing his wife and teenaged daughter.

Chaos reigned until Winterberry, Captain of the Guards, arrived and culled the Nobles down to D'Grove, the FirstFamily Grand-Lady and current Captain of the FirstFamily Council, Tinne Holly, and T'Ash.

Winterberry reported that the flatsweet tested positive for poison.

Then they viewed the memory spheres of Marin Holly and Nuin Ash.

Nuin Ash verified that he'd been called to observe a young woman Draeg had claimed was Loridana Itha D'Yew, and he had been observing her shopping when the FamCat Baccat had called for Draeg and Primross. Nuin's memory showed an extremely clear image of Lori. As young men did, he'd paid attention to the young woman. She *hadn't* been wearing work clothes, but a tunic and trous of a deep blue that were only a couple of years out of date and of a classic style. The tunic had long, rectangular sleeves that could be used as pockets.

Marin Holly's memory-image appeared rather like Nuin's, but both the woman's and the man's features were indefinite and blurred. The woman wore bright green with big bloused sleeves and trous ending in cuffs. The man's clothes also were of a current fashion, with epaulettes. And buttons.

Baccat had been treated and brought to the chamber. He remained closemouthed about several issues, such as why he'd been so fearless in his attack. The Fam staunchly insisted that despite his lack of memory he wouldn't have attacked his Fam-Woman, nor would she have struck him.

He'd never met Marin Holly before that evening, and Loridana Itha Valerian D'Yew had never seen the boy, would not know the boy, and knew no one outside the Yew estate.

It was Baccat's considered opinion that the pair who assaulted Marin were Vi Yew and Zus Yew, both of whom he knew, one of whom had already hurt him once in the morning but was too stupid to realize he'd been the same cat that evening.

While they had the Fam for questioning, they requested a mental image of the gliders that ran Lori down, and Primross confirmed that he'd traced one of the models to a minor Noble associated with the Traditionalist Stance. They were looking into his whereabouts the night of the glider accident, but there had been a couple of Traditionalist Stance meetings that night. Primross had not been successful in infiltrating the movement.

Before Baccat left, he requested a fee and a bonus, which caused a few chuckles. He was authorized funds paid by T'Ash with a small pouch of jewels. Then he gave a long stare at Draeg and teleported away.

Worried about the glider attack on Lori and his suspicions of her cuzes, Draeg found himself telling D'Grove, T'Ash, and Winterberry everything about his undercover mission to the Yews. Tinne and Primross had had his reports all along, and, of course, Draeg had occasionally spoken to Winterberry.

Shock and distress shook the group when he revealed Lori planned on leaving Residence and Family for a Valerian estate in the south.

Tinne had snorted and said that it was obvious the Residence and Family were evil enough to cause *another* young woman to run away from home. The Yew Residence should be stormed and the entire Family living there should be clapped in DepressFlair bracelets until the FirstFamilies Winterberry and Primross determined the killers.

Tinne was done with subtlety, and there'd be no stallion delivered to the Yew Residence to keep Loridana there.

D'Grove said she understood the position of the Hollys and ordered Tinne home to care for his Family.

When Draeg checked on his bond, he found Lori had returned to the Yew estate and had settled the animals—without him. He suppressed his need to pace the council room.

After thrashing various matters around for far too long—septhours—the group was adamant that they wished to meet Lori and judge her character for themselves. Draeg considered whether he and Lori could manage to leave that night, and looked up to see Primross and Winterberry watching him. So he knew that option—and Lori's own plans—could not be carried out.

Trying to run would only make everything worse, since it would alert the Yews to her intentions. Draeg thought she might never forgive him if that happened. He walked on boggy ground as it was.

And was torn between his mission to catch child killers, his friends, and love of his HeartMate.

He dared not tell her the whole thing. She'd throw him out of her life, and then she'd have only her Fam to defend her to the Nobles—and none of them could attempt to enter the Yew estate, whereas he remained an employee.

Finally, they agreed on a plan. Tomorrow night, Draeg would bring Lori into the city, and Primross and some of his feral cat informants would pace him and Lori.

At a street stall, they'd meet with T'Ash, posing as a peddler specializing in Flair testing. Draeg didn't know her primary Flair, wasn't quite sure she'd developed and practiced it yet, and T'Ash wouldn't be able to bring his full box of complex Flair Testing stones. But at least the GreatLord could measure the strength of her Flair and get a good look at her.

Marin Holly, too, would be there to observe her.

After that, Draeg would show Lori the GuildHall, take her to the FirstFamilies Council Hall, and the others could watch her reaction.

They'd decided on only three people: the Captain of the Council, D'Grove; the leader of the Holly clan, T'Holly; and Draeg's adoptive father, Straif T'Blackthorn. The words of all three would be accepted by the rest of the FirstFamilies. Those three would also be compassionate enough toward Draeg's lady.

A screen would be added to the decorations of the chamber, and they would wait behind it.

He didn't much like the idea but couldn't see any way around it without giving himself away.

*D*raeg *wasn't anywhere on the estate when* Lori *returned. Sick at* heart and irritated at his defection, she went immediately to the stables and ensured the animals had been tended. They all welcomed her with love and pressed around her. Tension she hadn't known she'd carried, as if eyes had watched her all the time she'd been in Druida City, dissipated. She stroked and murmured reassuring endearments to each one of her stridebeasts and horses.

FamWoman? Baccat mewled from a stall in the abandoned north stables.

The odd note in his voice had her hurrying to where he lay on his pillow that had been translocated from his shed, now that Zus believed him dead and he hid from the twins.

"What's wrong?"

My personal armor terminated at the wrong time. He panted a little.

"What? Were you injured?"

He lifted and dropped a forepaw. *Gravely, but My employer arranged for a Healer.*

Lori gasped. "I . . . I felt no harm from you." Reckless with her Flair, she ignited a bright spellglobe. His fur appeared a little dull, and his stomach looked less substantial. "Your *employer!*"

I acceded to a request to guard a youngster and was injured in the course of My duties.

She picked him up, to hold him, to make sure he was all right, and rocked him as he purred. Clearing her throat, she said, "Is the child all right?"

Yes.

"That's good."

We should have renewed My personal armor this morning.

"Yes." Running a hand along him, she spent more Flair ensuring the personal armor spellshield covered him entirely. For a moment she stood there, holding him, glad at the weight in his arms. "Where were you hurt?"

My skull was fractured and my left eye nearly destroyed.

A horrible hurt broke in her chest, from the idea that she might have lost her Fam, her closest friend, and that she seemed to have already lost her first lover. She let the emotion out in one harsh sob as tears burned in her eyes, then blessed anger came.

"Who did this to you?" For the first time rage fired her so that she wanted to physically hit someone.

My head injury prevented Me from remembering. I think We are wise in leaving this estate soon, and not becoming involved in any cliques or political—

"What?" Lori blinked, confused.

I am not impressed with the Nobles of this city. They lack intelligence and seem short-sighted.

With a snort, Lori said, "The only Nobles I know are me and my Family, and I'm not impressed, either."

We will do better on Our own. Following Our own rules.

Lori nodded. "Yes."

At that moment her calendar sphere popped into existence, and she sighed. "It's time for me to cleanse for the Last Quarter Twinmoons Ritual." She hesitated. "We will be in the main Yew grove under a weathershield. I am unsure how many of the Family will attend, but I would like you to be there, in the shadows." She smiled. "No, under my long robe, it's full enough, and I can cover your presence in the ritual circle and we aren't in the Residence so it won't be monitoring me."

You would like Me there.

"Yes" She rocked him again. "This will be the last circle I participate in with the Family. I don't anticipate many people will be there; most will gather next week for Ostara celebrations, but we won't be here. Tonight, perhaps there will only be Cuspid, Folia, me, and the twins, maybe a farmer or fisher or two."

I doubt that the twins will be there.

"Of course they will. They are on the estate, so they must attend. It's the rule."

Then they will have minimal Flair to contribute to the circle. I think they used up much of their Flair earlier tonight.

A terrible notion occurred to Lori. *Don't tell me they were the ones to hurt you!*

I . . . do . . . not . . . remember.

Her breath clutched. "Zus must know you still live."

Baccat huffed with ironic amusement. *You think he can tell one Cat from another?*

"Probably not." Her chin set. "We will leave the night after next. Two days' preparation is optimal. I can gather all the items on my list, prepare the animals mentally, and nothing will be forgotten because we act in haste."

And the weather will be slightly warmer and with no rain for an eightday, said My informant at the Mercenaries Guild.

"Good." Her ignored calendar sphere began to chime obnoxiously, and she set him back down on the pillow.

Good.

Two nights, counting this one, and two days, and she'd be gone with her animals. Good. But in the waterfall she let the tears come because Draeg would not be persuaded to accompany her in so short a time.

Thirty-four

*T*he next day went nearly as *Lori* planned—with regard to both her general duties and the final checklist she had for the last-day-but-one for escaping. Her tasks left her little time to slip out to the stables to see Draeg, and that was good. She knew he'd fed Baccat from the stables no-time that she'd restocked that morning.

During her regular session with the animals, he'd been . . . professional. Until the end when they groomed the horses. "Did you plan on going into the city tonight?"

She had, a last walk-through from the estate gate all the way to the southeast city gate. "Yes."

He stood at the end of the stall, and unless she teleported, she'd have to brush by him. Her whole body ached to feel those strong muscles again.

"By yourself," he stated. "Because I know Baccat is staying here at the stables. Resting. Let's talk about this in my rooms, after dinner and after your few minutes in the boathouse."

How she would love to spend a night in his rooms with him!

She closed her eyes, then shook her head. "I c-can't." Her voice broke.

"Just talk, Lori." His lips had curved in a small smile, but his blue eyes were serious. She couldn't resist him; even as her mind studied her schedule, thought wisped away.

"You're going to try to talk me out of walking away from here and the Residence and my Family."

He shrugged. "Not exactly."

"Try to control me with sex?" She'd meant for that to emerge lightly, but it came out more like a croak.

One side of his mouth kicked up farther. "If only I could. You are a strong-minded and determined woman, Lori. Come to my apartments before you go into the city."

"All right."

He dipped his head. "I'll go up and cleanse. You promise you'll meet me in my apartment after dinner."

Her imagination got stuck on Draeg in the waterfall, naked, but her head nodded.

"Say the words," he prompted.

"I promise."

His mouth curled more. "Later."

She nodded, finished her chores with the animals, stood in the stableyard and sent and received love to and from all. The next to the last time she'd do that here.

Then she went back to the grind of dinner with her Family in the Residence and thought of escape, and Draeg . . . and love.

*L*ori stood in *Draeg's mainspace, arms crossed.*

"Let me show you the city," he offered with a smile.

"You aren't going to convince me to stay, Draeg."

"Just be with me in the city. Something we haven't done before—be together in public. Unless you're ashamed of me."

"Of course not." She glanced down at her work clothes, then shrugged. "I have some clothes I can wear out." With a gesture, she translocated the tunic and trous she'd dressed in last night. No one would see her to care that she wore the same outfit.

Draeg stepped aside with a grin. "I'll be in the bedroom, otherwise we won't make it past the bed."

"I wouldn't mind," she said.

"Not this evening. I have something else in mind. Baccat and Corax will watch your animals." His brows went up and down as he teased her, then he left the room.

She dressed quickly. "Ready," she called, and he came back in, nearly a match for her in dark blue. Taking her hand, he led her to the teleportation area and centered them in the rectangle. He wrapped his arms around her and whispered, "I want to show you something special."

She wiggled her butt against his burgeoning arousal. "I agree it's special, but I've seen it before."

"Counting down to teleportation. One, Draeg and Lori. Two, Lori and Draeg. *Three.*"

And they landed on a teleportation pad in the corner of a small square—holding a festive market.

Pure pleasure washed through Lori at a new experience. She turned and hugged Draeg tightly, then drew in the scents of the place, let the feel of it soothe her with its not-Yew and excite her with its otherness.

He bought her cocoa candy with nuts with a fabulous taste that seemed to explode in her mouth and sift into her whole body.

"Look!" Draeg pointed across the small market square to a stall. "A Flair tester. Let's go see."

Lori frowned. "Haven't you had your Flair tested?"

"Yeah, but have you?"

"Of course, by my mother when she was alive and I was a child, then by Cuspid and Folia after my First Passage."

"Using your Family stones."

"Of course."

"With the Residence watching."

Lori shrugged.

Draeg whirled her into a close embrace and kissed her. "Come on, give it a try with other stones."

A wonderful kiss; she'd rather return to Draeg's apartment. But he stepped away and turned them back toward the stall, threaded her arm through his, and began crossing the square.

"The tester is busy with a child," Lori said, noting a handsome boy of striking coloring, hair so pale it looked white, and gray eyes.

"Come on." He smiled. "My treat."

"Everything has been your treat."

"Because I like treating you."

As they drew near, the boy put a red egglike stone into a box and studied Lori with a cool gaze.

Her smile faltered.

Then he nodded to her. "Greetyou."

She recognized the accent as Noble, though he dressed like middle class—and realized then that her own accent might have given her status away, though her clothes had usually contradicted that. A noblewoman down on her luck? A servant of an estate, like she'd told the girl the night before? But tension ran along Lori's shoulders.

"Greetyou," she replied to the youngster.

"Well done, Marin," said the tester, and she became aware that he was a big man with swarthy skin, looked quite tough, and moved a lot like Draeg.

"You're finished here, Marin?" asked a man in a rough voice behind Lori, causing her to jump. She stepped aside but met the gray eyes of a man who was surely related to the boy.

"Yes, Papa," said the boy.

"You have a fine son with strong Flair," said the tester in a smooth patter, holding his hand out for his fee.

With a crack of laughter lightening his expression, the boy's father paid.

At that moment a huge and scruffy black-and-white cat leapt from a stool, sauntered toward Lori, and stropped her legs, purring loudly and rustily.

Another laugh and a shake of his head and the man nodded to Lori and Draeg, then walked away with the child.

"Can I help you?" the tester said.

"Sure." Draeg nearly pushed her into the wooden chair with green sun-faded cushions. Faster than she could dust the cat hair off the seat, for certain. The cat leapt up on her lap and kneaded, and Lori winced. Baccat would scent the other cat on her and not like that at all.

"Here, try this one first." The big man caught her hand and put a warm clear stone in her palm, then curved her fingers over it.

Lori frowned. His touch had felt odd.

The cat revved his purr.

"Just concentrate on your Flair," the man said genially. "See if you can light the stone."

"All right." She sent a pulse of Flair to it and exclaimed when the stone shattered into fragments in her hand. Then she blushed as she opened her fingers. "I'm *so* sorry. I'll pay for it—"

The man choked, then summoned a smile. "It was flawed. Just put the fragments on the counter. One moment, please." He pushed aside the small box of egg-shaped stones and disappeared behind a curtain along the back of the booth.

Lori dropped the broken stone on the counter and dusted her hands. Returning a minute later, the tester carried a box a meter and a half square. Lori's mouth fell open.

"Does it look like we have the time and gilt for that to determine the type of her Flair?" Draeg demanded. "There is much more I want to show her after I leave you." He stared at the man from under lowered brows, then grabbed the smaller box. "Here, try these."

Since Baccat had assured her that her primary Flair of personal armor was a new and unique skill, Lori was sure this was a futile exercise. But she ran her hands over the stones, grimacing at the odd feelings: a hint of fur, a tiny shock, a touch of slime. No stone glowed.

"I'm hungry," Draeg said. "Let's get a snack." He placed a few coins on the counter and dragged her off, leaving the man scowling and the cat grinning.

They ate some meat pastries that Lori thought she could make tastier, then walked around the square, looking. She noticed a more than normal count of cats.

When they were done, Draeg cleansed her hands and led her to a wide street.

"One more thing." Though he swung their interlinked hands, his expression turned more than serious, hard with a touch of grim.

"Yes?" Lori asked.

He inhaled a deep breath, and a tingle at the nape of her neck warned Lori that she wouldn't like what came next.

"I want you to look at the FirstFamily Council room."

"No."

He turned to her and took both her hands. "You should know what you're giving up, abandoning."

Since she couldn't gesture, she jerked her shoulders. "It means nothing to me." She smiled but thought it looked bitter because it tasted that way. "My place as D'Yew, my status here as a FirstFamily GrandLady and in Noble society has not been made available to me by my Family." She paused. "And I don't know how long it would take for them to allow that." Her lips turned from smile to curl. "I don't need this. I have what I need, and I'll make the rest."

"For me, Lori," Draeg insisted quietly. "Look at your traditional seat, your Family ancestral place in the GuildHall for me."

She choked off anger. But she wasn't ready to teleport home—to the boathouse or the estate gate. She wanted to be with Draeg, and he'd made clear his price.

Through gritted teeth, she said, "Very well."

And the next instant, they'd landed on a thick teleportation pad in a large marble corridor.

This is the new GuildHall, or rather the newly extended GuildHall. The All Council and NobleCouncil rooms are newer and bigger. The FirstFamilies Council chamber only has—relatively—new furnishings." He coughed. "From thirteen years ago."

"Since the last time my mother and my MotherSire attended."

"That's right. Your Family has been waiting for you to reach your maturity."

She snorted, shook her head. "Draeg, you know better than that. They don't want me to be D'Yew until they believe I am firmly under their thumbs and will do what they and the Residence want me to." That would *not* happen. With every step she disliked this little side trip more. She should trace her escape route.

Since she'd become lovers with Draeg, time had slipped away in wonderful moments. And though they'd occasionally talked since he'd discovered she'd planned to leave, they hadn't made plans. Or altered the plans she'd made.

They hadn't spoken again about whether he'd come with her. She continued to hope and despair. After all, he loved the animals as she did, and when they settled in they could consider a partnership. Surely that would be fine with him. He wouldn't want to be a stableman on another Noble estate, would he?

And though she'd sensed the spark of ambition in him, most of the land that could be claimed in Celta demanded hard work; her Valerian estate was established.

Her palm within his began to sweat.

"The FirstFamilies did send a few inquiries to your Family requesting a regent be appointed for you," Draeg said.

She looked at him sharply. "How do you know?"

He looked down at her. "I'm sure that would be standard protocol."

She just stared at him.

"At least, it sounds reasonable, doesn't it?" he asked.

Most of the things he'd said to her sounded reasonable. But the ambience of this place worked on her, and doubts seeped in.

They walked down large, empty corridors, though they passed one or two "Clerk" doors that showed light spells behind the frosted glass. On the whole, the architecture and setup felt odd to her . . . felt *antique*, as if it had been brought to and imposed on Celta by the Earthan colonists themselves.

Draeg stopped at a door made of a striped combination of woods. She realized with a shock that they were all the trees of the Ogham alphabet, the trees that the FirstFamilies had taken for their names. With hesitant, trembling fingers she touched the reddish golden wood of the Yew.

Yews had been prized for bows, strong and flexible weapons. She didn't know if she matched the wood.

Her lover stood patiently as she stroked the door . . . surely she felt a tingle, a sense that she connected with this piece of wood; an ancestor of hers had blessed the tree and requested a long, thick branch, harvested it, crafted this piece with Flair.

When she let her hand stray to the left, tiny shocks zipped over her fingertips. Sighing, she set her hand on the door latch and pressed down. As she walked forward, light-spells glowed on, illuminating the chamber.

She saw a large room, and everything about it was exquisite. The marble floor had a pattern incised in it, set with gold lines and colorful mosaic tiles.

"You belong there." Draeg gestured to the end of the room where a dais stood and upon it, fifty chairs behind a massive wood table, again made of twenty-five sections of wood. Lavish thronelike chairs in different-colored velvet and various carved and polished woods stood for the FirstFamily Lady or Lord and their spouse.

Fifth from the end closest to her were the Yew seats. The sides of the chairs showed tight Yew leaves, spiraling up to the carving atop the back, a wheel, Arianrhod's wheel. One of the seats angled out as if inviting her to sit.

"D'Yew, look at your chair; go up there and see how you feel," Draeg enthused.

She thought she'd be dwarfed in it. "No," she said.

"Yes," Draeg insisted. He took her hand and led her to the deeply carpeted steps of the dais, drew her up with him, though her steps lagged. He walked with her along the thrones that were even bigger than they appeared from below.

He pulled the chair out easily, a strong man. Surely physical or Flaired strength might always be needed to use these chairs, to prove you were the equal of everyone else in this long line. She didn't like the implications of that.

Just glancing down at the floor where she'd been, along all the chairs, most of them obviously used while the two belonging to the Yews seemed pristine, made her feel like a great weight had thunked onto her shoulders. Her stomach tightened with the thought of the great decisions this group made. Life-and-death decisions.

Decisions she'd not been trained to make, decisions she had no experience to understand. She was woefully lacking.

The atmosphere inside the room seemed to throb heavily, and the hair on the nape of her neck rose. Her stare fixed on the corner of the room, where a tall wooden screen stood, slightly out of place. Great Flair congregated there. Other people? FirstFamilies' Nobles? Why would they watch silently?

She didn't know, and no threat came from the corner, so she looked at Draeg again. One muscular hand stroked the table in front of the Yew chairs—also cleaner and completely unmarred, unlike the rest of the table that had nicks and smears of writestick ink.

"This is yours. You could be here," he said.

Thirty-five

Everything twisted inside her as she stared at him, swept the chamber with her gaze, felt the massed Flair, the pulsing lifeforce of three people behind the screen.

She'd had her eighteenth birthday last year; she *should be* D'Yew in truth, the head of a Noble household, a FirstFamily GrandLady in fact instead of holding the empty title.

Baccat's words from so long ago, the morning after she'd met Draeg, echoed in her mind. *The other FirstFamilies are curious people and no Yews have been in their society for a long, long time. They do not know what is happening on this estate.*

Terrible understanding thundered in her ears with her blood, struck like lightning to her heart. The FirstFamilies had sent in a spy. Draeg.

Baccat knew. Perhaps he'd been trying to warn her, but he'd kept Draeg's secret. That hurt, too.

Nothing was true about Draeg. He'd persuaded her to stay, just by being himself, by having sex with her.

He'd lied and lied and lied.

She could see the way he liked this table, those Yew chairs, recalled how he looked over the Yew estate. How he continued to press her to fight for the property. Which she didn't want. Did he ever really believe her? That she'd be happy with a small estate and the love of animals?

He *was* the only lover she'd known. She'd even thought she might love him, and he returned that love. How terribly foolish she'd been. So naive and easy to fool. Such a simpleton.

Tears stung her eyes, and a rush of rage surged through her.

"This, *this* is why you want me. Not for *me*. Not because of *who* I am." She pressed a hand on her heart, saw the guilt shroud his face as he swung toward her. He reached out a hand and she stumbled a couple of steps back. "You want me because of the title I have, *what* I am."

Back and back and back away, hop down the dais steps, and see him prowl forward with a guard's grace. He was some Noble's guard, not a stableman.

She flung her arms wide, heard her tone shrill and didn't care. "You want *this*. You want the Yew *estate*. I just want to go away, and you want me to stay and want what I have."

His face hardened. "The title and the estate and the Residence and everything else *is* yours. You've tended it since your First Passage. You deserve it and I want you to fight for it!"

Without volition her head shook, no and no and no. She went chill and cold, and inside all the warmth of her crackled into ice. Words tumbled from her mouth in a long stream she couldn't stem. "You never wanted me, just me, Lori Valerian. You wanted, *want*, FirstFamily GrandLady Loridana Itha Valerian Yew. You want my estate. You're just like everyone else in my life, wanting something from me. The Residence and my Family want my energy and Flair. They want me to conform to what *they* think I should be. Like *you* want me to conform to what you think I should be right here in this council room. Become what you think I should be. Do what *you* think I should do."

Her chest pumped with ragged breaths and she fisted her fingers. "But I will not do that. Conform to what *they* want or what *you* want. You know what I want? I want my small Valerian estate.

Where no one has any expectations of me. Where, for the first time in my life, I decide what I want."

"You have responsibilities here," he said, his voice too calm for her.

"I *am* responsible. I am responsible for myself, and I am responsible for six stridebeasts and two horses. And you know what they want from me? They want food and shelter and *love*.

"I never want to see you again. So consider yourself *fired*. Don't return to Yew Estate until I'm gone—then you, and they, and the house itself *can descend to the Cave of the Dark Goddess for all I care!*"

Before she could teleport, he grabbed both her hands again, and she couldn't take him into the Residence, wouldn't take him with her at all. "Wait. Please. Listen to me."

"Let me go."

His mouth hardened and his eyes blazed. His fingers squeezed hers.

If he didn't loose her, it would be unforgivable.

He dropped her hands.

She took a shaky breath, and more understanding filtered through her mind. He *knew* this room, was comfortable in it. A whisper forced itself from her, putting her comprehension into words. "Who *are* you, Draeg?" She wet her lips. "Not Hedgenettle. What is your surname?"

"Betony."

She tilted her head at the shade of reluctance in that one word. "Betony?" she laced it with scorn.

"It's true. Betony . . ." He paused. "Betony-Blackthorn."

"Son of a FirstFamily GrandLord." Her gaze went to the thrones, five Families earlier than hers. Blackthorn, gold cushions, a gate carved into the top of the chair, signifying the opening to the Cave of the Dark Goddess.

"Adopted son." His voice sounded tinny against her ears.

"Adopted son to Straif T'Blackthorn."

"That's right."

His solid muscularity drew her stare once more. "You're not a Noble guard. You're a Noble *fighter*, like every FirstFamily Lord and Lady." She paused. "Except me." Her anger had dimmed under the sheer haze of unreality. She needed to find it again, needed to feel *herself* again before she returned home. So let him talk. That should erode this fog enveloping her in this strange, antique place. "And you think I should stay and fight. Why?"

Lori looked strange, pale and with widely dilated pupils. Her voice sounded thin, but she *listened*. Maybe he could convince her.

"Stay because of your loyalty to your Family." He winced as soon as the words were out of his mouth, hurried on. "I mean, not your immediate Family, the others who work the estate."

She blinked, then answered heavily after several seconds. "You think that me, fighting with my immediate Family, with the Residence, with Cuspid and the twins and Folia—and believe me, the fight would get nasty and I probably wouldn't win—wouldn't disrupt the rest of the Family?"

He jutted his chin. He wanted her to stay here in Druida with him. He waved toward the council table. "You could file a formal complaint against your immediate Family with the FirstFamilies Council."

"And the Residence? Oh, yes, that would please the whole rest of my Family, too, to bring in outsiders to deal with internal matters." Her eyes fired and she actually poked him in the chest. "Tell me, GrandSir Draeg Betony-Blackthorn"—she made the words a rhythmic pattern, nearly a taunt—"can you promise my Family will be better off than they are if I stay and fight the Residence—which isn't as easy as you think it is, since the house can drop a chandelier on me at any time, gas me—"

"That's not right or legal!"

"We're not talking about right or legal! We are talking about *practicalities*." She sucked in a breath. He shouldn't have noticed her breasts under her tunic, but he did.

"You can stay with me, with my Family at T'Blackthorn Residence," he snapped.

"Can you promise my Family would be better off if I stayed and started an internal war? And think of how *you* would feel with an internal war in *your* Family?"

That concept was a blow, all right. Draeg would defend Straif Blackthorn, the current GrandLord in power, to the death. He'd sworn to do so.

Lori simmered in front of him, awaiting an answer, and he could only reply honestly. "No, I can't promise that."

"Can you, GrandSir Draeg Betony-Blackthorn, promise me that if I went to the FirstFamilies Council, I, and my Family, wouldn't become an issue of contention in the Council itself? That the Council wouldn't use me to inflict penalties on my Family? That they wouldn't *use* me?" she spat out.

Like he had, he knew she meant. And thinking of the always shifting allies and political maneuvering of the Council, he couldn't give her a positive answer to that question, either. "No, I can't promise you that."

She made a disgusted noise, set her hands on her hips, raised her chin. "Can you promise me, GrandLord Draeg Betony-Blackthorn, that if I took you up on your offer of hospitality for me and my Fam and my six stridebeasts and my animals, that your Family, the First-Family Blackthorns, would welcome me?"

"Yes." He stood solid and tall, met her gaze. "Yes, that I can promise you."

The ends of her lips curved. "And I'm sure that my presence would complicate your Family's lives no end." Narrowing her eyes. "And how much would your father use me?"

Draeg stiffened. His jaw flexed. "As little as humanly possible."

Her head inclined a fraction. "Probably as much as you did, then, yes?" She turned and walked away.

Flinching, Draeg accepted the pain, the anger, the guilt. Her next words came stiltedly, with the hurt. "I think it's better for everyone, for me, for Yew Residence, for my Family, if I continued with my plans to leave for the Valerian estate. Right now the Residence and Cuspid and Folia have everything set up the way they want it, and they can continue that with my blessing."

Yeah, he'd hurt her deeply and didn't know how to make it better because she wouldn't let him try to fix her situation.

"You really are just going to walk away without a fight."

She whirled back, hands fisting, face flushed with rage. "Do you think that throughout my eighteen years I haven't tried to fight?"

"I—"

Slashing her hand through the air, she continued, "Don't you think I demanded my birthright? They ignored that, have ignored everything I've tried, like subtly endeavored to influence that? What happened? Nothing! I found a Fam I loved and brought him into the Residence and the twins tried to *kill* him?" Her voice rose. "I rescued him from a dungeon and had to fight my hardest just to keep him in the garden shed. To keep my animals. To get horses. Don't you talk to me about fighting."

"You need to report your problems to the authorities."

She panted, shaking her head. "You just don't get it. Fighting wouldn't be best for me, or for my Family. You think I haven't thought and thought and thought about this? You think this is *impulsive?*" She threw up her hands and gave him one last furious look. He wanted to grab her and hold her and help her, but the instant he took a half step forward, she backed up three paces.

"Even you, the one outsider who has spent weeks on the estate, don't understand my Family or the Residence—" Her voice broke. "Or me. Just go away, Draeg."

"Lori—" He grabbed her hands again before she could teleport again, rushed into speech.

"Your cuzes are dangerous; I don't want you hurt."

Gasping, she yanked away from his grasp. He saw, briefly, her eyes filled with tears, and her pain ripped at him.

"I don't want you hurt physically," he said, making the whole damn thing worse. Though she'd snapped their link down to a microfilament, her whole being radiated torment and he cursed himself again, everything about this fliggering situation. Swallowing, he tried not to feel his own hurt, tried to speak around it, lay out his conclusions. "Your cuzes are behind everything. They're secret members of the Traditionalist Stance and have conspired to harm others. And you, too. I think they're behind the glider accident. They want you out of the picture permanently."

"You. Are. Crazy," she stated, her voice rough.

Since it didn't look like she was heading anywhere, that she was listening to him, he settled into his stance. "No. I'm not." He angled his chin. "That's my conclusion."

She pointed a finger at him. "You're wrong."

He shook his head. "Don't think so."

With a snort, she said, "My cuzes, Vi and Zus, are not controlled enough to plan anything like all these accidents. Or kidnappings. They're lazy, and they aren't so smart."

"You believe so?"

"Yes. I do. They're selfish and they demand immediate gratification of their whims. Which usually happens because they've been spoilt all their lives."

"I hear you."

"So don't go thinking that they're some sort of evil masterminds." She gulped, and her eyes sheened again. "They're liars and spies. Like you."

"I—"

She slashed a hand through the air. "I don't want to hear it."

"You're not a good enough actor, if I'd told you."

Her gasp vibrated through the air. She speared her finger toward him. "Rationalization." Her lip curled in disdain at him before she said, "You didn't know I was leaving until I told you. The Residence and my Family *still* don't know I'm going." A toss of her head. "I've been acting all my whole life." Her smile sliced at him. "But I must admit you're an excellent actor, too. I had no id-idea—" Voice breaking, she stopped and inhaled, shook her head as her trembling lips grimaced downward. "I believed everything you said." She laughed harshly. "I thought you poor, and a Commoner, and that you lo—cared for me."

"I *do*!"

"Just stop the lies, Draeg Betony-Blackthorn. I don't want to hear any more."

"No lies!"

She shrugged and repeated herself. "I don't want to hear any more from you. Lies, truths, rationalizations, explanations. I'm tired of all that." Her lips moved silently in a Flair Word and her face looked better, eyes clear, flush gone from her cheeks. "Now, I'm leaving. Let the Residence and the Family determine their own future. You do what you want." Another tight smile. "Since, like everyone else in my life, you always do."

Baccat! she yelled mentally.

The cat appeared near her feet.

She held out her arms and the cat leapt into them. Dropping her head into her Fam's fur, she spoke, and her voice was muffled. "Time to go. Finally time to leave." She glanced at the twinmoons and shivered.

"It's late," Draeg said from between chilled lips. "The horses could take harm in the cold tonight—" he croaked from a dry throat.

Lori flinched, her face stilling to immobility. "That is my decision, is it not? You have nothing to say in the matter."

While revving a purr, the cat slitted his eyes at Draeg but projected his question so Draeg could hear it. *Leave D'Yew Estate? Leave Druida?*

"Yes. On *our* schedule. As planned. Everything's ready. I've had it with Nobles. We'll be gone tomorrow night." She seared him with a look. "I don't ever want to see you again. I'll inform the maître de maison that you have left for a better job." Her voice was heavily ironic. Then she teleported away.

No backwash of air flowed over him or around him, but the backlash of emotion, the snapping shut of the bond, made his heart twinge and his mind spin. He had to lower his head and soften his knees to keep his equilibrium.

He'd fliggering screwed up. Everything.

Indescribable pain saturated him, down to the cells of his very marrow. With each breath he wondered how he could survive the agony to take another.

Oh, the teenage angst," D'Grove, a matronly woman of late middle age, said as she stepped from behind the screen. "The drama."

T'Ash, still dressed as a tester, followed her, flushing a little under his swarthy skin. "Maybe so, but truth rang in her words." He stared at the dais and the chairs, his chair on it. "Lady and Lord know, sometimes I'd like only the responsibility of my Family, the pleasure of a small property, the company of animals." He paused and said with solid finality, "She's not involved in these abominable attacks."

"No," D'Grove said. She shook her head at Draeg. "And you've destroyed your relationship with D'Yew. For the moment."

Draeg knew that; his gut had tightened with horrible nausea and he struggled to keep his gorge down. A wave of heat had flushed through him at Lori's words, the kernel of truth in them. Then the heat faded, leaving sudden sweat clammy on his skin.

Thirty-six

A *heavy hand dropped on his shoulder and he glanced up at his* adoptive father, a sandy-haired man taller and leaner than he, and for once, looking at that determined and stern expression, Draeg understood he *did* have a hint of the Blackthorn features. Underlying bone structure, a little broader, but the same cast.

"You should have said you wanted to be my heir, a FirstFamilies GrandLord. I'd consider you for it—"

"I don't want to be your heir!" spurted from Draeg's lips before he thought. He winced.

"Yeah?" T'Blackthorn asked.

Draeg's turn to loosen his tight shoulders. "No offense." Discreetly, he stretched his back again, loosened his stance. "It's just that . . ."

One of T'Blackthorn's brows rose. "What?"

"This sounds stupid." Spit out the damn words so he could leave and try to fix his relationship with Lori! "I love the Yew estate. It's beautiful. Not too groomed, great view of the river, good chunk of forest. It feels right to me."

"That's not stupid." D'Grove's voice had gone soft, and so had her expression . . . as had the others', thinking of their ancestral land. Draeg didn't have ancestral land, and a need he'd never realized before he'd been at D'Yew's throbbed with ache.

"I like the Residence." Well, he liked the look of the Residence, even if he'd never been in it more than a few paces. He set his jaw. He bet he could take on a Residence and win. Cave of the Dark Goddess, *Lori* could take on the Residence and win. Why didn't she think that? Why wouldn't she *do* that? "I have a problem thinking someone could just walk away from an estate."

"Huh," said T'Blackthorn, a man who'd done just that.

"A simpler life has its attractions," T'Ash said.

"D'Yew would be young to oppose older Family members and an entrenched Residence personality. She obviously believes it isn't worth the effort," D'Grove said consideringly. "Obviously she has no love or support from her Family, and they've made demands and not offered sufficient emotional compensation to have her believe she is an integral part of the Family."

"Yeah, yeah," Draeg said. "I've heard a lot about that, seen how they treat her with disrespect," he admitted, then shook his head. "Still can't figure why she won't fight." He glanced at the faces surrounding him, saw mostly compassion.

D'Grove drew a breath. "She isn't involved in the attacks, and it's equally obvious that she has no influence over any Yew Family members who might be. She can't help us there."

"No. And I can't go back." He wanted to go back, back to just a septhour ago. Desperation began to creep through him as he realized the complete destruction of his life.

His father clapped him on the shoulder and he went down.

*T*he next morning, when *Lori* awoke, she lay on her bedsponge, quiet, as grief that Draeg was no longer here, no longer with her, would no longer *be* with her, washed through her. The waves of emotional pain crested, but she held them in until she reached the stables and fed and watered her animals. Their loving support helped her get through the worst.

As she did her dawn chores at the stables, she went through her list of preparations. The weather remained warm and sunny, and those of the Family members who worked the farm had said last night that the next three weeks should be good. Good enough for Lori and the stridebeasts and the horses to journey to the tiny manor in the south. They should all have time enough to reach the place before spring storms.

After she'd finished her time with the animals, she ran to the Residence—conserving Flair for the journey tonight—and cleaned up, letting the waterfall sluice away the remnants of bad dreams, negative emotions, and the tears she allowed herself.

Turning up the heat of the waterfall, dumping more herbs than usual through it, she cherished the luxury. Up to three weeks on the road to her new home could be challenging, cleanliness-wise.

She fixed on the future, not the past. Tonight, she and her small herd of stridebeasts and horses, and, of course, Baccat, would leave.

Today was the last day in her childhood . . . place. She was an adult and would leave the Residence and the Family who would not acknowledge that, not allow her to live an adult life.

She traced the final route in her mind. Moving six stridebeasts and two horses would be a challenge, and for sure, they'd be seen, but *no one* had the right to stop them.

Today she'd say subtle good-byes to her Family and the land, and the Residence. She'd have liked to spend some time in the HouseHeart, but she would do *nothing* unusual that might alert anyone that she and the animals were leaving.

The Family would stop her if they could, would punish her, perhaps might try to imprison her, though with the development of her Flair, that was less likely than it had once been. The Residence remained a threat, if it could trap her somehow. That had to be avoided.

As she dressed in one of her best daily gowns that the older members of the Family preferred her to wear, which she'd be leaving behind like most of her wardrobe, she continued to send images of the route to her animals.

At breakfast, in a small, last test, she brought up scheduling the loyalty ceremony to confirm her as D'Yew for Beltane, next month. Silence fell across the long table of twelve; her cuzes, Zus and Vi, snorted in unison. "Best if we do that later in the year," Zus said with the authority of his father, Cuspid. "The political environment is stagnant right now; do it closer to the elections in the autumn."

Lori thought that was exactly what he'd said last year. She chewed her good food—well, yes, she'd miss someone else preparing food—then allowed herself a small frown and a considering hum. "Wouldn't it be better if I take my seat at the FirstFamily Council table if I've been confirmed by a loyalty ceremony and acting as D'Yew for some months?"

A few people crossed gazes, and then Cuspid said, "We can talk about this later." He cleared his throat. "I am thinking that we might want to do a GreatRitual for the estate and the Residence at Beltane. To address the landscaping. Perhaps we can refurbish the other two stable buildings, too." That was a clear sop to her, to keep her happy, even though she knew who would be gathering the most energy, sending the most energy, anchoring the ritual and any other plans they made.

She finished a bit of pancake and let her frown deepen. "I was sure that we spoke midwinter about me being confirmed D'Yew and participating with the other FirstFamily Nobles at GreatCircle Temple at Beltane."

"Things have changed with regard to the Traditionalist Stance political party," Vi stated, placing her napkin on her plate and rising, looking as if she was ready to leave the room before Lori, a definite breach of manners. On another day, Lori might have stood, too, to emphasize that she was the titular D'Yew. Cuspid frowned at his daughter, but no one said anything.

If Lori hadn't already decided to leave now, that action of Vi's would have confirmed her conclusion. The Family had solidified into status lines around her. She might be a figurehead with absolutely no power.

But her own feelings had been validated. To fight for the estate as Draeg had wanted her to do would be a large and ugly battle, and simply not worth it to her.

Let them continue with their political maneuvering without her. Let them pile wealth on wealth. Let them take care of the estate they cherished and she didn't.

She was nothing to them but a person to be used, and she sure didn't care to be used by *anyone* anymore. Not the Nobles she'd met the night before. Not her Family. Not her Residence. Not Draeg.

That was over.

Lori watched Vi strut with satisfaction from the room. Zus got up and left, too.

Scanning the table, Lori considered each face and couldn't believe that any of these people could or would spearhead a plan to kill anyone, even the despised Hollys. Her relatives were, primarily, prideful isolationists who liked living in the past, when Lori's MotherSire had been a real power in the FirstFamily Council, years before Lori's existence.

And Vi and Zus had never impressed Lori as incredibly competent.

After folding her own softleaf as GrandLady D'Yew should on her plate, Lori stood, inclined her head to the rest of her Family, and wished them good day.

*H*er monthly duty had her walking the land today. Sentimentally she felt it might be an omen.

Yes, there were views that ached her heart with their beauty, and that she'd miss. And when she sat in the small grove where she'd spent so much time of tears and triumphs, learned to meditate and breathe and *think* for herself, she knew this loss would grieve her. So she stared until the last image of the wondrous place imprinted upon her brain and the memory sphere she carried with her.

She wondered a little what the bespelled globe would pick up of her emotions. She wouldn't be trying to impress them on the sphere. Excitement and anticipation, surely. Echoes of the lost love of Draeg? How much had he wanted her instead of her estate?

Biting her lip that nearly curved in a smile, surprising her, she reckoned that Draeg had had no thought of her estate when they made love.

She went to the gates of the estate and looked out, as she had so often as a child. Until last year and her Second Passage that marked her as an adult, she'd measured her height and age by these gates. Curling her hand around the edged bars, she felt the warmth. Yes, spring had arrived and it was time to go.

Her heart agreed with her head that it was past time.

She stood there until the late afternoon sun heated her and a brisk breeze swept from the ocean. She had enough mental pictures of such panoramas.

One last, very important task. Up to the parapet on the roof of the Residence and her tiny, hidden greenhouse tray that held the cuttings of the bushes and trees that she could propagate when she arrived at her new home. Including rootstocks of the main Yew of their most ancient grove, and clippings of others. She'd transfer each into a bespelled flask and be done.

Working in the sunshine and the quiet high above the estate, caring for plantlings, setting them in a container that would fit in her best saddlebag, she soaked in the atmosphere of her estate and said good-bye as the sun dipped toward the horizon, until footfalls broke the silence.

Lori turned. "Vi?"

"Here you are!" Vi yanked Lori from the roof onto the parapet walkway, slamming her against the taller, waist-high wall of the crenellation. Lori yelled as her body hit the stone, her whole side bruised.

She reached for her Flair, for her personal armor, but as in the glider accident, it didn't respond as quickly for her as when she coated others.

Zus arrived, grabbing her hair and spinning her away, this time with more accuracy as she headed for the lower, square opening in the wall. She'd fall three stories onto flagstones and die.

Lori flung out her arms, thought she heard a bone crack as her wrist crashed into the edge, fear and pain surging through her with awful nausea. She dropped to the floor, rolled as best she could away from the wall. *Residence!* she cried mentally. *Help me!* She sent a visual of herself, on the wall walk, hoping the Residence would buckle the stones beneath the twins' feet, or rearrange the wall to barricade her from them. Nothing.

When she tried to visualize the stables, the images faded from her mind . . . due to fear and . . . her head had hit the wall, too, at some point; blood ran sticky down the side of her face. Her thoughts were too foggy! She dragged in a big breath. Her mind was too misty to 'port!

When it stopped spinning, she'd have a chance. No time to be conservative with her Flair. Use it all as needed. Pulling from her own reservoir, she sent the best Healing spell she knew, one that she used on her stridebeasts, to her head and her wrist, even as she staggered to her feet.

Then she saw the gleam of the weapons in their hands. To Lori's horror, Vi held a blaster, and Zus a knife.

She stilled. "It might be hard to explain away knife or blaster wounds," she stated. Steadying her breathing, her *self*, so her mind would clear, she could use her Flair.

They had no notion of her Flair, or the power of it. No one here but Baccat knew of her personal armor. And they never considered her as a person. Now she knew that to Vi and Zus she was simply an obstacle in their way. A *thing*, not someone with hopes and dreams like them at all.

Zus grinned, nastily. "Better that you don't show a knife or blaster wound, but no one might notice when you're smashed from a fall and down on the ground."

"We can use our Flair to change you," Vi added.

Lori didn't think they'd ever seen a mangled body in their lives, let alone worked spells on one.

When they went out into Druida City, they didn't see the alleys with dead rats that Lori had with Baccat. Vi and Zus were transported by glider or teleportation, saw only pretty places, rich places as elegant as D'Yew Residence. Which, Lori thought distantly, confirmed Draeg's idea that the whole overarching plan had been made by Noble allies of the Yews.

"And no one will question *us*," Vi sneered.

"Why are you doing this?" she demanded, keeping them talking.

"You've ruined everything. The FirstFamilies are buzzing around our allies and they told us, *us*, to go away." Vi's nose pinched. "And the FirstFamilies are talking about *you*, Loridana. How do they know *you*? How could they *like you*? They weren't supposed to ever notice you."

"Which of you will take our title, become GrandLady or GrandLord?" Lori asked. The soles of her feet pulsed with power; she felt rooted not only to the stone she stood on but all the way down through the Residence to the bedrock of the planet.

"We will share," Vi said.

"We will share," Zus said at the same time.

They grinned at each other, and Vi lowered the blaster and moved it aside from Lori. She didn't seem to notice.

Lori began breathing deeply, wondering if she could—*no! Don't wonder. Do!* So, through her feet, she began stringing threads of power, of Flair, from the storage areas of the Residence, from some of the less-than-necessary spells. She wouldn't put the house in danger, but she'd use everything she needed to protect herself, reclaim what she'd funded the last couple of years.

This time when she pulled on her personal armor, she made sure she kept it invisible and thinner than ever.

Then she *expanded* it so it reached beyond herself, slammed her cuzes against the wall, pinning their arms that held the weapons.

Lori stared at her twin cuzes. In a battle between her and them, she'd always, *always*, lost. Her word had never been taken over theirs.

Draeg's furious words came to her mind, even as the remembrance of his voice stabbed her heart. "Aren't you going to fight for your legacy? For your estate? For your *home*?"

As she stared at them, the gray stone of the Residence edging her view, the land descending to the bluff and the river in the distance, the answer came to her.

No. Because this was not her home.

Her home was her sense of self. Her home was the love she felt for her animals and they felt for her, as once her home had been with Draeg. And the agony of that thought had her mind, her heart frozen for a few instants.

She swallowed, stiffened her spine, sent the hurt away.

Her home was her land in the south.

This had never been her home, merely the place of her childhood that she'd survived. She cared not for the wealth, or the big estate, or the power.

*P*ain! *It rolled through Draeg in a sickening wave, made him stagger a step or two.*

"What's wrong?" asked Tinne Holly sharply, slapping a hand around Draeg's biceps to steady him. Draeg was in a sparring room in The Green Knight Fencing and Fighting Salon, challenging all comers. Away from the whole Yew mess that the First-Families Council had convened to discuss.

Head smacking against a wall! "Lori!" Draeg snapped. Yeah, the pain wasn't his, but from his HeartMate. "Someone hurt her!"

Tinne's face set. "Bad?"

"Bad enough."

"Where?"

But Draeg followed the tiny link between them, still big enough to transmit life-threatening danger, and that's what she felt. As for him, blood drained from his face and cold sweat coated him. "She's on the estate, near or in the Residence, I think."

He checked the aura hooks he'd set in her Family. Yes! The

female twin hovered close to Lori. The male twin moved rapidly in the same direction.

"The Residence or her Family is hurting her?" Tinne questioned.

Draeg shrugged, stepped away from his friend. "I'm going there."

"Wait, take me, too—and, *Captain of the Guards Winterberry! SupremeJudge Ailim Elder, to me, emergency! Green Knight 'port stations!*"

The older man with a head of gray hair, Winterberry, arrived first, hopped off the pad, and reset it. A blazer showed in his hand. "What is it?"

"Assault and attempted murder of my HeartMate, Lori D'Yew," Draeg said through cold lips, "at her Residence."

Winterberry stared at him for too long, then waved. "Go. I'll muster the guard and do this legally, by the front gates."

"They won't let you in."

"Ruis Elder has Earthan machines that will break down the gates if they refuse to obey the law. The laws *all* FirstFamilies crafted and swore to at the beginning of our society and culture. The laws Ioho T'Yew reaffirmed, as did his daughter Taxa D'Yew, when they were confirmed as members of the FirstFamilies Council."

Thirty-seven

*S*tunned, Lori stared at the twins. *"You truly tried to kill me. And not just now. The glider accident."* After a noisy sucking in of air, shaking her head, she said, "And not only me. Politics. Alliances. You're part of the Traditionalist Stance"—she jabbed her finger at one of her cuzes, then the other—"and believe that hurting children is all right?"

"Whom are you referring to?" asked Zus in a bragging tone. "Watson Clover? Marin Holly?"

"Watson Clover." Lori had vaguely heard of the child, and of course all of the Yews had been scandalized when Watson's father, a former Commoner, had become the Captain of AllCouncils. She recalled that gossip since it had been talked about for a good three months at dinner.

"Watson Clover," she repeated. "His mother is a FirstFamily child. Like me. Like you."

"Sedwy Grove is defective," Vi said reasonably. "She was a part of the Black Magic Cult who killed people."

Zus grinned, and Lori definitely didn't like the light in his eyes. Carefully, warily, she tested her link between them, *felt* that he'd developed a taste for killing . . . or liked the power he felt when hiring a killer to end a life. He licked his lips.

Lori's throat had simply dried. "The Residence had me read that legal case. Sedwy was used by the Black Magic Cult. They mined her knowledge as an anthropologist for their dark rituals." Lori's next breath came softer. "And if you consider *her* defective, what about yourselves?"

They looked blank.

Flipping a hand at them, Lori said, "You've shown that you will attempt to kill and kidnap children."

Their mouths fell open at the same time. Zus laughed. Vi gasped, and she screeched, "How dare you! We are nothing like them."

"You are exactly like them."

Shuffling feet. Lori looked toward the nearest open door down to the inside of the Residence. Cuspid stood there, standing slump shouldered and nearly broken in the doorway. He'd overheard the conversation.

Her gaze focused on him, and she asked softly with no shrill of pain or surprise. They *couldn't* harm her. And soon she would be away. "You would let them kill me?"

Cuspid flinched. "They are merely . . . disciplining you."

"By trying to throw me off this wall? But disciplining me is what you all liked to do, isn't it?" She was surprised how much bitterness she had inside herself. She disappointed herself. She would have to work on that in the future, for sure.

"You don't see the knife they have, that they took from the armory? The blaster? Not that they are any good with them."

Zus tried a feeble struggle. Lori pressed back. Urine stank up the walk for a few seconds before the Residence, the very quiet Residence, whisked it away. A dark stain showed on the front of Zus's trous. Lori shouldn't have smiled, but she did.

Her gaze swept all of them. The two she had pinned against the wall with her expanded personal armor, the maître de maison who stood at the threshold of the door to the walk, others behind him.

But this action of her cuzes had freed her in a different way, a legal way she hadn't thought she could use.

"You can't expect me to stay here where my own Family tries

to kill me. You can't expect me to stay in a Residence that will not protect me. That would be stupid, and you did not raise a stupid woman. I'm leaving you, the Family, the Residence, Druida City." The inner strands of her muscles began to tremble as the strain of holding Vi and Zus against their will wore on Lori.

Everyone appeared stunned. Both the twins' mouths had fallen open.

"You . . . you . . . don't want to be D . . . D'Yew?" Vi squeaked.

"I was only called D'Yew here," Lori said quietly. "A far too empty title."

But she could not leave it until she did one more duty, tried to set the Residence and her Family back on the right path . . . where they wouldn't be alienating the rest of the FirstFamilies until those powerful folk ganged up on them and . . . dissolved them? Split up the Family and the Residence?

She let her anger off her reins, a little bit, not childish anger, a woman's anger. A decent person's anger. A Head of Household's sorrowful anger, though only she had considered herself that.

"But I am not the only one they harmed. I suggest that when the guardsmen come calling, and they will, you hand over this murderous couple."

"No, no, you can't!" Vi shrieked. "They might try to . . . to . . . constrain . . . us." She blinked rapidly as if she couldn't even process that thought.

"Constrain?" Lori said. "For murderous attacks against the children of the FirstFamilies?" Again her gaze went to the older people, whom she was reluctant to call relatives. "How did this happen? When did this happen?" she asked. Maybe she *was* full of pride and hubris herself. But she'd always had a fine under-standing of what would happen to her if she strayed off the line of what was acceptable.

"When did you think you are so special, so entitled, that you are above the law?"

No one answered her.

"Because the Family has wealth and power and we live isolated from the others? Is that what happened?" Lori spread her hands, shaking her head.

Finally, finally, she spoke to the oldest being of the Yews.

"Residence? Did you know Vi and Zus conspired to kill me?" She couldn't believe that. But it must have. Where else would they map out their schemes? And this pain was nearly as bad as when she'd discovered Draeg's true motives. "Not even the Residence respected me, *liked* me," she murmured. Her determination to leave solidified into titanium.

"It began with old Ioho Yew," Cuspid said. "He lived so long. He rose so high in the prominence of the FirstFamilies."

"As high as you think we deserved."

"He was a *power*," Zus snapped. "*The* leader of the conservative faction, the elders of the FirstFamilies council."

"So he didn't move with the times," Lori said. She made a cutting motion. "That doesn't matter. I'm out of this, free of you all. What you do with these two, I don't care." She didn't. She simply didn't care about her cuzes. In one way that fact saddened her, but in another, just looking at them as they were—miserable human beings with no decency or compassion, nothing more important to them than their own needs—she was glad to be shed of them.

"No one is truly free," Cuspid said with a trace of his old unctuousness. "You will find that your *freedom* itself has constraints." Then he winced at his own usage of that word.

Lori nodded. "I hear you. I may not know what will bind me . . ." She simply couldn't help it, she had to say the words. "Honor will. Fairness, the need to be just." Love for her animals, whose welfare she would hold as closely as her own.

"Stup!" Zus sneered.

A booming like thunder broke the air of the cloudless blue sky.

"Open these gates in the name of the law, under penalty of forced entry," echoed in the air across the whole of the estate.

At the same time Corax alit atop a spire and cawed, *Teleport HERE!* Three men appeared and rushed to them. Draeg shoved Cuspid aside and lunged for Lori. Her focus and her Flair shattered, but before Vi and Zus could do more than push against the wall, the other two men were upon them, subduing them. One was the father of the boy she'd seen in the market the night before.

"Who?" she breathed.

"Tinne Holly, father of Marin Holly, whom your cuzes tried to poison."

Lori swayed. "Let go of me."

"Lori—"

Tinne Holly and the other man marched her cuzes down through the door, followed by a bleating Cuspid. "Go with your friends," she said to Draeg.

"You're injured."

She thought her dry lips cracked as she smiled. "Thank you for reminding me." Using the Flair she'd summoned before, she Healed herself until she felt only bruising. Then she let the remaining energy and Flair she'd harvested sink back into the Residence and the estate. It would need energy and Flair in the future more than she would. A last gesture of duty. Of kindness.

"Go, Draeg."

Tinne Holly stuck his head through the door. "Better come down, Draeg and D'Yew. Winterberry and some of his guards are in, and so are some members of the FirstFamilies."

With a snarling swearing, Draeg released her and strode to the doorway, paused there.

"You go on," Lori said, picking up her satchel of cuttings and holding it against herself. "I am not really D'Yew. I am Lori Valerian."

"Lori, I love you."

The words held no meaning. Not much held meaning. She was probably in shock.

"I'm sorry," she said. "I don't think you do."

"Are you teleporting to the stables?"

She found herself shaking her head. "I must retrieve my bags before I leave this place."

"*Draeg Betony-Blackthorn*," a man's voice shouted.

"Captain of the Druida City Guards." Draeg grimaced. "We'll

talk later." He searched her face, and then, broad shoulders slumping a little, he disappeared from sight.

A few seconds later she began to move. With each reeling step along the crenellated walkway to the door and down the stone stairs, Lori drew in deep breaths . . . and a trickle of power through her feet to keep her going.

She stopped in her rooms for the bag she'd had ready for weeks, stuck in a clunky no-time. Then she headed down the main staircase. Three-quarters of the way down, she heard voices and caught the flash of a Celtan guard's uniform, and her stomach jumped. Guards would only slow her down, and she was determined to leave, right now. She should have taken the narrow back stairs, but it hadn't occurred to her.

So she used every bit of her natural physical ability to glide around the end of the large balustrade and slip into the long pantry that would take her near the back door.

"I thought you'd come this way." Folia stood tall and imposing, excellently groomed with perfect facial enhancements that seemed to add to the disgust of her curled lip.

To Lori's own distress, she squeaked like a mouse confronted with Baccat, added a clearing of the throat to the sound, and words tumbled from her instincts, not her brain. "You were the leader all the time. Not the twins. You liked it when I was hit by the glider, showed up first when I lay on the stairs down to the river. Would you have killed me then? And you . . . yes, I smelled your perfume that night when you came into my room, before I teleported away and into the HouseHeart."

Folia's expression turned cruel; it had never had a long way to go to do that. "Finally you demonstrate a shred of reason. The twins are selfish, uncontrolled idiots and now they're in jail." She made a chopping gesture with her hand, the heavy lids of her eyes lowered until only an evil glint showed. "Vi and Zus were easily directed by me and my . . . assistant, we who are the heads of the Traditionalist Stance." Her mouth puckered sourly.

Lori said, "Well, you're not an uncontrolled idiot, just bad and selfish and prideful."

Folia slashed with a hand that Lori dodged. She took a couple of steps backing up, trying to stay calm enough to visualize the stable area in the tricky light of sunset.

Teeth gleaming in a nasty, biting smile, Folia prowled forward.

"What do you want?" Again words spilled from Lori, more to delay, she thought. Of course the woman wanted to be D'Yew, the power and status of that in the outer world.

"To be D'Yew, you stupid, stupid child. Now there is no way I can discreetly obtain the title and take over the estate; too many outsiders know of our situation." Her teeth actually snapped; Lori heard them. Now Folia's face became ugly with loathing. She seemed to grow taller, wider. "Did you think I didn't know about those pitiful little trips of yours in Druida City?" She smiled, and it was worse than any of her other expressions. Lori got the distinct feeling that the woman liked her fear, was punishing her for the disruption of Folia's plans. "I kept track of you through a spell on those disgusting clothes you used. So much easier for a nameless young woman to die in Druida City than Loridana Yew, here. But you escaped the gangs and even Vi's and Zus's pitiful attempts like the glider." Folia pouted. "I think, though, you could yet have a fatal accident."

Lori saw it in Folia's eyes, *felt* it. She'd been positioned beside a heavy cast-iron pan on the top of the pantry shelf, ready to fall and shatter her head, with a little help from Folia.

This time Lori didn't hesitate; she yanked power from the depths of the building's foundation, coated herself with personal armor. Better. Getting better at this.

The pot flew and fell. She felt a slight impact and it *bounced* off her shoulder, heading straight toward Folia, who was yanked back by a thick arm around her throat—Draeg's arm.

The pot hit Folia in the knee with a sickening crack, then dropped onto her feet. She screamed. Lori realized the hum she'd noticed but hadn't paid attention to stopped—the drone of a lot of people talking in the Residence. Footsteps rushed their way.

Draeg lowered the shrieking woman to the floor, his face expressionless. The warrior she'd rarely seen.

"They . . . are . . . in the pantry." The high, hiccupping voice belonged to Cuspid.

"Betony-Blackthorn's missing," a man said. His voice rose, projected from one of the main rooms. "Betony-Blackthorn, what the fliggering hell is going on?"

Draeg ignored the question, so Lori did too.

Her spine straightened. "I'm leaving."

He closed his eyes briefly, dipped his head; when he opened his lashes again, she thought she saw anguish. "Stay with me. With my Family. We can work this all out. Here in Druida."

Draeg and she stared at each other.

"To be used as a pawn in FirstFamilies bickering?" she asked.

"I promise you, I won't let that happen." He offered his hand. His expression hardened. "I won't let anyone use you."

She looked at his hand, blinked tears away.

"I can't," she said.

"When it comes down to it, you don't trust me to help you, do you?" he asked softly.

"I can't stay!" Tears seemed to fill her whole head. She couldn't answer the question about trust. She didn't think she even trusted herself. Trusted no human at all.

His fingers fisted. "You don't trust me." He continued in a resigned tone, "You're leaving your Family in an uproar."

"An uproar of their own making? Yes, I am. My cuzes tried to *kill* me, and I should have Family loyalty?" Easier to think of that anger and injustice to herself than how she hurt her lover.

His jaw clenched and a flush came to his skin. He hauled in an audible breath, and then his head angled as if he heard someone speaking to him on a private telepathic stream.

She turned away, but flat words from him stopped her. "What of the general good of the City of Druida? You need to stay to

inform the guards—the Captain of the Druida City Guards—
exactly what happened here."

Her face simply froze as her spine stiffened into complete
rigidity and she panted breaths through her mouth. "Air the deep
problems of my Family to outsiders? *Whine?*"

He moved around her, seeming to fill the corridor, stance wide
and braced. Eyeing him, she didn't think that she'd be able to get
by him. Her head throbbed; her neck and all the way down to her
lower back ached.

"Your Family's problems are already subject to outrageous
rumor. Help the guards straighten this out." Now Draeg sounded
cool, professional, detached, and her heart twisted.

Stopping the most bitter words that coated her tongue about
him and his spying—she wouldn't stoop to his level—she turned
on her heel. "Very well. We shall see where all this shall go." Oh,
yes, she felt betrayed by everyone in her entire life. She was accustomed to that from her Family, but not Draeg.

On a wave of ire, she whisked out of the pantry, past others
watching, down corridors, and into the visitors' reception room.
As she entered, all snapping discussion, orders, and conversation
died. Several men and women rose and walked toward her with
varying expressions crossing their very Noble features, FirstFamily Lords and Ladies, she thought. The big, rough-looking guy
stared at her—the tester, and now she knew it must be T'Ash
himself—observed her.

Another, more elegant white-haired man in the uniform of the
guards turned toward her.

She held her palm out. "Stop. I will say my piece once and nothing more." She swallowed and she dug deep for a Voice she, herself,
had never used but only heard, a Voice of Command.

"Residence, project all recorded actions on the south roof walkway beginning when Vi confronts me onto the closed curtains."

Thirty-eight

To *her surprise, it complied. The image wavered as it followed the* dips and bulges of the curtains, but the golden silkeen color didn't show through the viz. She saw herself alone, setting a last cutting into a bag.

Then Vi came into view and attacked her. Zus arrived and pulled a blaster.

"Stop!" The rasping order came from an old-and-ravaged-faced Cuspid. "Lies. This is a *complete falsehood*. My daughter would not have acted like that."

The image flicked off.

"Denial," someone murmured, and Lori heard that truth. Cuspid had sunk into his own little world where his children were honorable and he wasn't broken.

"What say you, Residence?" demanded one of the other First-Family lords.

The house remained silent.

"We always believed Loridana Itha might go mad and tell stories." Cuspid shook his head. "Such a curious nature and imagination and rebellious streak the child has." A pair of bracelets appeared in his hands.

"I'm done, and I'm gone." Lori rapidly backed away to the door.

"Those are DepressFlair bracelets," T'Ash rumbled. "Who would use DepressFlair bracelets on the Head of a Family?"

"Who would even *have* DepressFlair bracelets?" a lady's high voice demanded.

Lori dodged around an appalled Draeg and ran toward the pantry, fairly sure that not one of the outsiders would stop her, and they *would* stop Cuspid with his dreadful bracelets.

She had to get away, now, because sickness washed through her in waves with every pounding footstep. Her worst nightmare had come true. She'd discovered that her Family had never even liked her at all. That the Residence would always listen to someone else before it heard her.

Yes, absolutely, let them all, Family and Residence, deal with the results of their actions and beliefs.

Too curious? She'd asked too many questions before she knew it best to keep silent.

Too imaginative? Because she wondered what life was outside the estate? Yes.

Too rebellious? That was true. And not in what she thought was a standard childlike way.

A weird sound came to her ears and she realized she mewled, even as her vision blurred. She scuttled along hunched over, her hands wrapped around her stomach as if protecting her internal organs. *Stop. Again, stop.* So she did, and straightened, and took a softleaf from her trous pocket and mopped up and stuck her emotions about her Family behind a mental door and slammed it and locked it.

At least the Residence wasn't paying enough attention to her to delay her. No doubt fully occupied with the powerfully Flaired humans in its mainspace.

"Fare well, Residence," she whispered. And, now, she sincerely hoped it would. She sensed it listening, and the floor creaked like bitter laughter, but it said nothing.

Without another word, and not checking the light, not really caring, going on instinct as she had all this time, she teleported to the stables.

Immediately a wash of love surrounded her. Her six stride-beasts and two horses. She let herself slump, lean against a sturdy corral pole, let tears trickle down her face in the painted colors of the sunset. She sobbed for a couple of minutes before her wretchedness eased and all the mantras and rationalizations and affirmations that she'd dredged up all day to deal with a lost love swirled once more in her mind. Taking a large softleaf from her pocket, she wiped her face, blew her nose, and flicked it clean once more since it had an inbuilt spell.

Distress still hummed through her, giving her energy. *Act, now!* "Whirlwind Spell traveling garments," she ordered, and suffered through the cleansing and dressing. But after a minute she wore good, thick leathers, the trous set with a multitude of pockets. She tidily folded up the softleaf and put it away.

A couple of cleansing breaths and she strode to the paddock gate, opened it wide. "We are leaving now."

She felt an upsurge of excitement mixed with anxiety from them. "I will keep you all safe, all protected with weathershields and personal shields," she vowed. "We are Family."

Except one wasn't here. *Baccat?* she called, her throat closing at the thought that he'd changed his mind. After all, she could stay and probably become D'Yew in truth, but she didn't want the responsibility of dealing with the Family, even the remnants of the Family, who'd held no respect for her. Better to be a responsible member of *this* Family. *Baccat?* she called again, this time unable to suppress a little break in her mental voice.

You are distressed! You are lacerated in heart and body! I will come!

She sensed him near the main gate of the estate, and his upset soothed her. *No, stay there, we will be there in a little while. What distracted you?* Because something had, she knew that with her next inhalation, and realized the little confrontation in the pantry had taken a couple of minutes though time had stretched long for her.

I have been watching the great Nobles gathered outside the Yew gates.

More like tormenting them with catcalls. She chuckled, and was surprised she could yet feel amusement.

For an instant she thought of leaving by the little northeast gate as she'd planned, but there was no reason to, and that wasn't the statement she wanted to make. *We will be there shortly.* She looked at the herd. They remained inside the corral.

She lifted her chin. "I *can* cover all of us with a weathershield, and give each of you personal armor on the journey. We've been planning for this. If we leave now, we should have no trouble making the wayspot where we can sleep tonight. With prime food."

Tossing her head with a whinny, Smyrna paced out of the corral; Ragan followed as did the rest of her herd—*Lori's* herd. Her Family.

Once they'd lined up, she brought halter, harness, and a pack for each of them and readied them with steady voice and strokes. This settled them and focused all minds on the journey ahead of them. She saddled Ragan but led her through the estate instead of riding, as she would through the entire city, according to plan. What wasn't going to be according to plan was her route. There would be no weaving through medium-sized streets in the middle of the night to the small southwest gate of the city, but a straight and simple path east, then south to the main south gate.

All those trips, the studying of the map, the imagining of the route, for nothing . . . but it had gotten her accustomed to being in the city, being around strangers, out on her own.

When the last curve of the gliderway revealed the pillared entrance to the estates and the huge greeniron gates—and more people than she'd expected on the other side, all dressed better than she—her steps hesitated.

Baccat, sitting atop one of the tall pillars, turned to look at her, and she felt his cat smile.

Who are all these people? she asked.

Most of the FirstFamilies' Heads of Households are here to observe events and Us.

Lori swallowed. "Oh, joy."

There is Zanth's FamMan, T'Ash.

"T'Ash," she nearly whimpered. "I left him inside."

Zanth said he got bored inside, wanted to look at YOU more. You made him curious last night. WE are very important. There is T'Vine and FamCat Rhyz's woman, Avellana Hazel.

The prophet of Celta and his HeartMate, worse and worse.

Straif T'Blackthorn and Mitchella T'Blackthorn are in the Residence. Draeg let them in.

"Of course he did," she said faintly. At least she wouldn't be meeting his Family.

Along with Captain of the Guards, Ilex Winterberry, and Captain of AllCouncils, Walker Clover.

"They're inside?" she asked, still aloud, though she knew her Fam could hear. One of the horses tossed her head and Lori clamped down on her anxiety.

Yes. Along with T'Holly and his heir, Holm Holly.

The enemies of the Yews. "I'm glad I don't have to face them."

But now she came closer, she saw more than those Baccat had told her of. "Who else?"

D'Grove, Captain of the FirstFamilies Council.

"Oh."

She and T'Ash and T'Blackthorn watched you from behind a screen in the FirstFamilies Council room last night.

So that's who Lori had felt. She slowed her steps to more of a march. Her Family behind her walked with pride. She'd reached the gates and gestured them open. Saw the man with silver-gilt hair, whom she recognized as Tinne Holly. His arm encircled the waist of a woman in her midthirties who looked a little frightened but determined. Much like Lori felt. The man's other hand rested on the shoulder of the boy she saw last night. Lori could see the blazer on Tinne's hip. A girl a little younger than Lori, *feeling* a lot younger, stood near her mother.

And the nuclear Family of the Tinne Hollys, Baccat ended.

Absolutely the worst. The woman Lori's MotherSire had wed

as a child, tortured, and been killed by in self-defense. The act that had driven Lori's mother mad. Lori would have to pass them to leave the estate and the city. Calm, deep, regular breaths.

Greetyou ALL! Baccat projected, leaping down from the pillar with grace and Flair and landing a pace outside Yew estate just before Lori stepped from her—former—land.

Lori's eyes widened as the first man bowed, T'Ash. He winked a bright blue eye. "Greetyou."

"Greetyou, T'Ash." Lori inclined her body . . . instinctively as trained, from one FirstFamily GrandLady to her equal, a First-Family GreatLord.

"Who are you?" asked the boy near Tinne Holly. "I saw you last night, but not the night before. I told everyone you weren't the woman who tried to give me a flatsweet."

Lori's stomach clutched. She didn't know all of the twins' evil actions, and didn't want to learn them. She nodded to him.

Her steps had slowed enough that Smyrna protested mentally, and she knew a shove in her back would be coming, so she picked up her pace. "I am Loridana Itha Valerian," she replied.

He scowled. "Not D'Yew?"

"No. I was never confirmed as D'Yew by my Family. Never had loyalty oaths sworn to me." Her glance traveled over all the Nobles, rested again on the boy. "I was never confirmed as D'Yew by any Councils, not the FirstFamilies Council, not the Noble Council, not the AllCouncils."

"You're nobody, then."

That hurt a little, but it had always been true.

"Marin," scolded his mother.

"I am Loridana Itha Valerian," Lori repeated. But she couldn't go on. She could *not* walk past this woman who had been harmed by her Family—by the human Yews to whom Lori was related.

She halted and held up her hand to her herd and they all stopped, too.

Standing in front of the woman, Lahsin Holly, under the fierce gaze of her husband, the wary eyes of her children, Loridana bowed deeply, not watching to see whether they studied her vulnerable neck to strike. Yet bent over, Lori said, "As the former Loridana Itha Valerian D'Yew, on behalf of the Yews and the Yew Residence, I apologize for the actions of my MotherSire, Ioho T'Yew, and all his great cruelties to you. I acknowledge the faults of his actions toward you and that any consequences of those actions were just." Now she peeked upward and caught an astonished expression on Tinne Holly's face, and then it relaxed into what she thought was his usual good humor. "I apologize to Lahsin Burdock Rosemary Holly"—Baccat had told Lori the names of the woman that he knew—"and to the Holly Family for the words and actions of my mother, Taxa D'Yew." She straightened and gathered the glances of everyone else. "I apologize on behalf of the Yews for the actions of Folia, Vi, and Zus Yew to any Family who was harmed by their recent threatening actions, and acknowledge the debt of the Yews and any reparations demanded."

"Well done," murmured D'Grove.

Then the gates shook as the land trembled—at her words or her last footstep. The stridebeasts shuffled and Lori walked away, focused on a prancing Baccat, nearly dizzy as a dark load she'd carried within her dissolved. Ill will and negativity lodged within her fell away with each pace she took.

The Nobles remained on either side of the road and bowed toward her in a ripple as she passed—a heady thing if she'd let herself believe in their honor and respect—and she walked to Bountry Boulevard and away from the estate.

She didn't look back.

Draeg paced. *He should go to Lori. He should find her and claim* her. He should carry her and her herd to T'Blackthorn's.

She wouldn't allow that.

He should go with her to the Valerian estate, accompany her. Walk along the public road with her. *Convince* her they belonged together.

But she didn't trust him to take care of her here, to fight for her. His heart felt skewered by that spear of distrust, barely able to beat around it. A deep and abiding ache.

Winterberry and the Hollys talked and talked and talked with Cuspid Yew, the maître de maison, and the Residence about . . . stuff. Penalties. Allies. Expectations.

They were all relieved that the Residence hadn't fought them, though the looming threat of a huge Earthan machine at the main back gate must have helped. Draeg's father, Straif T'Blackthorn, had murmured that all the FirstFamily Residences had hooked into the Yew Residence communication channels and were keeping it sane.

Draeg didn't think so, sort of thought it had slipped sanity a while back.

He wanted to be with Lori. In frustration, he banged on the wall with a fist.

"Stop that!" the Residence ordered. "Haven't you done enough, *spy*? Haven't you and Loridana done enough, bringing this scandal upon us?"

Fury popped words right out of his mouth. "Not true. Vi and Zus brought all this down on them because of their actions with the Traditionalist Stance. Because they are kidnappers and attempted murderers. Because your Family and you have been isolated and the twins spoilt."

Teeth hurting from the confrontation with Lori, Draeg stomped back toward the formal visitation chamber. As he went, he snapped, "Yew Residence!"

"I hear you." The voice came echoing hollowly down the corridor, and Draeg sensed it was dealing with several conversations at once. Too bad.

He translocated the button Tinne Holly had found under the faulty balcony from a drawer in Draeg's apartment over the stables, stopped and held it up to a scrystone so the Residence could see it. "Do you recognize this? It was found at the site of a murder attempt. Do you, with your prodigious memory, recall any one of your inhabitants walking your halls missing a button like this?"

Draeg demanded—and *his* voice echoed. Enough that he thought those in the visitors' chamber would hear him.

The atmosphere closed in around him, became leaden.

"Answer him," Captain of the Guards Ilex Winterberry said softly, and Draeg had no trouble hearing him.

"Zus lost a cuff button a few months ago," the Residence said dully. "A seamstress replaced it."

Draeg sucked in air and continued. "Look at you. No one wants to stay with you. No reasonable person, at least," he amended.

"You mock our grief," the Residence snapped.

"And which grief is that? Grief that *three* of your inhabitants are murderous? Grief that the Yew name is besmirched with dishonor? Grief that you must suffer through a scandal of your own making?" He laded his tones with scorn. "Certainly not grief that Lori left you." As she'd left him, wouldn't accept his support.

"She is an ingrate," the Residence said, but he thought he heard a wail of disbelief behind that, as though a wind blew through all the halls of the house.

"No. She is a woman and she is an adult and worthy of respect, which you never gave her."

"*She is GONE. My baby Yew, the last of the direct line.*"

She was gone. Draeg couldn't stand it any longer; he escaped the Residence, too.

Thirty-nine

Guards cleared the way for her and her animals; Baccat paraded in front, in his ruby collar he'd asked to wear and she'd put on him.

So many people watched her. So many people *saw* her now, it was scary.

Other people and Fams walked with her: T'Ash and his big black-and-white Fam, Zanth, and T'Ash's daughter, Jasmine—both humans telling her that she'd qualify to found a GrandHouse herself. But she didn't answer them, barely looked at them. So they dropped away and others took their place.

Avellana Hazel offered sanctuary at the new Intersection of Hope Cathedral for Lori and her beasts, but Lori shook her head, and the woman murmured an odd blessing and faded away.

Then Vinni T'Vine, the prophet, loped beside her. "I didn't see this coming."

She slid her gaze to his lined face. He looked older than he was. She shrugged.

"I knew of the plan that Tinne Holly and others of my age group formed. We asked Draeg Betony-Blackthorn to try to find out if any of the Yews were involved with the fanatics of the Traditionalist Stance. The violent fringe."

"And they were, and Draeg did."

"It was not a good plan."

Lori shrugged. "It's done."

Y*es, Lori had left. Was truly gone. And this place that had been* wonderful—well, the land and the trees and the river and the Yew groves, the natural atmosphere of this place—yet tugged at chords deep within him. Yeah, music in his blood.

But the damn Residence, and its population—if he thought about it, he could vomit, or worse, let the red of fury flow over his vision and fight and . . . maim.

Draeg made for the stables, and halfway there, he began to run. Yesterday when she'd dismissed him, she hadn't translocated any of his belongings to T'Blackthorn Residence—couldn't—so he went to collect them now.

The shadow of Corax kept pace with him.

I am sorry you are so sad, my FamMan.

Though his throat and mouth remained dry with anger and disappointment and guilt and other strong emotions blowing through him like a biting wind, his mental voice had none of those problems. *I am sorry, too. Sorry for me, sorry for Lori. Just plain sorry.* He stopped abruptly when the stables and paddock came into view—an open gate to the enclosure, the stables completely closed.

A kick in the gut, the place he'd lived and loved, and where he'd worked with and loved *Lori*, deserted and abandoned. His breath stopped, and his mind swam before he reminded himself to breathe.

Corax flew down to land on Draeg's shoulder, clicking his beak. *It is sad they are gone. But better they are gone than here with mean people.* A wave of sorrow came from him.

Draeg gasped in some air, continued telepathically, *You came here because of the horses, Smyrna and Ragan, to be with them. Yet they have gone and you're still here.*

The raven nipped Draeg's ear. He grimaced and grunted pain.

You are my FamMan, of course I stay with you. He paused. *I spoke to them. They love the woman and woman loves them. They like the other four-footeds as much as they like me and have more in common with the ground-bound.* Corax lifted his wings, brushing Draeg's cheek with feathers. *I FLY.*

Draeg stroked the bird. "I love you." He needed to say it aloud. "You will be the best one to help me get through this, I know."

Thanks. I love you, too. Woman should have stayed with you, but she wouldn't. You are right.

Shaking his head, Draeg said, "I wonder about that."

"Kyurk!" Corax vocalized. *And the horses have to put up with that CAT!* The feathers around his throat ruffled. *I am better here, with you.*

"You could fly and observe them," Draeg said, beginning to walk to the office door. He wanted to take time, and not to teleport. Besides, he didn't know if Lori or any other Yew might have cleaned the apartment, messed with his things, moved the furniture, and teleporting into a place you didn't know could be deadly.

I could, but I won't. I'm staying with you. She has other people, Lords and Ladies, maybe friends of yours, watching her. Probably through the city and all tonight. You should check with them.

Draeg's eyes widened; he hadn't thought of that. And he became aware of a low-level feed from his bond with Vinni T'Vine. Draeg accessed the stream of sensation-information. Vinni accompanied Lori and her animals through the city.

She was safe. The FirstFamilies would ensure she met with no harm on the road to her Valerian estate. Funds from that council had been allocated to hire a couple of mercenaries for her, perhaps help with nightly waystation fees. But . . . Vinni realized Draeg had tapped him and began a mental conversation.

My friend Draeg, I think that this lady, this former D'Yew, is such a matter of curiosity for the nosy FirstFamilies and other Nobles that she will have "exalted" company all the way to her estate.

That's good, Draeg replied.

Yes, since it appears she set out on this venture with minimal supplies.

What?

For instance, I am thinking how I can augment her food, and perhaps food for her animals, though I believe she has gilt and feed enough for them.

Nausea rolled through him. He hadn't known, hadn't made the mental leap, despite her lack of coin, her shabby clothes, that she was—would be on this trip—poor. But of course she wouldn't take anything from her Family, no gilt, and, of course, the Residence and the Farm would note if she'd stockpiled food, so she wouldn't have.

Vinni continued, *Though from my conversations with her Fam, HE will be fine.*

Baccat, Draeg sneered. That Fam would ensure his lifestyle. Didn't he have a pouch full of jewels? Did Lori know of that?

He is wearing a ruby necklace of great value.

Draeg sucked in some dust and coughed.

And, my pardon, but I must pay more attention to your lady.

Of course. Draeg hesitated, but he needed the information too much. *Do you see us together?* A whisper from his mind to Vinni's.

The future hasn't been narrowed down to a single option, yet.

Oh, Draeg said.

But I will remind you that HeartMates are forever, and I, personally, have never known a couple to stay apart for very long.

Draeg wasn't sure what Vinni meant by "very long." *Thank you*, he said.

It will work out, Vinni replied casually, then narrowed their bond.

Nothing about this whole fliggering matter felt casual to Draeg. He yanked at the office door, and it swung open easily, nearly unbalancing him. Striding through the office, he ran up the stairs and found everything as he'd left it. With a packing spell he'd mastered years ago, he drew everything that was his from the rooms and piled it on the bedsponge. More than he'd realized. Chanting a short chorus, he sent all his stuff to his chambers in

T'Blackthorn Residence, then turned and left, not quite inclined to quit this place.

A couple of minutes later, he found himself standing at the double doors to the northern main stable block. He knew what lay beyond there, but he had to see it again.

Pushing in a door, he opened it only wide enough to see the mosaic. The best he'd ever done. Beautiful.

He'd created it for Lori. She was gone.

With an oath and a sweep of his arms, he covered the whole floor with several centimeters of earth. He turned and exited into the last streaks of too-bright golden sunset, slammed and locked the door behind him, and teleported to T'Blackthorn Residence.

The journey passed quickly and with no outward trouble at all due to the fact that professional guards showed up every day to accompany Lori and her small herd. One was the Noble Cratag T'Marigold, who lived across the street from the Yews, as well as guards clothed in the colors of the FirstFamilies.

She and her Family of animals had been directed to the best places to camp, and she'd paid from her diminishing gilt for the best provender for her beasts. Then she'd been told the FirstFamilies would finance her. Her pride fought with her love of her animals, and love won.

Baccat had smirked the entire trip.

Misery had plagued Lori internally—too much time to think of Draeg and the past and suffer. So when they reached the Valerian estate and the end of the road, Lori was as glad to see the place as any of her stridebeasts and horses. Even more grateful that it wasn't in quite as good shape as she'd expected—which led to hard work, physical and magical, with a drain of energy and Flair that kept her concentrated on the here and now.

Though in the few minutes before sleep overwhelmed her in the dark softness of her bed, she acknowledged that her vision of the future was smudged by the ache of the past. But she'd get over

Draeg, second by second, minute by minute, day by day as time passed. That she promised herself.

And the use of her Flair in making the estate—land and house—a jewel, and in caring for her animals, was incredibly satisfying. Finally, *she* decided how to run a place, what to do daily, though she had to admit Cuspid and Folia and the Residence had trained her well.

She didn't think of her human Family much. Didn't receive the newssheets or keep up with the vizes about any prosecution of the Yews. Could care less about any scandal of her Family in Druida City.

As the weeks passed from spring to summer, she was satisfied, even content, but she wasn't happy. Having all her animals safe, the new animals she'd been able to purchase, training the horses and working on the estate, all those factors should have filled her life, her heart, to the brim.

But they hadn't. She still felt she had this gaping hole in her. And occasionally she could feel an emotion or two from Draeg no matter how threadlike their bond was. Those were usually fierce and intense. While she had worked on making her life serene, actually dull, he seemed to have reverted to old and violent habits.

She ached for them. Maybe, someday, she'd forgive him. She thought so, but couldn't quite visualize it yet. Actions and lifestyles she could imagine coming true, she could work toward. She wasn't ready for him, for all the immense changes he would bring.

The morning of her birthday, the day before the starships had landed, the holiday of Discovery Day, Lori decided to make an apple pie. She'd found a whole stack of cookbooks in the kitchen and the pantry and learned to cook, though this would be her first pie.

She'd just slid the pie into the oven, when her old-fashioned scry bowl played a short tune and she stared at it. Not the music denoting business—the buying of animals and grain, the selling of goods or services. Yellow swirled above the bowl. Someone with great Flair, then.

The song stopped, then began again. Dusting off her hands,

she walked over to the bowl on the counter, circled the rim with her finger to answer the call.

A man's narrow face topped by sandy hair stared at her, and her stomach tightened. She knew enough of distant family likeness to guess who this was.

"Greetyou, Loridana Itha Valerian . . ."

His words hung as if he waited for her to finish her own name with "Yew." She didn't.

"I'm—"

"FirstFamily GrandLord Straif T'Blackthorn."

He inclined his head. "Right. I'm scrying on my own behalf about my son, Draeg—"

"Has something happened to him?" she rushed.

His eyes bored into hers. "You left."

She pulled an impassive mask over her face. "He spied on me and betrayed me."

"I understand that you would think so. Know this, you can ask me *anything* about him and I will answer. No exceptions."

Her breath caught and a thousand questions crowded her mind.

"But I am also calling on behalf of the AllCouncils with regard to the Yew Family and the Yew Residence." A beating pause. "Which of my topics do you wish to speak to me about first?"

Lori swallowed. "Draeg. How is he?"

"Poorly. He grieves. He works at the Sallows'." Another pause. "Occasionally he stalks trouble in the city . . . and finds it."

She could only think to say, "I'm sorry."

"We all are. Especially Tinne Holly, whose plan it was for him to infiltrate you—the Yews. Both T'Holly, Tinne's father, and I have wrenched promises from Tinne that he would not bother you. Otherwise you'd've found him on your doorstep. Maybe his whole Family, too."

"I appreciate your restraint."

"Lori Valerian, do you love my son?" T'Blackthorn snapped the order.

"Yes," she replied without thinking, then bit her lip, sniffed back tears, and met his gaze. "Yes, I believe I do." Her turn to hesitate. "Does he love me?"

"Yes, indeed he does. How long are you going to inflict this suffering upon both of you?"

"If I . . . if I contacted him and . . . told him I forgave him"—she hadn't known until that instant that she had, that time had mended that wound—"and asked him to come and join me, would he?"

T'Blackthorn nodded. "He would. We, his Family, would be sad he is so far from us, but he should be with you."

"Does he love Yew estate?"

"He did and he does," T'Blackthorn stated flatly. "But he has not returned there since the day you and your herd left." The GrandLord smiled humorlessly. "Plenty of the rest of us have been back there, trying to fix things, but not Draeg."

Her face felt wet and she scrubbed at it, then realized she wept. "I hurt," she said, then cringed.

T'Blackthorn's expression softened. "You've had a lot of pain in your life." Another pause. "But you escaped a toxic environment, reached for and found your freedom. I congratulate you and I am proud of you."

Her mouth fell open. She didn't think anyone had said that to her in her life.

"You've made a new life; are you happy in it, Loridana?"

"I've been . . . content. But I miss Draeg."

"I am also pleased to hear that. Do you have his perscry locale?"

"I—no." Her hands twined in her apron. Somehow T'Blackthorn's scry should have reassured her. But he wasn't Draeg. She'd have to face rejection from Draeg.

"Do you wish his perscry locale?"

"Yes," she made herself say, then weakened it with, "I must think."

T'Blackthorn's brows dipped. "Don't think too long, and don't *feel.* Just do." His quick smile was lopsided. "I know what I'm speaking about."

She couldn't guess that he did, but she nodded anyway and said, "But he loves you and his Family and Druida City and . . . Yew estate."

With a cutting gesture, T'Blackthorn said, "Don't rationalize or put obstacles in your way. A man should be with his woman."

They stared at each other.

"I am also calling on behalf of the AllCouncils with regard to the Yew Family and Residence," T'Blackthorn repeated, and focused her thoughts on the other matter she didn't want to think about, though it was less painful than Draeg.

"I heard you."

His eyes piercing, T'Blackthorn dropped his next words like heavy weights. "Yew Residence is dying."

All the breath pumped from Lori as she fell against the edge of the counter. "What?" she squeaked, and then she said more firmly, "Impossible."

"It is quite possible. The Yew Family is in great disarray. The twins, Zus and Vi, were convicted of attempted murder, fitted with DepressFlair bracelets, and banished to the island where we send such criminals. Their father, Cuspid Yew, accompanied them at his own request." He cleared his throat and glanced beyond her left shoulder. "Folia Yew committed suicide before she came to trial."

"What?" Lori's knees gave out and she sat down hard on the kitchen floor. Impossible. Folia wouldn't have done that. "She's dead?"

"Yes. GentleLady Valerian?" T'Blackthorn demanded. "Are you all right?"

"One moment, please." With a weak gesture she slid a high stool from the breakfast bar to her, struggled onto it, stared blankly down at the concerned face of T'Blackthorn.

Softly he began again. "The Yew Family is in great disarray. There is no one person who has great enough Flair to become the

GrandLord or GrandLady. Yew Residence is dying. It has used much of its stored energy to sustain itself. It cannot, or will not, accept help from us, the other FirstFamilies. Our Residences inform us that the former masculine personality has fractured and, like the Family, other personalities struggle for sanity and supremacy."

Lori thought of the HouseHeart. Gentle, loving. Dying.

Forty

*S*o *my question, as the representative of the* First Families, *is whether* you, former Loridana Yew, will allow the Yew Family to be dissolved and the Yew Residence to die?"

Shock kept her silent and frozen for a good five minutes. T'Blackthorn did not end the scry. She got the idea that he'd wait septhours for her answer, and if *she* ended the scry, she'd have someone from the FirstFamilies on her doorstep . . . they probably already had someone here, or staying with one of the neighbors. That's what her Family would have done, and all the FirstFamilies were known for their manipulation.

"Loridana?"

He'd told her not to rationalize or put obstacles in the way of loving Draeg. But her mind did so now with this outrageous question.

"My Family will not want me," she said weakly.

"As opposed to being dissolved?" T'Blackthorn asked. He coughed and again did not look at her. "Much regarding your life in the Residence and the way the twins and Folia treated you was revealed during the trials. I'm told that shocked the rest of the Yews."

Humiliation flushed through her, hot and nasty. She didn't look at him, either.

"And, Loridana, can't you think of the other members of your Family that you valued?"

Too many faces came to mind. People she knew little, but respected, as they respected her—now.

"You want me to return." She focused on scanning the house she was making a home. "All of you. Every other FirstFamily Lord and Lady wants me to do this, to save the Yews and become GrandLady D'Yew in fact."

"That is correct."

"You're the representative of the AllCouncils. The AllCouncils want me back, too."

"Yes."

A thought occurred. "What happened to the Traditionalist Stance?"

"I'm afraid that political party could not survive the scandal of its fanatics," T'Blackthorn said with false concern. "Though many of us thought the whole thing nothing but fanatics in the main anyway."

"It's over."

"So it seems."

That had her meeting his eyes again. "What do you mean?"

"Folia Yew indicated to you that she had a partner in leading the fanatics?" T'Blackthorn asked.

"Yes."

"My son heard that, also. But she refused to say anything after she was arrested, and then she . . . died."

"Oh." Lori thought she heard all sorts of nuances in his voice.

"We continue to be watchful and alert. Her partner must be hiding. Sooner or later we will get him."

"Oh."

"Do you think any other Yews than Zus, Vi, and Folia were involved?"

"No."

"Loridana, are you going to let your birth Family be dissolved?

Your childhood home die? Your estate be confiscated by the All-Councils and parceled up? Your Yew trees destroyed?"

"They wouldn't do that! No one would do that!"

"No?" T'Blackthorn shrugged. "Who knows what happens to the land when the Family with ties to it is dissolved, and the Residence dies?"

He only let a minute pass this time before saying matter-of-factly, "We have a fast personal airship waiting to bring you here to Druida City on the estate to your north. It can leave in an septhour and you'll be here by noon tomorrow. I assure you, your remaining Family will welcome you with tears of joy." Something in his voice caught her attention.

"T'Blackthorn?" she asked reflexively.

"A Family should be cherished, Loridana. They should have cherished you. They failed. Can you find it within you to cherish them?"

She stared.

"As a young man, I lost all of my Family to a sickness, you know."

She hadn't. "No wonder you love the one you have now, and Draeg loves you."

T'Blackthorn nodded.

"But my animals! They *are* my Family. I will not desert them."

T'Blackthorn's nostrils flexed. "We have transports—"

"But—"

He lifted a hand, and she sensed the power of the man. "We have sufficient transports standing by to move your animals and bring them to Druida City as quickly as possible. They should not be more than a few days behind you."

She had to choose. To abandon her Family here to save those she'd already turned her back on.

Baccat hopped onto the counter and looked down into the scry bowl with a sneer, and she understood he'd been following the conversation. Smiling up at her, he said, *Took those Noble humans long enough to contact Us and request that We return to*

Druida City and the Yew estate. We should go back and be restored to Our rightful places. You can talk to Our four-legged Family mentally as we travel.

"I have a pie in the oven," she said blankly.

T'Blackthorn grinned. "Bring it." Then he asked, "What kind?"

*W*hen the First Families arranged matters, events proceeded at an accelerated pace. Before she left, she visited every member of her animal Family and, touching them, informed them of their journey, sent them love, and coated as many as possible with personal armor. She was still with them when the people who would transport them arrived; they studied each other and she finally met some of the Sallow Family. The Councils didn't shirk on paying for the best, either.

Convinced her beasts would be in good hands, Lori packed lightly. After all, she'd left a full wardrobe, though she'd filled out a bit more in the past months.

And all through the afternoon and night she planned, and dozed, and thought long and hard about what she should do, and when she should do what.

She carried Baccat from the airship and saw Straif T'Blackthorn there to meet them.

Her Fam didn't deign to greet the GrandLord. *I am going to Our estate NOW. To apprise everyone that We are back!* He licked her cheek, then jumped down and disappeared.

Be careful of teleporting! she shouted telepathically, then sensed he'd already arrived at the Yew estate, and her nerves began to twitch at the knowledge. He'd be rounding up the Family members and asking them to gather in the great hall of the Residence for a Discovery Day ritual.

"Loridana?" T'Blackthorn asked.

Donning the posture and the manner she'd been drilled in all her life, Lori nodded to T'Blackthorn and said, "Tell me where Draeg is."

The GrandLord grinned, took her hand, and tucked it in his elbow. "He's at the Sallows', I'll 'port you there."

"Not quite yet. I need to purchase something from T'Ash's shop, first." The wealth of the Yews had already been released to her. Appropriate that the first thing she bought with her own, her ancestral gilt, would be marriage bands. The copper with sapphire and amethyst ones she'd seen in T'Ash's shop.

T'Blackthorn's brows went up. "I can take you there, too."

Less than a quarter septhour later, T'Blackthorn teleported with Lori to the Sallows. The minute her feet touched the ground, T'Blackthorn disengaged himself, said, "Come to dinner tomorrow," and vanished, leaving Lori in a shadowy corner of a stable courtyard. Unlike her own—the Yews'—this yard was a full square, and in one of the corrals, Draeg schooled a magnificent black stallion. Both gorgeous males.

Suddenly, Lori wanted to look her best for him, beautiful for him. Her mind scrambled for an image of clothes, enhancements, for a Whirlwind Spell.

A shout interrupted her pondering and she looked up to see Draeg vaulting over the paddock fence, running toward her, his face showing desperate hope. Then he slowed to a walk, his expression impassive.

But she'd seen enough to ease her nerves, a little.

He came up to her and bowed. He was dressed like a trainer. So was she.

Her gaze met his hard blue one, then she glanced beyond him to the stallion watching them. "A very beautiful horse," she said. Like the ones in her books, the horses she'd dreamed of.

"He's mine." A pause, and quieter. "No, yours."

Courage. She stepped into him, her breasts touching his chest, her hands framing his face, eye to eye. "I . . . I love you, Draeg Betony-Blackthorn." A breath. "Will you wed with me and be T'Yew?"

He flinched and horror shot through her; she wheeled back, but he caught her and crushed her, and his lips were on hers and his tongue in her mouth and she tasted him and knew she was home.

Long minutes later, they separated and Lori flushed as she saw the audience of a dozen people grinning at her.

Loudly, Draeg announced, "Yes, I will marry you, Loridana Itha Valerian D'Yew, and accept the title of T'Yew."

Clapping rang through the yard. Then Draeg looked her in the eyes, claimed her hands, and said, "My HeartMate."

And she saw it then, felt it, the huge bond between them, and a golden bond waiting for loving to bind them together forever. She sniffled, but opened T'Ash's box to give Draeg the marriage bands. He took them and studied them with wonder, translocated them away . . . until their wedding ceremony.

After she'd been introduced to the stallion and they'd groomed him together, they borrowed a glider, drove to Yew estate, and parked outside the front gate.

Holding his hand, she opened the gate and once again stepped onto Yew land. Chimes echoed throughout the estate, as loud as Winterberry's voice months ago, but this time the sounds were lovely and musical. She heard shouts in the distance, from the Residence.

Draeg began to run, and she kept up with him. When the house came into view, she saw all the doors and windows open. The cook and some of the cleaning staff awaited them on the steps, obviously weeping.

When she and Draeg drew near, everyone fell back, and Lori scanned the faces, missing some, and, yes, cherishing the sight of others.

She and Draeg moved into the middle of the great hall. "Yew Residence?" Lori asked.

"Loridana!" The shout echoed throughout the house from roof to HouseHeart, and through every person in the great hall. "Loridana Itha Valerian Yew!" And as it recited her name the multiple voice refined into one, a female voice, but not the HouseHeart's. "I am Breva, the D'Yew Residence."

"Greetyou, Breva." On a shaky breath, Lori said, "I have

come home, and I have brought my HeartMate, Draeg Betony-Blackthorn, who is T'Yew."

Cheers erupted and Lori flushed. Glancing at Draeg, she saw a trace of red beneath his cheeks, too. She faded back and offered her right hand to the cook. "And now we will celebrate Discovery Day with a ritual."

In the ritual, she pulled energy from them all, cycled it among them, and the warmth of it, the shared bonds surprised everyone, and the *affection* they had for each other multiplied the strength of the Flair, of what she'd had to do alone all these years. A good lesson for them all. She would *not* be powering the Family spells, funding the Residence's spells, working on the estate in ritual all by herself.

She had a Family.

Perhaps a Family with strained and broken connections, but surely if she gave them kindness and . . . affection . . . they would return it. After all, what did she know about the individual members? Previously, what had they allowed themselves to reveal to the others, in daily actions, and in rituals like these? Not much.

But now they knew her, and knew that she demanded different things from them: openness, respect for her and each other, an acceptance of human frailties and mistakes.

This was not the Family she'd have built, but perhaps they could all regain—no, build together—a kinder household than she'd left.

From his seat on her feet, Baccat purred, and she felt the vibration move through her toes upward to her heart.

She heard the swish of wings, and Corax lit on Draeg's shoulder, made a throaty noise of satisfaction, leaned over, and plucked a thick strand of her hair from her bun, tugging gently enough that she wasn't hurt, and joined the circle.

No, nothing hurt about this circle, connecting with her Family. She thought her spirit expanded and theirs did, too. They'd lost Family members, people who might have been better if the Family had been built on love instead of fear, or greed for power.

Draeg turned his head and winked at her, and warmth, more

than affection, more than sex, true HeartMate and HeartBonded love filled her. She sent some of *that* around the circle, too.

She had him, her fighter, to help her.

Instinctively, she lifted her hands above her head, raising Draeg's and the cook's, too. All around the circle, arms went up.

"Welcome, Discovery Day! We are thankful for our planet and our land and our *Family*."

"Welcome, Discovery Day," said the Residence in throaty female tones.

Everyone else echoed the sentiment, and joy washed through them, doubled, redoubled until an effervescence of Flair filled them and spread from them into the Residence, restoring them all.

When they closed the circle, the Residence appeared pristine again, but also more cheerful. And after the party, when everyone retired, Draeg insisted that they walk to the stables. There, in the entryway of the north block, he swept away dust to reveal a fabulous mosaic of Ragan and Smyrna that he must have done months before.

Lori turned to her lover, her man, her HeartMate. "We're home and together and Family and you are my beloved HeartMate."

"Yes, beloved HeartMate." This time he put his hands around her face, and she savored the toughness in them. "I will always fight for you and with you." His voice sounded rough. "But if you need to walk away, I will be at your side."

She curled her hands around his thick wrists. "Thank you. I love you."

And he swept her up in his arms and they explored each other again in the warm shadows.